Horror Holiday

Selected and edited by

Scott David Aniolowski

Miskatonic
River
Press

Acknowledgements

Horror for the Holidays ©2011 by Scott David Aniolowski. Authors retain copyright to their stories, and unless noted otherwise stories are ©2011 per author.

"The Trick" ©1980 by Ramsey Campbell from *Weird Tales* volume 48, number 2, Spring 1981, edited by Lin Carter. First published under the title "Trick of Treat." Reprinted by permission of the author.

"The Christmas Eves of Aunt Elise" ©1989 by Thomas Ligotti from *Songs of a Dead Dreamer.*

"Keeping Festival" ©1997 by Mollie L. Burleson from *Return to Lovecraft Country*, edited by Scott David Aniolowski.

Cover image "A Krampus in My Stylus" ©2009 by Jeff Johnson.

Dedication

My love of horror and of books and reading comes from my mother, Linda Short, and it is to her that this volume is dedicated. Without the stories she read to me in childhood (*Grimm's Fairy Tales*—the gruesome original ones, among others), and the old classic horror movies we watched together (curled up behind her, hiding my eyes during my first movie—*Reptilicus*), I wouldn't be the person I am today. So good or bad, I have her to thank or blame! This one's for you, mom!

Contents

Introduction

Growing up, one of my all-time favorite Christmas stories was Dickens' "A Christmas Carol." Tales of jolly, red-clad, fat men with teams of flying reindeer or animated snowmen were all well and good, but nothing could beat a story that combined Christmas with the undead! The first time I saw the moaning, chain-rattling Marley appear to a horrified Scrooge I was hooked. Now, creeping toward the half-century mark of my life, I'm still enthralled by Marley and his cadre of Christmas ghosts; Dickens' classic remains one of my favorite books, and I have a collection of probably every film adaptation of the story.

My favorite childhood holiday was Halloween, the one night of the year when spooks and monsters and creepy things were encouraged to walk the earth. Like spectral Marley at Christmastime, the carved pumpkin jack o'lanterns of All Hollow's Eve became a beloved life-long iconic symbol in my life. As a child I went door-to-door trick-or-treating with the other neighborhood kids. In my early adulthood I reveled in my annual Halloween parties that would span the course of two or three nights with movies, gaming, good food and good friends. These days Halloween passes more quietly and unceremoniously and solitarily, but I carry the spirit of the holiday within my soul every day of the year, and it has shaped the person I am as an adult. Not a day goes by that I don't think, read, watch, write or otherwise wrap myself in some bit of horror or folklore or shadowy thing.

The inspiration for this volume came to me last year during the Christmas season. I was fully-immersed in the darker side of the yuletide holiday, watching my beloved "A Christmas Carol" films and re-reading another old holiday favorite of mine, Donald Westlake's "Nackles." I was also very much into the whole Krampus legend at the time… which is how I just happened to stumble upon Jeff Johnson's awesome piece of artwork that became the cover to this book! It had been a long time since I'd put together an anthology, and I was itching to get back to it. But I wasn't sure what sort of theme to do. The idea of a Christmas-themed book of Cthulhu Mythos and horror tales intrigued me, but I thought that that was likely too narrow a theme and I figured sales might be dictated by the season—how many people would buy a book of Christmas stories—horrific and weird or otherwise—in the summer? That's when the idea of a collection of dark HOLIDAY stories came to me. Spanning the whole year and any holiday, it would be the sort of thing a reader could pick up and enjoy pretty much any time of the year. And so, about a year later, here we are.

One of the greatest thrills for me as an editor is seeing what talented people create for me. I put out the call—some by direct invitation and some via open call—and the stories started coming in. Receiving a submission is like getting a gift—first I look at the title "wrapping" and try to guess what might be inside. Then slowly I begin picking at it, opening it up to fully discover what lies within. No two are the same. Most are surprises. Some I love, some I like, and some are just not right for me and I have to return them.

I am honored to have such talented people working for me on this one. It was nice working with some old friends, some favorite authors, and to see what some new folks had to say. I thank brilliant authors Ramsey Campbell and Thomas Ligotti for letting me use their work—both are an inspiration to me and to hordes of other scribes of weird tales. Thanks to all of the authors who submitted their work. Thanks to the talented artist Jeff Johnson for allowing us to use his fantastic painting for the cover. Thanks to my best pal Kevin Ross who is always a great sounding board, and who hooked me up with some fine folk who had written for his *Dead But Dreaming 2* anthology. Thanks to Tom Lynch and Miskatonic River Press for seeing my vision, supporting it, and taking on this project. And thanks most of all to you, the reader, without whom none of this would have been possible.

Until next time from the House of Secrets,

Unpleasant Dreams,

—SCOTT DAVID ANIOLOWSKI
Lockport, NY
November 4, 2011

The Tomb of Oscar Wilde

By W. H. Pugmire

And alien tears will fill for him
Pity's long-broken urn,
For his mourners will be outcast men,
And outcasts always mourn.

—Oscar Wilde (1854-1900)

"Why did you bring me here," I muttered, looking away from the grotesque defacement. "I find the sight exceedingly depressing. Please, let us flee."

But the poetess who signs herself "Celaeno" merely laughed at what she saw as my dramatics. "Don't be absurd, Yakov. What you condemn as disfigurement are the authentic love tokens of countless admirers."

"To mar a poet's grave with graffiti is the opposite of admirable. How many of the fools who have pressed their painted lips against this tomb have ever read 'The Sphinx' or 'The Harlot's House'? Or," and I pointed a long finger at her, "'The Grave of Keats'? If they want to pay homage to Wilde let them write a poem. But to blemish his tomb in such a manner! I had heard about these ugly lipstick stains, but I had no idea there was such a plethora of them. They have marred this sacred place with their Judas mouths and killed the thing they love. Away, away!" But my companion merely smiled and hummed a snatch of Chopin's somber Prelude No. 24. "Anyway, we shouldn't be here at this ghastly hour, and the last thing I need is to be arrested for entering this place past closing. How you knew about that other gate and the way in which to open it is a mystery I do not wish to think on. No, let us go, Rochel."

"But there's so much more to see. Let's go whistle at Chopin's tomb after we have conjured some magick here." She raised the portions of her black gown that fell from her shoulders toward the earth, looking very much like a winged and mythic beast. I was not enchanted. Some winged thing

9

soared above us in the Parisian sky.

"Conjure? No, no—I do not wish to commune with the poet except through the alchemy of his pages. No specters need apply. I need none of your outlandish witchery in this place. Oscar's poetry is sorcery enough."

She pointed herself, to the sky. "It's Rosh Chodesh, Yakov."

I followed her pointing digit and glanced at the sliver of moon. "I fail to see the significance."

"Do you remember Wilde's 'La Fuite de la Lune'?" Without waiting for my response, she began to sing the opening quatrain as it was set to music by the American composer, Charles Griffes:

> "To outer senses there is peace,
> A dreamy peace on either hand,
> Deep silence in the shadowy land,
> Deep silence where the shadows cease."

As though conjured by her song, a chill crept into the evening air, and a curtain of cloud covered the moon momentarily. The modernist angel on Wilde's tomb became a darker creature, seeming now like some somber sphinx that might at any moment whisper unfathomable riddle. I stood in the deep silence of a shadow-land, where the memory of wilted lives wafted to me on a gentle breeze. Queerly obsessed, a memory of Wilde filtered once more to mind, and I whispered a snatch of his verse: "A beautiful and silent Sphinx has watched me through the shifting gloom." As soon as my line was uttered the clouds melted from before the moon and my eyes were kissed by starlight. "Did you not write you own lines in memory of Wilde?" I queried, my face still lifted to the sky.

> "My song, imprisoned in this cave, my skull,
> Cannot be uttered by this clumsy mouth;
> My lips are thus consumed by poet's drouth,
> My song becomes a hymn unuttered, null.
> And so I sing with gleam of liquid eye,
> A prayer unuttered to the silver moon
> As liquid spills from lips of one dull loon
> Who aches to warble poesy to the sky.
> My mouth is clamped, but now my soul will glide
> To ancient moon as ache of silent hymn
> In which I pay homage, however grim,
> To one whose graceful language never died.
> Dear Oscar, take my song as silent token.

It is my gift, however frail and broken."

She finished reciting, glanced at me and shrugged. "Nu, it's rather poor, I know. Someday I'll polish and let it see print—maybe." I shrugged and smiled, then looked again at the mammoth tomb before us. A faint ache to whisper Kaddish came over me, however lacking I was of a Minyan. I remembered that this was Rosh Chodesh, the minor holiday of the New Moon. And that made me think of Oscar, who had been condemned to oblivion in his final years of mortality; yet like the moon Wilde returned and grew to fullness, so that now he shines in eternal opalescence through the magick of his Works and the tragedy of his story. And so I whispered a portion of prayer in Hebrew, which in English would be something like, "You have given to Your People the celebration of New Months, a time for Atonement for all their generations."

Rochel snorted. "Kaphar?" she pronounced in Hebrew. "What, you'd have Wilde repent? Feh. This poet deserves prayer to darker deity. How about this?"

I frowned as she began to recite her hymn to darkness, and yet I could not but marvel at how her small mouth pronounced the arcane language so perfectly.

"Y'ai, Shub-Niggurath! Y'gai h'yeh Aklo shoggoth! Ygnaiih...ygnaii...Shub-Niggurath!"

Darkness spilled into the sky once more, and wind arose. I watched as the lengthy sections of Rochel's long gown spread behind her like daemonic wings as her hawk-like visage leered at me in moving shadow, and I remembered why she had adopted her pen-name. She continued mouthing the obnoxious language, but now she combined it with Hebrew from a prayer with which I was unfamiliar. The monstrous sound withered my soul and froze my streaming blood.

"My heart!" I groaned. "You have emaciated it with your diabolic art. It withers still, and will soon be a thing of naught. I will wander the earth as heartless fiend, sans passion and poetry. Oh, oh!"

The witch laughed and drifted from my side, to the tomb against which she pressed her mouth among the horrid lipstick stains. I wanted to curse her but my limbs failed me and I fell to the ground as nameless outlines cavorted in the haunted sky and extinguished starlight. A thing of monstrous mist began to boil in the gulf of night, and I had no doubt that this was the "deity" that Rochel had called with her unholy art. Enfolded by gloom, I dug my nails into the dirt near Oscar's tomb. I saw his engraved name, obscurely, on the stone, defaced by the horrid red smears of lipstick, the animals fats of which caused havoc to the monument's stone and would cause irreparable damage. Gasping, I wept the poet's name.

The air had been tainted with a grotesque stench, a goat-like smell that fell to us from the cloud-like entity that Rochel had conjured in the sky. But now I sensed another fragrance lifted as perfume from the sod on which I knelt. With it another thing arose, a pale round luminance that seeped upward before the poet's tomb. I watched it shape itself into a semblance that was familiar and reminded me of Beardsley's irreverent illustration, "The Woman in the Moon." Reverently, I removed my clothing and struggled to my feet as nude acolyte to the poet I so adored. His spectral form took on a semi-mortal semblance, and I watched him wink at my companion and then lift his large face to the daemon in the sky. Pursing his lips, the prince of poetry exhaled sublime speech, the poetry of the ages. This magnificent and potent art penetrated the cosmic tempest and swept the paltry daemon from our view. Rochel fondled the jeweled tassel that dangled from the length of pearls around her pretty neck, and although her stance was defiant I could see the wonder that smoldered in the depths of her cloudy eyes as her alchemy was usurped by the Lord of Language.

Naked and heartless, I shuddered. Yet, although I lacked a beating organ in my breast, I still owned memory and mouth. My lips split and I heaved poesy.

> "Then turning to my love I said,
> 'The dead are dancing with the dead,
> The dust is whirling with the dust.'"

The poet gazed at me with star-like eyes, and I lifted my arms to him, reeling like a thing composed of mortal debris that might fall apart at his touch. But, oh, his caress was gentle! We danced among the dust of earth to a soft vibration that I seemed to recognize. I knew, at last, that it was the beating of the poet's eternal heart, and the sound of it brought tears to my eyes. He laughed and pressed his ghostly mouth to mine, and then he blew upon my liquid eyes as his hand rested against my breast. Momentarily, he frowned, not sensing the vibration he thought to experience from my chest. His gazing orbs seemed to read the misery of mine own, and thus he moved away a little and reached through his incorporeal frame. When his hand emerged I beheld the solid thing it held—his pulsating heart, which he offered me as gift of sacrifice. I took hold of the warm wet thing that seemed drenched with blood and martyr's tears. I held it to the waxing crescent of the moon, on this holiday of Rosh Chodesh that marks new beginning. I looked at Rochel, who was muttering to herself in Hebrew, and I winked at the sudden tears that had gathered in her eyes. Finally, I swallowed whole the poet's heart and laughed musically as it took root.

12

Love and Darkness

By Oscar Rios

Kira was dreaming again, dreaming of the deserted city beyond the gigantic brick wall. She walked the dark streets of this subterranean metropolis knowing her way through it by instinct. The young woman knew she'd never actually been there before, just as she knew she should be blind in this lightless realm. Yet in her dream, she saw everything as clearly as if she were walking in pure daylight. Darkness was no longer an enemy or obstacle, no longer something to be feared or dispelled. Darkness was her friend and father, her lover and mentor, her protector and master. It was sex and fulfillment, lust and life. Darkness was love.

Sometimes in these dreams, children would walk with her, holding her hands. They ran playfully around her giggling, overjoyed to be with her. Kira knew some of these children were hers, even though she'd never given birth. They were the children she'd aborted, usually with the morning after pill taken following a rave or lifestyle party: she disliked birth control and avoided barriers between her and her lovers, feeling such things were unnatural. These children didn't hate her for what she'd done. Here they lived and played and loved her. Kira knew on some level this should horrify her, but it didn't. To her they were the most beautiful children she'd ever seen.

Kira came to the center of the city where its lord waited for her, only for her. In her entire life no man had ever been special to her; none had ever captured her heart to the point of utter devotion. There'd been men who loved her, even a few who'd married her and she'd loved every one of them. But her love and desire knew no bounds; it was not a thing that could be contained or controlled. Kira had never been the monogamous sort, her sexual appetites simply too great for any one lover. But the lord of this city was different, for him she would do anything. With him, she knew peace and fulfillment, freedom, understanding and acceptance. To him she wasn't a whore or a slut or a freak. The darkness loved her and she loved him.

In her dream Kira was beautiful again, as she'd been before the incident. Her body was full of curves, pale freckled skin shining like the moon and her red hair fell thickly with abundant curls. She hadn't looked like this for almost two years, but in her dream she was restored. She knelt down before the darkness, knees spread wide and her arms open. With hands resting palms up upon her thighs she said in nearly a moan, "I am here Master, I am yours."

"My dumpling," the darkness replied, "I am coming for you. Each time you come to me here, I find my way to you. My steps carry me closer with each passing dream. You are my flower. I am your moth. Our reunion shall be soon."

Hearing his voice made Kira shiver. Her entire body throbbed with the need for his touch. "They won't let you take me. They are keeping me for something, trying to learn your secrets," she whispered.

"They cannot stop me," the darkness replied, "you belong to me and I shall have you. Any who stand between us shall be destroyed. You are paramour to the darkness, my pet. You are the beloved of a god, a hungry god who desires you above all others. These are the words of your master."

With that the darkness reached out to caress her, like a blanket of black velvet and silk. It slid over her skin, into her body and through her soul. It was energy, a living shadow of vitality and desire, all that lived and lusted and strove to reproduce fed into it. Her master was life and love and death. He was sensual and brutal, tender and overwhelming. The woman's body exploded in a climax so great she couldn't draw breath to scream.

Then the dream began to fade. She struggled to remain asleep, fighting hard to stay with her master. She didn't want to leave the city, which was supposed to be her home. She wanted to be with her children. It was agony to be cut off from the only one who'd ever understood or accepted her. She reached out to the darkness trying to grip it, but it was gone. Consciousness had her and she awoke back into her nightmare.

Kira was secured to her hospital bed, her body still throbbing in the final stages of the climax which had awoken her. As satisfying as it had been she hated that moment because it marked the end of her visit with her master. It was only a dream, and once again she was alone in her room, still a prisoner. She shifted and felt the pain swelling up within her.

Kira tried to resist hitting the button. She wanted to let the pain fill her so she could feel something real, but it was just too much. Grabbing the medication control she pressed the button and pushed morphine into her bloodstream through the IV. The pain faded instantly, and she started drifting back into unconsciousness. She knew she'd not return to the city, however, for she seldom had such dreams more than once every couple of weeks.

As the woman began to drift off under the affects of the narcotic, the intercom crackled to life. "Did you have the dream again? What did It say?" asked her doctor.

"He said you are all going to die. He's coming for me… I am paramour… to darkness…the words…of my Master…"

***

"Gentlemen, I believe we're running out of time here. I want everyone to give me status updates." The voice came from a video screen, a teleconference with the main office of Brighton & Cobb Pharmaceuticals. The man was in his sixties, in a suit that spoke of wealth and taste. His tone was crisp and controlled. Gregory Cobb—grandson of one of the company's founders—had the well-deserved reputation for being ruthless. Mr. Cobb was on the board of directors, and currently heading up Research Division Special Project Seven, of which Kira Ninesling was the key.

Dr. Dowd spoke first, "we're making some progress, but mostly in mapping out dead ends. We are slowly eliminating what isn't to better understand what is. We need to view our failures in finding the cause of the subject's immunities in a positive light. They're enabling us to zero in on what is, in fact, going on within the subject. We can isolate nothing abnormal about her on a molecular level. There are no foreign elements or compounds, no retro viruses or bacteria, no enzyme or antibodies within the subject to account for her resistance to infection or other cellular peculiarities. I think we can state that categorically at this time."

"So then why isn't she dead?" asked the man on the screen, causing the researcher to shift nervously.

"Well sir, honestly, we're not sure. The subject's wounds, which as you know have never healed, offer considerable surface area. Biologically it should be the perfect environment for bacterial infection but no infection has ever managed to take hold. Her cells are operating under… different rules. They don't divide, so she cannot heal. However, her cells can't be destroyed for more than a few moments, either. They don't make new cells to replace the old ones; the damaged cells simply repair themselves."

"How is that possible?"

"We're not sure sir, but it does offer some remarkable possibilities. The subject's hair and nails haven't grown since we've observed her. She has not lost or gained any weight, even when we've varied her caloric intake. There's been no sign of cellular decay of any sort in the entire time she's been with us. It's the type of thing medical nanotechnology is hoping to do but such realities are decades away at best."

Mr. Cobb smirked on the screen, "so you're telling me that this woman is what? Immortal?"

"Sir, at this point we can't definitely say that she's even alive, not as we'd usually define it. Her body seems frozen in time, neither healing nor aging while completely resistant to damage, disease and infection. Biologically the subject operates under different physical laws from any other life form known to man. Understanding how and replicating it would be the greatest medical breakthrough of all time."

"And where are we with that? Your best estimate Dr. Dowd. I know you can't give me a clear answer. Your best guess."

"With adequate funding, staffing and facilities, I'd say five years at best. We've only just started to understand what's going on with her. "

Mr. Cobb sighed. Five years was a long time but the payoff would be phenomenal. Everlasting life in a bottle, what could you charge for that? The military applications were limitless too, as he imagined soldiers regenerating from bullet and shrapnel wounds.

"Thank you Dr. Dowd. Mr. Rodrigo, what have we learned about the subject? Is there anything to explain how she might have acquired these abilities?"

David Rodrigo had been an F.B.I agent for twelve years before moving into the private sector. His training, experience and contacts had proven valuable to the pharmaceutical corporation, but sometimes facts and answers were not the same thing. "Sir, there isn't a lot to tell. We know the subject developed these abilities on or around the 15th of February, nearly two years ago. Before then she was a normal 28 year old woman. Her lifestyle tended to be extreme: heavy drug use and involvement with swing groups, raves—that sort of thing. She was a textbook party girl. Well, maybe a bit more than textbook. Her medical records show numerous abortions, sex related injuries, a few STD's, but nothing lasting or serious.

"She is the only survivor of a Valentine's Day rave at an abandoned warehouse in Huntington, Long Island," Rodrigo continued from his file. "The party ended in a fatal fire and Ms. Nineslling was the only one to escape the building. Arson is listed as the official cause. She was found by first responders lying in the snow outside with the injuries she still carries. However, my contacts with local law enforcement say the bodies recovered from the scene had injuries inconsistent with the nature of their death. There were a good number of blunt trauma injuries and most of the victims were already deceased before the fire began. Tire marks from a midsized vehicle lead away from the scene. One thing's certain; she was in no condition to exit the building on her own. In addition to her considerable injuries, she was too high to get far on her own, let alone probably have the where-with-all to escape a burning building. It's possible she was

16

carried from the building by the arsonist. That's all we know."

The executive frowned, "so we assume something happened to her at this party which caused this?"

"That's correct, sir."

"Dr. Dowd, could it be she took a mix of some odd synthetic drugs and her immunities are a side effect of that toxic cocktail?"

The researcher frowned, "that was our first guess too, but unfortunately we've eliminated that as a possibility in our research."

"Guys, this isn't good enough. Some filthy raver slut finds the fountain of youth and this is the best you can do? We've been at this for almost two years." Cobb ran a hand through his hair and looked over to a third man. "Dr. Hann, you've interviewed her extensively, what can you tell us that might help. What does she remember?"

"Gentlemen, Kira Ninesling is a very troubled young woman. I believe her experiences have caused her to retreat into a fantasy world. It's like a form of schizophrenia triggered by her post traumatic stress disorder. Even before the incident she was diagnosed as bipolar and suffering from hypersexuality. She barely remembers the party but says she met 'God' there. They allegedly engaged in very fulfilling sexual intercourse and that it was this 'God', or as she calls him 'her Master', who maimed her. As I said, Ms. Ninesling is not well.

"Since we allowed her to administer her own morphine she mostly drifts in and out of consciousness. She has recurring dreams ending in violent nocturnal emissions. After these episodes she mentions her 'Dark Master', an abandoned city, and makes threats against the staff. She says that her master is going to kill everyone keeping her here."

"Okay, on that. Legal, can we continue to hold her?"

Ms. Carolynn Johanson was one of B&C's top lawyers. It was her quick thinking and maneuvers that made Project Seven possible at all. That fact, much like her name, was more often than not forgotten by her employer. She barely reacted to such insults anymore.

"We can do anything we want," Johanson explained. "Kira Ninesling's death and cremation certificates are a matter of public record. So long as she's isolated and security protocols are followed I believe she can be held indefinitely." It was easy to make someone vanish. The system could be played like a piano if you knew what combination of keys to hit and Ms. Johanson was a virtuoso. A pay off to a nurse, a combination of drugs, knowing when a sloppy doctor was on his third shift, and Ms. Ninesling was declared dead. Who really cared? She was just another beat up, drugged out party slut—one more sad little girl who'd been used up and tossed over society's shoulder. Add the fact that she looked like something out of a horror movie and her death became a relief to the hospital staff, the police, to everyone. That she was worth her weight in gold as a subject for medical research was missed by nearly everyone on earth, except a few people affiliated with B&C.

"Well thank you everyone. A decision should be made soon. But I can tell you this, be ready to leave. Chances are high that this project will be moved onto an offshore research facility by the end of the month. Once this happens, space, staff, adequate labs and most of all security can be better maintained. Start breaking down what you can. Are there any questions?" Cobb didn't wait for a response before ending with "good." With a nod he terminated the communication, bringing the meeting to a close.

Everyone breathed a sigh of relief. Project Seven was moved into phase two, at last.

***

The nurse gave her only patient a careful sponge bath three times a week, but she never got used to it. It was disturbing on many levels. If it hadn't been for the excellent money and the fact the patient was bedridden and unconscious for about 16 hours a day she'd have quit months ago. The two previous nurses had quit; Ms. Nicolson had lasted longer than anyone else.

It wasn't the subject's appearance which bothered Ms. Nicolson. She'd seen horrible injuries before—pit bull attacks, gunshot wounds, stabbings, burns—a good trauma nurse got used to that. But Ms. Ninesling's wounds topped them all. It was sometimes difficult to look at her and accept that she was still alive. The nurse occasionally wondered what could have caused such injuries. The only thing her considerable imagination could picture was a school of sharks in a feeding frenzy.

The patient had six deep bite wounds on her body, each nearly a foot across. They were on both shoulders and hips, one breast and the right side of her face. Most of the young woman's left breast was gone, as were portions of her face: one entire cheek, part of her upper jaw and the radius of her right eye. All of the teeth on one side of her face and part of the optic nerve leading back into her skull were visible.

When Nurse Nicolson first saw the woman she though it had to be a mistake; no one could survive a year in this condition. Now, eleven months later, she just took it as fact. Ms. Ninesling wasn't going to die, she wasn't going to get an infection, and her injuries would never heal. For nearly two years these savage wounds remained as fresh and ugly as the day they'd been made. They'd gotten no worse and no better. The girl was the medical mystery which her generous employers were working hard to solve.

But the injuries were not what caused the nurse's stomach to twist every time she bathed her subject. It was the way the woman responded to the sponge bath. Ms. Ninesling moaned and shivered, even climaxed occasionally, as if unable to help herself. The nurse tried to fight her revulsion and struggled to be understanding. She reminded herself that the woman was clinically hypersexual. Her disfigured patient always apologized for making her uncomfortable, explaining how she couldn't control herself, but it did nothing to improve the situation. Nicolson wondered how it was even possible. The woman was usually in agony from her wounds or sedated nearly to the point of medically-induced coma. She was also on a steady regiment of anti-depressants, so clinically her libido should be non-existent. But nearly every time Kira was bathed she responded this way. The nurse just thought about the salary, nearly three times what she'd be making back at Mercy General.

When the bath was done she bandaged her wounds, even though infection wasn't an issue. She dressed the patient and brushed her hair, more out of pity than anything else. Sometimes the woman spoke but the nurse tried to ignore her. It often made no sense, schizophrenics seldom did. The patient blathered on about meeting God and being his lover, saying that they'd soon be together again. She'd explain that her master hadn't meant to hurt her, they just needed a safe word next time. Nurse Nicolson understood why the first two nurses had quit.

"Andrea, we've been together a while now," the patient addressed her. Her voice had a hissing rasp to it, caused by half of her mouth being open to the air. Her words were never fully formed and she drooled as she spoke.

It was rare that the young woman spoke directly to her; most often it was just talk. Actual conversation was discouraged by her employers. But the two women spent nearly every day together for almost a year so some dialog was inevitable. "Yes, we have Kira."

"I want to ask a favor, and in return I'll do something for you. It's nothing you'd get you in trouble for. I don't want you to get fired. We're friends. "

Ms. Nicolson didn't want to answer. She just finished brushing her patient's hair. But curiosity got the better of her and she finally asked, "What is it?"

The girl smiled, tears welling up in her eyes from the pain the gesture caused. "I need some makeup. Whatever you have on you. I won't let them know you passed it to me or get caught wearing it. It'll just be between us girls. Please. I need to be pretty for when my master comes. It's Valentine's Day soon, right? He's coming for me and I want to show him I made an effort for him. If you get it for me I'll give you something special."

Ms. Nicolson rolled her eyes behind her patient's back but went into her purse. She took out what little cosmetics it contained. She even included a pair of cheap plastic earrings which her niece had asked her to hold months ago at a family party. She put all of it under her patient's pillow, whispering to her "There it is. I'm sure he'll be happy you made yourself up for him." She turned to go, but the young woman whispered back "Wait, I said I'd give you something in return. One day I'll tell you to leave, to go home early. Tell them it's a family emergency or something. But when I tell you to go just do it, don't ask me why or tell anyone. Just go home."

After her shift that night, Nurse Nicolson stopped at a local dive for a few stiff drinks. Maybe it was time to look for a new job? But the money was so good and there were rumors the project was going to move to a bigger facility. She sighed as she sipped the last of her bourbon, thinking the worst day at work was better than the best day unemployed.

***

From a booth in the rear of the bar a solitary man watched a woman sipping bourbon.

The waitress finished hanging cardboard cupids and hearts all over the bar for its 5th Annual Valentine's Day Blowout. Now she moved about the room replacing the bowls of sourdough pretzel nuggets with sugary candy hearts. He picked one up and read it; LOVE YOU. He smirked. Love had been a foreign concept to him on every level, but it was now something which consumed him.

He felt drawn to the woman drinking alone but couldn't be sure at this distance. He walked over, pretending to head for the restroom. With slow steps he carefully avoided bumping other patrons with his bulk: he was a large man, the sort portrayed on sitcoms married to overly hot women. The man knew he looked to be just another comical fat man, another clown to laugh at in pity and disgust. In real life fat guys never got hot girls. They lived lonely lives and slept in empty beds. But he was different, very different, ever since that day the man knocked at his door with his bundle of books.

Mr. Hingley was peddling what he said was a rare set of books he'd picked up on a trip to England years earlier. An odd man, Hingley said he disliked the term "door-to-door salesman" and insisted on the title "The Mighty Messenger", and intimated that the books were some sort of religious volumes that would change his life. Intrigued, he purchased the books. What he read indeed awoke something deep inside him. His life did change and he was now part of something and it was part of him.

The itching burn in his palms intensified the closer he got to the woman. He noticed her purse hanging from the side of her chair and subtly knocked it to the floor with his hip. The ponderous man leaned over and picked it up. He offered it to her saying, "I'm sorry. This is yours, right?"

As his palm touched her bag, a scent raced up his arm and nearly set his blood to boil. This woman had touched the Paramour. Desire flared within him and he could feel power trying to push its way into his body, into this world. He fought hard against the urge, kept his head and maintained control.

"Oh, yes, that's okay. Thank you," she said as she took the bag from him and returned to her drink.

A short time later the nurse drove home, oblivious to the fact that she was being followed.

***

Kira bit down on her pillow and pulled hard against her restraints. Tears filled her eyes as bones snapped and her right hand slipped free. Ninety seconds later her hand was fully healed. She hit her medication controls, just once, filling her only with enough narcotics to enter a dream-like state. The woman then put her free hand to work, caressing her own body. Drifting away, lost in the effects of the morphine and the pleasures of self-stimulation, she focused on her fondest memory….

Kira exited the limo with some other beautiful women arriving at the Valentine's Day party. She'd been told there would be music and drugs, top shelf booze, only the hottest people at the clothing-optional event. Some rich fat dude was paying for everything, too.

Her first impression was one of disappointment, as the darkened warehouse didn't appear to be anything special. But after going inside, the party was off the hook. Her senses were assaulted by blaring music, lights, and smoke, dancing figures, glow sticks and bubbles. The room was strung with red streamers, lace hearts and cupids. A huge banner read "Happy Valentine's Day", there was even a cake shaped like two people doing it doggy style! The girls screamed and rushed the dance floor, Kira led the way. Someone handed her a drink, she drank it. Someone gave her a bag of pills and she swallowed the ones that looked familiar. Hands touched her, and she pushed into them. Someone kissed her, and she kissed them back… was it one of the girls from the limo? She didn't know, or care: it felt good. When had she lost her underwear? She loved this song. She loved feeling this way. It was hot, so she opened her shirt. The room was spinning, her favorite song was playing and she could see the music hanging in the air. It was red and pink for Valentine's Day. Someone said she had great shoes, so she went down on them. She laughed and laughed. Kira was home.

The music stopped, a huge speaker fell over, crushing someone. People were screaming, but not in a fun way. There was a strange smell, like jasmine oil, sort of. People gagged and threw up but she thought it was nice. Why did the music stop? Someone ran into her and she fell down. Someone stepped on her, so she rolled under a table. Something big stomped past her. People where running and hysterically crying. Something hot and wet splashed across her. Kira whipped some of it away and saw her hand was red. It was blood, she laughed. It was all so weird. What kind of a party was this?

When the screaming stopped, she crawled out from under the table and tried to stand up. She fell hard and saw someone turn toward the sound. He was huge, nude and thick around the center of his torso. She hoped he had long hair, but curiously no matter how she strained she couldn't see his head. He raced toward her, his footsteps making the ground shake. Somewhere in her mind Kira knew she was about to die, but she'd always known that one day her life would end at a party like this.

He grabbed her breast and her breast was gone. The pain rushed through her, even through the drugs, and she drew in a deep hissing breath. He spun her around and took her, holding her by the hips and shoulders. In that moment the party girl knew this was what she'd been looking for her entire life. A key turned in a lock, she was complete, even as she was about to die. It was worth dying to couple with such a man. Her last moments would be of pain and pleasure and fulfillment followed then by only quiet darkness. She lost herself in it all, surrendered to whatever he wanted from her. When she could speak she said, "I love you…" He caressed her face with a huge hand, a jagged toothed maw ripping away her cheek and part of her face.

It all became confused. She was floating then felt chilly air and smelled gasoline… There were sirens, a door slammed and a car raced off. There was heat… a fire nearby…the snow was cold… Through all the drugs the pain began to make itself known. In the ambulance she started to cry, but not why the paramedics thought. Sure she was hurt, badly so, but so what? She'd been ready to die, would rather have died than endure what had happened. He'd left her behind. The only man she'd ever really loved was gone.

***

The asphalt was dotted with patches of black ice making the narrow, twisting road a challenge. It was cold and the forecast called for snow after dark. Andrea Nicolson was glad to be on an overnight shift; she wouldn't have to face the ride home in snow flurries. Besides, it wasn't like she had plans. Since her divorce she hated Valentine's Day. The endless commercials about diamond pennants, flower delivery services and greeting cards, it was all bullshit. Hell, even the radio was filled with love songs dedicated from one idiot to another. Andrea hit scan on her radio as she drove and felt her tires slipping on a turn. For a second she had that sickening feeling of losing control before the tires gripped the slick road. The vehicle skidded back into its lane with a lurch.

Had she not been lost in the memories of her failed marriage, the nurse might have noticed the shift of weight in the SUV's trunk. But she didn't, her cargo settled back into place. They kept quiet, as they'd been told, but wanted to squeal in delight at the wild ride. It would be a special day. The lady was taking them to mommy.

***

Kira didn't want to fall asleep. They gave her no choice.

After freeing herself from the rest of her restraints, she'd crawled over to the door. She'd get away and maybe she'd steal a car, or something. She'd need some clothes, shoes for sure. It hurt to move but she had to get away. It was their anniversary and she wanted to spend it with her master. He was out there, somewhere, and she had to find him.

She wished she could do this with the IV drip, just feed her some morphine to cut the edge off. But she pulled the feed out as the short tube allowed her to go no more than a foot from her bed. Too late she noticed the flashing light on the medical console. Before she could react, the door yanked open and an armed security guard came in. Kira wondered if it would matter if he shot her?

It was pitiful, almost comical. She swung a bedpan but with a kick the security guard sent the makeshift weapon flying. The effort sent pain lancing through her. She screamed in agony and drew herself into a fetal position.

"Clear!" the guard called out, "Doctor! You got a live one in here. Come put your lab rat back in her cage."

A doctor and intern rushed in, hauling Kira back into bed. They strapped her down, reinserted her IV, and worked at cleaning up the blood she'd smeared everywhere. Two years old and still her wounds bled as if they were freshly made.

"Please, let me go. This is America, I have rights. He's coming for me, it's not fair. YOU HAVE NO RIGHT KEEPING ME HERE! I'm sorry, I'm sorry I screamed, please, just let me out for a day. I'll let you have a piece; there is nothing wrong down there… please…" She struggled against her restraints to arch her back and part her knees in display.

One of the doctors slipped in her blood. He shouted "somebody shut that slut up!"

The needle came out, driving into her arm. She felt calmer and her pain faded but she remained conscious.

"You fuckers, do you know who owns me? DO YOU? Master will kill you all! I'm his, not yours! I've seen what he can do… Master did this to me and he loves me. What do you think he'll do to YOU?"

"It's not working. Another 20 cc's," the doctor ordered.

Kira started feeling woozy but was still furious. "It's our…anniversary… It's Valentine's Day… limp…prick…mother fuckers…"

The intern was shocked, "there's no way she can still be conscious… what the hell?"

"Another 20 cc's, it's not like we can kill her. Just put her under."

"I'm his…beloved…paramour…." Kira could resist no longer. Her blood, assaulted by a flood of narcotics, finally surrendered. When the conscious world faded away she was home, in the empty city beyond the great brick wall. She laughed in surprise and joy.

***

The SUV pulled to a stop at the gate of the compound as the security guard stepped out from his little booth. He walked around the nurse's familiar car, peering in the back seat.

"Is everything okay, Mike?" she asked.

"Sure," he replied, "You're fine. Go through. Mr. Dowd told us to be extra careful today. Apparently someone nearly got out of her room."

Nurse Nicolson rolled her eyes and called out, "Yeah great, as if today could get any worse."

The guard turned toward the trunk, as if he heard something. He shook his head and waved her through. As the SUV moved to the research center he thought for just a moment he'd heard a child giggle.

Beyond a turn along the same road another car stopped. Its driver closed his eyes and concentrated. Yes, he could sense she was nearby; this was the place. He turned around and drove toward a motel he'd passed about three miles back. He'd get a room, maybe some food, and sleep. It was going to be a long night, but a good one. He reminded himself to pick up some flowers, maybe a bottle of wine. It was Valentine's Day and women loved that stuff. His little girl deserved a special day.

***

Traffic had made Ms. Johanson very late for work. It annoyed her. There was no way she was going to stay late to make up the time. Her husband had made 9pm dinner reservations for Valentine's Day. She pulled her BMW into her reserved spot and noticed the trunk of the SUV parked two spots over was wide open. She glanced into the trunk. It was empty but reeked. There were tiny tracks in the newly fallen snow all around the car. She mumbled "Raccoons. Filthy little vermin."

The tracks lead toward a basement window, which appeared to be intact. Nonetheless, she'd send the director an e-mail later to demand an exterminator. But then she reconsidered; why bother if they were going to move soon, anyway? She'd heard one option was a renovated hospital ship, a floating mobile laboratory. Security would be airtight and the place would be raccoon-proof.

***

"I tried to reach you but they stopped me. Master, may your girl ask some questions?"

The darkness paused before answering, as if pondering the concept, "You may, my dumpling."

"Why is your city behind that huge wall?"

The darkness answered "Men built it, to imprison me there. They thought to bar me from their world but their plan failed. Within every person is a potential doorway. Your world is unrestricted to me. It was in that way that I found you."

The young woman lowered her eyes and whispered "Yes Master, I remember. But…um…why did you leave me? You could have taken me with you. I'm not upset, just hurt and confused. Didn't you want me?"

The darkness paused again and the woman could almost sense it roiling in thought. "Girl…Master was…perplexed. Humanity is so young. What a girl showed her Master was something new, something he did not understand. But now He does. Master….loves his paramour. Leaving her was a mistake, one that will be corrected."

"Will it be much longer Master? I miss you so much."

"It has already begun. We'll not spend this Valentine's Day apart."

"SQUEEEEE!!!!" the girl yelled, rushing into the darkness with open arms. The wave of pleasure and release swept her back to consciousness. She awoke gasping and sputtering for breath but happier than she'd ever been before.

***

Andrea breathed a sigh of relief when her patient suddenly woke, once again in deep climax. The doctor had sedated her to a level that would be fatal to a normal person. But she'd been unconscious for only seven hours; even accounting for her patient's abnormal physiology, it should have been far longer.

"Kira, look at me, are you okay?"

The young woman smiled, "Yes, I'm wonderful. I was with him, two days in a row... and...." She suddenly sat bolt upright and looked around. Kira inhaled deeply through her nose, licked her lips and slowly blinked her eyes.

"Whoa, slow down. You're bound to be dizzy. They put you under deep after that stunt. They say you probably broke your wrist to get out, not that it stayed that way apparently. What were you thinking?"

Kira's body trembled, "Can't you smell that?"

The nurse sniffed the air but detected nothing. She looked at her patient, who seemed calmer and more focused than she'd ever seen her before.

"Can I see your purse for a minute?"

"See my... No. You need to stop this. You're going to... HEY!"

Kira's arm shot out. She captured the nurse's right hand in a vice like grip. Like a dog she smelled Ms. Nicholson's palm. The patient then let out a long, slow breath ending in a deep moan. It was a familiar scent, like burnt jasmine. Master had touched the nurse or touched something she had. He'd found her. He was coming.

Andrea struggled to pull her hand away. She was about to scream for the guard when Kira released her. The nurse stumbled backward, rubbing her numb hand and panting in shock.

Kira slowly turned to her, wearing a contented smile. She said "Go home. Don't think or ask why. Just get in your car and leave." She carefully retrieved her hidden cache of cosmetics from beneath her bed and began laying them out.

Andrea rushed out of the room, fighting against a sudden flight response. She glanced out a nearby window and saw light snow falling from the winter's twilight sky. For a moment she considered actually doing as Kira had asked. "This is crazy", she thought before marching straight for the director's office. The escape attempt, her assault, the warning and threat: something was going on and he needed to know about it.

***

An unfamiliar car rounded the corner and pulled up to the main gate. Mike figured they had to be lost, it happened sometimes. The car stopped and its heavyset driver rolled down the window. He was about forty with dark salt-and-pepper hair, easily 250 pounds or more. The driver said "Ho-Wan delivery. Two orders of steamed dumplings, eggrolls and a quart of pork fried rice." He nodded toward the back seat where a large bag sat beside a dozen roses. The guard smelled the Chinese food and was suddenly hungry.

Mike quickly recovered, saying "No, they don't allow food deliveries here. You must've taken a wrong turn. Where are you trying to go?"

The man frowned, "Shit. This stupid thing…." He pulled the GPS off his dashboard and tapped on the screen several times. "Damn it! It's says this is the place. Do you know how to work one of these?" He climbed out of the car, causing it to lift visibly higher once relieved of his ponderous weight.

"Lemme see… Well first thing, this isn't…" The last words the guard ever spoke. Three years working for B&C and he'd never had a single confrontation, never even drawn his sidearm. His moment had come and he'd missed it.

The hulking man stepped forward quickly, delivering a brutal upper cut to Mike's solar plexus. The punch was a powerful one, tearing through muscle as if it were tissue paper. He doubled over as he struggled to breathe. Time seemed to slow as the fat man grabbed his head and said, "You guys have something of mine and I want her back." Fingers curled into a fist in the guard's hair and the fat man's arm snapped down in a single powerful jerk, snapping Mike's neck.

It was a kindness. Mike felt no pain as his life ebbed away. A bit uncharacteristic but he was in a pleasant mood. He was going to be with the woman he loved on Valentine's Day. The fat man focused his consciousness, connecting his thoughts with those of his minions. The message was a concept, "Now."

Seconds later, the entire compound plunged into darkness. The rotund man opened the gate and turned off his car's headlights to drive up to the research facility in darkness.

***

Dr. Hann was in his office boxing up files, preparing for the move. When the lights went out he sat as his desk and waited for them to come back on. Maybe the ice or a falling branch had caused a power line to break, possibly shorted out a transformer. After several dark minutes he remembered the compound had independent power isolated from the commercial grid for security reasons and to insure a steady flow of power to the labs. Then he heard the first scream.

It was a woman, screaming once, then again and again. It began with a tone of fear but quickly changed to one of pain and sheer terror. Dr. Hann moved across his darkened office, fumbled for the door and opened it.

Suddenly, something small rushed into the room knocking the doctor off balance. He stumbled and fell backward to the floor. As the emergency lighting came on to bathe the room in dim illumination he saw them—a pair of filthy toddlers—rushing toward him. His mind struggled to process the image. The children had no eyes, just holes in their faces where eyes should have been. They wore dirty cloth diapers and their grayish blue skin was covered with dark black veins. Like blue cheese or marble, he thought. Corpselike.

The psychiatrist suspected he was hallucinating. Surely this wasn't real? The monstrous children leapt on him. They giggled and he saw sharp teeth in their mouths, but the mouths were on their palms!

"No…NO! HELP ME!" he screamed, his voice joining what was quickly becoming a chorus sung out across the compound. He tried to fight but they set on him like terriers with a rat. Within seconds blood sprayed from dozens of wounds. Eventually Dr. Hann stopped screaming.

***

Andrea's heart nearly stopped when the lights went out. She froze, holding onto the wall and wondering what to do. As the first of the screams began, a wave of dread washed over her. Mr. Dowd's office was straight ahead but the route to her car was in the other direction. While her body was frozen in fear her mind raced, she'd been given a warning and told to go home. Kira had always said her master would come to free her. She started for the parking lot when the desperate screams of Mr. Dowd shocked her into action and she raced to the director's office.

By the time she got there the emergency lights were on. Dowd lay moaning on the floor, covered in blood from numerous vicious bites. Although she knew it was futile, she rushed to the doctor's side. Suddenly there was motion in the shadows. She heard soft wet footsteps, a child's laughter. The nurse tried to back away but something tripped her and she fell. Andrea screamed as a pair of small dark figured charged out of the darkness.

Then there were flashes of light and thunderous roars which deafened her. One of the figures was hurled backward while the other went tumbling away. She heard it fall, rush to its feet and run off. It started wailing like a toddler.

A hand grabbed her. David Rodrigo pulled the nurse into the hallway, holding his sidearm skyward.

The screams were dying down and sporadic gunfire could be heard throughout the darkened compound. From the shadows echoed taunting calls in raspy childlike voices, "You're gonna get it…you're gonna get it…"

"What the fuck's going on? What are those things?" asked Rodrigo, the former federal agent.

Andrea replied through her panting breaths, "Its Kira…They've come for her…"

Tightly gripping her hand, Rodrigo rushed toward the patient's room. He triggered his radio and shouted into it, "All units, rally on medical, we have an escape attempt in progress."

As they neared Kira's room they could hear singing coming from inside. Children's voices were happily singing along with the patient, "A B, C D, E F G…" David kicked in the door and tiny figures went scampering toward the shadowed corners of the room, leaving Kira standing alone in the center of the room. David fired into the shadows. The small figures cowered, huddling together. One was crying pitifully in pain. They were all screaming, "Momma, momma!"

"Stop! Don't hurt my babies! They're only children!" Kira's voice was strong as was her posture. She was fully made up as if ready for a night of clubbing, and wearing the cheap plastic earrings Andrea had given her. She had tied and cut her hospital gown to create a makeshift mini-dress. On the breast of her garment she'd drawn a single four fingered hand in red lipstick. Blood stained the fabric and pooled under her feet from her never-healing wounds.

Kira's voice was sultry as she purred, "Andi, I told you to go home… You should have listened. You can't stop him, nothing can."

***

"Freeze! Show me your hands!" screamed the guard, his gun drawn and aimed at the figure entering the compound. The intruder was an obese man carrying roses. Across the facility the fading sounds of screams were replaced by whispers and children's laughter, taunting cries and the moans of the dying.

The stranger did not reply. With a roll of his eyes he strolled forward, unconcerned.

The panicked guard fired three times before his finger was uselessly pulling the trigger on the empty handgun. The fat man darted to his left unbelievably fast, almost a blur. The three bullets missed their target, but the bouquet of roses was scattered across the ground.

The obese man glared at the guard and growled deep in his chest. In the dim light the guard watched the stranger's clothing rip as his sallow flabby bulk expanded, rapidly swelling. The guard was unable to fully comprehend the terrible tableau. The enormous figure's head was gone and shark like jaws opened on the palms of its huge four fingered hands. His mind reeling, the guard dropped his weapon and began to back away. The still-swelling figure made swift work of the cowering, babbling little man.

***

"It's too late. Two years. For two years I've been asking you to let me go. I warned you all..." Kira said, in a deep lusty voice. "Master is here. He's come for me."

"Shut up!" Rodrigo screamed. "Nobody's going anywhere!"

"Kira, please!" pleaded Nurse Nicolson.

"I begged too, so many times..." the woman replied. She didn't hurt anymore and she wasn't afraid. The closer He came the stronger she felt.

Suddenly there was the sound of gunfire followed by a gurgling scream that ended abruptly.

"GIRL...GIRL!"

A shiver went through the young woman and she screamed back, "HERE MASTER! I'M HERE!"

"SHUT UP!" Rodrigo struck her hard in the temple with the butt of his pistol.

The nurse backed into a corner, muttering, "No...no...no..."

Small shapes crept out from the shadows, their childlike voices whispering "You're gonna get it...you're gonna get it..."

The ground shook under heavy footfalls which grew louder and closer. Suddenly an immense figure blocked the doorway. Two hands reached out and pulled away the doorframe and most of the wall, peeling it open like the skin of an orange. Kira sighed. Andrea screamed. David fought back the fear, shock and disbelief. It was only his years of training that allowed him to retain his reason. He didn't think, he just reacted and trusted his instincts.

The thing towered over them, a headless obese giant. In the palms of the thing's hands were mouths filled with sharp teeth. One toothy maw moaned, "Paramour, my dear one", while the other growled, "Release her and I shall make your end quick!"

David shouted, "I'll blow the whore's head off!"

The giant paused, breathing deeply. David could feel cold sweat slither down his back. His hand trembled in terror. His hostage shivered and asked in a breathy passionate voice, "Master, May I?"

The horror replied in a permissive tone, "You may, my pet."

"Thank you, Master."

Sharp teeth erupted from the edges of all of Kira's still-bleeding wounds. The newly-formed mouths on her shoulders bit into David's arm. He screamed in pain, dropping the gun as he tried to shove her away. But the mouths held and he couldn't dislodge his arm from her jaws. She spun around, turning back on him with a serpent's agility. Each of her terrible maws drooled, hungering for the man's flesh. Kira pulled him close. Mouths where her left breast and cheek had been gnashed their teeth. The many screaming mouths bit into David and he screamed as the paramour devoured him alive.

Guttural laughter came from the headless giant's hands as it watched its beloved feed for the first time. Slowly it began to shrink and change until by the time Rodrigo was dead it was once more an obese man standing in the shattered doorway.

Kira pulled herself to her feet, "Master... I ruined my make up... and my dress..."

He chuckled, "I had flowers too but I lost them."

"Oh Master, all I need is you!"

She rushed into his arms and they kissed deeply. Andrea watched transfixed as the fanged mouths on Kira closed and healed over. Not a scar remained; her patient was fully restored to her once-beautiful self. There stood a curvaceous pale women drenched in blood passionately kissing an obese naked man. Around the nurse, half a dozen filthy eyeless children whispered and giggled.

Andrea watched as the pair walked away, his arm around her and her head against his shoulder in some display of obscene romance.

"Finish her and meet us at the car," the fat man said over his shoulder. The children rushed forward with a squeal of delight. It was neither quick nor pretty but the nurse hardly seemed to notice. Mercifully her sanity had fled long before her life ended.

***

The pair washed off the blood and gore before dressing. The obese man had thoughtfully packed spare clothing for them both. The dress and shoes fit her perfectly. It was exactly the type of outfit she'd have chosen for herself. Master knew her, better than anyone else ever would. The Chinese food was still warm in the back of the car, and she ate an eggroll as her

Master secured the children. When they were safely tucked away in the trunk they drove off.

"We lost some, Master…" Kira said.

"I know, my pet," he replied, "Don't worry, there will be more. Many more now that we're together."

Kira ran her hands over her body and smiled. "I'm so happy I can be pretty for you again."

"You were never displeasing to me. I always saw the woman inside; the rest was just a shell." He reached out and held her hand. Master switched on the radio, the station was doing a countdown of the one hundred best love songs of all time.

"What happens now, Master?"

He chuckled, "We stay together. I take you home and we live happily ever after."

"I love you Master…Oh so much…" she purred.

"And Y'golonac loves you too, my Paramour," he smiled.

The woman began to cry, "This is the best Valentine's Day ever."

Be Mine

By Brian M. Sammons

Keith ran down dark, dripping tunnels of naked earth, feet splashing through puddles of filth, hand dragging along the soft wall on his left, lest he become lost in the labyrinth. His breath was ragged and it felt like sandpaper in his raw throat as he huffed and puffed, but he never slowed. His stomach churned and shot up the occasional spittle of acid bile as if he had just recently thrown up, and yet his guts felt swollen and bloated, like the aftermath of a particularly good Thanksgiving feast. His eyes were blurry with tears, which made moving through the benighted tunnels even more treacherous, but Keith could not remember if they were tears of fear, heartbreak, physical pain, or a combination of the three.

BE MINE.

Those two little words slammed into Keith as surely as he slammed into the wall on his right in their aftermath. They were not heard or read, but somehow known all the same. Perhaps they were felt? Yes, the words had a terrible weight to them, a crushing weight that caused Keith to double over and gag under their pressure. Once more, burning bile filled his mouth and again his stomach lurched, or was that squirmed?

Straightening up, he was oddly unaffected by the sudden absence of the tunnels, the ankle deep water, or the gloom that had surrounded him. Instead, all he could see was the face of a young woman that was beautiful, radiant, and smiling at him. With short reddish-blond hair, dancing green eyes and a splash of freckles across high cheekbones, she was a vision. This woman, no, this girl of perhaps at the most twenty years old, was his every adolescent fantasy combined with his slowly maturing tastes. But as maddening as the girl was beautiful, was the feeling that Keith knew her, and yet could not name her. The aggravation of trying to remember something, it being on the tip of the tongue, but still beyond any mental grasp, itched at the back of his brain, causing strange things to scurry into the light.

BE MINE.

Again the words, unspoken yet damnably real, and this time they brought forth the image of pale shades of pink, yellow, green and purple hearts. There were piles of them, all scared with words cut into them, etched in red like blood. *How cute, true love, my treat, be good, 4-ever,* and other sugary sentiments were inscribed into the tiny cardio-candies, but one sweet caught Keith's eye and held his attention until all other pastel hearts faded to black. It was a dark red, not the normal pink, and on its face, carved in deep black letters, was —

BE MINE.

Keith shook his head and his vision refocused on the blurry tunnel around him, only now it had changed. Gone was the damp, naked earth, replaced by old stones and crumbling mortar. His ankles were suddenly dry, but his calves felt crowed, pinched, and pricked by sharp bits. Looking down, Keith saw he was standing knee deep in bones. Thousands of them, yellowed, cracked and ancient beyond belief. They were of all sizes and of all kinds, but all were undeniably human. Worse yet, they moved.

No, something underneath the monumental amount of bones moved, causing the shattered skeletons to rattle and sway like a dull-white sea. And if Keith stood kneed deep in a sea of death, then he surely felt a huge tidal wave coming for him. In the darkness ahead the bones rattled, swelled, and parted for an as yet unseen bulk that trudged slowly toward him. Without glimpsing it in the slightest, Keith was sure that he didn't want to see what it was.

He turned and the tunnel behind him was as long, dark and clogged with the remnants of the dead as the other. Still there was no menacing presence that way so he surged ahead, wading through the clacking waves, using his fingers to grab the cold stone of the walls around him in an attempt to speed his passage. Yet he could still feel the doom at his back gaining on him. Slowly, surely, patiently, it would have him.

And when the words came again, they hit him harder than ever imaginable.

WILL YOU BE MINE?

***

Keith woke with a start in his bed of tangled, sweat-stained sheets and blankets. He listened for the unseen bulk, wondering if it was still moving toward him, but he only heard the hissing of warm air coming through his room's vents. His eyes darted back and forth, searching for the sea of bones and the moldering stone walls, but only total darkness was there. No, there was a single source of weak, green light to his right and parallel with him lying in his bed. It took him a moment to recognize it as the digital face to his radio alarm clock. Turning and leaning to see the time, someone suddenly twisted an invisible knife in his guts that caused him to groan and curl up into a fetal position, arms wrapped around his stomach.

The on again, off again stomach pain that had been plaguing him for the last few months was becoming both more frequent and severe. He hated the idea of seeing a doctor for many reasons, but the one he used as his constant crutch was money. As a fulltime student he had no extra cash to spare, and that meant going to the school's free clinic. Keith had always loathed seeing real doctors, so the idea of med students poking around his guts didn't fill him with confidence. But if the pain continued to get worse…

Keith tried to push the thoughts out of his head and focus on the source of his pain, his stomach. Placing his palms against it found that it was bloated, hard, and sore to the touch. Fear gripped him and caused the sweat that was still clinging to him to go cold. Like the bogyman, the word "cancer" crept into his brain and pulled up a chair to sit. No amount of pretending it wasn't there was going to ignore it.

"Fine, damn it, I'll go to the clinic," Keith whispered and rocked slightly on his bed. The little bit of motion seemed to calm his pain some, so after a while he once again reached for the clock to see the time. Its glowing green face said 4:47 AM and underneath that, in smaller numbers, was 02-06.

So on top of everything else, it was just eight days to Valentine's Day and he still had no girlfriend, steady date, or even a casual female acquaintance for a drunken night of "we're tired of being alone" sex. His two new roommates were already giving him hell for being such a loner, seemingly content to settle for internet porn and to date Ms. Michigan, the lovely Rosy Palmer.

"Oh God, can things get any worse?" he asked.

In answer, his stomach twitched and heaved again. The new bolt of pain was so intense that he just had time to turn his head before he vomited onto the floor.

***

Keith sat at the breakfast table, cup of cooling coffee in his hands. He had spent the rest of the night cleaning up his mess and then himself. By the time he was done it was only a half hour until he had to get up for class, so it looked like he would have to zombie it today.

Greg and Devin also sat at the little round table in the small kitchen. They chatted about this and that, but mostly about the upcoming Valentine's Day bash at the Kappa Alpha Psi house. It was an annual tradition, and even though none of them were members of the frat, Devin had an in with a buddy who was a brother. That meant they were allowed to come, but only if they showed up with their own liquor and ladies. The Kappas frowned on poaching of any kind at their parties. All too soon the conversation led to Greg and Devin telling Keith, for about the hundredth time, to get off his lazy ass and find a girl to go with him, or else miss the party of the year.

To this, Keith nodded and grunted non-committedly. His mind was occupied with more serious things than girls and parties this morning. Besides, Greg and Devin were really starting to annoy the hell out of him. They were ok guys for the most part. They paid their share of the rent on time and didn't freak out if you ate some of their cold pizza in the fridge, but they really weren't his friends. Last year Keith was a freshman and therefore condemned to the college dorms. This year he was lucky enough to score a room in an off campus house. That's how he met the dynamic duo, who were both a year ahead of him. While Greg and Devin sometimes palled around, Keith mostly just stayed to himself. In fact, he was sure they were only concerned about his lack of a love life out of fear of him being gay or something stupid like that. Their immature male egos would probably get all twisted out of shape if that turned out to be the case.

Thirty minutes later and both of Keith's roommates were gone, but still he sat at the table with the same cup of now half empty and cold coffee in front of him. His left hand sat next to the cold cup, while his right was inside his robe, under his t-shirt, and pressed against his abdomen. Last night's pain was gone, as was the weird bloating and tenderness. Keith was happy to write the whole thing off as remnants of his weird nightmare somehow aggravating a minor condition. He most likely had an ulcer, he surmised. He did seem to worry a lot about little things. Yeah, he would pick up some Mylanta and that would help next time.

Keith smiled at his self-diagnosis and was feeling a bit better about last night, when he happened to glance at the clock on the wall as saw that he was going to be late for his Psych class. With a curse, he leapt up from the table and ran for his room to change. He never noticed the tiny white globules that floated in the remains of his coffee. Nor did he see it when they moved by themselves to the side of his mug, and then began to slide up its interior surface to the lip of the cup and the freedom beyond.

***

It was two days later. Two days of no strange nightmares and only the occasional twinge of pain from his stomach. If Keith tried hard enough, he could almost pretend that nothing weird was going on, so that is what he endeavored to do. Currently his early morning Psych class was over and he had less than an hour before he had to go to Biology. There wasn't enough time for him to go home, so he decided to head over to the student union. There were a few classic arcade machines at the back of the Spirit Shop, and wasting quarters on them was a favorite way for him to pass the time.

Keith was halfway across Whitman's Field when he heard someone call out to him from behind.

"Hey, Keith, what's up?"

Turning, he saw Tom, a sort of buddy of his from last year. The two weren't really tight, but they were friendly.

"Hi, Tom, how's it going? I haven't seen you in a while."

"Yeah man, I know. So what you been up to?" Tom asked as the two shook hands. Tom said he was also on his way to The Union, so the two walked together, idly talking. The dialog was light, breezy, and completely forgettable, until Tom asked a question on the steps of the union building.

"So how's Chuck?"

"Who?" Keith asked.

"You know, Chuck, your roommate?"

For the briefest of moments, Keith had no idea who Tom was talking about. His roommates were two chuckleheads named Greg and Devin. Then it hit him; Chuck! Chuck was his roommate from the freshman dorms. Weird that he had all but forgotten about him.

"Yeah, well, I haven't seen or talked to Chuck since last year."

"Aw man, I'm sorry, are things still kind of weird between you two?" Tom asked and his cheeks started to get some red in them.

"What?"

"You know, with Kaytlin and all?"

Keith stopped in his tracks at the mention of the name. His stomach lurched and churned painfully, but his head suddenly felt light and fuzzy, so he hardly noticed.

"Who?" Keith whispered.

Tom grew a nervous, lopsided grin, and his eyes searched all over Keith's face, looking to see if he was putting him on, or if there was something wrong with him.

"You know, your girlfriend, uhm, sorry, ex-girlfriend?"

Keith stared at Tom like a boy studying a particularly creepy looking bug he had pinned with a stick and didn't know what the hell he was talking about. The last girlfriend Keith had was Naomi and that was back in high school. Who the hell was—

Then in a flash, it was there; the face from his recurring dreams. The beautiful, smiling, strawberry blond girl he had never met in the real world.

Or so he believed. And yet…

"Katie." Keith whispered.

"Yeah, Katie," Tom said, happy to see some sort of brain activity happening inside Keith's head. "I didn't mean to bum you out or anything. I know Chuck kind of stole her away from you or something like that. I just wasn't thinking."

"What? Chuck, what? He's seeing that girl?"

"Yeah, last I knew." Tom said with deliberate slowness.

Keith said nothing. His mind was racing. He had just found out the girl literally of his dreams was real. Not only that, but he had dated her last year and his closest friend at school, who he hadn't seen or even thought about in months, was dating her now. To top it all off, he couldn't remember a damn thing about the girl, other than her first name and face. So lost in thought was he, that Keith only half heard Tom say a quick and nervous goodbye before disappearing into the student union. Keith stood there on the building's steps for a few minutes more before turning and jogging for the student housing office.

Halfway across the campus, Keith's gut started acting up again, but it wasn't as bad as it had been before, so he gritted his teeth and pushed through the pain to keep going. By the time he reached the long, brick-faced administration building and found his way to the student housing office, the pain in his stomach was gone and he was completely out of breath. After a quick stop at a nearby drinking fountain, which forced him to slow his breathing while he greedily gulped down water, he opened the glass door to the office and walked inside.

Seeing that he was lucky to have no one in line ahead of him Keith walked up to the plump, but still kind of cute brunet behind the desk. He told her his name and that he was looking for Chuck Hampton.

"Chuck and I were roommates in the Freshman dorms last year. When the year was over we both packed up and went home, but when I got home I found out that I had accidently taken some of his stuff with me. When I came back to school this year, I tried calling him so I could return them, but his mobile number was disconnected. So I was wondering if you could please look up where Chuck is staying now, so I can give him back his stuff. I don't want him thinking I stole it or anything."

Keith mixed the lies and truth together and hoped that it sounded believable. Luckily it did, because while the girl behind the desk said that it wasn't usual policy to do that, she did an overly dramatic look around to see if anyone was listening, and then flashed a playful smile. She first quickly confirmed that Keith and Chuck had been roomies through the school's records. After that she told him that Chuck had a room at a boardinghouse on Fisher Street.

"I think it's great that you're doing all this," she said, still smiling. "Most guys would have just kept the stuff if they thought they would get away with it."

"Yeah, well, Chuck and I used to be pretty tight," Keith mumbled, oblivious to the little signs the girl was sending his way, and was already backing away from her desk. "We sort of just, fell out of touch, I guess."

He half-smiled and thanked the girl, then checking the time on his phone, decided that he had better get to class before he was late. Upon turning for the door, he noticed for the first time the small, four-chaired waiting area to his left he had briskly walked past before. It was the little table set in front of the chairs that drew his attention. Actually it wasn't the table, or the scattering of the usual magazines and school newspapers that rested upon it that caused him to stop. It was the little tin bowl filled with pastel, heart-shaped Valentine's Day candies. He knew that if he stepped closer to the dish he would see candies glaring up at him with 'Be Mine' etched into their little sweet faces.

Keith all but stumbled out of the office door and he heard the kind of cute girl inside ask if he was ok, but he didn't answer. Instead he took off running again, not only to make up for lost time, but to outrun the lingering memories of his nightmare that still lurked in the dark corners of his mind. To further distract himself, Keith also began to make plans for later that night when he would go to Fisher Street.

***

The boardinghouse was a large, two story wood building painted a light gray and set back in a good sized yard. It appeared quite old, for an American house, and at its front porch was an intercom that buzzed six different rooms. Above the intercom was a plastic sign that said, "Rooms 5 & 6 in back". So after checking the names listed on the intercom and finding "C. Hampton" next to number 6, Keith used a red bricked pathway, freshly cleared of snow, to go around to the rear of the house. There he found a twin set of wooden step that lead to a raised patio, divided in the middle by a low wall, and doors marked 5 and 6. All in all, upon first impressions, Chuck looked to be living in a much better place than Keith's rather shabby, crowded apartment. That and dating the girl of his dreams. Keith spit a bit of bile, both literally and figuratively, out of his mouth, climbed the wooden steps, and knocked upon door 6. When it opened, he felt as stunned as the man who opened it looked.

Chuck was looking good, surprised, but good. The last remnants of his teenage acne were all but gone, he had lost about thirty pounds, and he was dressed a lot nicer than Keith could remember ever seeing him. Then again, he still didn't remember much about his old roomie.

"Oh man, uh…what are you doing here?" Chuck asked.

"Nothing, can't an old friend stop in and say hi?" Keith answered, rather coldly.

"Well, yeah, but…come on man, you know—" Chuck stopped as there was a noise behind him that caused him to throw a quick look over his shoulder. It was a metallic clatter, like the sound of pots or pans clanking together.

"Got company?" Keith asked, and put a hand on the door to try to push it open. Chuck pushed back.

"Come on, what, so you found out, huh?"

"Is she here?" Keith asked. He stopped pushing against the door and just looked Chuck in the eye. The other man couldn't hold the gaze, but that only served to upset him.

"Hey man, you're the one who fucked up, ok? Don't blame me for picking up the pieces you left behind." Chuck all but snarled.

"What?"

"Last year, shit, right on Valentine's Day, you broke up with Katie. She said you broke her heart, came crying to me and everything. So don't get pissed at me for your mistake."

"But…I don't remember any of that." Keith said, bewildered. He tried hard to remember, but nothing came to him.

"Oh what, you going to say you were drunk or something?" Chuck snarled, then quickly shoved against his side of the door to close it. "Look, just get the hell out of here, she doesn't want to see you."

Keith tried to push back, but he was caught off guard. By the time he put any weight into it, he heard the door's deadbolt click home. Keith balled up his fists and began to hammer against the surprisingly sturdy door.

"Come on, please, let me talk to her. Please, just let me see her for a second, I need to see her!" Keith yelled.

"Dude, you're pathetic, fuck off!" came a muffled bellow from the other side. "I'm going to call the cops if you don't go away!"

Keith couldn't care less about the police and continued his assault on the door. He began yelling, "Katie? Katie, please talk to me. Please!" But then his stomach pain came roaring back, enough so that it doubled him over and caused him to cry out.

Keith staggered away from the door, put an arm on the patio's railing and rested his head against that arm. His stomach was an angry sea and his mouth filled with a bitter, acid taste. He began gagging, dry heaving, and his throat felt too tight. For a moment he couldn't breathe at all and it was like there was a large hand wrapped around his neck, choking him. Then he quickly lifted up his head, leaned over the railing, and vomited into the snow-toped bushes one story below him. A stream of yellowish-brown bile, and one white chunky mass about the size of a baby's fist, fell to the earth with a sickening splat.

"Man, what's wrong with you?" Chuck said from behind the peephole in the door, it sounded more sad than snarling. "Look, I called the cops. Just…just go away before they get here and don't come back, ok?"

Keith wiped his mouth on the sleeve of his coat. His stomach felt a little better after the expulsion, so he straightened up and walked shakily down the steps. Back on solid ground, Keith began to follow the path around to the front of the building, but at its corner he gave one last look back. At a window a few feet from door 6, Keith saw a small, slight figure with reddish-blond hair for a brief moment, before stepping back and letting the curtain she had been holding open fall back into place. Keith blinked a few times to stop any tears from coming, and slowly trudged back to his car.

In the bushes behind Keith, next to the stairs leading to Chuck's room, something rustled, shook like a wet dog and sent steaming spatters of vomit flying, then quickly scurried away into the darkness and safety beneath the old house's foundations.

**

"Come on, say you'll go, I want to show you something special." Katie said. She was naked and laying half on, half off Keith, with one breast pressing nicely against his left arm. They were both still warm and sticky with sweat from their love making, a nice contrast to the cold room. The couple was in her large bed in her very nice apartment since Keith was stuck in the dorms and he didn't want to rub his relationship in Chuck's no-girlfriend-having face. Especially not on Valentine's Day.

I don't think I've ever been happier, Keith thought, but to play things cool he only said, "What's in a dirty old cave that I'd want to see?"

Katie smiled and her eyes twinkled, "Well silly, you've got to come see if you want to know."

"But it's February and there's a ton of snow outside. It's cold as hell, baby."

"Yes, but it's also Valentine's Day, and you're supposed to do what I want." She said with a pout. It was a playful gesture, but one with a slight implied threat to it, something only a woman could pull off.

Keith laughed, "Ok, but a cave? Really?"

"Yes, it's on the land my family owns up north and it's a really special place." Katie said and her smile grew wider. And wider. And wider still. It was now an impossibly wide smile, literally ear to ear, and an opaque fluid started to drool out of the corners of her mouth to drip down from her chin in long, wet strings.

Keith gave a startled yelp, pushed Katie off of him and went to sit up, but he jolted up with such sudden speed and force that he toppled over the side of the bed. Only he didn't hit Katie's soft brown bedroom carpeting, but instead fell into a rainbow of soft pastel colors that crunched beneath him. Getting to his hands and knees, Keith saw he was kneeling in thousands and thousands of Valentine's Day heart-shaped candies, and as his face was just inches away from the sweets, he saw that each and every one of them bore the same inscription;

BE MINE.

"You must agree to the bargain." Katie's voice hissed out of the darkness.

Keith rose up from the candies and looked about for the source of the voice. He wasn't surprised to see the gray stone walls that had become so familiar to him as of late, disappearing into darkness. There was no sign of Katie.

"You don't have a choice. I'm sorry, but I had to do this." She said from behind him. Keith whipped around, but again saw only colorful candies and bleak, gray walls.

"Katie? Where are you? What's going on?" Keith yelled out. His echo was the only sound to answer him.

A rustling, rattling from his feet drew Keith's eyes down and he saw that the heart candies had been drained of their soft rainbow colors. They were now bleached bone white and were skittering and scrambling over each other, the floor, and even starting to crawl up Keith's legs. Keith sucked in breath with a hiss, bent at the waist to swat at the climbing candy-things, but stopped suddenly when—

BE MINE.

The pain in Keith's belly now swiftly, remorselessly spread up to encompass his chest. There was a burning tightness behind his ribs, his heart felt heavy and sluggish, and he had trouble expanding his lungs fully, so he had to resort to a series of short, sharp breaths to get any air at all.

I'm dying, he thought and deep down at the core of his being, he knew that was the simple, awful truth of it.

"If you love me, you'll accept this." Katie whispered into Keith's ear from behind. Turning around once more—

The hulking horror was only inches from his face and the thing's immensity was such that it eclipsed everything else from Keith's vision. To take in the full picture of the nightmare before him was beyond Keith. All he could see was creases, folds, and slabs of pale white flesh and muscle. Across that cracked and lumpy surface, countless hoary and many-legged things scurried about. The closest Keith could come to classifying the scuttling hoard was large, white spiders, but that didn't do justice to the alien wrongness of the things. Then across the face of this abhorrent moon, multiple murky-yellow eyes, the color of rotted squash, opened. The monstrous thing glared down at him, looked into him, and saw completely through him. Keith had never felt as naked as he did before the pale behemoth that impassionedly studied him.

Keith tried to scream, to let the raw terror inside him come bubbling up and relieve some of the mounting pressure he felt, but he couldn't. There was something solid yet squishy in his throat, blocking all sound, all air, and it was skittering and clambering its way up to Keith's open mouth.

WILL YOU BE MINE?

"If you love me, you'll say yes."

* * *

Keith awoke with Katie's words still buzzing around in his head. He ached all over, as if the persistent pain in his stomach had been equally distributed throughout his body. Looking around his room, Keith saw dim light creeping out from under his drawn curtains. He knew it was daytime, but that's all he could be sure of because there were too many other oddities that didn't make sense. First and foremost was the state of his room, which was not how it was when he went to bed last night. Piles of clothes were dumped here and there without rhyme or reason and they fought for space with the many dirty plates, bowls, and glasses, all containing the moldering remnants of various meals and drinks. Next, upon trying to check the time on his alarm clock, he found it busted and broken on his nightstand. Pieces of it were on the floor, as if someone hit it with a hammer. Groggily and sorely, Keith untangled himself from his blankets and sheets, got out of bed, put on his robe and left his room.

"Hey, it lives!" his roommate, Devin said as he walked by, coming from his own room and heading toward the kitchen.

"What?" was all Keith could mumble out and followed him, lemming-like.

"Feeling any better, sport?" Greg said from around a mouthful of milk and Cheerios. He sat at the table, dressed for school, eating his morning breakfast.

"What are you talking about?" Keith asked as he plopped down heavily into a chair.

"You know, whatever deadly illness you've had for about the last week?"

"What, my stomach thing?"

"Don't know," Devin said as he joined the others at the table with his own bowl of cereal in hand. "You really didn't tell us about it. You pretty much haven't talked at all for the last five days. All you did was sleep."

It was as if someone had thrown a glass of cold water into Keith's face. Suddenly the grogginess was gone and he had the crystal clear focus of a prey animal that just caught a predator's scent. "What do you mean 'five days'?"

"Ha, you really were out of it." Greg said. "You caught some sort of wicked-ass bug, and for the last five days, all you did was stay in your bedroom and sleep. You'd come out occasionally, to use the bathroom or get something to eat, but that was it. Dev and I tried talking you into going to the hospital a few times, but you would just mumble that you were fine and go back in your room."

"You don't remember any of that?" Devin asked, slightly bemused.

"No," Keith whispered, "No I don't."

"Yeah you had it bad. We could hear you retching all night, sounded nasty as shit, but the next day you always said you were fine or getting better or something. And well, neither of us wanted to get what you had, so we pretty much just left you alone." Greg said, then sheepishly added, "I mean, you kept saying you were ok and stuff."

My god, five days, I lost five days, Keith thought. "So what day is it now?" He asked.

"It's Wednesday. You know, Valentine's Day." Devin said.

"Of course," Keith replied and then was quiet as a jumble of frightening thoughts raced around in his head.

An awkward silence filled the kitchen as Greg and Devin ate breakfast and Keith brooded. The two roomies eventually got up, gathered their things for class, and left. Greg was the last to leave, and at their door to their rented house, he turned back and looked through the small living room and over the half wall that separated it from the kitchen at Keith where he still sat at the table.

"Hey, if you're going to stay home again from class again, could you call the landlord for us?" Greg asked. He had to repeat the question before Keith responded.

"Hmm, what? Oh sure, what about?"

"Tell him he needs to get an exterminator out here, I think we've got rats. Devin and I have been hearing things moving around in the walls for the last couple of nights. And well, since it looks like you're feeling better, I thought you could make the call. If you weren't doing anything else, I mean." Greg said and gave a weak smile.

"Yeah, ok." Keith murmured, but rats were the least of his worries right now.

Greg said 'later' and left, leaving Keith once more alone with his thoughts. Although this time it didn't take him long to decide what to do. He would get cleaned up, get dressed, and go back to Chuck's place and even if he had to kick down the damn door, he would talk with Kaytlin and get to the bottom of just what the hell was happening to him.

***

Keith returned to the large boardinghouse on Fisher Street, walked back around behind it to room 6, and pounded on the door for a good five minutes before their neighbor in room 5 opened up her door and told him, "Chuck and Katie are gone."

Keith looked over the top of the low privacy wall that separated the patios and saw a girl standing half out of her doorway. Using a variant of the lie that had worked earlier, Keith told the very young woman, who was obviously also a student at the college, about being roommates with Chuck, only this time it was Chuck that had some of his stuff, and Keith wanted the things back.

"I had my freshman roomie do the same thing to me. Bitch stole a bunch of my makeup at the end of the year and I never got them back." She sympathized with Keith.

"So any idea where they are?" He asked.

"No, sorry. Oh, but I did see them leaving. They had a couple of bags with them, so maybe they went out for a long Valentine's Day weekend or something? So you might want to try back on Monday."

"Oh…thanks." Keith said and he felt his heart sink. The girl nodded, stepped back inside her apartment, and Keith slowly walked back to his car on the street. Feeling miserable and terrified, he sat behind the wheel of his car and—

Suddenly he was in the same car, but heading north along I75, with Katie in the seat next to him. It was snowing and the roads were starting to get slick and he suggested that they turn around and go to her 'mystery cave' some other time.

Katie said no, that it had to be today. That today was special. It was Valentine's Day, after all.

"But you're sick, and you don't look that well." Keith said and that was true. For the last couple of weeks Katie had on again, off again stomach pains, and despite his best efforts to get her to see a doctor, she always refused.

Katie looked at him, grimacing more than smiled and—

Keith was back in his car, still behind the wheel, but he was alone and parked on Fisher Street. However, he now knew with certainty where Katie and Chuck had gone, just as surely as he knew how to get there. Turning the key in the ignition and putting the car into drive, Keith next tried to remember the easiest way to get to I75 from here.

***

The drive was long and dreamlike. It had been a fogy, half remember sojourn, stronger than a sense of déjà vu, but still something less than fully remembered. Keith was only sure that after three hours of driving north on the interstate, watching the cities fall away to towns and then the towns give way to hilly woodland, followed by yet another half hour on narrow dirt roads, he was finally back where he had been exactly one year ago. So too were Katie and Chuck, as he saw Chuck's car parked in the small clearing at the end of the long private drive that lead into the woods owned by Katie's family.

Keith got out of his own car, stretched, and looked around. Most people who owned a piece of land up north built cabins or parked trailers on it and use their wooded acreage for vacations or hunting trips. Perhaps in time they would build a little house so that when they retired they could "get away from it all". Not Katie's family. For as long as they had owned it, they had never built anything on it. Their land only had the small clearing to park on and lots of trees.

No wait, there's also a path, Keith remembered and he walked to the left side of the clearing. Sure enough, he saw a pair of tracks in the melting snow that came from Chuck's car and entered the woods through a narrow break in the trees at this point. Knowing what would be waiting for him at the end of the path, Keith returned to his car and retrieved a small flashlight from the glove box. Turning it on and off to check if the batteries still worked, and thankfully finding that they did, he slipped it into his coat pocket and returned to the start of the path to follow the tracks into the woods.

After a short walk, Keith saw what awaited him, a series of low hills in the woods with nothing out of the ordinary about them. Katie and Chuck's tracks lead directly to one snow covered mound of earth and to a hole in its side. Upon seeing the hill, a memory stirred inside Keith.

"So it's a hole in the ground." Keith said from a year in the past upon first seeing the cave for the first time.

"It's not just that. When my family came to America from England they were drawn to this spot. It's very special." Katie said and in Keith's mind, he could see her standing next to him. She was in obvious pain, although she tried to hide it, yet the smile on her face was genuine.

"Special how?" He asked, smirking.

"You'll have to come inside to find out." She teased.

The memory faded as quickly as it had come. Keith looked at the hole in the side of the hill, nodded to himself, and entered the cave as he pulled the flashlight from his pocket. The walls, floor and ceiling was naked earth, but being that it was mid-February, they weren't wet and dripping like they always were in his dreams. Keith chalked that up to random strangeness that happens in dreams. After all, he hoped he wouldn't find hallways filled with bones or heart-shaped candies either.

He was only a few yards into the hill, and steadily heading down, when another memory assailed him. In it, he and Katie had reached the end of the natural cave, only to find a completely different darkened tunnel continuing where it left off. This new passage somehow seemed older than the earth they were under and it was made of worked stone, mortared together by ancient, unknowable hands. Before he could make sense of what his eyes were telling him, Keith saw movement in the gloom of the newly revealed stone hallway. It was a huge shape, an oval bulk that almost filled the tunnel completely. It was bigger than his car, bigger than anything that walked on solid ground had a right to be, and worst of all, it was coming toward them.

Katie walked up close to him from behind and casually wrapped her arms around his neck. It was a hug, but a restraining one.

"I told you I'd show you something special." She whispered in his ear. "Behold, the Labyrinth. It touches all the dark places in the world. That is why my family came here after leaving the Severn Valley, the two are connected."

Katie gave him a light kiss on the neck before following Keith's gaze into the dark. She saw the monstrous thing lumbering toward them, and smiled at it.

"Don't be afraid. That is the Lord of the Labyrinth, Eihort. He is a god. A true, living god! One who rewards his faithful followers. He is my god and he—" Katie said, then cried out in pain, stepped back from Keith as she wrapped her arms around his chest, and doubled over. She began to retch so loudly and violently that the sound of it finally drew Keith's attention from the approaching horror to her.

Keith turned and saw Katie bent over a fresh puddle of vomit, shaking her head back and forth, trying to break streamers of spittle that ran from her mouth to the floor of the cave. Tracing those glittering strands down, Keith saw that the puddle of puke began to move as small, white, spider-like things crawled out of it to—

The ear-splitting scream shattered the memory and brought Keith back to the present. It was a high-pitched shriek of pure terror, obviously male, but the kind of sound no man should ever make. The scream filled Keith with dread and he wanted nothing more than to run from the cave, but then he heard Katie's voice and that held him in place. She was speaking loudly, but Chuck's continued shrieking drowned out most of her words, so that Keith could only make out a handful.

"…must…bargain…Eihort…survive…you love me…" was all that Keith could make out, but it was Katie's last three words that filled him with a nearly uncontrollable rage and drove him deeper into the cave.

He was two dozen or more running strides further along when it hit him.

BE MINE.

The words were not heard, nor were they a memory of some recurring dream. They were as real as anything else in this crazy, waking nightmare world, and they felt forced into his mind. It was like an invisible claw carved them into the folds of his brain, he had no choice but to understand them. Keith knew the words weren't directed at him, and yet their presence caused the pain in his abdomen to flare up like a bonfire.

"No," Keith called out, and stumbled the rest of the way to where the cave ended, and the labyrinth began. That is where he saw Katie and the terrible thing called Eihort for the first time outside of his dreams, in the flesh, since that last horrible Valentine's Day.

The large, pale, oval bulk of the ancient abomination was supported by countless fleshless legs, one of which, about as thick as a tree trunk, had Chuck pinned against a stone wall where the terrified student gibbered incoherently. Several feet away from the pair, Katie sat on the ground, covered in sweat despite the cold, rocking back and forth with her hands pressed tightly to her belly that even at a distance, Keith could see writhing and churning like a stormy sea.

"You must…accept his bargain if…you want to live, Chuck." Katie gasped out. "It's not that bad…"

"Lying bitch!" Keith shouted, one hand against the tunnel's wall to keep him on his feet. "Don't trust her or that…thing, Chuck. It's all a lie."

At the sight of him, Katie's eyes went wide. "No, Keith, I…no."

"Are you trying to have that thing do to him what you did to me?"

"Keith, I—" Katie began, but a sudden bout of retching stopped her.

48

BE MINE.

And with that psychic blast, the dam in his mind burst, and a rush of memories flooded in. Not just his own recollections, but thoughts and images from Katie also filled his head. Then there were the other bits, alien and grotesque memories whose source could only be that of the nearby obscene horror. The close proximity of Katie's damnable pale god joined the three of them in an inexplicitly and thoroughly unwholesome way.

He sees Katie as a young girl, the same age as she is now, but many years in the past. She has been brought to the cave by her father, to take her place in their ancestral worship. Her terror at seeing the Lord of the Labyrinth for the first time slams into Keith like a wrecking ball. Then he hears Katie's father's calm, reassuring words, telling her not to be afraid, to accept the bargain and be rewarded.

He skitters, low and stealthily, through a cold, dead city with architecture the likes of which Keith has never seen. The sky above is a writing mass of clouds, obscuring the twin moons above. He is not alone; he feels the presence of thousands of his kind, perhaps millions, and is comforted by them. Then somewhere deeper, somewhere darker, he feels the will of his sire, telling them that their time has come at long last. This world is now theirs.

He feels the ponderous weight of the bloated thing's thick leg on him, pinning him to the ground a year in the past on some other horrible Valentine's Day. Katie is there, kneeling next to him, stroking his hair, trying to calm him, and whispering, "You must agree to the bargain. If you don't, I'll die. You'll die. Just say yes and this can all be over."

He shares Katie's nervousness and feels her pain as the brood inside her crawls through her guts, skitters across her organs, and chews trails through her muscle and bone into her furthest extremities. This is her first sacrifice and she's afraid that she will do something wrong, or that the bargain won't be struck, and that she'll pay the price for displeasing her god. But there is also pity and sympathy for the young man she has brought here. He is newly home from Europe, still flush with pride over saving the world from fascism. His feeling of invulnerability at surviving the horrors of war, combined with the abundant amount of alcohol he had consumed at the bar, has him ignoring the fear and absolute wrongness he should be feeling. Even when her god first appears in the labyrinth, a monstrous blob of darkness in the sea of black, the young solider just giggles, points and asks, "What's that?" It is only when Eihort steps into the light that the screaming starts.

He is curled in the passenger seat of his own car; wet, cold, too exhausted both physically and mentally from the ordeal to weep, although that is all he wants to do. He has just been violated so completely that the word rape pales in comparison. Katie is at the wheel, driving them back to the university. She looks healthy for the first time in months, and she says coldly, "Don't worry, you'll forget all about this by tomorrow. It's all part of the bargain."

He walks alone through the dark halls of his labyrinth ceaselessly, eternally. He feels the presence of others encroaching on his domain. Not his brood, their presence is constant, but the feeble ones from above. They are dirty, ignorant, low creatures reeking of fear and filth. They worship him like a god, but he cares not for their veneration. They are only suitable as vessels for his brood to gestate in and nothing more. He will go to them and offer his bargain. Those that accept will be rewarded. Those who don't will be ended.

He sees himself through Katie's eyes as she first saw him; alone, confused, nervous on his first day at college. He's perfect for her needs. The brood squirm in her stomach, the time of their birth is getting close. She needs another to take before her god, to accept the bargain and take her place. Only then will Eihort de-age the growing offspring inside her, revert them back to their larval state so that she can continue to bring the Old One surrogates for its young to multiply in. And as the brood and her are linked on a level far deeper than a physical one, she will not only be spared for another year, but will remain young and beautiful. So she gets up, puts on her best false smile, and approaches the frightened freshman; a well-practiced predator on the hunt. Any traces of sympathy or humanity she once had has been lost over the many years, and countless boys she has brought out to her family's cave.

WILL YOU BE MINE?

The overwhelming will of the beast breaks the mental connection the three shared, brining Keith back to his senses. He looked to where Chuck was, sobbing and pined to the wall by a nightmare. He then turned to see Katie, sitting on the ground, a puddle of vomit next to her with a myriad of white spider-things crawling out of it. Lastly, he faced the abomination.

"No! Tell it no, Chuck." Keith yelled out to his onetime roommate.

"No, don't listen to—" Katie began, but was once more was interrupted by coughing, choking spasms of pain.

"That monster will put other monsters inside you, Chuck. They will grow and grow until they eat you up from the inside out. You don't want that to happen, do you?" Keith yelled out.

Chuck finally tore his watering eyes away from the horror that held him and looked at Keith. "N…n…no." He wept.

"Then tell it no. Tell it that you won't be his."

"No…" Katie called out, weakly.

"No!" Chuck shouted, "No, no, no. I do not want that, I do not!"

Then without any argument, cajoling, or the faintest hint of emotion, Eihort leaned forward with its massive bulk, and its thick leg smashed Chuck's chest against the stone wall like he was a bug. When The Lord of the Labyrinth lowered its thick appendage, Chuck fell into two pieces, with the lower part hitting the ground immediately, spilling blood, bowel and bladder, and the upper half sticking to the wall for a few moments before slowly sliding down, leaving a trail of gore in its wake.

The Pale God then turned its many yellow eyes on Katie where she cowered and trembled on the ground.

YOU FAILED ME.

Katie in turn looked up at Keith. "Why?" she asked.

"Because Chuck was dead either way. Because of all the other guys you've done this to over the years. But mostly because you broke my heart. You never loved me." Keith said and gave a cold, bitter smile.

Katie's face bore a mixture of sadness, fear, and anger for a brief moment before all emotions were replaced with incredible, searing pain. She began to shriek every bit as loud as Chuck had as a red gash started to bisect the skin on her forehead, causing a mixture of blood and a thick, off-white fluid to dribble down her screaming face. Her naked flesh began to bubble like the surface of a thick stew left on the stove for too long. Her cries of torment continued to rise in pitch, as she shuddered and blood began to well up out of her mouth along with a bubbling mass of pale, squirming, writhing things.

Keith turned around and closed his eyes. Although he hated the woman for what she had done to him, he didn't want to see what happened to her. He did hear it, however. Wet tearing sounds, gurgling screams of pain, a thick bursting splosh at the end, followed by the scampering of thousands and thousands of tiny feet.

Keith fell to the ground, physically, emotionally, and mentally spent. Wracked with pain, terrified beyond reason, and choking on the bitter taste of vengeance, he welcomed oblivion. Yet there was an animalistic part of him that would fight to the end to live. It would claw and scratch for every second of life it could, and even sacrifice others to do so if it had to.

It was a part of humanity that Eihort knew only too well.

WOULD YOU STILL BE MINE?

***

Another year, another Valentine's Day.

"Ok, you get some bonus points for this. I've heard of Valentine's Day dinners, but not too many girls get a Valentine's Day breakfast." Sheri said as she forked another bit of egg into her mouth.

The young couple sat in a small family restaurant just off of I75. She was all smiles, bright green eyes, and strawberry blond hair. As for him, the young man was pale and trembled slightly, often he brought his napkin up to his mouth to cough into.

"Well I have to reward you for coming along on this crazy adventure with me." Keith said, honey all but literally dripping from his words.

"I still don't know why we're going to some cave in the middle of no-where for Valentine's Day. Oh how romantic," she giggled.

"I told you, babe, this place is special. It's been in the family for years and I just want to share it with you." Keith said and then broke out into another coughing fit.

"Are you alight?" she said with sincere concern.

"Yeah I'm fine, just this damn cold," Keith said and shot a grin at Sheri. "Don't worry, I'll be better soon. Oh hey, almost forgot the second part of my reward-slash-bribe."

Keith reached into his winter coat and pulled out something small, brown, and fuzzy. He set the little teddy bear on the table in front of Sheri and turned it so that the pink heart it held in its little paws faced the girl. On the face of the stuffed heat were two words, stitched in pink;

BE MINE.

With appreciation to the master, Ramsey Campbell.

Cthulhu Mhy'os
by Lois H. Gresh

The door creaked as the night air wafted into the shack, and on the table, the whiskey shuddered in the Goblet of Anticipation.

"He has come," lisped Ahmose.

A trill of excitement swept through Dudimayos. The mighty one was finally here, and Dudimayos would see the promised land before he died. He would see it *tonight*.

He bit the arthritic bump on the knuckle of his middle finger. A tiny sting, like that of a mosquito, and a drop of blood welled from the incision. Dudimayos savored the tanginess, letting the blood swirl around his tongue before he swallowed. His great-granddaughter would do well, at this, her first seder. She was only four, but she was a direct descendant of Mhy'Os and her blood was infused with the spirit of He Who Cannot Be Named. Ahmose's trances were legendary throughout all twelve tribes. Dudimayos tried to keep his voice from trembling. "Let us begin. Drink your first cup, Ahmose," he said. "Unhindered. Free. And for the future." Ahmose lifted the Goblet of Anticipation, threw back her head, and swilled all eight ounces of 100-proof moonshine. She slammed the goblet down and smacked her lips. Her cheeks flushed yellow, and for a moment, her eyes glowed as a fishy musk wafted from her. She mumbled the first prayer in the ancient tongue, then scratched a fingernail on the oak table. Fire sparked from her nail and leapt to the table's end, where the two seder candles flickered to life.

In the glow of sacred light, Akeley's face loomed pasty and wet, his mouth a sliver of quivering flesh, his breathing heavy and his nostrils flared to capture every morsel of Ahmose's musk. To Akeley's right, Whateley's gibbering rose until he was shrieking the ancient prayers while beating his fists against his skull. To Akeley's left, violent spasms hit Peaslee's body, setting his chair clacking against the floorboards. From around the table, teeth chattered, eyes bulged and dripped mucous, facial tics spread over flesh and down limbs as if insects scurried beneath the skin. In the corner, Mason keened, Ward whimpered.

Dudimayos was lucky to have reigned over such an elite bunch: Dudimayos and Ahmose of the priestly Levite tribe, and one member from each of the other tribes: Akeley, Derby, Gilman, Jermyn, Marsh, Mason, Peaslee, Pickman, Waite, Ward, and Whateley.

Ahmose crawled onto the table and squatted on the seder plate, knocking aside vole skulls filled with herbs, nuts, and ossicles. She pressed her fingers to the candle flames and they died.

The gibbering and clacking shrilled and then ebbed to an undercurrent. A spotlight of moon streamed through the window behind Akeley, Whateley, and Peaslee, then centered on Ahmose.

"It has begun," whispered Derby.

"The blood," said Jermyn.

"The *meal!*" cried Mason.

Ah yes, the meal.

Dudimayos lowered his head in respect as Ahmose opened her mouth to speak. The last image Dudimayos saw was that of her face: ovoid and gray with foot-long whiskers and waxy eyes. The air thickened with her odor, dank and strong, and as tradition dictated, Ahmose recounted the story of Passover as if straight from the source, from Mhy'Os himself:

***

Ah, the swivel of hips—*said Ahmose*—the lilt of the flute, the whisper of the Nile breeze, the sweetness of dates, the seductress calling his name, "Mhy'Os, Mhy'Os," soft and low.

Feh, the bite of reality, the dry crackers, the flab on his wife Zipporah's hips, her voice as harsh as a sand storm. Mhy'Os had left their tent before dawn, and as always, was determined to stick it out under the hot sun and then head home long after sunset.

Mhy'Os wanted to cut loose, unhindered and free.

As his lambs grazed on the scrub, his head filled with fantasies about dancing Egyptian girls. He flashed to the Egyptian guard he had killed and Pharaoh's edict that he should either die or live the rest of his days in the desert. Already, Mhy'Os had been here for forty years. *Wasn't it enough?* There were no dancing girls, and Zipporah fed him nothing but lamb fat and dust.

The sand whirled into a haze on the horizon. The sun burned into his eyes, the rays like lancets. Before him was nothing, a bleak stretch of sand ending in the eddies that he knew would blind any man stupid enough to wander that far.

From the haze, something bright blossomed: it was red and orange, and it burst from the sky, crackling and spitting flames. Mhy'Os winced as he rose to his feet, then speared the sand with his shepherd's staff so he wouldn't fall. *This must be a mirage,* he thought, *for what else could it be?* Balls of fire didn't just burst from the sky, did they?

But this one was all too real. It blasted over the sand toward Mhy'Os and scorched the air, and the fire spit burning sand at everything below. As their wool went up in flames, the lambs shrieked and raced in circles, then fell into heaps of kicking legs and charred wool. Mhy'Os' heart clenched. The desert reeked of roasting meat. He staggered back and clutched his staff. A few final squeaks from the dying lambs, and then they were all gone. Just bones in the sand and trails of charred wool floating in the haze.

The fire hovered several cubits in front of him, singed his lashes, burned his face raw.

Mhy'Os would die. He would melt, like wax he would melt, and then he would die. His staff dropped, his hands flew to his eyes, but the merest scrape of flesh across his face hurt like hell, and he cried out and collapsed into the sand. The ball of fire flickered out, and in its place—yes, right there in front of him, coming out of nowhere!—was a burning bush.

A baritone voice boomed, the words hitting Mhy'Os like bludgeons. "Mortal thing! *You* are not circumcised."

Mhy'Os tried to speak, but his lips had melted into a tiny round hole. He didn't understand what the voice had said. Finally, he managed to squeak, "What? What do you want?"

"Mortal thing! *You* will serve me. All of your descendants will follow in your path. You will do as I say."

A bolt of fire hit Mhy'Os, and pain twisted in his stomach. He couldn't move, and then another bolt hit him, this time burning the white robe off his body in a bloody trail. Sweat gushed from his face, neck, and arms, and yet he was icy cold, and he knew, he just knew, that he was dying. This would be it, and let it be fast.

Fire engulfed his thighs, and as he gasped in horror, wishing he could fend it off—if only he could move—but the fire knifed his genitals.

Searing pain...

His eyes blurred.

"Let my people go!" boomed the voice. "Beg Pharaoh, then circumcise the men. Burn their genitals, and I will free them from Egyptian slavery."

Burn their genitals?

Mhy'Os was *not* going to burn anybody's genitals. He twitched in the sand and stared at his own bloody member. He could move his arms and legs now, but his crotch hurt like hell. "Who are you? Why?" he muttered from his melted mouth hole.

Leaves fluttered from the burning bush and formed words in the sky. Mhy'Os squinted. *I am. I am. He Who Cannot Be Named.*

Later, Mhy'Os had a hard time explaining what had happened to Zipporah. She demanded to know how an entire flock of sheep had burned to death in the middle of the desert.

Mhy'Os hissed through his mouth hole, "He Who Cannot Be Named."

She demanded to know why his face had melted off and why he limped. "Something must have happened! Who did this to you?"

"He Who Cannot Be Named."

She stomped her foot. "You tell me this, Mhy'Os! How does a penis just burn off, Mhy'Os?"

He hissed so loudly spit gurgled from his mouth. *"He Who Cannot Be Named."*

She fumed for a week until finally—deformed, hideously burned, and crippled—he limped from their tent, explaining that he had to trek across the desert to Egypt.

"I won't go with you, Mhy'Os," she said, eyes lashing at him like snakes. It wasn't as if he'd *asked* her...

Mhy'Os remembered the dancing Egyptian girls, and he turned his back on his wife. *I am circumcised*, he thought. *I am free of the past.*

***

Here, Ahmose paused in retelling the story of Mhy'Os. It was time for the second cup. Dudimayos grabbed the whiskey urn from the fireplace and filled the Goblet of Anticipation. It was time for Ahmose to shift quickly into the recounting of the ten plagues.

The dank fishiness of the room was laced with sweat. The fired crackled, and the scorched air made Dudimayos' mouth go dry. He stripped off his burlap shirt and flung it across the room, where it splashed into a puddle by the open door. In all the years he had led the Passover seder, Dudimayos had brought forth many of the plagues but only in weakened forms. One year, lice coated the table; another year, tadpoles flourished in all the forest streams; and yet another year, locusts blanketed the sky and sent the hypocrites and fools screaming into their houses.

Already, he knew that this year would be different. Ahmose would do what Dudimayos had only dreamed of doing.

Ahmose stretched her little four-year-old legs across the table and rubbed them. She lifted the silver goblet, tipped back her head, and swilled another eight ounces of moonshine. Direct blood, she was, straight from Mhy'Os through the ages to Dudimayos to his son and grandson, both dead from tragic accidents. Dudimayos gnawed his arthritic bumps and heaved his belly so it rested between his knees. He missed his son and grandson, but it was worth it. Ahmose was so pure, *so pure*.

"Let's get on with it," piped Derby. "Let's get to the meal."

"Yeah, tell her to skip the commentaries like you always did," whined Peaslee.

"She'll tell the story in her own way," said Dudimayos. "Ahmose knows what to do."

The little girl stroked her foot-long whiskers. Her eyes glazed. She was ready to continue.

"Blood," she lisped.

The first plague.

Dudimayos shivered.

It wouldn't be much longer now.

***

Water slapped the sides of the drainage troughs and gurgled through the streets. The color of sewage, it swelled over the banks of the Nile and seeped into dwellings and market stalls. Mhy'Os didn't mind the cool water on his ankles after his long hike through the desert, though it was odd to see fish flopping and muck floating around his legs. He couldn't wait to peel off his white robe, which was now yellow from sweat and dirt. A bath would be good. Some food. Maybe a dancing girl or two.

Egyptian boys raced around him, and he remembered enough of their language to discern that they were making fun of him. "Look at the old bum" and "He can hardly walk" and "Ha ha, he smells like dung" and "Have you ever seen such an ugly face?"

The young girls lowered their eyes and kept their distance. Before Pharaoh banished him to the desert, the girls couldn't take their eyes off Mhy'Os.

He limped past columns and bas relief images of Egyptian gods, pharaohs, and mummies, everything burnished and gleaming against a backdrop of blue crystal sky. Flowering trees swayed in the flood of the Nile, and the people here all looked beautiful and healthy. The hardships of desert life were unknown to them. Their translucent robes were pristine but for the muddy hems, their faces tranquil, their fingers smooth, their eyes painted with mesdemet made from dark ore and with glittering udju, the copper-green ore of the gods. Mhy'Os was acutely aware that his own eyes lacked decoration, that his lids had melted back into his skull, making his left eye bulge and his right eye blind. It was no wonder everyone stared at him. He was the only freak among perfection.

He drove his staff through the Nile muck that clogged the entrance path to Pharaoh's palace. His heart swelled as he remembered walking here as a child: the palace had not changed much. He brushed his palms over the row of huge Pharaoh statues, delighted in the fragrance of the floating lotus and the henna bushes, and plucked a grape from the vines draped over the stone walls. The fruit was a treat after forty years of lamb fat and dry crackers. He lingered by decorative pools where waterfowl splashed and bright fish whirled in endless loops, then finally limped up to Pharaoh's royal guards.

Four of them, they were much taller than Mhy'Os and quite muscular by Egyptian standards. They wore gold vestments and headpieces, and skirts of crisp linen. When they brandished gold-laced spears tipped in poison, Mhy'Os tottered back a step, and all four glared at him. He was indeed a wretch: filthy and burned into a grotesque blur of a real man.

He lifted his staff and turned to go. He knew better than to fool with the royal guards.

But then a baritone voice thundered in his head. "He Who Cannot Be Named demands freedom for Pharaoh's slaves. He Who Cannot Be Named demands the burning of the genitals."

Mhy'Os repeated the words, his voice barely audible as it squeaked from his melted mouth hole.

The guards laughed, their eyes no longer angry. Mhy'Os had given them welcome relief from their boredom. They probably thought he was a simpleton, an old fool. A spear descended, then two spears, both pointing at Mhy'Os, the poison tips only a hand-length from his belly.

"Tell Pharaoh," squeaked Mhy'Os.

They laughed, told him to move along, and threatened him with the spears.

Mhy'Os decided not to press his luck. He Who Could Not Be Named would have to be patient. Mhy'Os would bide his time by the Pharaoh statues and trellises, perhaps feast on some of the palace grapes when the guards weren't looking.

As he approached the decorative pool, where waterfowl had played only half an hour earlier, squawks rose and feathers filled the air. Mhy'Os stopped and stared at the water. Feathers and dead fish floated in water the color of blood. The hem of his robe was sopped in blood. Around his ankles lapped blood.

Suddenly, from all around, people were screaming and running through the water—*the blood*—that had overflowed the banks of the Nile.

The four royal guards remained rigid by the palace doors, but even at this distance, Mhy'Os' one good eye, the bulging eye, told him that the guards were staring at the surge of blood against the walls and stone edgings.

A baritone voice thundered in his head. "He Who Cannot Be Named demands freedom for Pharaoh's slaves. He Who Cannot Be Named demands the burning of the genitals."

Mhy'Os had to obey. He had no choice. The voice vibrated through him, it filled him and controlled him as if he was a puppet. So he sloshed through the blood and approached the guards, and again, he repeated the words. "Tell Pharaoh," he squeaked.

Again, they shooed him off, and this time, He Who Cannot Be Named filled the bloody waters with frogs. Croaking, belching, slimy frogs: they clogged the air as they leapt, making any movement impossible. Mhy'Os couldn't walk away from the guards, who once again slapped him aside and told him to get lost.

Over and over, the baritone voice filled his head, demanding that he issue the same order to the guards. The way Mhy'Os figured it, if He Who Cannot Be Named was powerful enough to turn the Nile to blood and fill Egypt with frogs, then clearly, He Who Cannot Be Named could inflict unspeakable tortures on him. Scared as Mhy'Os was, he complied with one order after another to demand freedom for the slaves and the burning of their genitals. The guards slapped him away time and time again, and finally, after He Who Cannot Be Named had inflicted Egypt with blood, frogs, lice, flies, and death of all livestock, one of the guards slammed Mhy'Os against the palace wall and shoved the tip of his spear against Mhy'Os' throat. One hair away from Mhy'Os's skin, just one hair, and Mhy'Os would be dead. In some ways, it would be a relief, but then he heard the voice in his head again; and this time, Mhy'Os didn't even have to squeak "Tell Pharaoh" before He Who Cannot Be Named inflicted another plague upon Egypt. Boils erupted on the faces and the bodies of the guards. Pus oozed from the open sores, blood streamed down their faces, arms, and legs. They screamed from the pain, but still, they wouldn't relent, and still, the poison spears trembled a hair away from Mhy'Os' neck. Hail, thunder, and locusts came next, followed by a darkness that was blacker than the mummy tar slathered on the dead. But still, they wouldn't relent.

***

Ahmose paused, gesturing at Dudimayos to fill the goblet for a third time. He grabbed the urn and sloshed moonshine into the goblet, and she anxiously swilled another eight ounces and licked her lips. The room reeked of sweat and musk. The end was almost near.

From outside the shack, people screamed in the night, birds cawed, and animals chattered with hysteria. Dudimayos could hear the effects of the plagues: the trees crashing to the forest floor, the fires erupting and sizzling through the brush, the thunder, the hail. The spotlight of moon no longer streamed through the window to cast its halo over Ahmose. Darkness was everywhere. The night was dead.

One more plague to go, and Dudimayos would finally see the promised land.

"We come to the tenth plague, the slaying of the firstborn sons," lisped Ahmose.

A tree crashed against the shack, and the vole skulls of herb, nuts, and bones rattled on the table. Dudimayos heard the candlesticks clatter to the floor down by Akeley and Whateley. Ward was sobbing and muttering, "Dudimayos, Dudimayos, Dudimayos, *no.*"

Dudimayos started to reply, but Ahmose cut him off. "Outside the blood is rising to the window ledges. Soon, it will burst through the glass and drown us all. I must continue with the story, and quickly. Or all will be lost."

Dudimayos gripped the table with both hands. He knew what was coming.

As the hail pounded the roof and the thunder brought mighty cracks of lightning overhead, Dudimayos saw Ahmose's face once again. It was ovoid but much larger, her forehead so high it grazed the ceiling. Her waxy eyes were solid black and protruded from her head on two throbbing stalks. The foot-long whiskers were replaced by enormous, writhing tentacles that swept the vole skulls off the table with one flick and slapped the front door shut with another.

Ward, Mason, and Peaslee all gasped and threw back their chairs, and they raced to the door and tried to pry it back open. It wouldn't budge any more than Pharaoh had budged in the time of Mhy'Os.

Dudimayos' chest tightened. It was hard to breathe in the heat, and he could almost feel death settling upon him. "He Who Cannot Be Named," he whispered. "You are here."

"I am. I am," lisped Ahmose. "Now let me finish the story, old man."

＊＊＊

Mhy'Os told the royal guards—*said Ahmose*—that all the firstborns would be killed that night if Pharaoh did not free the slaves. Pharaoh refused. And all through Egypt that night, people wailed over their dead sons.

***

A tentacle lashed out and coiled around Mason's neck, and squeezed. Mason's hands gripped the tentacle, tried to wrench it off, but the hold was too strong. Struggling for air, his face turned purple as he thrashed, and then his body went limp.

And the room went dark.

Another crash of thunder, and lightning illumed Ahmose again. Her eyes were now like black paste, no emotion or humanity twinkling from them. Her mouth curled into a wide grin, exposing white spikes that Dudimayos assumed were teeth.

And the room went dark.

And then lightning, again:

Blood coating the window and dripping down the walls from the ceiling.

This was all wrong, Dudimayos thought wildly. Ahmose had gone too far. He Who Cannot Be Named was too strong in her. Mason was already dead—*who next?* Dudimayos clambered to his feet, knocking over his own chair, and cried, "No, this isn't right, Ahmose! The blood is too high! We'll all die here! Only the firstborn should die!"

In the blackness came Ahmose's voice:

***

Mhy'Os did as He Who Cannot Be Named commanded. Mhy'Os took his own staff and whittled it into a sacred knife, and he sliced the genitals of all his people, the slaves.

He Who Cannot Be Named was enraged: "Mortal thing! You disobeyed my command. You did not *burn* the genitals!"

"I cut them," squeaked Mhy'Os through his melted mouth hole. "Was that not sufficient, oh great one?

"Just lead them from the land of Egypt, *now*, mortal thing, before I get angrier at you."

Mhy'Os gathered everyone, the men bleeding and staggering, the women weeping with babies in their arms, and he divided them under the leadership of those who would later evolve into the twelve tribes: Levite, Akeley, Derby, Gilman, Jermyn, Marsh, Mason, Peaslee, Pickman, Waite, Ward, and Whateley.

Then they trudged toward the Red Sea.

***

Tentacles shattered the window panes, and blood flooded the shack. Everyone scrambled to their feet and screamed.

"You've gone too far!" yelled Dudimayos. "You're killing us all!"

Ahmose no longer lisped. Her voice was a baritone, and her words hit Dudimayos like bludgeons. "Mortal thing, Mhy'Os led my people across the Red Sea. So shall I lead *my* people, *your* people."

"I don't understand!"

"I will take my fourth cup now, Dudimayos. Pour it for me, or die."

The other ten men huddled together by their slain friend, Mason. "Why did you kill Mason?" asked Dudimayos.

"He disobeyed the rules of my seder. He opened the door. You should learn from his mistake, mortal thing, and pour my fourth cup."

As lightning flashed, Dudimayos grabbed the matches from the mantle, and he scooped the candles off the floor and set them back on the table. His hands shaking, he lit the candles, then poured eight ounces of moonshine from the urn into the Goblet of Anticipation.

Ahmose aka He Who Cannot Be Named swiped the goblet from his grasp and swilled all eight ounces of moonshine. The fourth cup was the last. The seder was almost over.

Everything was out of kilter, imbalanced. Nothing like this had ever happened. Dudimayos didn't know what to do. Like Mhy'Os long ago, perhaps Dudimayos should lead the people from this horrible place and save them. By doing so, he would break thousands of years of tradition. Did he dare?

***

The Egyptian army raced after the fleeing slaves, for Pharaoh had changed his mind about letting them go. But Mhy'Os limped to the very edge of the Red Sea and implored He Who Cannot Be Named to save them.

Mhy'Os knew that he would never be able to make it across the sea no matter what happened. His body was racked with pain.

Suddenly, the waves shrank down to the floor of the sea, allowing the people to pass between walls of water. Mhy'Os limped to the narrow path and gestured at his people to follow him.

In the far distance, in the middle of the Red Sea, was a giant creature unlike any Mhy'Os had ever seen. It had risen out of nowhere, large enough to part the waters. Its tentacles flailed across the waves on either side of the path, and its wide grin opened to reveal what looked like spikes.

Mhy'Os' heart jumped. Was this *He Who Cannot Be Named*?

The slaves, circumcised to let go of the past and find their future, pushed and shoved and hurried across the sea.

They reached the other side, the promised land, and collapsed from exhaustion. Behind them, the giant creature fell back into the depths of the sea, and with him, the water crashed back down and drowned all of the Egyptian soldiers.

At last, the people were free.

All but Mhy'Os, whose dead body washed ashore the next morning.

***

"I could not let Mhy'Os enter the promised land," said Ahmose. "He disobeyed me and circumcised the people by cutting rather than flame."

The blood rose over Dudimayos' thighs rapidly to his waist. In the corner, Ward stood on Whateley's shoulders and clawed at the bloody walls. Peaslee and several others banged on the walls with their fists.

"What have we done to deserve this?" cried Dudimayos.

"*They* have done nothing wrong. They are only frightened servants, mere followers. *You*, on the other hand, have pure blood. You are a leader, and you disobeyed me more than once tonight. You fear me, Dudiamyos, and you fight my commands. You dare to question my authority, Dudimayos. For you, circumcision is no longer enough."

A tentacle knocked the candles to the floor, and the table went up in flames. Dudimayos ground his legs through the surging blood and flattened his back against the wall by the window. Blood continued to gush through the broken pane.

So this is how it feels to face death, he thought. After all these long years, finally, it comes to this.

His friends climbed on the tentacles, which shot up and whacked the roof off the shack. Splinters and shingles flew in all directions, raining down upon the bloody sea that once was the forest. The fires died beneath the sea, and Dudimayos floated to the surface.

"*I am. I am*," said Ahmose, "I am, He Who Cannot Be Named by human tongues. I am *Cthulhu*." The name sounded strange to Dudimayos, as if uttered in a rhythm of clicks and spit. Cthulhu continued: "I rise and part the Red Sea, and I take my people to the promised land."

Dudimayos' legs tread blood as lightning slashed the night sky and hail cracked against his skull. He wanted so badly to see the promised land. It was all he'd *ever* wanted.

The others clung to the tentacles high in the sky. They were safe. Only

Dudimayos struggled not to drown. "But I gave you my son and grandson," he said. "Was that not enough?"

Cthulhu, as he now called himself, lifted his enormous bulk from the bloody sea, and the surface sank and a path emerged between two walls of blood. Dudimayos dipped his head beneath the sea and swam toward the path, gulping air tinged with the tanginess of the blood. He would get there, *he would*.

Laughter thundered across the sky, and the spikes that were teeth gleamed in the snakes of lightning that thrashed in the clouds. The giant body sank, and the sea swelled and flowed over the path, sealing it.

Dudimayos rode a mighty wave, struggling to keep his limbs from snapping off his body. Finally, the bloody sea settled, and he floated upon the surface again.

From above, baritone words hit Dudimayos like bludgeons: "We return to the promised land. To R'lyeh, to my home beneath the sea." And Cthulhu sank back beneath the Red Sea, and with him, clutching those mighty tentacles and screaming from terror and joy, went the rest of Dudimayos' friends: Akeley, Derby, Gilman, Jermyn, Marsh, Peaslee, Pickman, Waite, Ward, and Whateley.

All of them drowned. All of them sank to Cthulhu's home, R'lyeh.

All but Dudimayos, who washed ashore the next morning. Alive, but wishing that he, too, had died and gone to the promised land.

And the Angels Sing

by Cody Goodfellow

Tuesday
April 3, 1945

The prayer before supper that night, their fifth in the rafts, started out the same as the others. Colonel Rowse led them in saying grace.

"Heavenly Father, we thank You for this bounty. We surrender our pride and we throw ourselves on Your infinite mercy, and we humbly pray for deliverance from this slough of despond. We do not deign to know Your plan for us, O Lord, but we beseech You humbly for water, just enough to keep ourselves alive, if that is Your will…"

The five men bowed their heads over steepled, trembling hands, watching their dinner gasp out its last in their laps. They'd caught a dozen of the ugly little fish out of the school of hundreds that skimmed under their rafts, using nets made of cargo webbing. Mostly eyeballs and spiny fins, yet something about their faltering death-throes made it vital to eat them alive.

But they patiently waited, and gave thanks.

Crushed into three rubber life rafts bound together by jute rope, they rode the rolling swells of the Pacific somewhere between Hawaii and the Marshall Islands, but in their hearts, the colonel reminded them, they sat in God's lap.

In the lead raft, Captain Ogilvy, Sergeant Wilcox and Corporal Hooper lay with their legs in a pile and their arms draped over the pontoons of the raft, which boasted of a six-man capacity, but must've been war surplus from Munchkinland.

In the middle raft, Colonel Rowse and Lieutenant Mundt were no less crowded, what with Mundt's crudely splinted broken leg and the empty food hamper and the Colonel's personal effects.

Corporal Trouba brought up the rear in a rubber dinghy little bigger than a bedpan. Trouba's ribs and both arms were pulverized in the crash. He moaned and sobbed and argued with the sky, but the rest of the crew

65

of the C-47 Skytrain they called Calamity Jane would have traded places, just for the solo berth.

"And Lord, we know that not all of us here have let You into their hearts, and we beg for You to shine Your light on them brightest of all, and break the chains of their sinful pride. If this is a trial set before them, and we Your agents in driving home Your lesson, then we humbly accept that task, O Lord, if it will hasten our rescue… in Jesus's name, we pray…"

And out came the crackers.

The C-rations were long gone, and they had less than an ounce of canteen water between them. In the hope of converting any "heathen natives" they might encounter, the Colonel had packed a box of Saltines and a bottle of wine blessed by a chaplain at Pearl that he gave out after prayers, "just for morale purposes." Only Hooper and Ogilvy had refused them, but now Ogilvy's stomach growled at him to convert.

Hooper tugged his prematurely receding widow's peak and said, "Amen, sir, except for that last part."

Rowse blinked as if stirred from a sweet dream. "Beg pardon, son?"

"Well, you've been leading us in prayer three times a day and calling our rations holy communion, but seeing as I'm a Jew… Why can't I just have the cracker and the wine?"

"Don't," Cptn. Ogilvy warned, but Hooper was studying to become a lawyer when he got drafted.

Col. Rowse closed his eyes. His heavy, measured breath whistled in and out of his flared nostrils like a pressure cooker venting steam. "I'm well aware of your people's denial of the Savior, Corporal. But that doesn't make it so." Nodding, he went on, "In Jesus's name—"

"Sir, I must protest. The Constitution—"

Ogilvy muzzled Hooper with his hand and got bit. Hooper foamed at the mouth, stood up in the raft. "We may be lost on the ocean and hopeless of earthly rescue, but for your information—"

The raft rocked like a seesaw. Wilcox called Hooper a stupid kike and pulled him back down. Hooper stumbled and fell straddling the starboard pontoon. He was about to say something else, when he looked down into the water.

The blue waves went white and parted like lace. A massive tiger shark shot out of the water and bit into his leg, just above the knee.

Hooper howled, "Oh God, don't—" He grabbed Wilcox's arm. Gnashing ripsaw teeth ground into his thigh until they met in the marrow. Dragged by sinew and shredded flesh, he slipped out of the raft.

Ogilvy locked arms with Hooper and clung to him until the raft almost flipped over. Wilcox kicked at the shark's blunt snout and black striped flanks. Rowse and Mundt fired pistols into the dancing red foam.

Hooper's eyes rolled back in his head. His body jerked, fingers dug even tighter into their arms. They let him go.

Nobody moved or spoke for a long time. Finally, Rowse said, "Say *Amen*, boys," and most of them did.

They ate in silence. The brilliant salmon sunset backlit a marvelous flying fortress of wine-dark rain clouds on the eastern horizon.

"Praise Jesus," Wilcox shouted, "it looks like rain!"

***

Wednesday

No ships, no planes.

No fish.

With every breath, Ogilvy had to remind himself not to try to undermine Rowse's evangelical fervor. The thrice-daily prayers had become the guiding light and inspiration for his crew after the plane went down, especially Corporal Trouba.

"We must stand together before the Almighty," Rowse liked to say, "for we will surely each die alone." He'd written these words in his inspirational memoir, *Angel On My Wing*. The crew was thrilled to bits to fly the celebrated World War I ace on his island-hopping goodwill tour along with their supply drops, and all of them bought a copy.

The crew knew each other pretty well, but after they'd talked cars, baseball, movie starlets and the likelihood of rescue, the rafts had become a confessional. Things no man should share with anyone but his priest got spilled out.

At first, Ogilvy had gently tried to deep six it, but they'd just as gently told him to shut up. Rowse just sat listening, encouraging them to make a clean breast of their sins. Rowse was the only one with cigarettes, and he'd rationed them out to reward the best confessions.

It bound them together before God and under Colonel Rowse, but separated them from their captain.

He should be grateful someone could keep their spirits up. His own attempts had come to nothing. He tried until last night to get them to row north towards Hawaii, but a bone-deep fatigue, born of terror and despair, had settled in and claimed them.

Wilcox had already confessed twice, but he still had lingering guilt about the redhead he bedded in Melbourne, just before they lit out. "Tits like flippers, but she was like a bucking bronco, boy... stay on eight seconds, and you'd win a prize, beg pardon, Lord." He fondled the memory for a bit, long enough for Ogilvy to wonder how remorse could make a man drool.

"Y'know that corny Johnny Mercer tune about the angels? That was our song, I tell you what. It's crazy, but last night, I thought I heard her singing it out there, in the—"

"That's enough, Mark," Ogilvy said. He was staring into the water, like a desert of dirty glass. He searched it until his broiled brain filled the azure void with sharks and Zeroes.

Rowse sat up and stretched his rangy, sun-bronzed arms. "Believe I'll go for a little swim. Care to join me, Captain?"

Ogilvy shaded his eyes to scan the surrounding water for fins. "I don't know how good an idea that is, Colonel…"

"No sharks out there, now." It sounded more like a command than an observation.

Ogilvy pulled himself up, ashamed at the luxury of space Hooper had left. The water was cool and inviting, until he slid into it. The brine bit into his blistered skin with a million tiny teeth, but it cleared his head.

Rowse belly-flopped and bobbed to the surface like a big red walrus, chopping the water with easy, powerful strokes. "You boys try not to sail off without us, now." The crew pursed their cracked lips to whistle "When The Saints Go Marching In," to help them find their way back.

Ogilvy kicked and clawed after Rowse, nursing his cramped legs. The old man was way out ahead of him. His regal white mane dipped in and out of sight among the jumbled swells. Ogilvy's stomach clenched, but he couldn't show fear. It would not just ruin him with his men, but somehow, it was feeding the colonel.

He'd worked out what he wanted to say, but before he could catch his breath, Rowse growled, "If you want to give the orders, you go on ahead, Captain. But if you want to come between these men and their God, I'll have something to say about it."

Ogilvy fought to keep the rolling waves from sucking him under. "I just don't want to lose another man to a stupid accident, sir. And these men aren't dead, yet. They need more than a 24-hour prayer vigil. We mustn't give up hope, and we must not give up trying—"

The Colonel rolled on his back and floated effortlessly. In the ocean, his bulk was buoyancy. "We'll be rescued or we won't, son. It's in His hands."

"I beg to differ, sir. It's in *our* hands, yours and mine." Ogilvy struggled to keep his head afloat. Every kick felt like he was telegraphing *Come & Get It* to the sharks. "I've been watching the stars whenever the skies cleared up, and I know our position."

"We talked this to death already, Ogilvy. You figured out where we are, without a map or a sextant?"

"I've been taking compass readings. We can't be more than a few hundred miles east of Christmas Ridge and the Line Islands. If we rowed from dusk to dawn, we could—"

"You could fill them full of false hope and run them so ragged, even the sharks wouldn't eat them."

"Colonel, the current is pulling us east as we speak. There's nothing east of us until the Panama Canal. The important thing is to stay focused. You're propping up the boys' spirits pretty good with prayer… But you've got them expecting a miracle—"

"I'm fighting for their souls, Captain. Their bodies might survive, but I've seen what men can do in situations like these. Men without hope, or a healthy fear of God, are no better than beasts." In the molten sunset glow, the thick white hair all over his body gleamed like a golden fleece.

"I know my men a bit better than you do, sir. And I hardly think one needs church to keep from turning to cannibalism. What's more—"

The Colonel dove out of sight with a powerful kick that threw spray in Ogilvy's face. Ogilvy spun around and around, waiting. He didn't hear the Colonel surface behind him, was still looking for him down below, when a powerful arm wrapped around his neck.

Ogilvy twisted impotently in Rowse's grip. The colonel grinned, but raw, seething rage carved animal angles in his jovial face. "I wouldn't expect you to understand, Captain 'Decline To State.' That's as strong as the personnel form lets you put it, but you marked it up pretty hard."

Ogilvy barely remembered the last time he went to Mass, before Dad came back from the Great War and said if the bastard wanted a cheering section, He should become a football player. "Get your hands off me, you bastard—"

Rowse ducked him under. The brine rushed into his sinuses, but the colonel held him up so he could hear. "Think of this as your baptism… your crash course in Sunday School. This is all you need to know about God, boy. If you can't beat it, if it holds your life in its hands and could crush you at its leisure, and there's not a damned thing you can do about it but pray for mercy, that's God. When we pray, you'd damn well better join in, and if you can't get through to heaven, well then, you just go ahead and pray to me. You understand?"

Drowning, Ogilvy emphatically thrashed his head against Rowse's chest. The colonel let him go.

Ogilvy kicked away from the colonel and turned to defend himself. Rowse laughed and shouted, "Gracious, Captain, I thought you said you knew how to swim!"

Still fighting for breath, Ogilvy coughed, "What in the hell is wrong with you?"

"I wouldn't fly with someone who doesn't trust in the Almighty, but war is war, and your record looked solid. But you were riding for a fall. God struck you down, and these poor boys had the bad luck to be stuck with you."

"We were struck by lightning."

"Ha! Well, there you go!" Rowse swam up close to Ogilvy, his broad, powerful hands strangling the water. "You'd rather play the Devil than go creeping to the cross, eh? Suits me. This game's a lot more fun, with a Devil in the deck."

Behind the orange fire of reflected sunlight, Rowse's eyes were flat black disks, revealing something that would not think twice about holding him under until the bubbles stopped. "I offer them hope, when no earthly hope remains. What can you offer them, son?"

Ogilvy backed up, but the buffeting waves held him helpless. He scanned the plunging horizon, but he couldn't see the rafts or hear them whistling. *Pick your battles.*

Laughing, the colonel kicked lazily back toward the rafts. "You don't know where we are, Captain. And you can't really believe we can just pick a direction and paddle for home. Because if you think you're the master of your destiny, then where were you on Sunday morning, when your plane fell out of a clear blue sky and dumped us in the sea?"

* * *

Nothing in the nets for dinner.

Wilcox dangled his foot in the water and babbled about how, if you pickled it real good, you could eat your own foot without pain or bleeding to death, and it didn't even taste like human flesh, but just like deviled ham.

They said a special prayer for Trouba, who begged for a priest, when he made any sense at all. Colonel Rowse administered last rites.

"God has a special purpose for us all," Rowse preached. "You can't ask to be saved, without first pledging to serve. I know in my heart what my purpose is, and it's to be a vessel of His goodness, to save men who can't or won't heed the call, or who cling to Him only in imminent peril. Such men are less than dogs, sick in their own sin as a beast in its own filth, for their pride blinds them to the evil that they do."

Ogilvy said nothing, but his teeth worried at the dry meat of his cheek. He had seen the beast Rowse kept at bay. If he threatened the colonel's grip on the men, he would corner it. What then?

"Body of Christ, amen," Rowse said as he fed Trouba a soggy Saltine. The corporal had thrown up all the water they'd given him, but somehow he kept down the cracker and a mouthful of wine. Another miracle…

At dusk, just after they finished singing "Nearer My God To Thee," the golden face of the waters sparkled with dancing ripples, like a pot set to boil. A flock of flying fish jumped into the boats. Laughing and cheering like asthmatic crows, the boys caught and crushed them in their fists.

"God works in mysterious ways, his wonders to perform. He has decided that we should live another day. Give thanks, boys."

Bullshit, Ogilvy thought, as he mouthed the words.

***

Holy Thursday

They awakened just before sunrise and ate the last of the flying fish for breakfast, after a lengthy morning sermon. The men were thirsty. Ogilvy ordered them to piss in their canteens and drink it.

Ten minutes after they said, "Amen," it began to rain.

"Hallelujah!" Rowse cried, and the others echoed him.

Under his breath, Ogilvy said, "He probably does that when coffee comes out of a coffeepot, too."

Wilcox punched him in the throat. He didn't look at his commanding officer. He didn't say anything. He just shot a quick jab and crimped his windpipe.

"Look here," Wilcox growled. "If it ain't a miracle, what's it hurt to believe it? Just keep your goddamned doubts to yourself from here on out, I'm warning you, sir."

The rafts jerked as the nets snared something longer than the whole convoy. The lead raft nosed down into the rushing water and was swamped. Ogilvy flipped over the top and hit the water headfirst. Wilcox clung to the raft, praying, "Please God, please."

Ogilvy dove after their first aid kit, but the blood-warm water abruptly turned pitch black, grave-cold and thick as concrete. His ears popped and his lungs smoldered when he turned back, and bumped into something.

The big gray body sent him spinning. He expelled his last burning breath in a scream of bubbles and chased them to the surface.

He clawed at the raft, but with nothing to kick against, he could only flail in the water. "They're here! Wilcox, help me!"

Wilcox took his hand, but didn't pull him into the raft. "*You* lost our fishing net."

Ogilvy dug his fingers into the Sergeant's arm. "Pull me in, goddamit Mark, there's a shark down there—"

"You don't believe in Him, but you'll call on Him to curse. And you lost our medicine."

"I didn't lose anything! Let me into the fucking boat!" He tried to throw a leg over the pontoon, but it was weak, dead meat. His thrashing would only bring them faster. He needed to calm down.

Something brushed against his back. A cautious, curious shove.

"Help your captain, Mark," Rowse said. "Judge not, lest ye be judged."

Wilcox didn't meet Ogilvy's eyes as he dragged him into the raft.

***

Sunset.

No planes.

No ships.

No miracles.

Rowse checked his footlocker and found all the Saltines missing. Mundt accused Wilcox of eating them.

Wilcox put on a show. "Why would *I* eat them? They were *holy* crackers, Lieutenant. It'd be a mortal sin—"

"They're just crackers," said Ogilvy, "unless a priest administers them, right?"

"Not like that would stop a chow-hound like Wilcox," Mundt added.

"Well, what about *you*, sir?" Wilcox pointed at Ogilvy. "Me and the Colonel were asleep all afternoon. Begging your pardon, sir, but if they're just crackers to you, and you're an officer, then maybe—"

Ogilvy pinched his temples to hold his brains in. "Are you accusing *me* of stealing the crackers, Wilcox?"

"Well, somebody sure as hell took 'em," Sgt. Wilcox snapped, "and it'd be the hot place for sure… if a guy believed in it."

"And if he didn't," Ogilvy said, "then anything goes, is that it?" He had slept for two blessed, dreamless hours after swimming with the sharks. The last thing they needed was a fight.

Sitting beside Mundt, Colonel Rowse kept his hand on his footlocker, and his eyes off on the horizon, plotting his next sermon and licking salt off his lips. "I'm not angry, boys. Just disappointed…"

"Ah, come on, Colonel!" Wilcox crawled as far as he could away from Ogilvy. "We all know who done it!"

"Mark," Ogilvy said, "stop and think what you're saying. It's absurd, and it's insubordination."

Rowse smiled at the sun. "'Come and let us cast lots, that we may know for whose cause this evil is upon us.'"

Rubbing his eyes, Mundt stared at the blue on blue horizon until he was sure of what he saw. "Sharks!"

The shifting plain of water tilted beneath them to become a wall of blue-green glass studded with sleek black shapes.

"Come on then, you devils!" Rowse stood up in the raft and fired a shot at the armada of scythe-like fins. The rest took up oars and leaned back from the pontoons.

The clear azure water turned to shaving cream. Trouba's tiny dinghy bobbed and danced as sharks passed under it, homing in on the rippling waves of agitation from the terrified men in the bigger rafts.

"It's every goddamned shark for a hundred fucking miles," Wilcox snarled, then added, "Sorry, sir. But that fuckin' sheenie Hooper rang the dinner bell."

The middle raft bucked and slid sideways. Rowse almost fell out, but Mundt caught him and tugged him back down.

A fourteen-foot great hammerhead reared up from the froth and sank its teeth into the port pontoon. The heavy, oily green rubber popped like a daydream and shredded in its threshing jaws. Water gushed into the maimed raft. Mundt and Rowse shot its eyes out, but the hammerhead beat the water like a runaway torpedo, hurling its ponderous bulk onto the raft.

Mundt smashed his oar over the monster's back, then slid across the tipping raft on his splinted leg and fell on top of the hammerhead. He threw out his hand to Rowse and screamed for help. Rowse draped his body over the food and tried to reload his gun.

In the forward raft, Ogilvy and Wilcox huddled back to back as they fought off circling tiger sharks. Ten feet long, at least, their black stripes cut through the churning white foam like slices of night. Ogilvy jabbed their snouts away from the raft, but he wondered at their markings. They weren't stripes at all, but bands of black diamonds in intricate, arcing bands down their perfectly streamlined bodies. Sleek, perfect, hundreds of millions of years in the making.

"God, help us!" Rowse roared, and struck the hammerhead with his Bible. The blind shark snapped it out of his hand, raging to get at Rowse, but a tiger shark leapt out of the foam to maul the hammerhead's flank. Dozens of frenzied sharks homed in like iron filings charged by the magnet of blood in the water.

Ogilvy was looking at the other raft when a shark bit his oar and yanked him off-balance. He jerked backwards into Wilcox, who bumped or shoved him into the water.

A torrent of streaking bodies bumped into him, driving him down into the cold darkness. Silver, black-banded skins stroked him like cat's tongues. God no, he thought, not like this—

He inhaled seawater and sank, gagging. His foot touched something and kicked off it. Climbing out of the water on the bodies of sharks, Ogilvy vaulted back into the raft.

"Help me, Jesus, please!" Mundt screamed and clawed at Rowse, who clung to his footlocker. The tiger sharks ate their way into the stranded hammerhead like rats in a cheese. The dying hammerhead silently roared and rolled off the raft, taking Mundt with it into the midst of a feeding frenzy.

Ogilvy leapt onto the starboard pontoon of the middle raft and grabbed for Mundt's hand. The lieutenant looked right through him and reached out to Rowse.

Rowse threw out his other arm and caught the rope tethered to Trouba's raft. As Ogilvy grappled Mundt into the raft, he saw Rowse tip the little raft just enough for Trouba to roll out.

"They're eating me!" Trouba screamed. "Captain, help me—" His broken ribs ground him up inside as he flailed at the whirlpool of teeth. Bloody foam jetted up like a scarlet halo. His hands shot out to wave at them with no fingers on them as he was pulled down out of sight.

"You son of a bitch!" Ogilvy wheeled on Rowse to find the gun in his face.

"Get back to your raft, Captain."

At their feet, a couple dozen sharks battled for scraps of Trouba and the hammerhead. The rafts danced on the heaving sea, but they were not attacked again. They drifted away from the feeding frenzy as if they were already dead, or marked by God for something else.

Rowse reached into the water to fish out a gobbet of meat and sank his teeth into it. For all he knew, it was human flesh, but Ogilvy was too tired to go for another swim, right now.

No more Body of Christ, but Mundt and Wilcox numbly polished off the last of His blood.

Ogilvy lay in the raft alongside Wilcox, but he did not sleep. At least, he did not feel himself sleep. He dreamed he heard beautiful voices singing weird, wordless hymns, way down in the sea, like silver waves crashing on some undiscovered shore.

And he woke up to find something wet and cold lying on his chest.

The first aid kit.

***

Good Friday

No ships, no planes.

No rain, no fish.

Hot before the sun came up.

The Colonel recited the Book of Jonah. "'We beseech Thee, O Lord, let us not perish for this man's life, and lay not upon us innocent blood.'"

"You murdered him." Ogilvy's throat was parched and swollen halfway shut. He had some water left, but he had to hold it. He'd offered it to Wilcox, who had a raging hangover, but he refused.

"Your lies shame the devil!" Rowse shouted. "I saw you fall into the sea, and the sharks spat you out! He delivered you, and you have heard His angels singing in the deep, and yet you still deny him!"

"Mermaids," Wilcox slurred. He stared into the bottomless sapphire depths as if searching a crowd for a familiar face. Urine and the blood from his cracked lips were all he'd had to drink since the last rainfall, unless he'd been drinking seawater. His breath smelled like rubbing alcohol.

"Rowse fed Larry Trouba to the sharks, Wilcox. Isn't there anything in the Bible about that?"

"She's out there." Wilcox hummed, mangling an oddly familiar tune.

"I am an old sinner, son," Rowse crowed. "I make no bones about that. The Lord makes enough of us, and for good reason."

"I don't want to hear your reasons, Colonel, or His."

"He made his peace with the Lord, and was ready for the Lord to take him. But I won't hear you accuse me of murder."

Mundt stared into the empty sky. "The Colonel saved our lives. Trouba was already dead."

The sun got stuck at noon and camped out overhead for a year. No rain, no wind, no fish.

Hotter. Sharks circled like vultures under glass.

"Your doubting will be the death of us all, son," Rowse said. "God has a plan for us all, even you. *Especially* you, I think."

Ogilvy's mind drifted on seas teeming with monstrous visions—his whole fighter wing vanishing in a cyclone of steel over Manila, as if the hack cartoonist who scribbled this funny paper of a war had just erased them; Calamity Jane sinking beneath the gunmetal waves, transformed into a giant hammerhead shark; Colonel Rowse, smiling and walking like Jesus on red, shark-infested water…

"Hey Colonel, she's here!" Wilcox hung over the side. He threw his arms around something in the water.

Ogilvy reached out for him, blearily moaned, "Wilcox, don't—"

"So long, suckers!" A sleek gray shape rose up to kiss Wilcox's grinning face off. Before Ogilvy realized that he was awake, Wilcox was gone.

Rowse delivered a heartfelt eulogy. Tears cut through the salt crust on his ruddy cheeks. Ogilvy screamed, "Balls!" in the middle of it. Rowse ordered him into the aft boat. "If the Captain can't abide the stink of us Christians, maybe he'd prefer Corporal Trouba's berth."

"You go to hell."

"Ha! There're no atheists in foxholes, Captain. Get in that raft, or I'll shoot you in the leg and let you swim back to Hawaii. You're so sure you know the way."

Ogilvy turned to appeal to Wilcox, but he was gone. Mundt jumped into his raft. Ogilvy caught the blade of the oar across his temple.

He toppled into the water. Kicking away from the raft, he looked down and saw something circling him.

Rowse pointed the gun at him, but was all smiles as Ogilvy paddled back to the tiny dinghy at the tail of the convoy.

"You're insane, Colonel," Ogilvy shouted. "Why don't you drop the mask and show us what you really are? Why can't you just kill me, too?"

Colonel Rowse laughed and laughed until the last light died. He looked like a big shaggy dog, perched on the drooping edge of his raft. "I want to hear you admit that you don't disbelieve, Captain. You just hate Him. Well, you don't have to love Him. You just have to recognize who is in charge, here."

Ogilvy heard the water come unzipped behind him. Mundt giggled.

Ogilvy screamed, "God damn you!" and threw himself into the dinghy.

That night, softer and sweeter than tears, it rained.

***

Saturday

Ogilvy awoke to the ungentle rocking of the raft. For a second, it felt like Sunday morning at home, with the kids sneaking up on Mom and Pop, and the dog pulling the covers off the bed…

He rubbed his eyes with his left hand. It was still dark, but the eastern horizon nursed a low rosy glow. On his chest lay a waterlogged, half-digested black book. Rowse's Bible.

A twelve-foot bull shark tugged almost playfully on his trailing right arm.

Fighting nausea and panic, he whipped his hand back and counted his fingers. He had eleven on each hand.

His head throbbed like a fire alarm. His gut ate itself. He heard someone singing the sweetest song he'd ever heard. It wasn't his crew. The dinghy floated alone on sloping, slanting swells like an endless field of slate-gray rooftops.

The water boiled and went red. The bull shark whipped around and leapt out of the water as something below tore off its tail.

A pack of tiger sharks devoured the crippled bull, but never touched the dinghy. The black diamond swirls around their fins and tails were not natural markings, but stylized bite wounds, sacred scars.

He opened the Bible. The ingots of tiny text dissolved in brine and stomach acid. He tore the pages out and ate them.

Swarms of remora and smaller fish swooped in to mop up the debris, but the tiger sharks followed and circled the dinghy like gray guardian angels. The current flowed faster now, dragging him along like a crumb on a vast blue tablecloth.

They cut him loose in the night. He didn't remember sleeping, but he must've dropped into a coma soon after he lost the last argument with Rowse.

He was laying on an oar. Also, the wrappers from two sandwiches, four empty C-rat tins and three Cracker Jack boxes. He doubted Trouba had enjoyed any of it.

He upchucked the Old Testament, but he had better luck with the Gospels.

There had to be a reason. In any God's book, he deserved to be punished. He had failed his men. He was half-asleep at the stick when the plane went down in that freak storm. He had let them fall under the sway of a lunatic. He had failed to keep them alive.

The sun rose like a fever. Its first tentative rays struck his blistered arms and chest like the lashes of a whip. He paddled with the current until his emaciated muscles twanged and tore under peeling, cracking skin. He hunched over and tried not to retch up the last fluid in his belly, held it down with Revelations. He had to catch up to them, save his men from Rowse—

Fins darted around him as he paddled, doubled and trebled and turned into a kamikaze fighter wing, lost forever in the mirror of the sky. Sharks flew overhead, too—white ones, screeching at him to give up and die.

No, damn you, I won't.

He cursed the sun in a raw, rasping croak. "OK, I give… Uncle, mea maxima culpa, I admit it. I'll never love you, but I kneel, I bow, I humbly acknowledge your everlasting power. Do with me as you will…"

He paddled until his arms revolted and he dropped the oar and fell into a stupor of delirious agony. He heard angels singing "When The Saints Go Marching In" in thundering baritones that shivered the raft like the skin of a drum, and he knew they were watching over him.

Just let it be for something, Lord. Just let there be a reason…

***

Sometime after nightfall, he woke up to an old familiar friend, the sounds of shooting and shouting.

He opened his eyes and checked his watch. Almost midnight. The rolling, moonlit hills of quicksilver parted and sucked him into a momentary valley.

The rafts rode the high shoulder of the next swell. Rowse had maneuvered Mundt into the sinking raft, and now held him at gunpoint.

"Rowse! Stand down!" Ogilvy could barely hear his own croaking voice. He reached for the oar, but it was gone. They didn't see or hear him. He paddled with his bloody, ragged hands, screaming at the top of his lungs.

"'What shall we do unto thee,'" Rowse bellowed, "'that the sea may be calm unto us?'"

Mundt shouted, "*Colonel Rowse, I relieve you of duty!*"

Rowse fired a flare gun at Mundt, who caught the phosphorus round in his mouth. Jets of scarlet sparks blew out his cheeks and eyesockets.

The ocean rolled under Ogilvy's raft like a restless sleeper, shooting him down a sheer slope toward the rafts.

Rowse broke open the flare gun and calmly reloaded it. In the moonlight, his teeth looked like little knives.

Mundt folded and fell into the sea. Ogilvy saw the red Roman candle of his skull fizzing underwater as he sank out of sight.

When Ogilvy was thirty feet away, Rowse fired. The flare punched into the nose of the dinghy and melted it.

Ogilvy felt the water throbbing with their presence, their gray angelic chorus. His muscles rebelled at the furious exertion of swimming. The fear of drowning, of being eaten or shot in the back held no power over him, anymore. He was driven solely by the one human motivation the blind, idiot god of this world should have applauded: revenge.

Something surged under him and flung him from the sea. He crashed into Rowse and smashed both fists into his face.

The colonel dropped the flare gun and flopped back, grabbing his heart. "I'm the one they chose, damn you… you don't even believe…"

Ogilvy took Rowse by the throat and shook him. "You were right, Colonel! God is real! You ready to meet Him?"

"*I'm the one who heard the call!*" Rowse curled into a fetal ball. "*I'm the one who was chosen—*"

Ogilvy threw him over the side, and tossed his footlocker after him.

Shaking and short of breath, he lay down in the raft. He heard hymns from deep down below, felt it through the rubber hull, and he thought he heard Col. Rowse singing along.

***

Easter Sunday

Ogilvy woke up to see sharks in the sky. He rolled over and looked around. He was alone. But he was alive.

The boat rocked like a cradle in the lacy breakers on a deserted beach. Ogilvy looked into the shallow water for a long, heart-frozen while, then rolled over the side, but found his legs quite unable to hold him up. On elbows and knees, he wallowed out of the surf and planted kisses on the coarse black sand. *Thank you, whoever you are—*

It was a tiny desert atoll of naked lava rock with a few tortured thorn trees engulfed by creeping morning glory vines. On a low bluff above the lagoon lay a cluster of huts made of driftwood, scrapped canoes and whalebones. A low, blunt hump of a volcanic mound rose up behind it, with a ramshackle clapboard shack perched on its peak: a church, surrounded by crude but authentic crosses.

Ogilvy lay back and melted into the sand. An insect alighted on his forehead and sipped from the bloodshot oasis of his left eye. His hands couldn't get the trick of brushing it away, and that was just fine. But he was not at ease in his mind, for he felt unseen eyes peeling him like an onion.

He rolled over to find a girl smiling shyly down at him. Her long black hair, almost auburn at the ends and woven with garlands of morning glories, cast a veil of blessed shade across his face.

"You came! We prayed for you, and now you come! Now no one will go hungry…"

Captain Ogilvy smiled up at her. She was a beautiful Polynesian girl, somewhere between fourteen and forty. Even draped in a garish sackcloth muumuu, her slender, fragile form reminded him how long it'd been since he saw or touched a woman. Never one half this beautiful. "You speak pretty good English for a dream come true, ma'am. What island is this?"

She laughed shyly, covering her mouth with one fist. "I am Kalei." She knelt over him and put her hands on his chest. They were tiny delicate things, with no fingers. "We are good Christians, Lord." Her glossy black eyes searched his with earnest need.

Evading her hopeful gaze, he nodded, looking out at the ocean. "Our plane crashed, and we—I guess I'm the only one…"

"He sent you!" She jumped up. "We pray to you to come every Easter just like Father say, but you never come! But we love you, Lord. We never give up hope."

"I was otherwise engaged…" He fogged out her crazy chatter as he watched a pack of boys come bounding down the beach to frolic in the surf.

"Hey, what gives?"

The oldest was maybe twelve, the youngest only six or seven, but only two of them had legs. The others hopped along on stumps and fingerless paddle-hands.

Another miracle. He'd washed ashore on a leper colony.

They found something in the surf. Dancing and clapping their flippers, they hauled it out onto the black lava shore.

It was Col. Rowse. He threw up an arm picked clean as a chicken wing to fend them off.

"Don't touch that!" Ogilvy got up. He felt faint. He had to get away from here—

"Come, we make ready!" Kalei eagerly tugged his arm, dragging him up the beach to the circle of huts. She had no legs below the knees. He noticed the patterns of scars down her arm, swirling around and above the shiny scars of her amputation. The bite marks were stained black from charcoal rubbed into the wounds. He pulled himself to his feet and walked after her.

He saw the children and the girl with new eyes. They weren't lepers. Throughout their lives, they'd been eaten, a bite at a time, by sharks.

He shuddered with disgust and shame. Theirs was not a sudden ordeal, but a ghastly way of life. The ocean was infested with sharks. There was nothing else to eat.

The children laughed as they pulled Rowse's mouth open by his straggly white beard and stuffed a sea urchin into it. Foaming at the mouth, he bucked on the sand. The children played a game of trying to ride him in his death throes... *Stay on eight seconds and you win a prize.*

Ogilvy asked to see the priest, the chaplain, the missionary teacher. "Or the doctor. Surely, you've got to have a doctor or a nun, if this is a, uh…"

"We pray for you to come," she repeated. She led him to an empty hut and lay him down on a mat of woven human hair and fed him cool spring water and candied eel meat. Her strange accent slowly melted, and her voice became almost manly, as she told him.

They were the children of Nanaue, a great chief of Maui and the demigod offspring of Ka-moho-alii, the god-king of sharks. The offspring of his many dalliances in his human and his true form, they rallied around Nanaue when he was hunted for devouring human men and women. Driven out of their sacred caves at Hana by jealous tribes who feared their mastery of the sea, they followed their chief to Molokai. When Nanaue was dragged from the sea and burned, his children turned away from their true nature and swore never to eat flesh, and to live and die on land.

But then the king exiled the lepers to Molokai, and the people of Nanaue had to flee in canoes, for Ka-moho-alii had forgotten his grandchildren.

"The cruel sea brought us here to die," Kalei said, wiping away a tear. "We had no choice but to eat our cousins, even as they ate us. We were hated and forgotten by all, when the Father came to us." With a graceful spade-shaped hand, she indicated the ruined chapel on the hill, and then pointed at a framed picture on the wall of the hut.

Through corrosion and salt crystals, he saw hollow, haunted blue eyes in a wasted, ascetic face with a straggly beard. Jesus, he thought. It was a mirror.

"He taught us that Jesus would come to heal us and end our hunger. We read the Bible and were baptized and our warriors took Holy Communion, and they were born again."

A croaking, barking riot erupted outside the hut. Kalei tried to fend them off, but they would not be denied. When they came piling into the hut to worship him, he thought he had nothing to fear.

They hopped like frogs out of a French kitchen. They humped over the black sand like caterpillars and snakes. They led blind, faceless monsters who hummed "Ave Maria" through naked, sun-bleached bone and teeth filed to needle points.

Leprosy, famine and the sharks had whittled them down to shiny gray botched shark-shapes that slithered and hobbled towards him and groped his salty rags and called him Jesus.

They herded Ogilvy out into the moonlight with their mangled stumps, urging him down the path to the beach.

Kalei took his hand. "The Father saved those who came to him, but there was not enough of him to save us all. We prayed to God to let us swim with our blessed brothers, and we feared not nor despaired, for He promised us His only begotten son!"

"No, you can't believe that!" Ogilvy shoved her away, stumbled over crippled children and broke for the beach, looking for his raft.

He couldn't heal them, he couldn't do miracles. This was a cruel cosmic joke, or a nightmare he'd conjured up to punish himself for breaking down and begging God to save him. The last refuge of a scoundrel…

His raft lay on the shore, but all around it, the shallows churned with slashing fins and mutely howling mouths. A tiger shark twice as long as Ogilvy was tall beached itself on the shore, gasping its last. Another leapt out of the surf and lolled on the sand, gills flapping.

Ogilvy backed away from the waves. Eight gigantic tiger sharks lay between him and the raft. The nearest one swelled up as if the gases of decay had collected inside it for months. Silver chainmail flanks split open like rotten fruit, and a human hand reached out of its mouth.

The islanders scuttled over the sharks and ripped them apart with bony flippers and needle-teeth, gorging on the suddenly putrid meat and peeling away cartilage and gristle to reveal a sac like a giant egg pouch in the wreckage of each shark carcass.

The pulsating sacs burst and men climbed out, to the wordless croaking adulation of the village. Eight feet tall, they walked unsteadily on long, muscular legs still pink as the new skin beneath a scab. Their bottomless black eyes goggled out the sides of huge, torpedo-shaped heads. Their gasping jaws praised him through rows of blood-rimmed bayonet teeth. Wobbly as cartilage slowly turned to bone in their newborn bodies, they converged on Ogilvy.

Backing away, Ogilvy turned and ran towards the hill and the church between fluted fangs of lava dripping perfumed flowers. The jagged rocks scourged his feet like rusty razor blades.

He shaded his eyes and scanned the church and the crosses on the rocky hill. A skeleton in bleached black rags hung from the nearest one. Colonel Rowse's corpse hung on another, stripped to the bone from the hips down. His poisoned meat was *tabu*, but a naked child too young to call a boy or a girl yanked a dangling strap of bowel, causing his slack mouth to open and close, silently preaching, *forever and ever, amen…*

Legless women and children clamored around Ogilvy, lifted him off his feet and carried him down to the water. Too weak to run, too tired to try to fight, he knew that God did indeed hear prayers and work miracles for His favorite children. And it was no secret, now, who His favorites were.

"Say the words, Lord," Kalei whispered in his ear, as the warriors began to sing. So eerily beautiful underwater, their voices on land were harsh, guttural as they croaked that corny Johnny Mercer song.

Ogilvy opened his mind, and the words were just there, as if he'd eaten them.

"Take, eat… this is my body," he said.

She kissed him and boldly probed his mouth with her tongue. She bit his lower lip and peeled it off with a toss of her head, skinning him down to his chin.

He screamed. Stumps and claws caressed his flesh.

She pried his jaws wide and bit his tongue. It burst in her mouth like an overripe plum and deluged her widening mouth with hot arterial blood.

Shed for many for the remission of sins—

Drowning in himself, Ogilvy tried to say, "Drink ye all of it."

They did not wait to say grace.

They didn't need to.

The Last Communion of Allyn Hill

by Peter Rawlik

From the Notebook of Phillip Sherman
Wednesday, April 1, 1931
2115

It is a fine feeling to put pen to paper once more. I found a blank field book in one of the station's supply cabinets, so I can finally get back to routinely making entries. It has been weeks since we passed through the Panama Canal and I filled up the back cover of the last journal. I am grateful, a new journal helps bring closure to what has gone before, and I would rather forget what I can of those days.

It took fifty-eight days for *The Miskatonic* and her sister ship *The Arkham* to bring us back from the frozen wastes of Antarctica. We had set sail from Boston, but it was always our intent to return directly to Arkham. Circumstances being what they were, Pabodie felt it "prudent" to divert the bulk of our specimens to a more remote location rather than bringing them directly into Arkham. So we, the crew of the *Miskatonic* and I, came here ten miles off the coast of Kingsport, to Miskatonic University's Orne Marine Research Station situated amongst the islands known as the Shallows. There are few people here, thirty or so villagers who live on the big island of Allyn, and who not coincidentally supply crew for *The Miskatonic*, and a lone graduate student named Shane Atkins. Atkins is a wiry little biologist with blue eyes, a wild mane of blonde hair and a quick wit. He's been here at the station for a year studying the behavior of seals and several species of shorebirds, and is nominally in charge of the lighthouse.

He tells me that visitors to the Shallows are rare. Perhaps here, on this tiny cluster of scrub islands, I can work on the samples in peace, away from prying eyes. The failure of the expedition will surely be the subject of much speculation, not only amongst the faculty but also the ravenous and insipid individuals that pass for newsmen.

We docked in rough seas early this morning, and it took most of the day for us to unload the *Miskatonic's* holds. Atkins and several of the men from the village helped us maintain a break neck speed. Weather reports from the south spoke of a storm that had formed in our wake and the captain was eager to be on his way to a more sheltering harbor. It was near dark when the ship finally sailed, leaving the windswept docks strewn with the crates, trunks and equipment of the expedition. I stood on the jetty with Christian Larsen, a crewman, who has been my friend and assistant since we first began our expedition, and together we watched as the majestic vessel receded into the sunset.

Over the next several hours we moved the cargo into the station's warehouse. Larsen is actually from Allyn so he left to spend time with friends and family. Atkins is a decent cook, but not much of a conversationalist. After a small meal of shellfish and winter vegetables I spent an hour exploring the station buildings and the small island of Orne on which it sets. There is little here to write about.

Thursday, April 2, 1931
1015

Up early, and Atkins and I have spent the morning going through the smaller crates, and dealing with their contents. We're finding small errors and discrepancies, but nothing major. We found a box with a packing slip listing nine of Lake's star shaped stones, but actually containing only eight, all bearing handwritten, sequentially numbered inventory tags. The number sequence was complete, so I think this was just a documentation error. Lake had described them as being comprised of soapstone, but they aren't common steatite, a kind of talc, but rather pyrophillite, a mineral that forms radiating fan-like clusters of metallic crystals. They were all about six inches across and a half an inch thick, and although you could see the patterns of cleaving, the whole thing was curiously smooth.

Packed in with the samples were some of Lake's notes, which being written by a biologist I understood only a little. Thankfully, Atkins was able to decipher Lake's cramped handwriting and explain some of the thoughts contained within those hastily scribbled paragraphs. Much of the content referred to the pervasive foolishness that influenced poor Pr. Lake to name the frozen specimens "Elder Things" and helped drive my fellow expedition member Danforth, to the brink of madness. This in itself has its roots in the teachings of a member of the Miskatonic University faculty, a man named Wilmarth. I knew that several members of our expedition had met with Wilmarth prior to our departure, and one or two had taken some course work with him, but I was not privy to the nature of those conversations, nor of the teachings expounded on in his classes.

According to Atkins, who has taken several of Wilmarth's courses, the core of the man's scholarly work is cobbled together from several volumes in the University's restricted section. Atkins was a bit vague on the details but Wilmarth's teachings, drawing from occult sources and myth patterns from around the world, suggests that for millions of years the primal Earth was visited and ruled by a succession of creatures that had seeped down from the stars. Amongst the more successful of these alien species were, according to the Al Azif, the "Elder Things", also known in the Pnakotic Manuscripts as the Q'Hrell or "Progenitors" which dominated the Earth and waged war against a variety of enemies for millennia.

Lake does not explain why he drew the link between the specimens and the Elder Things, I assume there must be some physical resemblance, but cannot confirm this. Once I return to the university I'll look into the matter. Lake's notes make the link a *fait accompli*, and further suggest that the star stones that had been discovered with the bodies were the *pentateuchos*, or five-fold tool mentioned by Theodoras Philetas. Such things were supposed to be used as wards by the Elder Things to drive back or imprison their enemies. It seems so ridiculously melodramatic, and I keep having this vision of one of the alien things wielding one of the stones menacingly, holding off an unearthly and undead ghoul.

1145

The weather has turned, and the wind is becoming quite fierce. Atkins is going to show me how to operate the lighthouse, including pumping fuel from the main tank to the holding tank at the top. Apparently if done incorrectly the fuel can mix with the air and be ignited via static electricity, much like the dust found in corn silos or coal mines. Something I need to learn how to avoid.

1300

Larsen has returned with an invitation to the evening festivities. At first I thought it was simply a celebration in honor of Larsen's return but as the conversation continued I realized that my sojourn to Antarctica had caused me to lose all track of time. Sunday will be Easter; which makes tomorrow Good Friday, and today Holy Thursday, marking the events of the Last Supper. Tonight, the residents of the Shallows will hold a mass, followed by a community feast to which both Atkins and I are invited as honored guests. It is good to be back amongst people again.

2330

Have just returned from Allyn, and must say I had quite an enjoyable time.

The entirety of the main island of Allyn is little more than a hundred acres all sparsely covered with low shrubs and a few thin trees through which a small herd of goats roams freely. The village itself is wholly un-remarkable, consisting of homes built in the salt box style, along narrow avenues of crushed oyster shells. The village, properly Allyn Hill, is built on a low rise around a single large building, which had once been an inn back when the entire island served as a resort and spa. The Great Hall as the locals call it, now serves as a communal center, and this evening it had been laid out for a great feast with long rough wooden tables and benches well supplied with fruits, vegetables and breads. Several casks of wine and water, an important provision on the island, were also available and I was relieved that the community was not one that prohibited the consumption of alcohol. Off to the side a fire roared within a massive granite hearth, tak-ing the chill out of the air, and warming a variety of stews, and chowders. A few birds were slowly roasting on a spit, as were a pair of rabbits, an obvi-ous delicacy for these people who seemed to draw most of their sustenance from the sea. The smells that wafted from these dishes mingled with those coming from the kitchen proper and I am not ashamed to write that my mouth watered at the thought of fresh food prepared by skilled cooks.

Not unexpectedly, the evening began with a religious service, initiated by the ringing of dozens of small handheld bells scattered throughout the congregation. The bell ringing ushered in an ornately dressed priest and a procession of altar boys. It wasn't until the clergyman had reached the cen-ter of the room that I recognized that it was Larsen. All that time together and he never told me he was a man of the cloth. Atkins noted my surprise and whispered to me something about Larsen being a church deacon, the actual priest had fallen ill.

From my makeshift pew I listened politely as Larsen embarked on a traditional sermon full of holy fire and celebrating the life and sacrifice of the Son of God. Surprisingly, the sermon was in English with a smattering of Latin, though for the life of me I cannot remember the subject or any of the actual content. I do remember how the altar boys brought forth the wafers and the wine, and how the townsfolk, Atkins included, lined up. I however, remained seated, routed in my own status as an agnostic and in my disdain for such ceremonial pomp. One by one they went and knelt before the priest. One by one Larsen offered up a thin wafer, which they accepted as he blessed them saying time after time, "I am the resurrection and the life, through me the dead shall live again. This is my body, which is for you. Do this in remembrance of me."

I will not dwell on the details of the last few hours. The feast lasted well into the night, and when the bell tolled eleven I urged Atkins to return with me back to the station. He declined, choosing instead to remain and revel in the night's festivities. As I stepped outside and made my way across the breakwater a wicked wind rose up off the sea, soaking me with a blast of cold wet air. By the time I made it to the station proper the storm that Captain Thorfinnssen had so feared had finally arrived. I am exhausted and slightly inebriated, and after writing this I shall collapse into the warm embrace of my bed and deep peaceful slumber.

Friday, April 3, 1931
0830
The storm has grown in intensity, the wind now continuously roars through the rafters and driving rain lashes the windows. Atkins' bed has not been slept in and I assume that he is still over at the village and now trapped by the storm. I have climbed the tower and watched the storm from a height. I am fascinated by the way the wind moves across the island scrub like ocean waves. The frequent lightning competes with the lighthouse for dominance, and both cast weird shadows across the island and the village.

I have spent the last few minutes watching the village and I am growing increasingly concerned that something is terribly wrong. Even in the dim light of the storm wracked sky I can clearly see into the heart of the village, and there are no lights visible on the street or in any of the windows. The only sign of life in Allyn Hill is the small herd of goats wandering the streets, seeking shelter in the shadow of buildings. Unfortunately, I can also see that the breakwater is being violently lashed by wave after brutal wave making it all but impassable. I shall attempt to make contact using the wireless.

915
I have been unable to contact anyone in Allyn Hill or on the mainland; the only sound from the wireless is a steady drone of meaningless static. I am a qualified operator, and following my training I have checked all of the components in both the transmitter and the receiver. I found nothing that was in disrepair. The only explanation I have is that the storm has somehow interfered with transmission and reception. I am extremely frustrated, and it seems the only option available to me is to brave the storm and

breakwater. There is a suitable set of foul weather gear in the storeroom.

1030

The villagers of Allyn Hill seem to be suffering some sort of reaction either to a toxin or an infection. They are strewn about the room in chairs or on the floor, unconscious and unresponsive. They are feverish, with clammy grey skin from which an odor, a sweetness exudes. Thankfully the fire in the great central hearth was still burning, providing a modicum of warmth. It bothers me that amidst the ashes and embers there are what appear to be fresh logs, but I have no time for such things. I need to get warm and attended to the afflicted.

1200

It took me more than an hour to arrange the bodies in an orderly manner on the floor around the hearth. I am sorry to say that two have died, not from their strange affliction, but rather from associated circumstances. One man seems to have fallen backwards out of his chair and broken his neck against the stone floor. The other was a woman who apparently went face first into a large bowl of chowder and asphyxiated. That no one had attempted any sort of aid to either of these poor souls suggests that whatever happened occurred quickly. There were more than twenty men, women and children laid out about the room, including my colleague Atkins. However, oddly absent is my friend Larsen.

I am in the kitchen drinking coffee and eating some bread leftover from the night before. I have tried the wireless set that is down the hall. My efforts were wasted; whatever has affected the station's set is also interfering with this one. I need to rest, am exhausted both physically and mentally. The wall calendar reminds me that today is Good Friday, and I can't help but chuckle morbidly over the irony.

1545

I was awoken by a chorus of screaming and I started from the chair in a panic and dashed out of the kitchen. My charges were awake and from the sound of their moans and anguished cries they were in agonizing pain. I found Atkins who had curled up into a tight little misshapen ball and tried to comfort him. His breathing was shallow and fast, between gasps he told me that he was cold, and that he couldn't feel his arms or legs. To the touch his forehead was hot, and he was sweating profusely. I took his right arm and tried to exercises it and then dropped it in revulsion. The flesh had a strange color and consistency and as I moved it back and forth, it did not bend at the joint. As a child I had watched my grandmother make sausage by filling long greasy tubes of intestines which would then flop and twist on the table like massive grey worms. Atkins' arm was like that, it curled like a long thick sausage. As I looked I could see that the appendages of all those around me had suffered the same shocking metamorphosis.

As I pulled away something more caught my eye, and my curiosity overwhelmed my revulsion. The back of Atkins' shirt was soaked not just with sweat, but also with streaks of crimson. Carefully I rolled the fabric up and by the light of the fire examined the source of the fluid. Three great wounds had opened up on his back, one vertical along the spine, and the other two parallel to the first but almost to either side. A watery and bloody discharge seeped slowly from these lesions and for the life of me I thought perhaps that someone had assaulted my friend. I know from my courses in folklore and comparative religions that some extreme sects re-enacted the more horrid events of Christ's life, going so far as to flog and then crucify a volunteer. Looking at the wounds on Atkins' back it seemed a plausible explanation, but as I scanned about the room I noted that many others were showing the same crimson stains. I quickly realized that this was not the result of a physical attack, but yet another symptom of whatever the villagers had been exposed to.

As I sit here, I am completely incapable of rendering any further sort of aid. I can hear the low distant sound of other victims who were not in the hall but rather are scattered about the village. Like their fellows they too are screaming and moaning in agony. At a loss for what to do I once more shall don my foul weather gear and brave the storm. It is better I think, that all those who are suffering be brought together in one place.

1630

I followed the screams, breaking down doors where I had to and gathered up what stricken villagers I could find. It was not an easy task. Two I found could walk or limp, and together we hobbled down the shell strewn streets. Another, a large woman suffered more severely from that strange softness of the limb bones, and I had to load her into a wheelbarrow. I found one woman in the street outside of her home, her legs and arms like rubber, but she had found a way to move about by crudely lashing out her limbs and then pulling herself forward. I gagged as I watched her do this, for her appearance reminded me of octopi that the crew of *The Miskatonic* had brought up in a net one afternoon off the coast of Cuba. The ship's cook would cut off most of the creatures' limbs for use in the kitchen, and then toss what was left of the wounded animals on to the deck where they would flail about in a desperate attempt to return to the sea.

Dusk, and the agony of the villagers seems to have subsided somewhat, or at least they have become accustomed to whatever pains wrack their bodies. The storm shows no sign of letting up and I am fearful of crossing the breakwater in the dark, I am resigned to staying in Allyn Hill for the night. Though I will admit I am uncomfortable with the thought of staying in the Great Hall.

1745

Have been watching from the second floor of the Great Hall. It took me a moment but I realized that something was amiss. Yesterday when Atkins and I had refilled the fuel tank, he informed me that the fuel would last for at least four days. Yet here it is little more than a day later, and the sweep of light has ceased. Something or someone has interfered with the operation of the lighthouse, and I have a suspicion that the condition of the villagers, the failure of the radios and now the failure of the lighthouse are all connected somehow. I even suspect that the source of all these problems may be anthropogenic, though I am still unclear on the why and how of it all. Against all better judgment, I am going to try and get back to the station and restart the light.

2000

Larsen is deliberately sabotaging the equipment. As I came into the station, he burst through the door knocking me down and then dashed down the path to the breakwater. It took me a moment to regain my footing and in that brief span of time Larsen was moving across to the other island. I gave chase, but stopped at the breakwater. As I hesitated, Larsen whipped out a large fish knife and sliced the guide ropes before lopping up the stair toward Allyn Hill. I called after him, but he either didn't hear me or, given his unusual behavior is purposefully ignoring me.

I've got the lighthouse working again, but the wireless is a total loss. I think initially he just cut the antenna lead on the side of the tower, which explains why I can't reach anyone at any distance, now the damage is much worse, while I was gone he took a hammer to the set. Chances are that he has done something similar to the set in Allyn Hill. I've found a shotgun and a box of ammunition, mostly birdshot but a few of the shells are loaded with buckshot. It's not much but I would rather have this than go hand to hand against Larsen. I've pulled all the storm shutters down and I've barred all the doors. I've tied empty cans to all the doorhandles and climbed the tower halfway to a landing. There's a window with a view of the breakwater and Allyn Hill beyond, and enough space for me to stretch out and sleep. There are three heavy doors between me and the rest of the world. I won't try the breakwater unless the storm lessens.

The Last Communion of Allyn Hill

Saturday, April 4, 1931
0700
The storm has passed and the sun rising in the east is a welcome sight. I've slept a little and found something to fill the emptiness in my belly. I'm cold though, the storm must have dropped the temperature by at least ten degrees. The gun is little comfort. I need to find Larsen. I also need to get back to the Great Hall. As soon as the waves relent I'll try to make it back over to Allyn Hill.

1230
Atkins' condition has worsened. The strange transformation of the limbs has spread to the rest of his body. My medical training is limited, but from what I can all of the bones have suffered some sort of transformation, a decrease in rigidity that seems to have been transferred to the skin, which has become grey and rigid, at least on the chest and abdomen. Their backs however have become soft and pulpy, and the three vertical wounds no longer are oozing red fluid. Instead strange fibrous green tendrils have appeared. I've never seen anything like them before. I poked at one of the tendrils with a knife, and it recoiled back inside.

After I rest I am going to search the island for Larsen.

1700
No luck in finding Larsen, but I have found the priest, he's dead, strangled. I think Larsen killed him so that he could take his place in the ceremony the other night. I'm still not sure why, and I really have nothing to support such an idea, but it is the only thing that makes sense.

In the same house where I found the priest I found a star stone sitting on a work bench. It has a collection tag that identifies it as the one missing from the crate. It's been damaged. One of the arms is split open along one of the edges, the exposed interior is incredibly complex, with dozens upon dozens of tiny black crystals. These crystals are no bigger than a pinhead, all curiously pentagonal trapezohedrons. There are very few minerals that produce such a shape, which should make it readily identifiable, but right now I have neither the time nor the inclination to do so.

There are things nagging at me, things that I think I should be thinking about, but I am so tired. I am not thinking clearly. It's still very cold out, and I think that is contributing to my exhaustion. I need to sleep.

1900
The villagers of Allyn Hill are all dead. I can write no more.

2145

I've made it back to the station. Another storm, or perhaps the same one coming back, is rolling over the island and the wind is picking up. It's bitterly cold out. I would have thought that all that time at the pole would have made me more resistant. I've barricaded the doors again, still no sign of Larsen.

As I have written, the villagers are all dead. I don't know why or how but somehow in the few hours I was exploring the island they all succumbed to whatever malady they were suffering from. Curiously, either through their own action or that of Larsen, they were all clustered together into small groups. They had been arranged in sets of five, with their backs to each other and their legs splayed out on the floor. Some of them seem to be clutching their neighbors with what use to be their arms.

As if that weren't odd enough, the clusters themselves seem to be oddly grouped. All the young children are sitting together, as are all the adolescents. Even the adults seem to have been sorted by size, height I mean. If this was some last dying attempt at community, I would have thought they would have clustered into family groups.

Tomorrow, if I can I'll take one of the small boats to the mainland.

Sunday, April 5, 1931
0230

I'm back at the top of the lighthouse trying to make sense of what I am seeing and hearing. About twenty minutes ago I woke to a chorus of strange high pitched keening noises. At first I thought it was the birds or seals, but it was coming from the village, so I came up here to get a look. I can't see much, but I can see shadows moving about within the Great Hall, which means that somebody is alive and has turned on the lights.

The noise is definitely coming from Allyn Hill. It's an eerie throaty sound, like air moving through an organ. It repeats every few minutes, but in different pitches, like its being repeated by different sources, but always the same tones and pattern. Tek Tek Tek Tek E Li Li.

I'm going over to investigate.

0430

I made it across the breakwater and carefully crept up to the kitchen door of the hall. All the way I could hear that eerie inhuman sound, but as I crossed into the hall I could hear other things as well. I could hear the goats bleating incessantly and beyond that there was a man talking loudly, speaking as if to a large crowd. Just as I reached the doorway from the kitchen to the main hall I realized that it was the same voice that I had heard just a few nights ago offering Communion to the faithful. Larsen was preaching and even now I can remember his words.

> I am the life and the resurrection
> Those who believe in me even if they die, shall live forever
> For I am the child of God and wield his power
> I give you life, first on this Earth as mortals, and after the resurrection, life eternal
> I come amongst you know, to remind you that this is the image of God
> And that all men shall be as I, made in His image

As I watched him through the door, Larsen was standing on a table, a bound goat held in one hand, a knife in another. With ease he drew the blade across the animal's throat and allowed the blood to pump out in a torrent onto the floor. Then, effortlessly he tossed the now still beast down to the floor.

God I wish I had not seen the greedy crowd that waited below.

The villagers which I had thought dead had undergone yet more of a transformation. The clusters of five had grown into each other, traces of their left arms were still visible but like a parasitic tree on its host, melted into the neighboring flesh. The right arms, all boneless now had become thin and whip-like, the fingers and thumb elongated into a tentacular mass that constantly seemed to flex and grasp. Likewise, the adjoining lower limbs had wrapped around each other, no longer ten legs but five thick, grey tentacles that flailed about dragging the creatures clumsily along. The toes were gone, and in their place each were developing a fat triangular paddle. Like the fingers the paddle curled and flexed in a seemingly useless exercise. But most horrid of all were the heads, or what once were heads. Though the features still remained, the once semi-spherical craniums of men were gone, crushed and remolded into a pyramidal structure, the mouth shoved down toward the base and pinched into a tube, while the eyes had been forced up to the apex. Ten eyes seemed unnecessary to whatever it was becoming for without variation one of each pair of eyes was dangling limp from strands of necrotizing flesh, while the other was frantically whipping about on the end of a short fat stalk. It was as if some alien Prometheus had grown jealous of man's bilateral morphology and had seized the flesh and molded it into a new pentaradial shape. A shape I was not wholly unfamiliar with. For the things that crawled about in that great hall resembled to a striking degree the ancient and enigmatic specimens that Lake had excavated out of the ice in Antarctica and had dared to call "Elder Things"!

I shuddered at the sight of the seven things that were once the proud residents of Allyn Hill. Shuddered even more at the way the monstrous things grasped and tore and sucked at the flesh and bones of the goats that Larsen tossed to them. Then my eye caught the thing that flailed in the corner. There were by my count thirty-nine victims in the Great Hall, thirty-five of them had melted into seven sinister protean things, but the other four were incomplete, and this imperfect monstrosity lay in the corner whimpering. It was less complete than the others, and therefore less inhuman, and on one of its faces I could still see the bright blue eyes that rested beneath a shaggy golden mane.

Cautiously I slipped out of the kitchen and made my way along the back wall toward the pitiful thing. The others and Larsen were so distracted by their feeding that they failed to notice as I knelt down beside the mewling, simpering defective changeling. I stared into those bright blue eyes, and for an instant I thought that there might still be some humanity left within the deformed mass of writhing flesh. Those eyes stared back, and there was a spark an instant of recognition and hope and I reached out to touch what I knew was all that was left of Shane Atkins. In a flash all traces of humanity were gone and a great grey tentacle whipped around my hand and dragged me forward. I pulled back, but to no avail. The eldritch mass of tumourous flesh pulled me closer and another tentacle flailed about trying to find purchase and strengthen its hold on me. In unison the four bulbous mouths whistled out that howling unearthly refrain Tek Tek Tek Tek E Li Li!

Without hesitation I swung the gun up, pressed it against the face of the thing that was once a man, and pulled the trigger. The ensuing recoil pushed me backed toward the kitchen door, which all things considered, was fortunate for my action had attracted the attention of both Larsen and his flock. I quickly crawled backwards, closing the door and bracing it just as something large heavy and wet slammed against it. The door cracked and I could see the latch straining under the pressure being applied on the other side. I threw the lock hoping it would buy me a few seconds and then slid a kitchen knife into the space between the floor and the door, wedging the door closed. I backed away from and surveyed the kitchen for options. Somehow, even in my panic, I knew that these monsters needed to be destroyed. I dashed about the kitchen and one by one snuffed out the flames of the lights but left the gas work valves wide open. I even stopped and turned on all the valves for the stove. Stepping outside I frantically grabbed a box of matches and an oil lantern. I smashed the glass of the lantern against the door handle and lit the wick. I set the broken lantern inside the door, shut it and ran as fast as I could.

I was at the bottom of the stairs that led to the breakwater when the explosion lit up the night. The pooled water around the shore rippled as the shock wave blew past, and I stared as flaming pieces of debris careened in arcs across the sky. I sat there for a while and the glow from the top of the hill slowly grew stronger. It took me quite some time to cross the breakwater and get back to the station. The pain in my back is getting worse and my legs ache horribly.

I've climbed to the top of the tower again. The whole village of Allyn Hill is burning, in a few hours, I doubt there will be much left at all.

0530

I think I understand now why Danforth was driven mad, and I suppose why McTighe tried to kill himself on the way back. The things Lake found, the Elder Things, that rose up and slaughtered our colleagues, I cannot deny that anymore. They laid dormant in the ice for millions of years. If they could do that imagine what else they could do. Imagine their resilience.

The explosion in the great hall and the ensuing fire wasn't enough, three of the things survived. They're down below now, clamoring about desperately trying to find a way into the lighthouse tower.

I can't move much, my legs aren't working well, but I've been able to douse the light, disconnect the fuel line and turn on the pump. The ground level is covered with kerosene, and fumes are slowly filling the tower. I'm going to place this field book in a tin and throw it out into the ocean. Then I'm going to light the wick. It's crude but when the fumes reach the top of the tower I think the resulting explosion will be enough to kill them and me.

Pr. Pabodie, Dad, If the stones survive what I'm about to do here, you need to make sure to destroy them. Use a kiln if you have to. I also want you to know that despite our differences, I couldn't have asked for a better step-father. I appreciate everything you've done for me over the years. I also need you to know that what happened here wasn't your fault; I wanted to go to Antarctica. It was Larsen who caused all of this. He figured out what the stones were and stole one of them. It was madness what he did, I suppose he was like Danforth and McTighe. I think maybe all of us who survived the expedition might be just a little mad.

The stones, they're not stones at all. They aren't a magical ward, or even a weapon, not at least in the manner that we think of. But we should fear them; they could destroy us all. I keep thinking back to when we excavated those star shaped snow mounds back at Lake's camp and how the dogs went wild with fear. I think they instinctually knew something we've forgotten. The star stones, they're theca, protective cases filled with parasitic spores. I don't know when it happened; it may have been in the communion wafers but something else as well, the bread maybe. Everybody at the feast that night was infected. It makes some sort of inhuman sense. They transform the very flesh of their infected host into something else something akin to those ancient things that so long ago ruled the entirety of the planet.

0630
The sun has risen, Easter morning.

Glory, Glory, Hallelujah!

Father, remember me as the man I was.

They've nearly broken through the last door.

I don't have much time. The pain is unendurable.

I wish my arms were still

Mrs. Spriggs' Easter Attire

by Joseph S. Pulver, Sr. and Tara Vanflower

Easter. Night after an unbroken storm, first burst to cascade, that sheared and ate. Limbs and branches and roof tiles up and off, gone with the wind or to Oz. Night that put two inches of warm rain in the ground. Night with a hide-and-seek moon stretching out its light in search of purls and cracks... and collisions...

30 feet below what dramatic tonight put down—

Brittle decades without soft or bright hues. Lot of dirt. Dark loam. Blunt passages and tiresome rooms. Little or nothing human. Hinges broken by prying hands and rust. Insects, and worms, dangling roots, and once fine molding in the cool clay.

No lick of new.

Until the new arrival shone. Waved its sunflower sunshine right in Ada's eyes, no halfhearted river, hurled it right straight. Said its brilliant patch large.

"Such a fanciful bonnet *here*?"

Remake. Remodel. Fitting for Easter. Renew. Ada warm lighter, swells.

Maybe some notoriety—"Oh, to be lovely again." And that feeling of sun—sky smiling joy, touched by the bright sparkling beams of heaven. Enough of Lodge's *Wits Miserie*. Enough full to bored and flared cold.

One more admiring sigh, "Who *is* that?" Clean as quiet sin and yummy. Handsome to turn rue to away from the kind favors of clean gravestones.

Eyes on her. Only her. "Oh, Ada. How charming."

Eyes that dote. "Lovely, Dear. Lovely."

Eyes that adore. "Oh joy. So delicate. So soft."

Fawning again.

Maybe.

Maybe John or Mister Robin would notice her—he certainly had a hundred years ago on Main Street. She'd noticed him, a gentleman who was a paragraph where others were sentences, smiled back. Thought, "Able. I'll take that one, please." And self-hypnotized for a time, drifted on a wedding march and pillow talk and blue eyes that were moonbeam mercy. In them she would, if he'd asked, climb to any night of come closer my love.

Maybe Mister Robin, smiling, tipping his eyes to her bright sky. One more southward to womanly charms. One more soft moonlight and the carpet of "Sweetheart". How long had it been?

Decades packed under tight and foul. A tomb with the stink of lonely. A tomb without noble radiant.

Maybe this yellow would do it, this soft yellow gift. "Pretty." Pretty yellow, nice as a light carnival of kittens purring in your lap.

"On me." The whisper of dream's river.

And Trouble's eyes hiss. Inhuman-red gone hellfire jealous. Got her claws on it.

"Slip your claws off *mine*."

"Return to *your* place, Gil-*da*."

"My place?" Pushed by a tongue sharper than her fangs the fleet quicksilver of her hiss stirs the dust motes in the semi-darkness of the muddy crypt.

"Care and respect for one's *place*, before your words bring about instincts that draw blood."

"You would be the wise to raise your ears. Mine is mine. And *yours* is a hole of nothing."

Ada leans forward. "And you'd do well to mind St. James. Your tongue, should you not temper it, could well be the source of your destruction."

Ever the balance, John's moon-soft tone, "Ladies. *Ladies*. Is there a need? Joy blooms here. A heavenly feast has been brought to us. We can step away from spiders and beetles and moles and grumbling bellies." Feels the pangs in his own. Tongue caught on the bitter taste of beetles, his eyes narrow. His smile does not. "We can share this. Can't we?"

A pair of hiss. Shines in harmony with shatter growing wild. Dark feathers are readjusted, sharpened.

"Tis merely a bonnet, Ladies, please conserve your diabolical for other seasons."

Ada slips into a tone she hopes will please. "This spider, not I, shall catch slow and sleeping. I saw the sails of this ship before she even arrived."

Gilda's scorch scalds. "This is my Day. Not hers. *My Day*. Mine. She has one of her own."

"True, Dear Gilda. True. This is your day."

Ada, in a flare of scalpel tongue, is unhappy with John's attitude and comment. "I have the Right of Catch. Her eyes know that to be true."

Gilda's burn slashes. "Day rules Catch."

"Not in *this* warren. Here I own what I own. When there were only three, Mister Robin and I wrote the laws. Simon was here with us. He approved them. He gave his blood."

"Would you have me leave and make some lodging away from St. Echo?"

Eyes blare yes; slap a hard now on it. "You may hang your dress and fancy of childhood anywhere you care too. For now somewhere over there might be fitting." Ada's crooked grey claw points to a stout beam and a web-cocooned noose where her brother Simon hung himself. "The ceiling matches the tone of your raggedy mane. Perhaps its medicine would cure you of crude meanness?"

"I shall not leave this party. Not when we have this to give thanks for. This is my sign of rebirth. A very fitting one as I see it. Fitting to be brought here, to me, on *My Day*."

Gilda's day. Was. According to some. She was reborn on Easter. Rose. Remade. Walked around with the Gift. Tried to wear it well. Hard your first day. New muscle, new legs learning to stand, to move. Hands learning to grasp and hold with grey claws that look like they could have been chips of stone from a quarry.

Eyes. Trying to *see*. Newborn's eyes adjusting to the darkness studded with dead shadows. Wanting to cry, wondering if she still could.

Feeling the teeth in your mouth, the worm-knot gnawing in your belly. Gilda Stern. Popped up. Her Day. Wasn't fresh as a daisy. Wasn't still a wonder or a hot little number, not fit and beautiful. Grey. Hair a mess, a few bugs in it. Missing one hand, the one she favored, drove with—burst of that BLACK grid bumper-thing on the pickup truck suddenly a crushing wall. Missing smooth cheeks and they'd sown her torn lips together; she had a song for that tailor and his or her stitch-work. A song of nightmares. Must have been drunk or held in the tongs of some idiocy loaded with inept to sow her up like an old potato sack.

But Gilda found an old pair of scissors (and a cigarette pack-size chunk of a mirror) and cut the sutures. She was afraid to open her mouth. Afraid to speak. Hoped she would not sound like a monster. Simon came and the ribbons of her confusion fled. In Simon's kindness, Gilda found her voice.

That first night, conscious for an hour or so—felt like it, searching the smudged light of this rank cellar place. Shaking, wondering. Fragmented, rummaging experience for handholds. Just plain scared, the tension of mild panic wanting to get louder, until Simon came. Whispered. Took her hand and spoke of ways and need, spoke of reborn and the Gift.

"It will soon be Easter, less than an hour. And you are resurrected. You are the Easter gift."

Those few minutes before Midnight arrived and became a new day. Saturday reborn as Sunday. Easter Sunday. Out of good Fridays. No more happy hours in the Red Light with Nancy and Nunz. No more laughs—till you're in stitches, or shows of action and fun and funny. Years and she still missed the shows, how they ganged up on you with that BANG. And she missed the adoring eyes of the men. Those feasts were dead and buried. Never to be resurrected.

St. Echo. That first Easter morning under the brown-consumed cemetery, under the longing veins of dangling roots ready to carry the power of spring's flow of liberation above. Found the mirror fragment, cracked, only a piece. Wiped off the dirt, white of her sleeve now soiled by grave. Eyes looked at her. Gone blue. Radiant bright blue, shining with hopes and dreams and all the joy of happy Caribbean seas. Gone. Red. Sour red. Vivid, haunted. Stained with the same cold fire that boiled in her belly.

No coffee. No cigarettes. No lipstick, gone *Say Yes To Dizzy* red buzzing my branches are precious.

On the way to good-time rich detoured.

No fashionable boys, saying yes to dizzy. Confident men, hard and smooth and ready to shower her in the candy of summer harmonies, prophets begging and promising to refashion her spine with quakes of discovery, gone, gone and GONE. Their devouring gravity not. Her tremors as their arrows flew… Out on the floor—then alone somewhere, hands on. Saturday night vibrato, knitting together, skin, sheets, tucked in the taste of excited, flexing on the colors of the trumpet…

Sunday morning. Atoning—

No soft hand of Dear Sweet Lord or scripture of *a new birth into a living hope*—yet, somehow, she was resurrected.

And here was Easter again. Her Day.

And that bonnet was hers.

Ada could stick it.

Gilda would help her. She'd bury something, claws or a hard snapped off root. Bury it deep. Then she'd go off with Mister Robin. Ada could bark or howl. If she was still alive—

And there was the dead woman's body. Not lovely. Not young. Was it once, she wondered. Fleshy, abundant. All that meat. What the morgue didn't carve out. Lot to go round. Enough to renew the warren's empty bellies.

But only one bonnet.

"Mine."

Hunger and want. She wanted the bonnet and she wanted Mister Robin. Same as Ada. Same as the few other women here, if you could call any of them women. Still had breasts, and wombs, not that they would ever embrace born. And they all had desires; the clocks might be dead, but their hearts still built scaffolding from the gravity that curved and spoke swiftly.

John prays they don't rip each other's eyes out before Mister Robin arrives. He saw Ned dash off, knows Ned is Mister Robin's man and would run to his master with any and all news.

Ada, cold as a hiss, sears. "Not today."

Mister Robin shook his head. "Ada dear... *Ada*." Tipping his head, leaning toward her. "Today is Sunday. *Easter*. Simon told us she was the Easter child. And we have always followed that."

"My brother looked at things differently. You know that. Even here he whispered of God and things we know do not have a bearing on our ways. I only went along with this being her Day to maintain the peace. But he is gone now and we should set things, and this matter, right. This is not her Day."

Gilda takes Mister Robin's hand. Eyes plead.

Ada runs her finger over the yellow ribbon around the corpse's neck. Looks at the old woman's neck. Charcoal grey. Drying up and wrinkled like fried pig skin.

Mmm, pig skin. A time from before, the ripe then when food was food and it was everywhere. A flash of memory; of big Sunday feasts where little girls and boys run about in the sun with sprite dogs weaving play with heels and Japanese beetles buzz and glisten green like jewels, and robin's-egg blue sky with the puffy white cotton clouds that morph from animal to tree to army man. The tables set with feast, with renewal.

Cakes, and ham, and salt and butter—Jam and loafs of fresh, still warm bread...

Laughter and full mouths.

She picks up the ribbon tying the silk into raggedy brown hair that once glistened in that sun. *Did. Did. Then.* Now dull and lifeless like she is. And she feels warm, lighter—fragrant within, remembers the day she took the rough tip of a jagged claw to the cuticle of that dead woman, peeling back long strips of flesh from fingertip to shoulder for her betterment. Wasn't a pretty ribbon, but it was a ribbon. Worked well enough. Thinks of other ribbons—a drawer full, much prettier, quick pink and energetic red and smelling so sweet. Not the grey of death, like everything here. Dried up like husks. Dead, some frozen closed in the dry teeth of the abyss. No red that tastes like kiss. No blue. No green lark of sun-ripe springtime. No silver. Dead and grey. Like everything here.

"I want those," Gilda said reaching for Ada. "It's my day!"

Ada stood up in a flurry yanking her hair back, scowl intact. Eyes shining dull like an old penny covered in the gunk of age. "I... *These are mine.* Get your own." Her voice raw, boots moving over wet gravel.

"Greedy old bitch," Gilda snarled.

"Ladies." With the influence of a lion Mister Robin cut through the chicken squawking swift and sure. "I'll take the bonnet and the ribbon for now... Perhaps a peek upstairs?" His grin belied his intentions.

Ada removed the ribbon from her neck. Gilda handed him the bonnet. The women looked at one another, a blade strikes a blade promising I will write in your flesh. The yellow magic in Mister Robin's hands calls their eyes back. Eyes are filled with music, rapture.

"Ladies, please."

They were slow to turn their fastened faces from the treasures' immense beauty and toward the stairs.

"I want it," Ada purred. Her memories (Yellow butter sun. Brilliant daffodils and fluffy dandelions. An ice cream social dress with polka dots and crisp white gloves, pressed and fresh with starch.) swarming like whirring beetles.

"It's my day! You could have the ribbon!" Gilda whined.

"Ladies, patience," Mister Robin warned, voice stern but ambassadorial honey.

Ada turned with a smile, grey as it was, and acquiesced with a nod of her head. With a sly step retreated to his side. Sliding past and keeping close enough to brush her womanlies against his arm as she ascended the stairs.

Gilda looked back at the bounty with pleading, jealous eyes, and followed. The cluster of teeth she assembled to smile intensified, only she dared placing a hand to Mister Robin's broad chest as she passed.

He didn't mind.

Let the bitch eat dust, she thought, swaying her backside at the face she knew followed three steps behind.

Unnaturally slow, as if carrying grief they entered St. Echo silently.

Ada dropped down. How many Easters since she had last walked across this floor and sat in the family pew listening to the Good Reverend William Harvey's language of piety? No rebirth came into this abandoned church. Time ate.

Many things died. Sections of the floor were lost in the bellies of worms and a corner of the roof the wind had driven away. The waxing crescent of moon lit the boards. Night fell and the dead began their rest. Beneath the dirt they began their corruption. The bacteria ravaged as worms and unseemlies found their way into the casket from the surrounding earth. Time would win out and wood would crack. But here there would be no body. The clan would see to that.

Mister Robin's hand invited Gilda to sit.

She took a pew on the opposite side of the aisle.

And they waited.

The shape of Mister Robin's back. Looks up at the stained glass Christ cradling the lamb, no blur or ecstasy of prayer or crucifix-relic comforting the fingers to proclaim faith. "You are an impossible mountain. Never were a doorway." Doesn't spit like he did that first time.

His first steps here. Sitting in that pew. Claws biting into his palms. Fear and the taste of corpse meat on his tongue. Hated the taste. Belly liked being full.

St. Echo. 188 bodies in the larder then...

Then. When he licked his lips and the corpses were fat and many...

Then they were gone—

Sure as a knife and a fork had had played seizure.

Hard came. Squeezed. Chewed up prudent right along with the blood and the intestines, heart and thigh. The plate was empty and no deliveries arrived. No occasional drunk bedding down for the night. No urban renewal infringing. Not even a suburban housing development nearby. No historical relevance to save it or bring onlookers. The few family farms ringing St. Echo crushed into ruin.

Decades since a body was buried here. This one's arrival only springing from the desire to be buried beside her Beloved Mother. Decades since the local teens stopped using St. Echo as a party house. Few were the rats and rabbits that were to be found on St. Echo's lot these days.

Meat was becoming foreign to the tongue. Fresh unknown.

Ken had exploded on a man in black suit who'd come to visit his parents grave nearly twenty years ago. There were tears above, and there was murder. And the body had barely been carried away before a swift current of police descended when the man's car was found.

No one had been taken after that. The risks were too great. But as the years passed that became less an issue, fewer and fewer came to grieve for their loss.

St. Echo, small but once quaintly grand, rotted inside and out and bellies stayed vacant.

But not hungry hearts...

Mister Robin walked to the casket they'd carted upstairs and placed on the altar. Opened it. He gave Susan Lordes her yellow attire back. Tied it neatly and just so.

Susan Lordes lived alone. No cats, no purse-size lap dog to attend her loneliness. No ball, no waltz on her dance card, just Susan and her TV and her chocolates... and pastries and cookies and that yummy bowl of jelly beans... and her bags of snacks... She sat and watched dances of romance and obsession—fueled need, and ate, sometimes by the fistful. Four hundred pounds of desire packed on four inches over five feet of bones. Four hundred pounds of sensual dreams. Each kiss of chocolate her lover. Each salty snack the velvet caress of her new sweetheart. Until her heart, full of cravings, could take no more passion...

Susan had her plush sofa and her soft slippers and three snuggle-thick lap-throws and her 3-layer yellow boxes of foil-wrapped sweets and her piles of "Celebrity Glamour" magazine. Napped in the afternoons so her evenings were free to watch reruns of *Dynasty* and *Desperate Housewives* and when her heart was filled with sin and fear and shame, she grab the handset and call Pastor Jesse Ted Fuller's tele-ministry, 1-800-SEED-GOD. Twenty five dollars and she'd get her two minute Blessing. Free of sin, reborn to new pasture—green pasture of soft and pure square one. Again, abundant Life. $25 and sin-free, and she'd begin the feast again.

No rainbow-colored Easter eggs. No solid chocolate bunny. No feast of maple-cured ham and buttery sprouts and yellow layer cake under daisy-swirls of buttercream frosting this year. They buried Susan with the bonnet she never got to parade in church.

Shakes his head. "My Dear Ladies, we can all partake of this repast, or, if you cannot put aside your desire, I offer you Right."

Then he closed the lid. Let them sit. Stew. Walked away and sat. Sat with his hands folded as if in prayer.

And he waited for John.

John would conduct the dance.

A grey color slow as graveyard fog walked by the women. Didn't turn right or left. Stood quiet waiting to unfold. John cracked the lid, in a coalblack voice, "It dazzles you." Looking back at Mister Robin and those surrounding him, dripping grins like poisonous lizards. One bite would kill. Rot you from the inside out. The church's hollow air outlined empty to edge with bent hunger and driven expectancy.

Eyes turn face right.

Eyes turn face left.

Neither frightened. Stare. Not studying. Hating. Grudge shoved and shoved back.

Bolted to place, mouth ready for violent, one thinks she'll go mad.

One accelerating.

John raised his hands looked up at the stained glass window. The Good Shepherd holding a lamb. "The feast of abundant rebirth."

Velocity on a face netted with invade. "My bonnet!" Gilda exclaimed rushing the box and knocking John off-kilter. Her eyes were wild, fingers tearing at the sunshine ribbon. "It's my day! It's my day!"

"Mine!" Ada rushed, pushing Gilda, yanking the hat from skeletal fingers.

John steady. Steps away.

Mister Robin watched in delight as the two ragged women fought over scraps of fabric, scraps of memory. They weren't great beauties now, and one had never been. But pride comes before a fall, and he would watch the show.

Ada smashed the bonnet down over crispy crumpled hair.

"It's my day!" Gilda complained ripping the bonnet from Ada's head and rushing off into the shadows.

Mister Robin looked up, watching Ada sneer off into the darkness. He rose and walked to her. Held her hand, patted it.

"Children." Ada snorted. Sauntered over and dropped down in a pew smoothing her hair, adjusting the old leather ribbons tied in sick bows in her hair.

Gilda held rusty old scissors. Heavy in her hand, she trimmed the crooked hair across her forehead. Pulled her fingers through her hair to smooth the matted tresses, trimming along the bottom edge as straight as she could. She set the scissors in her lap and lifted the precious bonnet placing it reverently on her head and tied the ribbon beneath her chin, big yellow bow above her right ear. Blinding bright, like the face of god, against the dirty pallor of rot, she wished she had a mirror to admire it. Not so long ago she was breathing summer air, bathed in the beautiful blue sky, sunk into velvet green grass. She was drunk on it when she closed her eyes. Every swollen curve of fertile, the rhythm and meaty ripples, she could feel it, smell it. Birds singing, trees swaying with wind-music. Spinning in circles, arms wide, face raised towards the light.

And she had nights—impulsivity. The temperature of free-range music, soaring on the physics of dance. Marvels of carved lust, her wings wide, a flock of lanterns. Wild, scent of the moon breathing on skin, hips awakened, interlocked in truthful confession. Nights, filling mine with felt!

And this yellow gift brought it all back.

The minutes of THIS melt…

gone the casket-box and its blizzard tongue smelling like mud. The shackles of joyless-BLACK that tear at beauty. Gone worms and dark-dirt filth…

SUN—every side right, hung over simple things, the river playing, licking panes and feet…

b i r d~ s~S   waltzing through the anatomy of the rising year—

...light...

laughter   Jack's flashing

                Jills—no limits to the pink peaks of feminine with unwinding plans and bells that believe luck...

Yellow in her hands. Playful yellow. Unsoiled. Dawn fresh...

Gilda beaming, sunny as an 8-year-old fingers full of tall and rising. Wearing it—vibrating brightness, now a nightingale, some bonfire Genesis, in the sirenwaves of sweet fables. This is better than the scent of soap or his sweaty hands on her gorgeous ass when she slammed her hips against his energy. "Oh." Almost happy enough to cry.

"*Mine. Mine.*" Laughs as she expands. "I'm pretty." Looks up at the stained glass Christ. Smiles. "Not that old bitch."

The black-weight shade of Ada, a plenty about to splash and spread. Sharp fangs bared. Froth of graveyard hissing air. Ada. Crowd of witch-hag stink and dust. Sniffing. Hands snatching the pretty yellow bonnet. Holding it. "There you are." Voice so low and filled with hatred. Acid churning over tumbled rocks. "Sweet, sweet spring... And mine."

Hands come up to take it back.

Yank —pull —twist. Scrape. Nick. Claws in a razor tug of war.

Gilda has the bonnet. Presses it back on. Spits on Ada. Mad-wind howl laugh, barks, "You lose bitch."

Iron hands of quarrel, twisting, pulling hair out by the roots, blood seeping into the bright cloth. Red expanding like paint in water. Ribbon biting throat, suffocating. Seams popping. "Bitch? I'm a bitch? Who's losing now?"

Ada twisted the satin fabric in her fist, tightening the ribbon around Gilda's windpipe. Gilda's arms flailing, reaching for something to hold onto as her eyes bulged, night-sight red glare bursting. Groping for a key or a hammer—the scissors... Suddenly feeling them in her hand, cut her way to free.

Ada's hiss. "I'm going to wear this as I feast on your entrails."

As blackness consumed her vision, Gilda, ready to tear to pieces, thrust the rusty scissors up and shoved the blades into Ada's chest. Slicing. Ripping. The crack of bone gripping the hallways of loud as the metal shattered a rib and forged definite in muscle. Gilda tried to smile. Eyes venom-hot, as Ada channeling rage, crushed her windpipe.

Didn't stumble or strain just up and out of avid and prattle. Gilda slumped over, all life gone now. Brilliant yellow atop dead grayish flesh.

Ada stumbled back sucking in a gasp of air. Like a dying fish at the surface of the water, mouth biting for breath, air hurrying from the situation of her lungs. Her eyes began to close, blinking to stay here, to stay focused, flash of yellow, flash of yellow. She lunged forward ripping Gilda's eyes from the sockets. Popped them in her mouth, snapped her bony neck. Bite down. Vessels pop. Scarlet like the most vibrant rose. Scarlet as the soft insides of a freshly disemboweled corpse, the sour claret tang on her tongue, on her lips, the taste of gone raining on her drought. Ada gasped, swallowed. Smiled at the warm yellow. Her hands were young, sudden. Barked joy as she placed the torn bonnet on her head, tied the ripped ribbon around her neck. Adjusted it by feel, no mirror. Fit. "Pretty." Chuckles. Rattles and chatters. No longer a spoiled postcard edges tattered. Alive again—flashing sunny. Ready—

To take in the zephyr-fruit "Yes" of Mister Robin's appreciative eyes. Ready.

"Ready."

And then slid to the floor greasy with cobweb-cursed centuries and cut with things fangs didn't care to articulate.

Mister Robin smiles over the pocked-hide biddies crumpled muzzle to muzzle. Gilda's features swollen purple and black, cheeks ground meat, neck's familiar slipped from strength, helped to ludicrous by a bear-grip ending in snarling claws. Dismissed from the tiger exhibition of the melodrama, part of a once delicate ear hung. Chunks of blood-damp hair around her shoulders with strips of scalp still attached.

Ada, bonnet tied to her head, smiling, smug with satisfaction, as her torso still wept thin grayish blood.

"From one loaf... Bountiful day," John said standing beside Mister Robin who turned and smiled.

The bonnet. No longer cooing luminous yellow and lofty fancy. No longer bright butter sun and dandelions. The sails of its exuberant song ripped, its DAZZLE dialect trampled, covered in dirt and muck from covetous hands and saturated in blood's rejuvenating wine. Mister Robin, remembering hot night air and the melody of a garden tryst with Gilda untied the dog-eared sun-bonnet and set it atop Gilda's crooked head. He tied the bow as nicely as he could and gently lifted her hand.

"Now let us pray," he said raising Gilda's hand.

"It was her day, John," he said. "To be reborn." Slow grin. Long teeth. *As flesh for our flesh.*" he said, and bit into her hand as a man would place a kiss.

Season of Sacrifice and Resurrection

by Adrian Tchaikovsky

he absence of a quiet man: Kevin's loss is felt in many small ways. The labs cleared poorly, jars and samples never quite back in place with the millimetre-accuracy that they once were. Late hours of silence without that tacit presence near midnight, for the new man knocks off at ten. Most of all it is the department's museum, its T-shape of narrow galleries, that misses Kevin. He had been its tender and its master. Now he is gone the exhibits grow untidy, the displays lack the precision of his touch, mislabelled, out of place, a garden growing wild.

I never loved another human being as I do the ancient dead. The more ancient the better: fifty million years is a bit fresh, for me. In other walks of life this would be the doorway to psychosis, but a doctorate in palaeontology has reworked me into a productive member of society. I have been at the department here at the university for over a year now, nominally teaching—though it is debatable whether my students learn anything from me—but hired on mostly because I was and am a ferocious publisher for the greater glory of the department, churning out papers every few months on such world-shaking matters as the precise function of trilobite morphology, or an overview of our current state of knowledge on the Tommotian shelly fauna.

One would think that this would qualify me to become part of the team, but in truth my academic colleagues have fuller lives than I: pub, telly, amours, divorces, talk of which is as dry and dull to me as I always suspect my lectures are to my students. Home holds no amenities for me beyond my bed, which is never jealous of the time I spent working late. I can find in the microscopic intricacies of a fossilised mollusc an infinite fascination that the rigors of human contact denied me. Working late was how I got to know Kevin, in as much as anyone ever did.

His real name was something like Cieven Slovornik, but he was introduced to be as Kevin, and it was Kevin that stuck. He was from some-where in Eastern Europe, I guessed, or else the Balkans, or somewhere, his speech accented and queerly stressed. He spoke little to anyone, little enough to me even after I struck up our acquaintance. His job description was lab technician, and he had been there four years before I joined the department. In the manner of many quiet, formidably efficient and skilled men, he made his job look effortless, and was consequently underappreci-ated by everyone. He tidied and filed, categorised and dusted. He cleared up the labs after the students had been in, and he helped classify new finds that came into the department, leaving them with whoever was the best specialist without being asked to, every decision impeccable, invisible. By the time I came along the entire department was running on a frictionless substrate of Kevin's attentions without anyone ever quite realising.

I didn't know what his qualifications might have been, over in Belarus, or even if he had any at all, but his understanding of the field was broad and detailed, more than many men with letters to their name. Night by night, the two of us the only living souls in the place, I discovered that he would confidently take on tasks I would not trust to my most senior students, performing them swiftly and to the minutest detail: preparing slides, clean-ing and uncovering fossils with picks and acids. Most of all he tended the museum, that odd appendix to the department that was mostly ignored by staff and students except for sudden bursts of activity ahead of open days or summer schools, when members of the wider public might be enticed by it. Without Kevin the place would have been an embarrassment, but he spent many painstaking, nocturnal hours turning displays into dioramas, matching predators and prey, creating miniature wonders of juxtaposition and revelation. He was the Balkan Michelangelo of the display case. I have no idea whether the work was actually in his job description or not.

On one occasion I had landed a contract for a children's book about dinosaurs, a task that failed entirely to mesh with my usual technical writ-ing style, and only Kevin saved me from ignominy. In his halting, Slavic speech, he sat by me for three nights, retelling the story of the Cretaceous period in a way that I had never envisaged, slowly gaining in confidence as a raconteur while I scribbled down every word. The sounds! The smells! The bellowing clashes of the armoured reptiles, the sudden quiets, water rippling to the silent coursing of leviathan. I, who had lived for things long dead for decades, discovered them again in Kevin's passionate retelling. The book was, if I say so myself, a modest success, but I have Kevin to thank for it.

"You make them live," I told him when we were done.

"But they do live," he insisted. "They are there, in the Then, alive, all of them. They leap and stride and crawl." He, who normally said nothing, was now in the full flow of his eloquence. "Put your hand here," touching a chain of vertebrae from a plesiosaur, "and in the Then it is moving, swimming those seas, swift and hungry." I had never before come across a man who so shared—and exceeded!—my passion for the subject. It was the beginning of the closest thing to a friendship that either of us really owned to.

He was a fugitive, and that explained a great deal of his reticence. From where, precisely, nobody was sure. He never named a country, but there were plenty of places east and south of central Europe where having the wrong ancestors could abruptly become hazardous to your health, fossil feuds from generations back springing to life and howling for the blood of the living. He had come to England fleeing persecution, that much was known, his people under threat from some ancestral enemy. Years later, he still lived in the shadow of it. His daily routine was an exercise in getting in nobody's way and attracting the least attention possible, his diligence, I assumed, born from memories of a land where any excuse might suffice to move him on or worse. Even at his most relaxed, as we talked over the latest articles in *New Scientist* past midnight, sitting in the museum and surrounded by his handiwork, I always felt that he was looking over his shoulder, an edge of nervousness never far from him.

Then there was his religion, another topic he never addressed directly. I soon learned from colleagues that Kevin was a member of some odd little sect, some import from his unmapped homeland. Certainly he had sporadic days off for some observance or other. Doctor Rillental, the department head, whose doctorate was apparently in inter-departmental politics, was far too aware of the number of minority boxes Kevin ticked, and never demurred.

So the days went on, smoothing seamlessly into months, and then close to a year of our odd camaraderie, a friendship sutured together around an interest in the dead stone relics of forgotten times, which were more real and immediate to both of us than any of our fellow staff members. I settled down to the job, bored my students, published my papers with a frequency and regularity that became the envy of the department, and assumed that the pattern of my life had been set for the next decade or so.

It was not to be.

One night in mid-March it was, that Kevin came to me. I had not seen him that evening at all, but this was not unusual. A defining feature of our friendship was a lack of obligation, and he would drift by as and when he had the time and the inclination. At one in the morning, however, just as I was typing up notes on ammonite shell perforations and the probable causes thereof, he was there at my shoulder, strangely reticent, some new nervousness to his manner.

We exchanged a few words and it was clear that he was ill at ease, but I did not press him. Eventually in his own time he came out with, "I have a request, a favour from you."

I think that, discounting immediate family who have a claim on one's loyalties regardless of actual like, nobody else had ever said this to me, nor been in such a position of intimacy from which to venture the question. Faced with that realization and self-knowledge, I nodded for him to continue without hesitation.

"I need you not to be here one night next week, on 20th March," he explained, a little awkwardly. "It is a very important favour."

"What's this about?" My mind was completely blank. I could not imagine.

"I need to... use the museum." He was not looking at me, staring fiercely at the desk.

"You need to?"

"We—some of my—my people."

Something was nagging at me, the desk calendar catching the corner of my eye. The date he gave was marked there: vernal equinox.

"Kevin, is this to do with your... religion?" I asked carefully.

For a moment he was not going to admit it, but then he nodded, once, sharply.

I frowned. "Your religion needs the *museum*." I was being rude, I knew, but the thought baffled me. I knew Kevin to be a man of broad scientific knowledge, and in my experience religion and science seldom touched hands. Certainly Kevin had made the museum a very temple to rationality, every detail intricately researched. I could not think what any religion might find to exalt in there.

"We are very greatly interested in the things of the past," he said slowly, picking his way through the English words with more hesitation than I had ever known. "They are of much importance to us. Each year since I came here, there has been a... ceremony in the museum. Before you came there was never anyone else, at such an hour, to object. Now... this year, this is very important to me. To me, more than any other. This year is my ceremony." His eyes met mine at last. "You must tell nobody. I have trusted you with this."

"Nobody," I echoed, and the thought of mentioning it—to Doctor Rillental or anyone else—never crossed my mind. "Kevin... this is that important, to you."

Again that curt nod.

And then the point that I took a step too far, presumed too much, forgot myself. The question that should never be asked. "Could I watch?" because I was intrigued, as no human activity had ever caught my imagination before. A religious ceremony (or was the word *ritual*?) in a museum, some strange sect that revered the past. I felt as excited as if I was describing a new species of bivalve.

The silence stretched itself out, until even I, social inadequate, felt moved to fill it with, "I mean, I'd be interested to see..." and "If it isn't..." but the pause I had taken for offence was instead Kevin thinking patiently over the request I had made of him, weighing pros and cons, considering the chance of a betrayal if I refused, and other variables inconceivable to me.

If the reasons for my asking had surprised me, the reasons for his agreement were a closed book. In retrospect, though, I can only think that, whilst our odd friendship had led me to greatly overestimate the ways in which we were alike, his own assessment of my similarity to him had been so much wider of the mark. And in the end, I think that he valued my companionship on a level that I could not appreciate. He was, after all, very far from home, and I think that he was lonely.

"You must promise not to interfere," was all he said. I wasn't sure why I might be moved to interfere, at the time, and—again in retrospect—I should have thought more about it.

∗∗∗

"It is a matter of practicality," Kevin explained to me, on the chosen night. "We value rationality above all other things. You know that the calendar on your desk, it is a recent thing, yes? In truth, in logic, without sentiment, that point when the days are starting to grow longer than the nights is the start of the year."

We were waiting for his co-celebrants, approaching midnight, 20*th* March. Kevin could not keep still, and he spoke in halting rushes, more words than I normally got from him in a week.

"But there is sentiment, even for us. Your people have always known that the turn of year is a special time: for death of the old, birth of something new. You have your own celebration, yes."

"Well, Easter's not for a month, yet but..."

He shrugged, casting off all the complex ecclesiastical negotiations that had placed Easter where it was in the year. "Death and renewal," he insisted doggedly. "The year, your saviour's sacrifice, is all from the same thoughts."

I wondered then, and not for the first time, just what brand of religion Kevin espoused. I had always assumed some splinter of the Orthodox church, some offshoot of Slavic Christianity with its own proud and almost extinct traditions. His words suggested otherwise. "So what is it that you celebrate now?" I asked him. In truth I had never seen anyone less celebratory.

"It is to do with the land we have left, and the land we will go to," he told me, quite seriously, leaving me quite at sea, wondering, Is he Jewish then? This promised land business? Or does he mean an afterlife? He watched me try to assimilate this, and touched my arm slightly, more human contact than either of us had initiated during the year. "You are aware we have enemies, and that we are fleeing them."

Have, or had? Fleeing or fled? But all I did was nod, and he seemed satisfied.

His compatriots arrived then, and all at once, a little band coated and scarfed against the chill of the early year. Kevin let them in without comment, without introduction. They did not seem surprised to find me there, although their gazes were narrow and suspicious. There were half a dozen of them, and they had heavy duffel bags and rucksacks, bulging awkwardly with rigid contents. Their manner, entering, was less celebrants and more tradesmen here to perform some task with the minimum of fuss. With their coats off—and meticulously hung up—they were a strange spectrum of humanity, none of them seeming to have much ancestry in common with Kevin or each other. A broad-waisted man wore overalls, a woman in a skirt suit, a dark man in shirtsleeves, an elderly lady in woollens, a broad-shouldered man with a gym-toned body. One was a young man with a strange cast to his face who had the most striking snake-eye contact lenses I had ever seen, or at least I hoped that was the case. There seemed nothing to connect hem, save that they moved with a uniform efficiency and determination, exchanging barely a word as they followed Kevin into the museum, with me trailing behind.

Our museum was fitted around other rooms, a meagre T of galleries with an open space in the centre that was the only place that a group of any size could possibly gather. One gallery of the T's long crosspiece was currently devoted to a time-ordered display of fossils from the Cambrian to the Cretaceous, while its opposite hall had a presentation on continental drift, climate change and sea levels. The spur of the T had been given over to Pliocene and Pleistocene exhibits, mostly early hominids, and a little set of stone tools. All Kevin's work, of course, and now I began to wonder whether there was some deeper significance to it all, invisible to the uninitiated.

"What now—?" I whispered but, even as I began to speak, they were in motion, setting down their bags, pulling zips, releasing ties, revealing a variety of pieces, fragments—components might have been nearer the mark. Each neatly-packed container held rods and wheels and clips, and dozens of pieces of metal and glass that I could not even comfortably categorise.

They set to work with the careful speed of professionals—professional what, I could not say, but still there was nothing of the sacred in what they did, merely a complex practical task that they were plainly all very familiar with. As they assembled their shrine or idol, whatever it was, they spoke to each other, not conversation nor catechism, but something that was plainly technical instruction and interplay. None of it was in English, but neither was it anything that would have fit Kevin's accent or the Eastern Europe that I had assumed for him. This was when I started wondering about the wisdom of staying on at the department that night, but by then it was too late to back out.

The language they spoke was comprised of strings of hard monosyllables interspersed with slurred sibilants, a weird agglutinative speech that made me think of old Sumerian, that proto-language from the dawn of human civilisation which seemed to spring into and out of history with neither heir nor ancestor. Aside from a tentative reconstruction of that ancient tongue I had never heard anything like the language those men and women used between themselves. It was as distant from me as the speech of stars, of bees.

Occasionally one of them directed a brief string of sounds at Kevin, who replied effortlessly in the same manner, with none of the awkwardness he showed with English.

I had thought they were constructing some art deco altar or reliquary at first, but then as their quick work progressed I guessed that it was some sort of three-dimensional model representing some religious truth, for the internal construction was complex but ordered, and yet not merely symmetrical. That there was a functional plan was plain, what that plan was eluded me.

"You don't..." I gestured at the work, voice hushed.

"Last year, other years, I did," he told me. "Tonight is... my night. Tonight it is my turn. I am spared this." His body language had not changed, nor his voice, but something beyond these overt tells communicated to me that he was sad, and perhaps a little frightened.

"Kevin, tell me what this is about," I hissed.

"It is about our people," he replied, plainly including everyone in that room except me. "Where we were, our enemy, whom we once cast down, rises up. Our stay there comes to an end. We move on to where we will be. Each year, at the year's turn, we must... the phrase 'test the waters' is good."

I thought at the time that stress was bringing the worst of his grammar to the fore, his tenses hopelessly muddled.

"You believe in a promised land?" I pressed.

"There is such, and that is where we will go, where we have gone," he told me, sincere and baffling in equal quantities.

The construction was nearing its close, the end result a far smaller assemblage than I would have dreamed possible from all the parts—a loosely cuboid structure of glass and metal rods dominated by a great curved lens.

"It looks like the time machine," I said wonderingly, and then stopped, for the complete and combined attention of all of them there, motionless and silent, unnerved me more than I could tell. "Like in the film, or the Wells book," I managed, my voice abruptly hoarse with the perception of some hidden danger, and a little tension leaked out of the air, and then went back to work.

By then, though, I knew I had hit on at least something—it was a machine. I could see no moving parts, nothing that would hint at any technology I ever saw, but everything about it, every line and piece, insisted on function and functionality.

Were they some sort of spiritualists? I remember thinking. *Are they going to try and speak to the dead?*

Up until that point I was still clinging to the idea that, any moment, they would begin some service or invocation, or gather around and join hands. Even fits and speaking in tongues would have fallen within the bounds of my expectations. Then one of them turned the machine on.

I thought all the lights had gone out, at first, although I could still see. The bulbs in the ceiling were still glowing like embers, but they illuminated nothing but themselves, nor did the machine appear to shed any radiance. Instead there was simply a brooding, undersea light that had no origin at all, but hung in the air and touched everything with an unhealthy pallor.

At the same time, something happened to the ends of the three museum galleries. From being some twenty feet distant at most, their ends receded abruptly and then were gone, lost in a kind of creeping mist that seemed less an obstruction in the air than a limit to my meagre human perception. There were shapes, though, backlit by a silvery light and only dimly perceived in the fog. I had been looking down the fossil gallery when the machine came on, and what I saw finally convinced me that there were more things in heaven and earth, as the man wrote, than are covered in my philosophy.

The shapes themselves did not stir overmuch alarm. I saw structures, or what I thought were structures at first: great conical forms with nebulous, shifting caps—or then I thought they must be plants, for there seemed to be some manner of branches growing from their narrow points. They were still, though, wreathed in the unnatural mist, mere silhouettes against the deadening white glimmer. The movement that claimed my attention was not theirs, but resided in the exhibits of our museum for, where the mist touched, I saw flickers and shapes, and then more than that, clear glimpses of our little relics of stone coated over with flesh: a trilobite waving its whiplike antennae, an ammonite shell buoyed up in an invisible medium, tentacles emerging tentatively from within. When the mist touched the partial plesiosaur skeleton that Kevin had mounted on the wall, I saw the marine behemoth twist and writhe, the reconstructed head rolling its yellow eyes and baring needle teeth.

I backed up, mind devoid of anything so substantial as a thought, and ran into Kevin, who steadied me with a firm hand. His expression was fiercely engaged, as I had never seen it, and I remembered his words of months before: *They are there, in the Then, alive, all of them.*

"That is the Then," he told me, as if reading my mind. "My people are in the Then, under threat from the resurgence of our great enemy." And he gestured toward the far gallery, where climate change and global warming had been consumed by mist that was enlivened by a thousand scuttling, shelled things so that I could only parrot, in my mind, *an inordinate fondness for beetles.* "That is the Yet To Come, when our enemy, though they are the child of three hundred million years, have ceased to be."

My asinine words recurred to me. Time machine. "Will they come...?" I waved toward the great conical shapes, the moment-to-moment animation of the fossils, imagining some stream of refugees like Kevin, stepping out onto our museum floor en route to some unguessable refuge.

"All that is flesh, there, shall perish," Kevin said. There was fear and mourning in his voice. "Only our minds, the most gifted of our minds, can leave the Then and escape that ending. Only those few minds shall find new homes in the Yet To Come."

"And...?" I could only point down the spur of the T, where the handaxes and ancient human detritus had been swallowed by a limitless dark abyss, where a fickle, reddish light touched on great tumbled stones of black basalt. Not for one moment did I doubt him, or think him mad or misled. He spoke the words as they were unshakeable fact. Any scepticism in me died before that certainty.

"That is the Now," Kevin explained gently. "That is the Now, in the last places of our enemies, their deep strongholds at the edge of their time." He looked at me searchingly, seeking that kinship we had pieced together over the year, and he must have felt that he found it, because he was moved to try some few more words to enlighten me. "We are not safe in the Now, my people. Only we few conduct our experiments at the turn of each year. A time for resurrection that predates any reason your people might assign to it. Resurrection and sacrifice."

"Your experiments?" Each answer had only spawned more questions. I could not stretch my mind far enough to understand him. I expected more of the same, every word a cipher, but this time his response was such that even I could comprehend him.

"Each year we must test to see if our great enemy has succumbed to time. Each year one of us must journey to their haunts in the Now."

He had taken a few steps away to me, toward that dark, far place, where the ancient, vast stones lay, and I remembered him saying, *This year is my ceremony.*

Although the half-life of the fossils, the Then of Kevin's people, was at my back; although that dreadful, beetle-haunted Yet To Come chattered and thronged at the far end, it was that offshoot, that sideways glimpse into the Now that truly chilled me. Those stones had been worked, no natural formations, and yet the scale and the aesthetic were something inimicable to me, far beyond than anything else that I had seen that night.

"You have to go...?" My hands made inconclusive gestures at it. "But what if these... enemies are still there." I knew beyond doubt that the nemesis he spoke of was not simply some other tribe or religion of man, that far more than ethnic differences lay behind the enmity.

"They are," he told me softly. "They are not gone yet, nor for many of these years to come. They are tenacious of life, while they wait for our return. In the Yet To Come, we know to the year when their last scion shall fade and decay."

I did not understand, as with so much else. "But if you know, then why go now? Why not just wait?"

His face creased, and I saw there his fondness for me, shining from an expression that there were no human names for. I saw also that he was very afraid of those black stones and what lay behind them, far more than I. As loathsome as I found them, my ignorance was yet my shield.

"How else will we come to know the extent of their time, unless we experiment? Without our ritual of the years, where would our minds in the Yet To Come find the knowledge that they have? We do what must be done. We do what we know we did. The turn of the year demands it: for resurrection, there must yet be sacrifice."

He was past the machine now, standing at the mouth of that spur gallery, the stalk of the T, and I saw a wind start up, amongst the black stones, swirling the dust into unwholesome patterns.

"You're going to die?" It was a fool's question to ask anyone, save someone whose life, and the ending of it, was apparently already written in the histories of the far future.

"Something will die," he replied calmly. "But I shall live on." The thought seemed to sadden him, but then he gathered his resolve, and was walking away into darkness. Now I could hear the moaning of the wind out there in the lightless reaches, hungry, strung with wordless sounds that yet promised meaning, for anyone mad enough to listen for it. I started after him, just one step, feeling the tensing of the machine-builders as I did so. *You must promise not to interfere*, he had said. In truth, it was my own fear that stopped me, more than obedience to his wishes.

His walk seemed to take far longer than was possible, passing down and down into that place, far beyond the museum's walls, until the true size of those great basalt blocks became apparent, and he was just a tiny form moving amongst them, as the wind whipped at his clothes, growing stronger and stronger, its unseen voices raging and fluting.

He turned about one block, lost to sight on the instant, and a moment later I heard the scream that has stayed with me ever since, and lurked in every dream I have had. It did not seem, to me, like a sound Kevin would ever have made, but it was human, without doubt, lost and alone and in dreadful fear, and then gone, cut off and silenced by some invisible stroke.

The machine-builders showed no discernible emotion, simple scientists whose experiment has demonstrated some unfortunate but undeniable conclusion. They looked towards the Yet To Come, as if confirming that whatever lurked there, amidst the hints of mandible and carapace, had made its own record of the result, and then they looked back to the Then, and I did too.

One of the cone-shapes, those hazy-edged silhouettes, had moved, come closer until it seemed almost within the confines of the museum. Seeing it, I saw something living, but of no classification of animal or plant that Linnaeus had ever known. Even so, some part of my mind was instantly casting my thoughts to odd, strange fossils I had seen, unnamed and indecipherable, curious relics that seemed to match no known phylum, incomplete fragments that might, yet, have once belonged to this: a great cone-shaped thing, with four snaking limbs sprouting from its top, one of which terminated in a nightmare bundle of tendrils and eyes, for without doubt it was looking at me.

I saw something, then, that I have tried to deny to myself ever since, but the sense of it was so strong that even now I cannot dissuade myself from it. Staring into that alien gaze I touched a spark of something I recognised. No expression, no stance, nothing of the man I knew could have shown itself in that huge, unthinkable form, and yet I knew instinctively that what

I looked on had last spoken to me with Kevin's voice.

Only our minds, he had said, and if they could send them forth, why not drag them back as easily, to mount another expedition at some later date, to some later date. What limits could a race know, for whom time was a road they could travel at will?

Then Kevin's compatriots did something to the machine, and the world I had known sprang back, leaving me blinking in the electric light as they dismantled what they had built. None of them had anything to say to me, and I knew that Kevin was gone, and that they would find some other suitable place for their tasks next year. My mayfly part in their aeons-long story had come and gone.

And now Kevin is gone, too, and the department decays in a hundred subtle ways without his constant attention, and despite everything I saw that night, despite everything that I know, about him, about the world, I would welcome him back, if I saw him again.

And I have faith, atheist as I am, that I will see him again.

Some days, when visitors come, or when I must travel amongst strangers, I find myself watching their faces, looking for that spark of kinship that was enduring enough to cross the boundaries of species and ages to make itself clear to me. He is out there, in the Then, living amongst the living, breathing exemplars of the fossils I have loved all my life. He fights his peoples' enemies and plans their exodus, and one day, I am sure, he will find the Now again. Any man, any woman, no restrictions on colour or creed or country. Sacrifice and resurrection: Kevin is gone, but Kevin may yet return.

Mother's Night

by Ann K. Scwader

May moonlight lends these waves a spectral glow
Akin to phosphorescence fathoms down
Beyond a dark reef only locals know
Which haunts the harbor-mouth of Innsmouth town.
One night each year, a shambling, shadowed horde
Assembles on the cobbles of this shore
To crouch in silence, faces turning toward
Those depths where ceremonies long before
Brought forth a strange deliverance—or bane—
To mark their blood forever. Siblings all,
They wait for Her on whom their fathers called,
& glory in the knowledge of her reign
Beneath immortal seas ... where her embrace
Shall welcome every child of Hydra's race.

Free Fireworks

by T.E. Grau

Jacob let loose of his father's hand and took off across the cobblestones of Independence Square, slaloming through the statuary as he headed for the brightly colored booth advertising "Free Fireworks!" William smiled, readjusting his grip on the bouquet of red, white, and blue carnations. Jacob acted just as surprised and excited as he did last year, as he did every year. Children never tire of the familiar.

In Old City, fireworks were distributed free of charge by the federal government, which knew all too well that those who became accustomed to the explosion of gunpowder made for better soldiers. And in this city, as it was in all the free cities that were left, everyone was a soldier.

It was thirty minutes until the parade, and two hours before sundown, but already the crowded streets were alive with pops, flashes, and booms from 60 tons of liberated Mexican fireworks, doled out one bag at a time. Excited hands couldn't wait to bring spark to gunpowder and ring in the holiday with roaring concussion. M-80s and bottle rockets, Black Cats and spinners. Smoke bombs, snakes, and sparklers for the girls. There was a certain power to the dangerous alchemy. War games, played by children, watched by adults.

Across the top of the Square, below the breeze line, tendrils of smoke hung like lazy apparitions in the sticky July air. Jubilant groups of people gathered on stoops and balconies veined with ivy; drinking, grilling, and laughing under strung lines of tiny liberty bells. Revelers spilled out of apartment building doorways and onto the narrow sidewalks, taking the party into the street. Security was high and conspicuous, but citizens were allowed free reign today, and knew it.

This was Independence Day, the most important holiday of the year. The day to howl freedom in an explosive symphony of a million tiny bombs. All other holidays were shadows now, their backstories muddied by generations of tears and rivers of blood.

Jacob clomped back over to William in oversize steel toes, eyes as big as saucers. "Look what I got, daddy!" he said breathlessly, opening his bag.

The fireworks were a bit sparse this year. Budget cuts. The war had been dragging on too long. Insurgencies were like that. Ones fueled by religious fanaticism were even worse. Without hope for treaty or surrender, they could suck a country dry while every last zealot with a death wish was pried from a hole and liquidated. Pricey stuff, this business of hunting and killing.

"Let's show mommy!" Jacob said, taking his father's hand. William's wife Abigail was back in their apartment, listening to jazz with the windows closed, a bottle open and curtains drawn. She hated the 4th. Hated the fireworks, and what they meant. Hated that her husband might someday join the parade that started in 25 minutes. So she hid her patriotism made poor behind four walls and a ceiling, waiting out the day, especially the night, peering into a glass and drinking what came out. Abigail missed the old days, when the 4th of July was about picnics and skinny-dipping and explosions that would never reach you. William missed the old days too, but knew that looking over your shoulder at the golden glow behind wouldn't change the unlit road ahead when you finally turned back around.

"Don't you want to watch the parade?" William asked his son, not ready to go back home yet. Jazz always confused him. Made him edgy. Especially that bebop shit. What ever happened to Lionel Belasco? Abigail never could hold her liquor.

A firecracker went off nearby. William jumped and reached for something at his belt that wasn't there. "Can we light these on the roof, daddy?" Jacob asked, holding up a handful of roman candles. "I want to send them into outer space!"

William chuckled, tousling his son's hair. "Let's go lay the flowers first," he said, peering over a sea of heads crowding around a tall bronze statue. "Okay, dad," Jacob said absently, squinting at the labels of his fireworks, trying to work through the inscrutable Spanish to get at the secrets. "But can we hurry? The parade's going to start any minute!"

William glanced toward the east end of the Square that opened up into the city proper, where a group of disabled veterans and the local battalion marching band were gathering in the shadow of a converted church. A hobbling man, his face pinched and whorled by shrapnel scars, jerked his body in that direction, still trying to come to terms with the rubber and titanium that now served as his left leg. Jacob jumped in front of him, pointing finger pistols at the teetering man. "Pow! Pow!" The old vet staggered dramatically, feigning a mortal wound, then smiled and winked before continuing on.

Jacob held on tight to his father's thick, military-issue belt as they wound through the jostling crowd, arriving at the center of the Square.

William laid his flowers near the base of the statue, adding the bouquet to the thousands already stacked wide around the monument. This one was built higher and grander than the other eleven statues arranged in a half moon on each flank. William stood back, taking a moment, before bending to his son and recounting the story he told him every year. Jacob smiled. The magic of the familiar…

This was the statue of Sheik Nazir, the first member of Group of Twelve, a handful of popular, firebrand religious leaders, politicians, and mullahs who turned their back on extremism and joined the side of law and order. This shocking movement flipped the field in the Time Of Terror that erupted after the dawn of the New Enlightenment over a decade ago. It was then that the New League of Nations bonded under one banner of unmitigated truth, fighting back against those who shut their eyes and held close to lies taught by the generations that came before. Those who didn't know any better.

A giddy squeal came from nearby, interrupting William's story. Jacob looked over to a group of kids who had somehow hollowed out a pocket of space in the rowdy crowd. They were setting up a line of beer bottles, anchored by pouring in grit through clenched fist dug from a purloined sandbag. Jacob's face brightened. "Bottle rockets… Sweet." He looked up at his dad, who nodded. Jacob ran over and joined in, speaking in the fast, clipped language of little boys.

William looked past the children at the arching line of mismatched statues. These were the Twelve Infidels. A dozen to turn the tide. Their bold organization in a time of chaos helped prop up the flailing collective of hastily treated governments as wave after wave of catastrophic suicide attacks on all free countries nearly brought civilization to its dusty knees. Loaded oil tankers were turned into half million ton napalm bombs. Passenger trains filled with ammonium nitrate burrowed deep into city centers, leveling financial districts. Dirty bombs depopulated 17 major metropolitan areas, while a massive fleet of truck bombs took out governmental installations in 42 others. In the outlying areas, groups of heavily armed men burst into shopping malls, movie theatres, and grade schools, mowing down everything with a pulse. Sleeper cells in military platoons fragged fellow soldiers and blew themselves up, taking as much of the brass with them as they could carry. Brother killed sister, only to be killed by father. Ordered society broke down, melted away, congealing in a pool of splattered organs and chips of bone imbedded into bedroom walls. Ultra religious savagery reared the many heads of the hydra, as holy warriors wrapped in death cult dogma sought to plunge the globe back into a new Dark Age.

And they came so dangerously close. Two million died that First Day... July 4*th*, eleven years ago.

But the infidels fought back on the 5*th*, spreading hope like a spider web creeping up from the underground to cover the globe.

And so the war began in earnest. The new War of Independence. The last Great War, everyone said. Everyone was probably right.

William's modest Midwestern city stumbled to the brink of extinction after the First Day, as the kill ratio was so astronomically high. But the frontier was built on DIY, and the old mettle bubbled up. Soon, a small but determined group of police, ex-military, and even the local football team picked up hunting rifles and used their innate knowledge of deer trails and secret ravines to track down the remnants of the murderous cell that just days before killed thousands of locals. The remaining city leaders decided to pull back into Old City, walling off the blood soaked suburbs of what became known as New City, and hunkered down. That's what people did on the Plains. They hunkered down when the world turned foul, as it often did out here.

That was seven years ago. Pitched battles were fought in the meantime. Bombs of various sizes went off almost weekly. Always testing... Spies were sent, and spies were captured. The stench of waiting death hung over everything, as the souls of the free citizens calloused under the weight of daily, lingering fear. Some trained. Others drank and listened to jazz. A few split themselves open on the cobblestones. Everyone prayed and watched the skies.

But Old City was still free, and today was a celebration of that improbable fact, wrapped inside the stars and blood red stripes of a nation that was now just another wounded part of the wider world. Wave the flag, crack a year old beer, and toast to the Fates. Death came not on this day.

Fight like they do. Die like we do.

And they did, and so did we.

Four bottle rockets fizzed up from the group of children in near syncopation, whistling past the bronze image of proud Nazir, who looked out with fierce eyes under raised, haughty brows to the city skyline, toward the bombed skyscrapers and scooped out remains of New City just visible over the 30 foot concrete security wall. A wickedly curved scimitar was housed safely in its scabbard at his waist, but a knotted hand was on the hilt, always at the ready to take down insurgent filth of any stripe, any tribe. Even his own.

We were all infidels in the image of Sheik Nazir and The Group of Twelve, and we of the free lands wore the title as both a blood oath and badge of honor.

William walked over to Jacob, who was staring at a tiny rocket still resting inside its bottle. "Mine was a dud," Jacob said quietly, a smoking punk held in his hand like a stick of incense. William lifted his son into his arms with a grunt, reminded that the day was fast approaching when he wouldn't be able to lift him up anymore. He pushed back a bit of Jacob's unruly black hair. Hair like his mother's. "I promise that'll be the last dud of the night." Jacob smiled and hugged his father, wrapping his legs around him like he did when he was a baby. With his boy in his arms and the entire city holding them close, William walked back into the crowd, melting into the swirl of citizens, celebrating like it was their last night on earth.

***

The sun was setting, finally, and the cicadas took up their song. The daylight hours of July 4th seem to last an eternity, adding anticipation to that moment when the night sky first goes from dead to alive, thrilling and frightening in equal measure.

From the rooftop of their apartment building, William took a deep breath, and caught a waft of countryside air, blowing in from the west, pushed on by the sunset. For a brief moment, he could smell the honeysuckle, flavored with fresh tilled loam of the farm where he grew up, where he used to run through the wooded creek beds and crawl through culverts, playing war. It was mid summer now, and the crops would have been growing so quickly you could hear the corn stalks creaking and popping in the fields as they thickened and reached up toward the hazy sun. The beans needed to be walked, and the hogs were fattening in the mud, looking for a low spot in the fence. The bailers would be out, scooping up the first cutting of fragrant alfalfa drying in the fields, exposing a hidden civilization of earwigs and clicking beetles that gathered under the hot wetness beneath. William closed his eyes and took another breath, hoping to uncover more memories, but this time only smelled smoke. A neighbor had just lit up one of those ridiculous cone fountains on the far side of the roof. Children danced around the guttering sparks like wild Indians; like the heathens we all once were. Jacob got up from his contemplation of a late-lingering Junebug and joined in.

William frowned. He had grown to hate the smell of smoke, of burning things, which now filled him with horror when it was such a pleasant experience in his youth. He hated that he was an expert in smoke, noticing the nuanced differences of chemicals and wood, rubber and flesh. He hated the things he had done while other things burned. He missed the smell of burning trash on the farm, when the sharp pungence of combusting plastic was just a Kool Whip container dripping into the coals, when the odor of burning hair and muscle was just the calcine remains of a bird shot squirrel.

Down below, a muffled hush swept the Square, nudging William from his reverie, as the mournful strains of "Taps" began. This was the lament of the widows and the heartbroken left behind. William looked back at the door leading to the roof. He fetched Jacob and brought him close, listening to the song begat during the Civil War—the first Civil War—but made so common the last few years that it became an Independence Day hymn. It was written by a youth from the North, who ran away from his family to attend music school in the South. There, he wrote a simple, mournful tune. That young man died on the field of battle, fighting for the Confederacy, and the song was discovered in the pocket of the bloodied corpse by his shocked father, who was an officer in the Union Army. The officer asked his superiors if the Union band could play it for his dead son. They refused his request, as they'd be damned if their band would play a tribute to the enemy. He pleaded, and was finally offered a single bugle. The grieving father gave the song to the bugler, who played the funeral dirge to the lone body who had written it. "Taps."

William looked down at Jacob, who was watching the veterans' parade with right hand raised to brow in a stiff salute practiced for so many hours in front of the mirror. His grandfather, who fought, killed, and died a little in the haunted jungles of Vietnam, would have been proud. William smiled sadly, wishing that Jacob would run away to music school, to leave this city and this war and this grim and uncertain future behind, but Jacob would have nowhere to run. Music schools were the stuff of fairy tales these days. Music was the drum beat of battle and schools were now campuses of war.

The battalion band took over, playing John Phillips Sousa as the parade proceeded through the Square. A shout went up, and grew. Men saluted. Women threw flowers and blew kisses. Children watched with wide eyes. It was a celebration of those who survived and sacrificed so much to keep this country free.

As the sun dipped below the horizon, bathing the world in that sweet hue of magic hour blue, the first volley of organized fireworks launched into the air, exploding in bellowing showers of multicolored sparks taking on fantastical shapes... Flowers, sunbursts, fiery spirals like the flash of galaxies. Jacob jumped up and down, clapping his hands and trying to whistle through his fingers like his father taught him. Somewhere in their apartment, William could almost hear the dissonant sax music rising in volume. Abigail needed to be up here, but she just couldn't. William understood that, as best he could.

The fireworks continued, unleashing burning glory in the sky. Brief, fiery sketches thrilled the crowd. The Square cheered each glimmering salvo. Bellowed like Vikings. People were drunk now, forgetting their fear in the haze of liquid hope. William watched the burning patterns branding the darkness reflected in Jacob's eyes. He picked up his son, so he could get a better look.

William heard a sound behind him, and turned. Abigail stood in the roof access doorway, holding a lit sparkler in her hand, a tired, bleary smile on her face. He set Jacob down and went to her; took her pale face in his hands and kissed her deeply, like they used to kiss when every second mattered before the porch light came on. He looked into her bloodshot eyes, and pressed his forehead against hers. "Thank you," he said. Her soft hand against his face told him everything he needed to know. She held up the sparkler as it fizzled to a red, glowing stick, then frowned, pouting like a little girl. William laughed and kissed her again, sometimes feeling as much her father as her husband. He took her by the hand and walked her to the edge of the building to their son. Jacob's eyes lit up, but he said nothing as he hugged her tight around the waist. William put an arm around his wife, and brought his son in close between them. For the first time in a long time, it all felt right. The way it was supposed to be. The way it once was. The All-American family, enjoying the 4th of July under a dying sunset, with fire in the sky and without a thought for tomorrow.

Just then, a boom much lower and louder than the others shook the cobblestones. The parade stopped abruptly, the band's trumpeter trailing off like a deflating balloon. Fireworks continued to fly, as the fuses were already lit, but no one was watching anymore. Murmuring silence choked the Square. Abigail looked at William, whose face told her everything she needed to know. Another muffled blast sounded, and another. Triangulation. The citywide PA system croaked to life. Orders chattered into the night. Sirens wailed. Abigail fell to her knees and wept. William looked down at her, as if it was happening in slow motion.

A plume of black smoke billowed up from the Old City marketplace, four blocks over from the Square. The throaty belch of a heavy machine gun fire chewed through the din. Screams littered the Square, as the crowd scattered, grouped, rallied.

God damn them… On our holiday. Just like last time.

Jacob looked down for Abigail, but she was gone. His stomach turned. He didn't want to gear up and head out like this. William took a deep breath and turned to the roof door. A hand stopped him. It was Abigail, holding Jacob in front of her. She blinked away tears and smiled, laughing in spite of herself. He walked to her and she kissed him, whispering into his ear. William smiled, gripping the small of her back, re-etching the familiar curve into his memory. He then hugged Jacob and looked into his son's eyes. William wanted to say that he loved him, but he did it so rarely, that he was worried that the boy would take it as a final goodbye. So he just nodded. Jacob nodded back.

And then, only two stood on the rooftop, and William was gone. White smoke drifted over the Square. Black smoke rose beyond. Abigail closed her eyes.

***

William strode quickly onto the street, wearing starchy fatigues, a modified M-240 in his hand and a heavy pack slung over his shoulder. He blinked a few times, trying to orient himself to the frantic commotion of the Square after dressing in the silent apartment. All around him, fellow soldiers, male and female, young and old, kissed their loved ones goodbye, while others emerged grim faced from apartment blocks still littered with bottles and trappings of the party that hid them from the outside world just hours before. A banner of red, white and blue dangled limply from the awning of a shuttered storefront. Under it, an old man leaned on a cane and looked up for the stars of his youth. He didn't move, only stared. William looked up at the roof, where he knew Abigail and Jacob were watching, and waved.

Another explosion two neighborhoods over shook the ground and shot red-gutted smoke into the sky. Infiltrators. Spies gone active. Peace had made security soft. Made all of them soft, William thought, adjusting the tight Kevlar vest under his jacket that always fit him so loosely before. He was adding inches, while the city was giving them away. Give them an inch, they'll blow up a mile. Gunfire ripped into the night, sending everyone but the soldiers scurrying for doorways. The man under the striped banner was gone.

William jammed a receiver into his ear and a walkie talkie to his mouth, as he jogged toward the outer wall ringing Old City, receiving intel and barking orders. He had to man his post.

***

The walkway cresting the wall was crowded with crouching troopers, weapons bristling outward like deadly whiskers, just like the days of castles and keeps that thrilled William's childhood. A teenage private, still a bit woozy after fear burned off most of his drunk, lit up a cigarette. William shot a glare in his direction. The kid blanched and quickly stamped out the smoke under heavy boot tread. William shook his head. A glowing cherry earned you a sniper's bullet exiting the back of your mouth. Some of these guys need more training, more time. There was never enough time anymore.

William returned his gaze down his scope, scanning the frustrating darkness below. He knew they were out there. Knew they were watching, praying to the empty sky. He could smell them. Smell their smoke. Exhaust, campfires, dank Turkish cigarettes… What were they waiting for?

It had been hours since the last of the suicide attacks rattled the city and dawn was on the creep. Insurgent recon was lacking, as they leveled a recently emptied ammo dump and part of the Old City prison, freeing two spies awaiting trial just long enough for proper justice to be rendered with the gavel fall of hollow points. Their slapdash Trojan horse failed to open up the enemy from the inside. Terrorists didn't win many battles. They just wore you down until you gave up and lowered your head. But tonight, there would be no 'wearing down'. This would be to the death, and whatever waited beyond.

William's earpiece crackled to life. Air support was on its way, but they were coming in from the nearest base in the Rockies, a good thousand miles away. William tested the breeze, hoping to find a westerly tailwind. Nothing. Everything was still. Quiet, within and without. The holiday was over. The air force would be late.

He looked up to the queer stars arranged in new constellations that knew not nor cared not what was happening below. He didn't think he'd ever get used to them, even after all he'd seen. A shooting star carved through a patch of grayish black with a dim trail of stratospheric sparks. Free fireworks.

A commotion went up from the troops manning the west section of the wall. Dots of light appeared on the hilltop about a mile outside Old City, on the grounds of what used to be a high school. William looked through his scope as the sun groaned through the pre-dawn, dimly lightening the sky and giving the first glimpse of what was waiting in the dark.

Flags decorated their front lines. Flags with symbols of religious zeal-otry and indiscriminate terror. The Crescent moon. The star of David. The Cross. The insurgents—from Pakistan, Korea, Italy, Ethiopia, Iran, England, Indonesia, India, and the barely United States—raised their collection of mismatched firearms and took aim at the city wall ahead. They had a half squadron of banged up tanks. Aging howitzer barrels bristled behind them. A battery of Russian-made rockets flanked each side. Ragtag military equipment patched together with a soldering iron and chewing gum. By the collection of this hard won gear, this looked to be a last stand. We'd send them to paradise, good and proper.

Fight like they do, die like we do.

William sneered and shook his head, as all around him the flags and battalion banners of Old City were raised, catching the growing breeze. These were the flags of organized statehood against those of anarchy. These were the flags of the Twelve Infidels. Those of fang, of eye, of tentacle. That of the Elder Sign, which tied them all together under the primordial bond of The One Faith. These were the believers in the Blind Chaos swirling at the center of Time, as revealed to the bug-eyed world through The Great Priest, who cracked the foundation of the earth and rose from the sea to re-claim his earthly province. To wipe away with an atmosphere splitting roar all the lies that filled the vacuum in Its absence. It came back to remind us all of how it all began, and how it would never end. After bursting from the South Pacific, the Old One straddled the earth for The Three Days, crush-ing mountains and displacing seas. Destroying certain myths and validat-ing others. 100 million died in the unnatural calamity, a fitting sacrifice for our forgetfulness, for our arrogant creation of our own gods and fathers, in the absence of alien reality. Then, without a glance at the fleas weeping in the circus below, It leapt into the sky and disappeared into the ether, leaving behind a New Order of Things, staying just long enough to give us a glimpse of stark, mad reality, tended by those Things that awoke with it, crawling from the earth and screaming down from forgotten mountains where they had waited for a billion years to reclaim Eden.

But still, many did not believe—refused to believe—branding the Old One and the Elder Things as spawns of the devil, even though the accused progeny were incalculable eons older than their supposed father. These religious extremists clung to their upstart monolithic god and his handful of dirt scratching prophets with violent resolve, spurning an older pan-theon, just as they did with the Pagans, the Babylonians, the Egyptians, the Hindu, the Greeks, the Native Americans... Where was their god now? Was it cowering in the corner of eternity, or fled altogether? Did it ever exist in the first place? No one knew. There was no proof. There was only the faith of a bawling child, waiting on an errant father who promised to come back and take them to paradise. The paradise was lost before it could ever be found. But still they believed. They needed to believe, because to not would mean they were wrong. That they knew nothing. That they were nothing but a handful of chemicals given mass and the electric spark of life. They wanted back the magic of the familiar.

William's grim musings were interrupted by the deep, humming peal of the curiously shaped bell that one night just appeared in their abandoned church four years ago. He turned back as the Nameless Acolyte of Old City emerged from the cathedral, now a Temple to the Starry Wisdom. He wore a cowled robe of yellow, stitched with intricate patterns that dazzled the eye, even from this distance. No one had ever seen the Acolyte's face, and none wanted to. Old City was devoted to the New Enlightenment adopted by the American federal government and so many others, at the behest of the Twelve Infidels. But that didn't change the fear that twisted the hearts of humanity still coming to grips with this new religion birthed amongst dead stars in a reality not compatible with our own.

The Acolyte raised his wrapped hand, and made several quick, arcing movements, as if carving the air with tortured geometry. These gestures were now familiar but no less unsettling to William, who pulled on his helmet that had the appearance of a cuttlefish, and checked his chamber. His fellow soldiers did the same, as the clarion call of horn and dissonant flutes split the early morning quiet. The Army of Justice and Truth—the Army of the United States of America—took their positions on the wall, taking aim at those far out and below.

William set up at the head of his platoon, and from around his neck took out a figurine carved from a greenish gray stone. He brought the tiny toad-like shape to his lips and kissed it. "Elder Gods protect us on this day from the non-believers," William said, looking up into the dark sky. "May the infidel triumph over the lies of the usurper."

A shout came from further down the line, as three trucks without headlights sped toward the wall, bucking and pitching over the cratered ground. Suicide attack. Grinding trident. The men on the wall of Old City opened up with .50 caliber fire, thudding the turf with heated lead. Several Katyusha rockets whooshed from the ground behind to cover the desperate attack, and slammed into the base of the wall, rocking the graves of smashed strip malls.

One of the trucks spun out and flipped. The other burst into flames. The last truck, chugging lower to the ground under the weight of three inch thick armor plating, withstood the barrage and was still coming. The decoys were dead, but the stuffed duck still remained, moving to within 100 yards of the wall. Just then, from behind the Old City lines, a boy no more than 12—just a few years older than Jacob—jogged forward, a LAW rocket launcher bouncing casually on his shoulder. All the men and women parted, allowing the boy to reach the edge of the wall. He hoped up on a box set down for him, took aim just ahead of the truck and squeezed, sending a whistling anti-tank round arcing downward. The truck stayed on course and met up with it 60 yards out, unleashing a mini mushroom cloud fueled by five hundred pounds of C-4. The terrible boom blew back the fighters on both sides. A mobile bomb that would have torn a 30-foot wide hole in the wall. A Hail Mary in every ironic sense.

As everyone picked themselves up, the cottony silence after a huge explosion was filled by a clicking and chattering coming from the sky, peppered by piercing shrieks. Many on the wall smiled. Many more shook off a shiver. The terrorists sometimes had choppers, even an occasional jet, but the free nations also had things that flew. The air force had arrived.

William looked up into the sky, where winged, insectoid creatures—alien inkblots against the bluish smudge of the Milky Way—moved in bizarre but graceful formation, sizing up those on the ground below.

Small arms fire rang out from the enemy position, before the anti-aircraft guns mounted on the back of pickups roared to life, pouring death into the heavens. Phosphorous tipped tracer rounds stuttered across the sky, trying to bring down those Things that flew above. Some took bullets and crumpled, falling with unnatural speed to dent the earth with a monstrous impact. But others found their targets, swooping low to rend metal and flesh, scattering survivors and sanity as they swooped back up into the unquiet sky.

William crouched low and took aim, squeezing off rounds into moving figures that could be friends and neighbors, but who had all become The Enemy. Fuck 'em. The worms would eat them all just the same.

Bullets rattled the wall, as defenders dove for cover. William reloaded and reengaged, when an RPG exploded to his left, blowing him onto his side. His ears rang, his eyes bled, but he could still see flashes of fire, the rockets red glare, the bombs bursting in air, that were lighting up the sky above the city, carving rivulets of light over the towering bronze effigy of Sheik Nazir and as his eleven fellow infidels. A Baptist missionary. A venerated Vatican Cardinal. A Micronesian king. A Muslim scholar. Three Presidents, two rabbis, a swami and a Mormon leader. All those who lost their faith in the lies of the One God, and embraced the horrific but undeniable proof of the Many Gods.

The fighting increased, as both sides vented their righteous hate through sizzling metal. William got to his feet, clutching the figurine around his neck. All he could smell was smoke. July 5th... The day the Twelve fought back.

William looked up, unbowing his head. Tracers and explosions ripped across his view into the universe that was closing its eyes, turning away. Showers of sparks from exploding shells took on beautiful, terrifying shapes, creating a new show, an encore of brutalism and death that danced atop the sky, below the mute stars that saw nothing.

Free fireworks.

Doc Corman's Haunted Palace One Fourth of July

by Don Webb

It was the last time I shot fireworks professionally. It was the last time for many things. For my friends it was the year they started to say, "Something's not right about Rob." It was the simultaneous gaining and loosing of *certainty*. In the big picture the change of the world-view of a restaurant-and-book critic in a Texas town is not very cosmic, unless it is the flap of the butterfly wings that They use to bring about a human hurricane. But I think that I am rather small butterfly indeed.

For almost thirty years I reviewed the restaurants of Austin, Texas and the books of its astonishingly large literary crowd for the local free paper. I bet if you look around your library you'll find a couple of sentences on some book that bear my praise. Check out your Austin titles: Caroline Spector, Bruce Sterling, Don Graham, Neal Barrett, Brad Denton, Walt De-Brill, Lawrence Person, Rex Hull, Bill Spencer. Yep, Rob Kenyon that's me. Of course it might just say *Austin Chronicle*. I also do the Day Trips section, occasionally movie and band reviews (we are the Live Music Capital of the World). And I write *Ron's Ramblings*. I write about stuff I do. I began before blogging.

My friend Ragan Falconer has a small-time pyrotechnics firm. He shoots little shows with his brother Clyde. You, if you live in a city of any size, have never seen a hand-lit fireworks show. Mainly they've gone the way of the dinosaurs. You've seen an electronically-fired show. They're safer. They're faster. They cost more money, but not *that* much more money. Each shell sits in its own canon (a length of black PVC pipe) and has an electric fuse that runs to its quick-match fuse. Flick a switch, it lights. The outer part of the shell explodes and flings the inner shell, the one with the stars in it, into space. Shells fly up about one hundred feet per inch of diameter. Three-inch shells go up three hundred feet, four-inch shells go up four hundred feet and so on.

In a hand lit show, the pyrotechnic team buries the canons in the earth rather than in a sand-filled trailer. A lighter walks alongside the row of canon carrying a lit fusee, one of those red flares that come in auto safety kits. He or she lights each firework's quick-match fuse and bang off it flies. As the fireworks launch, a runner from the ground crew drops a new shell in the empty (and smoking) cannon. A crew consists of lighters, runners, and folks that watch the ready boxes, picnic coolers dragooned into once-a-year pyrotechnic purpose. Ragan's crew had shot shows for three years when he first called me to be a runner. Some cousin had the flu or some son had a headache or something. Anyway I knew Ragan and I had always wanted to shoot a show. We had to drive to the small town of Flapjack, Texas—one of those little dying town in the Texas Hill Country. Flapjack lay twenty minutes to the southeast of Austin. Most of the residents worked in Austin, those that didn't seemed to either sell antiques to those that did or Dairy Queen frozen custard cones to each other. Decades ago, between the World Wars, Flapjack had had a minor boom as an agricultural center. The town had a few grand homes from that period, and not all of them had become bed and breakfasts.

Flapjack could afford a $5,000.00 dollar show, that meant thirty minutes of show—"No black sky!" hand-lit. The Falconer brothers liked their shows in those days to be hand-lit. It's exciting. It's fun. It's dangerous. Everyone on the crew risked life and limb for seventy-five dollars and a ton of hard work. But we would have done it for free. So would you. I am talking *professional fireworks* here.

I rode with Ragan in a yellow rider truck. We had magnetic decals on the side warning other motorists of our explosive threat. No one ever seemed to notice. Do this for me, will you? Next time you see a bobcat truck on the highway with a dangerous **Explosives** sign on the back door or the sides don't tailgate. Thank you.

Ragan had joked with me on the way down about how patriotic and right wing the Flapjackers were. I could tell he was being ironic, setting me up for something. When he pulled the truck into the city park by the little hill, I saw the joke. There were three things on the hill. One was a fabulous three-story redbrick mansion, a multi-winged Gothically embellished piece of Richardsonian Romanesque. This lordly estate was the "Corman Place"—the home of a railroad baron, who had had the bad taste to get rich in the 1870s rather than the 1920s. For you non-architecture buffs, I won't be offended if you go google the style. Two billboards shared the hill. One had red letters on a black ground. THE US MILITARY KILLS OUR BOYS. The other shows a mainly gray and green scene of American soldiers in the jungles of Vietnam, and bore an legend in white, "Why do some people choose which fair-haired boy must die?" Both billboards faced the park; they would be the back-drop of our show. I hoped that they would not be lit at night—this proved a vain hope.

I stared at Ragan and he grinned. "Doc Corman's anti-war protest. Get the sheriff to tell you when he shows up."

There was a small artificial lake in the park. There were cottonwood trees and post oak and gray green buffalo grass. Across the lake a barbecue company was setting up next to the rows of picnic tables, beyond them were the small brick buildings that served as restrooms, a playscape full of kids enjoying the July heat, and a fenced-in tennis court.

Clyde Falconer and his two sons had arrived in his blue Lexus. Ragan and I opened the back of the truck and took out the picks and sharpshooter shovels. We began digging the holes for the canon. Six three-inch canon four feet apart, six four-inch, four six-inch and five single shot eight inchers. It was hot work, and we were glad when Sharon Falconer showed up with her big brown SUV that held a giant cooler of sweet tea.

We had arrived just before noon and were finished burying the canon by four. The sheriff drove up across the grass in his tan and brown sheriff car. He was a big man with a sweat stained Stetson and a white handlebar mustache. He liked to talk and we had sat out the lawn chairs by then. Following Ragan's clue I asked about Dr. Corman.

He wasn't a medical doctor. He was a teaching doctor. Specifically he had taught anthropology at the University of Texas half an hour north. The name vaguely rang a bell; there had been some articles about him a few years ago.

The sheriff was not a stupid man, but higher education had passed him by. He had also been in Vietnam when Randy Corman encountered a landmine. Not in the same unit of course. The sheriff had just warmed to Randy's story when I saw the infantryman near the base of the pictorial billboard. He was a blond haired white guy dressed like the grunts appearing twelve or so feet above his head. But what caught my eye was the machine gun he was carrying. The bombing Oklahoma City had happened in April of that year and to my thinking men in combat fatigues carrying machine guns weren't a good thing.

I pointed him out to the sheriff, who just said, "I'm getting to that." The sheriff was like my mother, a Southern storyteller who views his narrative as shots of bourbon to savored slowly so that the intoxication of the tale builds up over the whole of the evening. I could see how happy he was that the solider had made his dramatic entrance.

The sheriff paused in his story and gave me a brief sketch of the Cormans. The founder of the line had merged two small Texas railroads and one Louisiana-to-Oklahoma railroad, making Flapjack a major hub in the world of post-Reconstruction commerce. Timber from East Texas, cotton from the Dallas area, cattle from hereabouts had access to New Orleans and Galveston ports. The manufactured goods from Europe and the east coast could come to Texas and Oklahoma markets. He built his "Palace" on the hill. I felt smart—it really had been designed by Henry Hobson Richardson just after his asylums had been in built in New York (1870) and Arkham (1872). The townsfolk hated him for his conspicuous consumption—the mansion had ten fireplaces—all of which had won a prize at a fair or exhibition. You can build great stuff if you own the railroad and shipping costs you nothing. His children were set for life. His son Markham had sold the railroad to the Atchison, Topeka and Santa Fe at the beginning of World War I. His grandson Roger had opened the chain of markets and movie palaces across central and south Texas between the wars. His great-grandson Hiram added to the family fortune by opening savings and loans in Austin and Houston, and beginning the first large scale Texas winery, Hiram's boy Thomas devoted himself to education gaining a doctorate in anthropology at the University of Chicago and a further PhD in Indian and Burmese Literature at Princeton. This took us to Randall. By this time the barbecue was ready. Brisket and chicken, ranch style beans, cole slaw, German potato salad. A local band was playing Willie Nelson covers. Clowns were making balloon animals for the kids, and coolers everywhere showed forth ice, Lone Star and Shiner Beer—and I knew when the sun went down I would be running from the big yellow cooler full of three inch shells to the first canon line. It was great! Some locals shared watermelon with us—from their own patch.

Randall and Sheriff John Haggard went to Sam Houston High School at the same time. Flapjack had been on decline in the sixties and the graduating class of 1972 was a mere fifteen souls. John Haggard had been captain of the football team—but of course every boy in school played on the football team. Randy had been president of the Spanish Club, leader of the debate team ("We called him a master debater. Get it?") and even president of the Photo Bugs. Our country was four years short of its 200*th* birthday, one of the last Japanese soldiers had surrendered in Guam, the war had gone for decades for the poor SOB. We watched *Maude* and *All in the Family*. There were great paperbacks that year: *Journey to Ixtlan* and *Fear and Loathing in Las Vegas*. There was also a little something called the Vietnam War. Now simple high school boys in central Texas didn't know that Nixon was going to end the war by bombing the pucky out of Hanoi come Christmas time, they just knew they might have to go to the unhappiest place on Earth. The graduating class of 15 was six girls—they were safe—two black boys—they were going—one Mexican—ditto, and six white guys. The draft board had to pick two of the Anglos.

John Haggard was born on the wrong side of the tracks, so he was an easy pick. The richest kid in town was an easy pick as well. The serfs had risen up. These choices were not only hard on the Corman and Haggard familes, the boys had been dating the "Pridy twins, and boy were they pretty." Gloria for John and Jeanie Mae for Randy. They would wait for their boys.

Randall Hiram Corman had his leg blown off by Charly. He was airlifted to Saigon and then on to Tokyo, and there he died of an acute infection. He had graduated Sam Houston High in May, was drafted in June and his body was delivered home a week before Halloween.

Randy's mom drank herself to death in six months, so she never even heard of the Paris Peace Accords. "Southern Comfort," a fruit, spice and whiskey flavored liquor is a good drink for Southern tragedy. With a cruel twist of fate, a report that was meant only for Army brass was mailed to Doctor Corman. Turns out that Randy got very inferior care. In fact negligent drunken care, and the Corman's lawyers got a lot of money. So the rich get richer. Dr. Corman gave the town a library in Randy's name. He paid for Jeanie Mae to go to school. She came back as an English teacher at Sam Houston. Then according to the sheriff Dr. Corman began writing them books till UT fired him. Having reported on excesses of professorial eccentricity, I knew "them books" must be something.

At the next Halloween the Haunted Palace started. The good doctor had his mansion made into a haunted house filled with all sorts of anti-war scenes—villagers broiled in napalm, mine fields, field surgeries—as well as the standard Frankenstein's monsters and vampires.

Grisly and macabre, it even got a write-up in *Texas Monthly*. In about six years the trouble started. Reagan was President by then and we would all be saved by Star Wars "for real." Dr. Thomas Emanuel Corman put up the anti-military billboards. Some people were so mad they wanted to move the Fourth of July festival, but the Mayor had said the Fourth of July was about free speech. Dr. Corman got in some kind of trouble at the University of Texas at Austin, his graduate class on East-West interaction had some kind of party with drugs or something, and the Sheriff wasn't clear on the issues.

The Sheriff's wife spotted the first solider on patrol around the Corman place. It was just before the Fourth. Dr. Corman had hired an actor that looked like a Vietnam era US solider to patrol the area near the billboards. Well some people had threatened to burn them down.

But it was worse.

The actor looked a great deal like Randal Hiram Corman.

It was awful hard on Jeanie Mae.

Everyone else came back from the war. The Sheriff had married Gloria, the black boys had come back black men and started a gas station/convenience store. The Mexican boy started a taco place. Everybody was settling down, but Jeanie Mae—she still waited. Jeannie got to watching the solider on patrol. Jeanie got to thinking that it was Randy. She told her sister, her sister told then-Deputy Haggard. The Deputy told her that Randy was dead—they had all been to the funeral. They all knew his ashes were in an urn. It had a blue spot light on it every Halloween. The Deputy told her to get therapy.

Jeanie Mae snuck onto the ground one night with her little cocker spaniel. The solider made her dance naked, killed her dog and cooked it, making her eat some, and finally raped her. She stumbled into town all bloody. The Sheriff and Deputy Haggard went up Beacon Hill and found no solider. Dr. Corman said he run off at dawn. The Doctor was burning a big bonfire. He invited them to search. They searched and found nothing.

Then a few months later, he hired another actor to impersonate a solider. This guy looked like Randall, but there was something wrong with his face. People were mad. But there are no laws against such poor taste and insensitivity. The Sheriff used these words in his narrative; I wondered what lawyer had taught them to him.

It was time for the show. I had loaded two three-inch red shells for Ragan to light during the "...rockets' red glare.." part of the anthem. Then came white titanium slautes, Super noisy—they set off the car alarms all over Flapjack. Each shell drives the smoke into you, weeks after a show you will smell of gunpowder at the oddest times. I ran my butt off. Sharon Falconer sat on one of the white plastic lawn chairs and did the count.

You count for duds. If 101 fireworks are lit and 100 make their flower-fire in the sky you have one dud. As I mentioned each shell has two parts. The outer shell that explodes to lift the inner shell into the air, which that ignites the stars—the pretty stuff that lights up the sky. If the inner shell should not ignite it falls to earth. It looks exactly like an oversized cartoon firework. It practically begs kids to light it, and cover themselves in burning papers and salts. You have to find every dud after a show—no matter how long it takes in the dark.

Now the Gentle Reader will think that I ride back to Austin the next day and looked up Dr. Corman. In fact I wrote an amusing story of my night of shooting off fireworks in Flapjack. I completely forgot about Dr. Corman.

I didn't remember at any of the shows we shot for the next three years. I moved up from a runner to a lighter. I set off the three-inchers the night that I thought about Corman again. Another of his actor-soldiers had made the news in a terrible way. A Vietnamese family had opened Ng BBQ in nearby Comesee, TX. The actor-solider (at least somebody dressed as GI Joe) had torched their house. No one could prove it was Dr. Corman's employee—but said employee could once again not be found. Corman had a little trouble on his own, a fire in one of his storage sheds had burned out of control the late the same night. The Sheriff was perplexed, but relieved that Corman hadn't hired yet another "solider" to guard his acreage.

But just before sunset, I saw the gleam of the burnt orange Texas sun on the M16 barrel as Corman's re-enactor made his martial patrol. I was gleeful. I could smell a big weird story with a big Rob Kenyon by-line.

So the next day in Austin, I drove to the Perry-Casteñada Library on the University of Texas campus. I researched Dr. Thomas Emanuel Corman. He wrote 14 books, 15 counting his dissertation. You could line them up in chronological order and they stretched from solid scholarship from academic publishers to pseudo-science bullshit from gosh-wow paperback houses. It seems that everyone agrees that Dr. Corman went mad, the dissent is about which of the books marked the French-frying of his gray matter.

His studies focused on the Pre-Buddhist cultic practices that was assimilated into early Buddhism in Burma. Buddhism of various unorthodox sorts (heavily mixed with Tantrism and Tibetan shamanism) encountered the Bagan culture of Burma in the sixth century. From this heady blend, a group of wonder-workers called weizzas arose. These forest sages combined the worship of spirits (called Nats) with Indian and Tibetan practices especially astrology and alchemy. The later was more focused on the prolongation of life by certain regenerative measures than in the transformation of base metals into gold. If the name "weizza" sounds like "wizard" to you, it is because it is a cognate. In fact, in Miramar today, it is still the honorific for a BA degree.

Dr. Corman studied these alchemist sages. As more orthodox Buddhism showed up in the seventh century, the weizzas needed to become organized. They became a monastic order of "Ari Buddhists." These fellows were a little looser in their ways—they could drink alcohol, practice some Tantric sex and made good money as fortunetellers. They wrote in Pali, the orthodox Buddhist scriptural tongue.

They hid some of their magical beliefs as a sort of scholarship: they decided to write down the words and practices of a group of older and even wilder magicians, the zawgyi. Their scholarship was a window to the more obscure civilizations and peoples of Burma.

After his sixth book, Dr. Corman had begun the re-translation of a seventh century Ari Buddhist named U Pao. He was a master alchemist and a devotee of a powerful Nat, Yog-Sothoth. U Pao wrote a Pali sutra in praise of He "Who orders the planes and angles of existence." The so-called *Black Sutra* had been translated by a German Indologist in the nineteenth century, but great strides in comparative Indo-European linguistics had taken place since then. And the University of Texas is the hotbed of Indo-European linguistics. Dr. Corman began his translation in 1972, about the time his son came back in a body bag.

His next book *Alchemy East and West* was slightly controversial. He theorized that the medieval Indian Siddha Alchemy tradition, the Burmese zawgyi tradition and the European alchemical tradition were in fact a single multi-cultural scholarly/scientific endeavor. He named it the "White College"—apparently deriving the name from some Welsh alchemists Cur-Gwen *Cur = College, Gwen = White as in Guiniviere) , whose name eventually became "Curwen." In an obscure footnote toward the end of the book he noted that the name had variants: Curwin, Korman and Corman.

Then his wife died.

He couldn't find a scholarly house for his *Glimpses of Immortality*, but as a popular occult book it brought him serious coin. He suggested that the purification by fore motif in alchemy might actually work. He suggested that some of the long-lived alchemist like Count St. Germain or Ludwig Prinn might have discovered the real process. A trio of popular books followed. Dr. Corman because big man on the New Age lecture circuit—and since he gave his hefty fees to anti-war charities became something of a saint to some.

Then the year he hired the actor, he had to find an even less stringent publisher. His remaining books became collections of odd events and Fortean moments suggesting that alchemists know how to be immortal and they work for some ultra-mundane group of powers that want to change the consciousness of the world, one "endarkenment" at a time. They books are full of standard New Age tropes—the hundredth monkey, morphic fields, pyramid power, ancient astronauts. His employers at the University were not amused. However he scarcely seemed to mind.

I spoke with some people in the Anthropology Department. Dr. Corman became neglectful of dress and hygiene. He browsed the personal papers of Aleister Crowley, which are part of the University of Texas HRC collection. He may have bought drugs from students. He may have sold drugs to students. However, tenure doth protect the odd and odder.

He finally went too far. His class, "The Alchemical Tradition: East and West" met one night in the middle of the football stadium to "Open a Gateway to the Gatekeeper." Nude co-eds and a goat were said to be involved. You can risk your reputation as a scholar, but you can never risk the reputation of football. The apparently risqué sexual magic (or perhaps I should write "magick") was enough for the regents to ask Dr. Corman never to return. The next year, one of the physics professors went off the deep end and shot some students from the infamous clocktower. Some uncharitable types speculated on a connection between the two rogue faculty members.

His last books degenerated into collections of speculation and paranormal incidents. Lovecraft's agent Julius Schwartz points out a freakish bird death to Eric Frank Russell and the later writes Sinister Barrier. A researcher vanishes from dolphin studies, a peculiar clown festival in Miroclaw, Fortean happenings in the Sesqua Valley. He randomly gives fragments of spells and sections from outlandishly named grimoires. I made a note of a phrase of recognition between Yog-Sothoth followers, I felt it might come in handy.

When the Fourth rolled around again I bought a very powerful LED flashlight. I wanted to meet the man on the hill. I realized this was a dangerous idea, but I have always been attracted to danger. Dangerous drugs and dangerous women, fireworks and mountain climbing, interviewing gang members and extreme religious types. I was not the sensible one in my family. I lit the four and five inch shells and lit one of the finale racks, which launch eighty three-inch shells in less than a minute. You light it, run and fall backwards to see the red, lilac, white, silver and gold you have painted the sky with. Sharon told me the news I wanted to hear. There had been a dud, one of the four-inch shells. I told everybody that I was climbing Beacon Hill to look for it. I moved quickly before anyone could realize that might not be the smartest idea.

It had been a wearingly hot day and the dry smoky air was thick with the smell of gunpowder. Ragan and Clyde were putting out a little grass fire. Clyde's sons were looking for the dud nearer the firing line (i.e. in the logical place). I grabbed a bucket (to the put the dud in), a big glass of sweet tea and my flashlight.

The hill proved easy to climb and I came to a three strand barbed wire fence after I had gone about twenty feet into the sparse oak. Using the weight of my bucket I pushed down the top strand and stepped over. I had been getting over barbed wire since I was ten. I grew up in Amarillo, Texas; where barbed had been invented for Christ's sake. Now logically the weather on either side of a barbed wire fence should be the same, but logic didn't hold near the Corwin place. The air turned steamy and smelled of animals—like the reptile area of a zoo. Mist hung near the ground like milk, and I could hear jungle birds. I had never been in the jungles of Vietnam save through the miracle of movies, but I felt as though I had crossed to that place. I could hear tropical birds, and the base of the billboards looked like the creeper covered pylons of Ankor Wat.

I pointed the light at my face. I wanted him to see I was white. I was an American; although that knowledge hadn't seemed to help with his girlfriend. The jungle grew thick. It took me twenty minutes to go up another fifty or so feet. I couldn't hear anything from the firing line, as though a three-strand fence were effective sound-proofing. I was unprepared for the loudness of the burst of machine fire. A small bright comet flashed above and to the left of me, bark exploded off a nearby trunk. My ears rang. Machine guns are much louder than exploding firework shells, then I realized that I had taken my earplugs out. I knew the solider was playing with me. He could have literally cut me in two at this range. I yelled the recognition phrase, "Kyron Yog-Sothoth Bolon Yokte' K'uh!"

I expected the counter-sign of "Yog-Sothoth Neblod Zin!" Instead a solider stepped out from behind a live oak. He raised his machine gun and shot three rounds in the air. "That would impress my dad, but it's not the password, Sarge." He said. I turned my flashlight on him. I recognized Randal Hiram Corman from his yearbook picture. He was still 19. At first I thought he had put black grease paint around his left eye, but I saw that a thick and wiry *fur* surrounded the eye. The pupil of the left eye was a vertical slit. "Well, Sarge, we have a problem, you and me, because of time."

"Randy?" I asked.

"Private First Class Randall Corman, sir!"

I saw that his arm was in a green sling. The fur around his eye moved. It seemed to be a mass of feelers. "Not the handsome son of a bitch that you were expecting." Private Corman remarked. There was a fallen log between us; he motioned me to sit with his free hand. I expected that the gunfire would bring the sheriff soon. Maybe I wasn't in real danger. I hated the brilliance of my flashlight; I didn't really want to see his eye.

I sat and he sat next to me. Private Corman said, "I think I may have talked to other people since being stationed here. Sometimes my mind works a little, didn't you say you knew my dad? He teaches at UT."

"Randy do you know what year this is?"

"I saw the fireworks so it's July 4, 1973. I didn't think I would last this long at Ngoc Linh. How'd they get fireworks? USO?"

"Randy what did your father do to you?"

"He's an old zawgyi these days. You want to know something funny? He could end war now. He knows all the angles. He knows how to eliminate the problem of humanity. Think he will?"

"Randy, we're in the twenty-first century now. Do you know what your father did to your ashes?"

"'After calcinations, the essential salts may be reassembled if the One-in-All Re-Members the being. Care must be exercised for the purity of the salts, lest Otherness seep in.' You know I haven't got a letter from Momma since I been here. I hate 'Nam. It's Disneyland in reverse."

"Randy do you remember Jeannie Mae?"

"I've got her picture."

He moved to lay down the M16. I saw what the cloth hid. He and the rifle were grown together like a Giger painting. Human, insect, gunmetal— all fused. He seemed confused that he couldn't release the rifle. Finally he grabbed at his pocket with his free left hand. There was a mildewed wallet. He couldn't open the wallet, which had mildewed shut. Finally he threw the thing away from him. He was crying. He stood up quickly and fired his machine gun at the wallet. I thought he was going to fire at me.

"You know I can't point this thing at myself."

He demonstrated his inability to point the weapon at himself. "The worst part is sometimes I think Their thoughts. Dad didn't know that. What year did you say this was? 1976, I bet. Were those Bicentennial fireworks? Did we make it to the Bicentennial?"

"Yes. Randy. It was the Bicenetnnial."

"Damn war has gone on too long."

"It sure has solider."

"You know I can't die. I tried once in Tokyo. Dad just starts me over. Can you tell Momma I'm OK? She's back in Texas. My little town there is called Flapjack, can you believe that, Sarge?"

"I believe you Randy."

"Sarge, you don't want to think Their thoughts. It makes the nights too long."

"I bet it does Randy."

"Tell my daddy just to end it. He can end it all. My daddy is the most powerful man in the universe." He sounded just like the eight year old blonde boy he once was.

"I've got to move on solider."

"The password is *Kung Fu*. You ever watch that show Sarge? I saw it on R-n-R."

"Best show on TV." I said.

"No," said Private Corman, "The best show is *M*A*S*H*."

I saw that the shadow Randy Corman cast by my LED flashlight was much less human in shape than he seemed to be. I turned off the light because I didn't really want to see it clearly. I knew that I didn't want to remember this Fourth.

"I got to go now, son." I said.

"Don't let your meat loaf Sarge."

I stood up and headed down the hill. Just before I passed over the barbed wire I heard more gunfire. I wondered if he as shooting at me. I wondered if he was shooting at anything that existed in my world.

When I got to the firing line, Clyde's sons had found the dud. Nobody said anything about gunfire. Of course, tonight of all nights gunfire might not be correctly identified. I helped finish the cleanup, digging up the rest of the cannons. Sharon asked me what had become of my bucket. I said I had dropped in the dark and couldn't find it. I looked up Beacon Hill, I thought I saw some lights flicker around the base of one of the billboards.

We drove home.

But I can't quite *believe* in home anymore. I wonder if Randy's father can end it all. The problem of humanity. I wonder if he understands the special hell he has made for his son. I wonder what Their thoughts are like, and some nights I wonder so long and hard that I think I might start to know.

For Walt DeBill

Translator

by James Robert Smith

enjamin Landis, Captain in the United States Army, retired. August 14, 2012. That's today's date. Sorry for the pauses. It feels strange talking into this digital recorder. I'd rather you had been present for the interview. Oh, well.

There aren't many of us around, these days. The men who worked in the Japanese POW camps here in the USA. So many people don't even know we brought Japanese POWs over here. Of course the camp I commanded was specifically for those Japanese prisoners who it was suspected were of use to the war effort. As far as intelligence was concerned. That's how Lieutenant Akashi Omura came to be there.

And to answer the question you asked me earlier, during our online chat, I guess I did what I did and the way things happened that way because.

Well, Hell. This is going to sound maudlin, but it's true. The day it happened was our holiday, you know. VJ Day. And it fell out the way it did at the camp because it was 1945 and I was a Jew. It was pure compassion. It was a mistake, I realized later, but at the time I was so ecstatically happy, and I just felt sorry for Omura and the other POWs.

Since late Spring of that year I'd seen the reports coming out of Europe. My parents had heard the rumors—odd notes from friends and relatives and acquaintances who'd been fortunate enough to escape. For what happened with Omura and the other prisoners…well, it was just compassion for a strange man trapped in a bad situation. Even his own fellow Japanese hated him.

I felt sorry for him.

That's all it was.

Misplaced compassion.

I commanded Camp Norland, on the shores of Lake Dodd, in the Adirondacks for Pete's sake. It was a relief, I have to admit. I'd been stuck in the Pacific for the previous three years. My outfits had all been part of the island-hopping campaigns against the Japanese Imperial Army. If there was ever a more intransigent, single-minded foe than the members of the

Imperial Japanese Army…well, I frankly don't want to know about them.

Sometimes I think it was a miracle that there were any Japanese POWs at all. They say that the war in the Pacific between the USA and the Japanese was the most racist war ever fought. I think it's true. Each side genuinely figured the other for devils. And that's a fact.

Well, you don't want to know about that particular Hell. And I guess enough of us have talked and written about it to fill a million books. You want to know about what happened that August 15 of 1945. That was a particular kind of Hell, and almost no one knows about it. How you pried it out of those expurgated files I'll never know. But since you did, and you know the bare bones, and I'm too old to give a damn, I'll give you the rest. Or at least as much of it as I can. Frankly, I don't think anyone living can make much sense of it; not even me.

I was made commander of the camp for a number of reasons. First of all, my own CO felt that I'd earned it after going through what I'd endured north of Australia to just south of Iwo Jima. I was up for promotion, my health was shot, I was ready to be rotated Stateside, I could speak a bit of Japanese, and I'd been in Medical school before the war broke out. I never did go back to that, you know. Something about that incident…it made me less interested in Psychiatry than before.

Sorry. I had to shut the thing off for a while. It's saved. Nice device.

Camp Norland was located in New York state. It's gone now. Go looking for it and you might find some old foundations in the woods, maybe some rusty fence posts. They took it down after it was closed. I think the military kept nominal possession of the property or else it would be houses now instead of woods and marshlands leading down to the lake. They closed it up not long after the incident, but of course I wasn't there when they packed up the remaining prisoners and sent them elsewhere. The ones who'd lived through Omura's…rampage…most of those were sent back home. Japan, I mean. All of them ended up there, I suspect. No war criminals were among the lot, as I recall. They were all mainly enlisted men and low level officers we'd picked up along the way; but only a few officers were even as high a rank as Lt. Omura.

The thing that I noticed almost immediately after being placed in charge of Norland was that Lt. Akashi Omura was something of an outcast. Whenever the other prisoners had any kind of gathering or celebration, Omura was always conspicuous by his absence. He wasn't welcome among the others.

If you know anything about Shinto—and I admit that I know only a little, even now—it's that every region has their own special holidays or celebrations. Since the camp was home to some three hundred men from all parts of Japan, I would routinely get requests for some type of holiday or ceremony on an almost weekly basis. Sometimes it was just for two or three of the prisoners, but generally many more than that would take part. As a Jew, I like to think that I was sensitive to those placed among a larger population who feel nothing but animosity for them. So I did my best to allow such ceremony to proceed.

But every time I would notice that Lt. Omura was nowhere to be found. Or, worse, he'd be almost present—sometimes skulking along the boundaries of the gatherings. At first, he reminded me of a lost or outcast dog. I should have known better. But it's like I said. I felt compassion for him.

I visited his room from time to time. Because of his rank, we'd given him separate quarters. And also to butter him up, of course. We wanted what we thought that he knew. On one visit I saw that he had a series of crude sculptures on a makeshift altar beside his bed. He allowed me to pick them up and examine them. I don't know what they were made of—I'm no geologist—but I asked them how he'd come by them.

He told me that he'd made them.

I asked him why the previous commander had allowed him to keep them.

He told me that they were harmless.

I decided to take them out, to examine them. And so I did. I could tell that Omura did not like this, but I had to be sure he was not up to something. Each sculpture was perhaps the size of large potato. Five pounds in weight. I had a couple of orderlies bundle them up and bring them to my office for inspection.

They were—I wish I had photographs of them—but there is no way to describe them other than as monsters. I supposed then that they were some kind of demon or fetish. Each was different from the other. One was aquatic in design. Not so much fish-like as mollusk. One was all jaws and fangs. Another was like a cat; one a bear. Or bear-like, I should say. And of course the thing that I noticed straight away was that none of them was finished. They were each in some stage of development. The underlying surfaces were of a kind of hard, black stone—almost like onyx. The outerlying stone was more like sandstone. And Lt. Omura seemed to have stopped each of them in some kind of midpoint. They were all unfinished.

The things disturbed me, but I decided that they were harmless and I had my men return them to Omura's quarters.

Occasionally, if our resident translators were not around, I would find it within my capacity as commander of the camp to at least try to debrief some of the prisoners. My Japanese was picked up in my months fighting those soldiers and is nothing like proficient. I'd learned most of it through a woman who'd come to be captured by my unit in the Pacific in 1943. I'll never forget the first time I used my Japanese language skills on some soldiers and they'd laughed at me. They said later that I spoke Japanese like a woman!

But I could generally muddle my way through such a thing and between the English that the prisoners knew or had learned, I could write a decent report and pass the information along the line.

We were then, of course, still looking for intelligence that might shorten the war. Leading up to August, none of us knew that the bombings of Hiroshima and Nagasaki were on the horizon, or that the Russians would wipe out Japan's Kwantung Army. And even if we had, we'd still have been at our jobs. Because we were soldiers and it was our duty.

Since Lt. Omura was one of the highest ranking prisoners we had at the camp, I had occasion to interview him and to sit in on other interviews. My impression of him as the meek outcast was eroded in such encounters. There was something…well, now I can say it was sinister… but then I couldn't put a word to it. He was, somehow, disturbing to be around. It was in the way he looked at us, and in the way he spoke to us. There was nothing of fear at all in the man, and I wondered how we'd managed to capture him in the first place. Unlike most of the prisoners we had in our care, he was tall and muscular. Tall for a Japanese man of the time, at least. He stood an even six feet tall, had a pronounced jaw, a slash of a mouth, and a heavy brow that recalled some kind of cave man. This caused his eyes to be almost perpetually in shadow. I never saw him smile but two or three times. Never for any good reason I could name.

It was during one of the Shinto celebrations that I happened to speak with him. It was one of the larger ones—I believe he was the only prisoner not taking part—and I decided to have him in to my office. Since we'd arranged for the other prisoners to have wine with their meals that day—they'd asked specifically for it—I brought in a bottle of sweet wine to share with Omura during what was, in fact, an interrogation. I thought that he might betray some secret, feeling alone and cast out by his own countrymen. So there we were, in my office, talking and sharing wine. Yes, there were three guards in attendance, but it was as friendly as any such exchange could be. I wasn't, after all, there to kill or torture him.

As I said, my Japanese is rudimentary, but Lt. Omura had a decent grasp of English, and so between us a conversation could be held. He was not, like most of the other prisoners, either part of the Imperial Army or the Imperial Navy. He had been, in fact, an officer of the Kwantung Army.

I already knew that he was attached somehow to Lt. General Ishii Shiro who was a war criminal on a level even beyond that of Joseph Mengele, but at that time I did not know it. We merely suspected that he could be of some use to us, and so we kept prodding him, irregularly, for bits of information.

After some time the ice seemed to break.

I'll never forget it. With half a bottle of wine in him, and a glass or two in me, he smiled, ducked his head in the only sign of submission I'd ever seen in the man. And he asked me:

"May I complete my works?"

"Your works?" I asked him.

"What you took. What you returned. May I complete?"

And then I understood that he meant his sculptures.

I asked him what he needed, and he pointed to a pen on my desk. I asked him what good a pen would be to him to finish a sculpture, and he struggled for the words, as did I, trying to bridge the gap between our languages.

"Metal," he told me.

"You need a sharp tool," I said to him. And he nodded.

"I'll consider it," I told him.

Up to that time I'd felt that he was close to giving up something important to us. If he didn't know something that would put the war to an end sooner, then he might know something that would defend us in the future. The world in 1945 was a pretty awful place, and you never knew where you could find something that would be needed someday. Even among the enemy.

Over the course of the next few days I realized that the situation between Lt. Omura and his fellow prisoners had deteriorated. I could see the hatred in the eyes of the others whenever Omura would appear. And always he stayed on the periphery of their social comings and goings. He was always in the shadows, Omura was. Once again I'd had him brought into my office for interview. It was more of an intercession, because I was genuinely worried about him. To keep things relatively quiet I'd had him brought to me in the evening. In hopes that the other prisoners wouldn't take much note of his absence, or his presence among their captors.

That day we hadn't had a competent translator on hand because all three of my fluent Japanese speakers had been called out on detail, one of them to DC. I figured something was up with some operation for which they needed those men's language skills. Of course I had no idea what it was. But now it's all too obvious.

During my conversation with Lt. Omura I bluntly asked him about his problems with his own countrymen. It couldn't have been that he'd surrendered. Half the men in the camp had boldly done so, the rest of them had fallen into our hands in some other way. And for the second time since I'd met him he made a small request. He asked for wine, and explained that he wanted it for his own celebration that should occur within an hour or so.

Seeing one more opportunity to break the ice with someone who might be able to provide intelligence, I had a bottle of sweet plum wine brought in. For some time Omura just sat and made what I guess we'd call small talk. Occasionally he would just eye the sweating bottle and then, toward evening, he finally leaned forward and bowed, asking if we could enjoy the wine.

"Of course," I told him. I had one of the security detail pour and I raised my glass in a toast.

"To your people," he said to me. "To the Americans." And he drank.

All at once—and I discussed this later with the other three men in the room with us—I felt a distinct tingling run through my body. My first thought was that some prisoner had poisoned the wine and that we'd fallen for some kind of trap. But of course I'd watched Omura drink from the same bottle. Certainly he wouldn't commit suicide. And then—this is the thing that my own men corroborated—we all felt a sensation like something had passed through us. Each of us could taste something, like lead or some kind of metal on our tongues and in the backs of our throats.

And I remember that Lt. Omura was grinning. From ear to ear. It was most unsettling.

"A celebration," he told me.

I had him sent back to his quarters, only later discovering that while we were talking and toasting, Paul Tibbets was dropping the Little Boy nuclear device on Hiroshima. I know now that, somehow, Omura had known this. And had celebrated it, and had caused me to celebrate it with him. If I'd realized it at the time, my subsequent meeting with him would have been completely different, and I like to tell myself that what happened in the next few days would not have occurred.

But then I realize that he'd have figured a way no matter if I cooperated or not.

The next day, finally, the tension broke. Omura was assaulted. I happened to be nearby and arrived just as some of my guards were breaking up the melee. Lt. Omura had been attacked by six men, and while he'd obviously given a good account of himself, one against six is not going to be a winning combination for the one. His attackers were calling him "devil" as they were pried off of him. I had his assailants placed in solitary and Omura taken immediately to hospital where he was examined and patched up for numerous minor lacerations and contusions. He had a broken rib, I remember, and he lost a tooth—a molar I believe.

I went to see about him in recovery, and inspecting his battered face and bandaged torso, I made my decision. That pesky compassion, it was.

"You can finish your sculptures," I told him. "I'll arrange for tools. Under strict supervision," I added.

Again, he smiled, through the bruises, despite the bandages. In the light of the day, it was not a pleasant sight.

Because I figured that there would be some kind of breakthrough with the man, I had him not only under guard, but guarded by others. We provided him with some basic metal tools with which he could work the stone. During his times working the sculptures I had him under close watch, and we made sure that he was never able to pocket anything we provided to him. He did not seem to find the constant watching by my soldiers to be a hindrance to his progress. Unlike some artists, he did not mind in the least for someone to watch him at work.

Finally, one of my men, a Sgt. Andrew Novick, asked me to come look at what Omura had done. Novick—a strict Catholic fellow as I remember—thought that there was something wrong with what the prisoner was doing. I made time in my schedule and met Novick at Lt. Omura's room.

At once, I could see what the Sergeant meant. If the sculptures had been intimidating before, now they were absolutely disturbing. Each seemed to be like some creature in the midst of being born. It was as if the stone had been their womb and their black flesh was slowly being exposed to the world. Both of us watched while the artist chipped away at the stone, working diligently.

I stepped forward and lifted the sculpture on which Omura was laboring. I had to admire it, for all of the monstrosity that was being created. The thing's limbs were almost completely formed; I could see the claws like daggers ready to be revealed out of fingers too much like those of men to be attached to limbs so much like those of a starfish. Hidden behind the white rock but creeping ever out was something like a mouth, and filled with teeth that were more needles than ivory.

I asked Lt. Omura how he did such a thing, how he created anything so amazing. He could see both the horror and the admiration in my face.

I chuckled at his answer. And then I returned his work to him. I instructed his handlers to allow him to continue until curfew, and then to retrieve the stone-working tools as they'd been ordered to do. Sgt. Novick followed me out.

Novick asked me what was said between Omura and myself, and why I'd laughed.

"I asked him how he made such monsters," I told the Sergeant. "And Omura told me that he chipped away everything that didn't look like a monster."

I recall that Novick said only, "Jesus."

And two nights later, we all know, it happened. For my part, I'd been admittedly negligent that day. It was, after all, the day Japan surrendered unconditionally. I try to tell myself that it was all right to let my guard down. I had allowed my entire command to be almost lax in their duties. All I could think all that day of August 15, 1945 was that no more Americans would have to try to wrest Japanese territory by sacrificing their own blood. No more island hopping campaigns. The fear of millions of American men laying down their lives to inch across the Japanese archipelago were now safely interred in the territory of 'what if'. So I let my command relax. I allowed my men to smoke, to stand at ease, to sneak bottles of beer and wine onto their very posts with a wink and a nod.

That was a mistake and I had to admit that to one and all. I stand by my own guilt on that count.

My house was not within the compound, but was not far away. In those days I was single, but I had a big place. It was still strange to me to be living with the luxury of a home with three bedrooms and a bathroom. No blood-sucking bugs. No leeches. No malaria. No comrades with stinking wounds full of maggots. But I'd been dreaming of such nightmare stuff when the alarm was raised. It was Sergeant Novick himself who arrived to take me by jeep on that short ride to the prison camp proper.

The screaming, I was told, had started an hour before. It had mostly died down by then, but in fact had moved from the fore barracks toward the one farthest from the front gates and closest to Lake Dodd which lapped the shores about a half of a mile to the east. Light flooded the compound and there wasn't a shadow that had not been dissipated. The first thing that struck me was the smell of human shit. When you are accustomed to flushing it down the toilet as soon as it's produced, you don't give it much thought. But when you're stuck with the stench of it—well, that's something that's not going to fade from memory once things are back to normal.

The next thing I realized was the blood. It was everywhere. It poured out of the barracks doors. It stained the windows. I could see walls spattered with it. My Japanese prisoners who weren't dead lay screaming on the turf either in pain or in abject fear. Those who were coherent were screaming the same thing. "Devil! The Devil!"

I asked after Lt. Omura. It was the term *devil* that had brought him foremost to my mind.

"He's missing," Novick told me.

With a score of armed soldiers we followed the trail of mutilated bodies and screeching wounded through the rooms and barracks, plodding through pools of hot blood as if poured from barrels. Somehow, I knew that Lt. Omura would be at the end of that path of gore.

In the end, though, he wasn't. We only came to the eastern fence, rent like paper. There were five small trails of tacky black leading up to that fence, and a pair of footprints, sodden in human blood seeming to follow them, as if someone had been forcing hounds before him.

The trail led to the lake, and ended there. None of the guards had seen how Lt. Omura had cut through the fences or even how he'd gotten through. The excuse of each of them was the confusion and panic as something had cuts its way through scores of Japanese prisoners like razor blades through warm cheese.

Camp Norland ceased to exist within the following two days. And Japan's surrender was a solid fact. My surviving prisoners were rolled up and carted off to other places, some of them home to Japan. I was carted off to military retirement a month later. That was all right. I was ready to leave, to forget what had happened. But you never forget. Not that kind of thing.

And then there was the investigation and debriefings. They finally brought in an officer who was far more proficient in Japanese than I, and he gave me a good going over. They were all interested in Lt. Omura, and rightfully so, in retrospect. I don't know what he knew about his mass murdering bosses, but I do suspect he knew more about darker things than even they suspected. Somehow, his fellow prisoners knew that much about him, and deservedly hated him for it.

My own hard-ass interrogator hammered at me for a week before I finally realized what I should have known all along. It was at the point where we came to the exchange Sgt. Novick had told them about the funny joke Omura had shared with me that day I'd approved his work with his lumps of stone.

"What, exactly, did he say to you?" I was asked. And you better believe those guys know how to pull the exact nature of the truth out of you.

"Omura said that he carved away everything that didn't look like a monster," I told him.

"Can you repeat what he said? In his native tongue?"

And, amazingly, I recalled it just the way he'd said it.

Watashi wa monsutā de wa nai subete no mono kara kiriwakeru.

And that's when my interrogator—a man who was proficient in Japanese—told me what Omura had really said.

"I carve off everything that **isn't** a monster."

I still hear Omura laughing. I can still see that smile of his, and that taste of metal on the back of my tongue, and those strange and horrible carvings that were not what they seemed to be.

Hallowe'en in a Suburb

by H. P. Lovecraft

The steeples are white in the wild moonlight,
   And the trees have a silver glare;
Past the chimneys high see the vampires fly,
   And the harpies of upper air,
   That flutter and laugh and stare.

For the village dead to the moon outspread
   Never shone in the sunset's gleam,
But grew out of the deep that the dead years keep
   Where the rivers of madness stream
   Down the gulfs to a pit of dream.

A chill wind weaves thro' the rows of sheaves
   In the meadows that shimmer pale,
And comes to twine where the headstones shine
   And the ghouls of the churchyard wail
   For harvests that fly and fail.

Not a breath of the strange grey gods of change
   That tore from the past its own
Can quicken this hour, when a spectral pow'r
   Spreads sleep o'er the cosmic throne
   And looses the vast unknown.

So here again stretch the vale and plain
   That moons long-forgotten saw,
And the dead leap gay in the pallid ray,
   Sprung out of the tomb's black maw
   To shake all the world with awe.

And all that the morn shall greet forlorn,
    The ugliness and the pest
Of rows where thick rise the stones and brick,
    Shall some day be with the rest,
    And brood with the shades unblest.

Then wild in the dark let the lemurs bark,
    And the leprous spires ascend;
For new and old alike in the fold
    Of horror and death are penn'd,
    For the hounds of Time to rend.

The Hindmarsh Abomination or Moonday

by Will Murray

The original town fathers would not recognize Arkham, Massachusetts, as it survived into the 21st century. The celebratory Wiccan counterculture would to them be a scandal of the worst order. Witches presiding over curiosity shops instead of being clapped in stocks! The profusion of New Age tea rooms and Tarot parlors would horrify them. The statues of witchy celebrities such as Margaret Hamilton and Elizabeth Montgomery would have confounded them.

Cotton Mather would no doubt curse the police prowl cars with their bold witch-astride-a-broomstick emblem as an abomination under the Lord. Never mind that the doughty Puritan would mistake the commonplace vehicle itself as a cursed conveyance of Satan loose upon the Earth.

The World Turned Upside Down, they would mutter. And shun the old cobbled streets they knew of old.

It is most offensive at Halloween, of course. Halloween—a holiday inconceivable to the Puritan mind.

During the weeks immediately preceding All Soul's Days, the tourists arrive in a noisy flood. To shop. Get their cards read. Visit the Witch Museum. Marvel at the turning leaves which ranged from dull umber to riotous scarlet and gold. Harmless Autumn fun. And good business, in the opinion of modern Arkhamites.

Those who had driven out the witches long ago were long ago relegated to the category of cranks and charlatans. The *Malleus Malificarum* is consulted no more. The stocks and the dunking stool are quaint antiques consigned to the Witch Museum.

But those who had suppressed the witch, had suppressed them for good reason. And in the 21st century, a hoary witch-spawned contagion was stirring to life once more....

***

Halloween in Arkham begins early. The first commercial decorations begin appearing in shop windows on September 30th. House decorations reveal themselves during the first day of October. Pumpkins are carved, and Jack O'Lanterns show their leering faces by the end of that first Autumnal week.

Others preparations and portents of the coming holiday take place in secret, behind closed doors, or in remote pockets of the storied seaside town.

There are Wiccan ceremonies conducted upon the small islet in the winding river Miskatonic. Convocations of rival witches take place in the woodsy earth depression known as the Arkham Kettle. Dead animals are sometimes here discovered. And other, less identifiable bones. Spells are cast within its earth walls. And sacrifices made. Their products are often unknown.

For this is the season of Samhain, marking the end of summer and harvest time.

On the other side of the fence, the Massachusetts National Guard is called up and put on ready status. For memories are long in Arkham. And while the witches of the latter generation are not taken seriously by the locals, they are taken *very* seriously by authorities with access to sealed records.

Halloween fell on a Sunday in the year recounted here. No one outside of the Wiccan community suspected the significance of that simple fact. And among the rival covens, there were groups in the know and groups who were ignorant of The Plan.

On the Saturday before the day of Halloween, unusual activity began taking place in the remote pocket of the town known as Hindmarsh. The name was a corruption of the original Hind Marsh, so-called because it was a marshy stretch of coastal plain situated at the uninhabited southern portion of Arkham proper, vaguely in the direction of Dunwich.

They began arriving in one and twos and threes. They did not resemble witches, or wizards, but that is what they were. And this was their greatest holiday.

The ritual they initiated was one that would not have been entirely familiar to the notoriously public Wiccans who practiced the old ways in the open. The four quarters were marked and the watchtowers invoked. But there were no supplications to revived godlets such as Pan or Astarte. For these practitioners belonged to an older, unbroken line of their craft.

After night fell, queer lights were seen over Hindmarsh. That was the only portent the town received in advance of its greatest holiday....

***

Arkham police officer Kevin Mulroy responded to the call reporting the unusual lights.

"Marsh gas, probably," he told his dispatcher

"People have been seeing marsh gas over there for generations," the dispatcher returned curtly. "It's something else. Check it out."

"Maybe some tourists got lost," Mulroy suggested, turning on his roof lightbar and heading south, oblivious to the irony of the black witch decal on his doors.

The problem with Hindmarsh is that you can't get there from here. Officer Mulroy was obliged to pull over onto the highway and hoof it into the boggy patch of no man's land. There was no path. But amid the marshy ground, there were streaks of higher land capable of supporting a man—if he tread carefully.

It was very dark, so he brought his long steel-barreled flashlight. Mulroy soon discovered that he didn't need it.

The night sky shone with a lambent light. It was vaguely lavender. Above the light, a mackerel sky revealed waves of rolling clouds resembling a smoky washboard.

The clouds hung unusually low. They seemed to press toward the Earth like a massive hand.

Mulroy shook off the weird sense of something happening in the sky and concentrated on his feet.

It was while picking his way amid the reeds and cattails and salt grass that it happened.

The lavender night sky swelled like a mouth. The shifting light made Mulroy gaze up. His own mouth sagged downward.

For there was a hole the purplish sky...

Beyond it was a glassy blackness. Something inserted itself into the hole. It was massive, horny, shaped vaguely like the thorax of a gigantic wasp.

At its tip was no stinger, but a russet bud. This convulsed, irised open.

Down spilled a squirt of dark matter. It landed with a mushy noise. But the noise was not the worst of it.

A horrible stench came to Mulroy's nostrils. It hit him like a putrid fist. The first malodorous wave overwhelmed him, and it was if his respiratory system rebelled against something so alien, it shut down rather than endure any further assault upon his senses.

Gasping, strangling, Mulroy collapsed. His mind went as dark as the hole in the heavens….

***

Dawn found him coming to in a private room in Witch's Bay Hospital, a Lucite oxygen mask over his lower face. His mouth felt moist.

A nurse saw him awake and retreated. Detective First Class Alan Gaunt popped his serious face into room next. He was with the Vice Squad.

"Tell me everything you saw, patrolman," he instructed without preamble. Nothing like getting down to business…

Mulroy gave it to him straight, unadorned and without apology.

Gaunt took it all down in his notebook and asked no questions. He only said, "Thanks. Share this with no one."

***

The stench Officer Mulroy described so vividly was no longer as strong as it was the previous night, but it was offensive enough. Detective Gaunt got within a hundred yards of the ceremonial site and no further. No amount of Vick's Vap-o-rub applied to his neat mustache kept Gaunt from retching uncontrollably. Finally, he had to give it up and requested a mobile Hazmat unit.

Enveloped in clumsy white protective suits, the Hazmat team swarmed over the area, taking samples. Even these were hard to handle. They contaminated everything—sample containers, shovels, boots, gloves, everything. No one wearing white came out of Hindmarsh that same color.

***

The forensics lab had a preliminary report within two hours.

"Stool," was the consensus.

"Say again?" asked Gaunt.

"Excrement."

"Human?"

"Hardly. Whatever evacuated that matter was larger than an elephant."

"Anything else?"

"Yes. It's contaminated by undigested seeds or pods of some type."

"Contaminated?"

"Technically, yes. These seeds aren't like anything we can place."

"That's not good," said Gaunt.

"No, it's not. We're quarantining all samples and cordoning off the Hindmarsh area. We could have an invasive species here."

"We could have something far worse. I'll be in touch."

* * *

Officially, the Arkham Police Department did not have a Witch Squad. That would have been politically incorrect, not to mention bad P. R. So Gaunt was assigned to Vice. But unofficially, he was the Witch Squad.

Detective Gaunt didn't understand what was up. But he did know one thing. Anything weird that happened in the weeks leading up to Halloween always went back to the Wiccan community. Count on it.

Gaunt made it his business to know who were the players in the neo-pagan subculture—every witch, wizard and New Age warlock in town. With the unique stink of the Hindmarsh droppings still clogging his nostrils, he began to make the rounds.

The Official Witch of Arkham traced her ancestry back to a German coven that was still operating in Bablesburg. She ran a gift shop, did spirit readings in the candle-lit back room with a Rohrig Tarot deck. Complaints had been few and far between since her first bust back in the late '80s for soliciting to remove a curse. These days she was going by the name of Ethel Goss-Geist.

Gaunt found her in the back room of her shop, cracking open dark brown nuts and separating the shells from the nutmeats and filling candy dishes with the latter. He got right to the point.

"What went on in Hindmarsh last night?"

"I don't know them," Ethel said thinly. Her elongated face was the only thing witchy about her. Her ebony hair came out of a bottle two shades too dark to accentuate her pale skin.

"Don't know who?" countered Gaunt.

"The riff-raff who have taken over Hindmarsh. I mean really, who would do spellwork in that miserable cesspool?"

"You don't know the half of it…"

"What?"

"Let's skip ahead. Point me toward someone who knows what's going down."

Ethel resumed her noisy toil. "Ever heard of Moonday?"

"No. Is it a person or a place?"

"It's not a person. Or a place." A queer look came and went in her hazel eyes. "It's a time, I guess. You didn't hear this from me, but it's the day between Sunday and Monday."

"Come again?"

"Riddle me this: At midnight tonight, what happens?"

"All the trick or treaters go to bed," Gaunt ventured.

"Try again."

"It stops being Sunday?"

"It stops being *any* day."

Gaunt sighed. Magical thinking was not this favorite kind. "Spell it out for me."

"Unintentional humor. I like that."

Gaunt grimaced. "What you're describing is impossible. You know that."

"Not if you know the proper spell with the correct ingredients, sirrah."

"Who the hell would want to prevent Monday?"

"I'll pretend I didn't hear you ask me that. But it's not about Monday. It's about Samhain. Halloween to you mundanes. The time of year when the veil is thinnest. What if it could be engineered to be an all-year-round event?"

"Take the magic out of it," Gaunt muttered.

"No. It would mean my kind and their kind would rule. *Your* kind would tumble right into the dustbin of history."

Detective Gaunt eyed Ethel the witch skeptically.

She continued. "The legend goes like this: The proper spell stops Sunday at exactly midnight. Dawn never comes. The sun fails to rise. Monday doesn't happen. Instead, it's *Moonday*. Eternally."

"You're not serious?"

Ethel shrugged. "The question is: how are they going pull it off?"

"Assuming it can be done," Gaunt said dryly.

"I discard no possibilities," she said dryly. "I've lived through the Witch Wars of the 1980s." She crossed her forearms and shivered. "And this is the work of an Innsmouth coven. Those people are the pits."

"Where can I find some of these Innsmouthers?"

"Try the Pickerel Inn. Ask for Candiru Rezendez. Don't mention me."

"Never fear."

***

The Pickerel Inn used to be an ale house with a Georgian hotel squatting atop it. Now it was a hotel with a restaurant. Gaunt hadn't been inside since its last incarnation.

Today, it was tricked out like a haunted house. Skeletons dominated the seasonal decor in the windows. In the old days, the lobby walls had been decorated with game fish mounted on polished pine plaques.

A fishy odor crawled into Detective Gaunt's nostrils as he stepped into the old-fashioned lobby. He noticed that the wall plaques had been replaced with mounted skeletal fish. Both marked the owners as hailing from Innsmouth.

Gaunt wandered into the bar and ordered a Becks.

"Looking for Candiru Rezendez," he told the barkeep, flashing his gold shield.

The barkeep drew his draft and slid over a tray of candy and nuts, saying, "Try these. Just in."

Gaunt sipped his beer and ignored the tray.

The bartender dug blunt fingers into the tray and helped himself.

"I'm him," he admitted. "Rezendez."

"What do you know about what went on in Hindmarsh last night?"

"What makes you think I know anything?" Rezendez said through a mouthful of nut meal.

"Understand it was Innsmouthers. You're Portuguese. Two and two makes four."

"Since when are proto-pagan religious ceremonies against Arkham town ordinances?"

"When they stink up a marsh."

Rezendez grabbed another handful of nuts and fingered them into his mouth one by one. His lower face made thoughtful shapes, like a fish working its gills.

"I heard it was Estevao Suarez's coven."

"Where can I find him?"

"Innsmouth, of course. Go there. Ask around. Just don't bring up the name Rezendez, understand?"

"You got it." Gaunt finished his Becks. He laid a five dollar bill on the table.

Rezendez asked, "Sure you don't want some Portuguese nuts? We only set them out for Halloween. There're sweet. Like candy. Better for you."

Gaunt took a handful. "They look like filberts."

"Better than filberts. Bigger than Brazil nuts. Healthy too."

Gaunt left the Pickerel House, jaws working thoughtfully.

***

Innsmouth air clogged the nostrils like no other. Driving into the fishing port, Gaunt closed the car windows and turned on the air conditioner to keep out the pervasive sea and salt odors as he asked around for Estevao Suarez. It smelled like clams having sex.

Halloween decorations were surprisingly sparse. It was as if the holiday was not observed. Innsmouth had always prided itself as being an opposite to Arkham. But this was talking it too far, Gaunt thought.

He received little cooperation. No one had heard of Estevao Suarez. Gaunt tried the decrepit police station, the Gilman House hotel, and assorted random persons. All he received for his pains were fishy vacant stares and monosyllabic grunts. Innsmouth was that kind of burg.

There was a Portuguese church, St. Vasco's. Gaunt paid the rectory a visit and met with Father Joa. By contrast with the average Innsmouthian, he looked so normal it was startling.

"I have heard of this man, my son. He lives in Arkham."

Gaunt frowned. "In Arkham, they say he lives in Innsmouth."

"Who is your authority on this?"

"I'd rather not divulge the name of my informant."

Father Joa shrugged. "If you cannot say, I must respect the confidence. But anyone who knows of Estevao Suarez is not to be trusted. Do you understand my words? The people who possess such knowledge are not God's people. They deny the Savior. They worship nothing clean. There is a word for these people—copro—"

Gaunt frowned. "Do you mean coprophages?"

"Yes, that is the term. Eaters of excrement."

Gaunt stood up. "Thank you for your time, father."

"Go peace, detective."

***

The drive back to Arkham seemed longer than it should. Dusk had come. Night was creeping in, painting the western horizon with autumnal hues. It was as if the blaze of reds and golds that were daily transforming the dying leaves had suffused the sunset.

From a pocket, Gaunt chewed the last of the Portuguese nuts. He hadn't cared much for them at first, but they were growing on him.

Realizing his cell phone had been unusually quiet, Gaunt checked the screen. It had been left on vibrate, and there was a text message from the Forensics lab:

CALL ME ABOUT HINDMARSH MATTER.

But when Gaunt did, no one answered. He left a message.

***

Stopping at the Arkham station precinct house on Saltonstall Street, Detective Gaunt accessed the national law enforcement database. Punching in Estevao Suarez, he muttered to himself, "Why didn't I think of this before?"

A list of aliases popped up on the screen.

One name made Gaunt curse.

CANDIRU REZENDEZ.

"Damn!"

***

Gaunt rushed over to the Pickerel Inn, blowing through red lights and nearly knocking over early trick or treaters as he did so.

He shouldered past assorted munchkins and superheroes as he entered the place. A placard in the window proclaimed: TRICK OR TREATERS WELCOME!

"Looking for Candiriu Rezendez," he told the young waitress who was dropping paper wrapped packets into yawning Halloween bags.

"He has gone home to give out the treats," she told him.

"Where is home?" Gaunt demanded.

She gave an address beyond French Hill, then added, "Would you care for some Portuguese nuts?"

Gaunt hesitated, urgency pulling him half out the door. But he snagged a paper packet on the fly.

As he exited, he could hear a kid in a traditional witch costume complain, "These aren't candy!"

"Nuts are better for you, dear."

***

Gaunt munched nervously as he drove, ruminating that lunch was a long time ago. It felt like an eternity. And that wasn't only his stomach. Time seemed to be dragging. He kept looking at his watch, as if expecting it to be later than it was.

Renzendez' home was on the other side of the tracks, but the drive seemed to take an hour. Night had dropped down like a velvet curtain. The trick or treaters were out in force now.

Some of them wore unusually realistic costumes. Adults. Strangely, they were not accompanying children. They wandered about like drunken tourists, opening newspaper boxes and trash cans, as if looking for food. A few were unnaturally tall….

"This town gets weirder every year," Gaunt told himself.

At the Rezendez residence, a woman was handing out handmade paper sacks, the tops twisted shut by hand. An old Portuguese tradition, no doubt.

Gaunt showed his badge. "Looking for your husband."

"I have no husband."

"Candiru Rezendez then."

"Ah. He is my mate. He is out."

"What about Estevao Suarez?"

The woman gave Gaunt a strange look. "He is out too."

"Where can I find him?"

"Which one?"

"Don't give me that! I know they're the same person."

"But not at the same time," the woman returned.

"Skip the New Age doubletalk. Where?"

"He might be visiting Ethel Goss-Geist, the witch."

"Figures. Thanks."

"You are welcome. Take some Halloween nuts with you."

Despite himself, Gaunt accepted the bag, thinking, "These things are addicting."

It was a short drive to Ethel Goss' gift shop. Short, but surreal.

The streets were full of ghosts, shades and phantasms. They knocked on no doors, and therefore weren't after candy. They gave Gaunt the shivers. Even for Halloween Eve, they looked out of place, dislocated, like wanderers out of some distant desert.

A lean ebony-skinned man with a blank-featured face attired like an Egyptian pharaoh was striding down Pickman Street, surveying the neighborhood as if he owned it. Even though he possessed no face, somehow Gaunt knew that he was smiling. How can you smile without a mouth? Must be an optical effect of the Hollywood-quality makeup job, he decided.

Above in the night sky, scattered clouds seemed to cluster lower like aerial lions, eyeing prey. The shadows they cast had an unreal quality, not dark, yet not light. Something partaking of both, which struck the retina with a contradictory impact.

Turning onto Boundary Street, Gaunt was stunned to slide into a milky area of fog. It was as if the thick vapor had been poured into a container whose walls were the street itself. He slowed to a crawl, feeling his way forward.

A block along, he was forced to pull over. It was impossible to see. Gaunt exited his vehicle, looked about. A halogen flashlight failed to penetrate more than a few inches. It only illuminated the whitish murk like lighting does a thunderhead.

The fog was pearly and dry—nothing like the type of moist, clammy haze that hangs over the Miskatonic River, only a few blocks away. It reminded Gaunt of cigarette smoke, but it was impossibly dense.

He sniffed it. The scent was odd, half-familiar. But Gaunt couldn't place it.

Going to his radio, he tried to call it in. But the radio was dead. Not even a hiss came out of the radio speaker.

His cell phone still worked. At least, it showed three bars. Gaunt had to hold the screen almost to his nose to see it though.

Dialing the station house, he got the duty sergeant.

"I ran into a dense pocket of fog on Boundary Street," he reported. "Visibility is virtually zero. And my radio is out."

"We'll send a unit."

Hanging up, Gaunt turned. A pair of headlights came racing around the corner. He rushed to get out of its way.

As the vehicle blew past, Gaunt saw that it was no automobile, but something other. It sported baleful, yellowish lamps. And there was the rataplan of hooves, and a feral snorting that suggested horses if horses had been interbred with tigers—or worse.

Something like a whip snarled and cracked. Then the apparition was gone in the direction of Hangman's Hill.

A coach! In 21st century Arkham?

When an even more unnerving commotion drew near, Gaunt ducked into his vehicle and locked the door.

What sounded like an elephant lumbered past. But this was no stately pachyderm. Gaunt had seen circus elephants walking along. This thing had too many legs. And those legs made sucking sounds as the beast squished past.

The smell of its passing penetrating the closed car reminded him of the stench that hung over that blighted patch of Hindmarsh.

The fog was entering the car, too. Gaunt was soon sitting in an unsettling cocoon of dense hazy cobwebs that tickled the skin like crawling ants. He wondered if it was safe to breathe.....

***

Gaunt was nervously digging into his stash of Halloween nuts when his cell phone buzzed. Unable to see the screen, he answered it.

"Hello?"

"Detective Gaunt. This is Foley from Forensics. I wanted to follow up with you on those seeds we discovered in the Hindmarsh material."

"What have you got?"

"Turns out they're not seeds or pods. They're nuts."

Gaunt stopped in mid-chew. "Say again, Foley?"

"They're just like nuts. Crack open the shells and out rolls the meat."

"Edible?"

"I wouldn't even try. But they resemble filberts. In fact, they look a lot like those nuts a lot of people have been passing to the kids out tonight."

Detective Foley began spitting the crushed mealy contents of his mouth into the seat beside him.

"Are you there, detective?"

"Yeah," Gaunt said thickly.

"As I started to say", Foley continued, "the nuts must have passed undigested through the intestinal tract of whatever dumped that load out in Hindmarsh, just like unchewed kernels of corn in human feces. As a cross-dimensional delivery system, it's primitive, but effective. Sounds like time to call in the National Guard and declare martial law until we see what it's all about. This could be as wild as the Halloween of '69."

Gagging, Gaunt said, "I'll get back to you."

He fumbled for a water bottle, got it open and washed out his mouth. His heart was pounding now. He felt trapped in his own car, but dared not exit. Things were abroad in the night. Their comings and goings registered as unquiet disturbances, ripples in the cottony murk.

Gaunt checked the time on watch. Eight sharp. A full moon was rising. Its ghostly light seeped through the fog, bringing out leering faces that were too animated to be the products of imagination, but far too unearthly to be real.

Those disembodied faces were the last thing he remembered for a long time....

***

When Detective Alan Gaunt woke up, he was still sitting in his vehicle.

He could feel the familiar seat cushions. The world was otherwise opalescent smog that smelled like something from deep in his memory. Maybe it was the fact that he was emerging from subconscious sleep, but he placed it now.

The scent was a muted echo of the stink of the Hindmarsh abomination, made subtle and sweet as if scrubbed of all noxiousness. It brought to mind an alien incense.

Checking his watch, Gaunt discovered it was midnight. Exactly. The unreality of falling asleep at exactly eight and waking up at the precise stroke of midnight gripped him momentarily.

Gaunt listened. The silence was eerie. No traffic sounds. No footfalls, human or otherwise. Arkham was very, very still.

The full moon had risen until it was a small, defaced coin high in the night sky, visible through a rip in the overhead murk. It seemed out of place somehow.

Abandoning his vehicle, he used his halogen light to pick his way forward. The nearest landmark he knew was Ethel Goss-Geist's gift shop. Unlikely to be open this late, but with these pagans, you never knew....

***

Feeling his careful way out of the hazy zone, Gaunt found the place. Lights were on. At least, Jack O'Lanterns were glowing. Halloween closes late in Arkham, Massachusetts.

When he entered, one carven countenance swiveled to regard him with blazing foxfire eyes. In a deep voice, it announced, "Visitors!"

Gaunt almost jumped out of his skin. The triangular features swiveled back to sentry position. The eviscerated pumpkin sat on a taboret with no sign of mechanical support to account for its automaton-like animation.

When the Official Witch of Arkham poked her narrow head out of the back, Gaunt snapped, "You lied to me!"

Ethel Goss-Geist looked unconcerned. "Which time?"

"Rezendez and Suarez are the same person."

"Now that you finally figured it out, come back and meet the man himself."

Gaunt pushed through the beaded curtain. He stopped dead.

There were several people seated around the backroom Tarot tables. Most appeared translucent, like holograms—or something equally unnatural. They regarded him steadily with orbs as pale as their wan countenances.

Ethel the witch said in a deceptively casual voice, "Detective Gaunt, say hello to my grandparents and great grandparents. They dropped in to pay a visit."

The visitors registered on the eye as semi-solid. They were also old—

ancient of face and eye. They were dressed Old World European, circa the Great Depression.

"What's going on here?" Gaunt demanded hoarsely. For he recognized ghosts when he laid eyes on them—even if it were for the first time in his career.

"The veil has opened wide—wider than ever imagined," laughed Ethel. "And all because the rival covens of Arkham and Innsmouth have laid aside their old grievances and made common cause. Cotton Mather never dreamed of this glorious day." Her voice grew bitingly grave. "It was his nightmare."

"Make sense," Gaunt growled.

"Have you forgotten our talk already?"

Gaunt reached back into his memory, but his brain was as foggy as the streets of Arkham. He was still trying to shake the sleep from his consciousness. What was it she had said...?

"Cobwebs on your brain?" asked the voice of Candiru Rezendez, AKA Estevao Suarez. He emerged from a deeper room, looking confident. He was dressed in a black tuxedo, a white satin-lined opera cape shrouding his shoulders like a maestro of classical music.

"You're too slick for your own good," Gaunt charged.

Rezendez gave a courtly bow of agreement, inquiring, "What time is it, detective?"

"Past midnight. Why?"

Rezendez smiled thinly, "Look at your watch."

Gaunt checked it. It said 12:00. His cell phone displayed the same thing. "What the hell!"

"It's been midnight for almost three hours now," Ethel Goss laughed. "The veil has been wide open for over five hours. It is the greatest Halloween in the history of mankind."

"And other kind," chuckled Rezendez, displaying the tiny pointed teeth of a barracuda.

The ghosts of the departed Goss family murmured their accompanying mirth.

"You see," Rezendez explained, "knowing the correct spell was not enough to freeze the forward march of time. Since duration is an illusion experienced in the brain, it was necessary to chemically alter the cerebral chemistry of the local population, creating a spreading hive-mind effect at the quantum level of reality. I believe some call this effect morphogenetic resonance. Our allies on the Other Side of Reality provided us with the agency to effect that necessary adjustment."

"The damned nuts!" Gaunt croaked out.

"The blessed fruit of a new dawn and a new day," returned Rezendez, gesturing as if to encompass all of the world.

His tongue lying cold and dead in his mouth, Gaunt realized that he had been a part of it all. A dupe of these unclean communicants with the Other Side. An instrument of their unclean, coprophagic triumph. The bitter taste in his mouth was mealy and foreign.

His service weapon jumped into his hands. Gaunt pointed it at Candiru Rezendez, and said with more nerve than he felt, "You are under arrest."

The other grinned devilishly. "What is the crime of which I am charged? Dispensing unregistered and unclassified Halloween treats? Soliciting with intent to transform? Perhaps I am in violation of the Food and Drug Administration's alien nutmeats regulations."

From one corner of the room, a semi-human skull poked in through solid brick, looked about in curious glee, and then entered fully despite having no feet other than a blurry ectoplasmic skirt.

It floated up to Alan Gaunt, eyed his pistol curiously, then took it into his toothy gullet. The weapon made gritty sounds as it was methodically pulverized.

"Do you know what day it is?" Ethel the witch queen asked brightly.

Detective Alan Gaunt surveyed the surreal scene and nodded dumbly. It was the day after the last day the human race ruled its natal planet, the first day in which the Astral Realm supplanted all grosser matter as the dominant vibrational plane.

Moonday had come. It was Halloween, now and forever…

The Trick
by Ramsey Campbell

As October waned Debbie forgot about the old witch; she didn't associate her with Halloween. Halloween wasn't frightening. After the long depression following the summer holidays, it was the first night of the winter excitements: not as good as Guy Fawkes Night or Christmas, but still capable of excluding less pleasant things from Debbie's mind – the sarcastic teacher, the gangs of boys who leaned against the shops, the old witch.

Debbie wasn't really frightened of her, not at her age. Even years ago, when Debbie was a little kid, she hadn't found her terrifying. Not like some things: not like her feverish night when the dark in her bedroom had grown like mould on the furniture, making the familiar chair and wardrobe soft and huge. Nor like the face that had looked in her bedroom window once, when she was ill: a face like a wrinkled monkey's, whose jaw drooped as if melting, lower and lower; a face that had spoken to her in a voice that sagged as the face did – a voice that must have been a car's engine struggling to start.

The witch had never seized Debbie with panic, as those moments had. Perhaps she was only an old woman after all. She lived in a terraced house, in the row opposite Debbie's home. People owned their houses in that row, but Debbie's parents only rented the top half of a similar building. They didn't like the old woman; nobody did.

Whenever the children played outside her house she would come out to them. "Can't you make your row somewhere else? Haven't you got a home to go to?" "We're playing outside our own house," someone might say. "You don't own the street." Then she would stand and stare at them, with eyes like grey marbles. The fixed lifeless gaze always made them uneasy; they would dawdle away, jeering.

Parents were never sympathetic. "Play somewhere else, then," Debbie's father would say. Her parents were more frightened of the witch than she was. "Isn't her garden awful," she'd once heard her mother saying. "It makes the whole street look like a slum. But we mustn't say anything, we're only tenants." Debbie thought that was just an excuse.

Why were they frightened? The woman was small, hardly taller than Debbie. Boys didn't like to play near her house in case they had to rescue a football, to grope through the slimy nets, tall as a child, of weeds and grass full of crawlers. But that was only nasty, not frightening. Debbie wasn't even sure why the woman was supposed to be a witch.

Perhaps it was her house. "Keep away from my house," she told nearby children when she went out, as though they would want to go near the drab unpainted crumbling house that was sinking into its own jungle. The windows were cracked and thick with grime; when the woman's face peered out it looked like something pale stirring in a dirty jar. Sometimes children stood outside shouting and screaming to make the face loom. Boys often dared each other to peer in, but rarely did. Perhaps that was it, then: her house looked like a witch's house. Sometimes black smoke that looked solid as oil dragged its long swollen body from the chimney.

There were other things. Animals disliked her almost as much as she disliked them. Older brothers said that she went out after midnight, hurrying through the mercury-vapour glare towards the derelict streets across the main road; but older brothers often made up stories. When Debbie tried to question her father he only told her not to be stupid. "Who's been wasting your time with that?"

The uncertainty annoyed her. If the woman were a witch she must be in retirement; she didn't do anything. Much of the time – at least, during the day – she stayed in her house: rarely answering the door, and then only to peer through a crack and send the intruder away. What did she do, alone in the dark house? Sometimes people odder than herself would visit her: a tall thin woman with glittering wrists and eyes, who dressed in clothes like tapestries of lurid flame; two fat men, Tweedledum and Tweedledee draped in lethargically flapping black cloaks. They might be witches too.

"Maybe she doesn't want anyone to know she's a witch," suggested Debbie's friend Sandra. Debbie didn't really care. The old woman only annoyed her, as bossy adults did. Besides, Halloween was coming. Then, on Halloween morning – just when Debbie had managed to forget her completely – the woman did the most annoying thing of all.

Debbie and Sandra had wheeled their prams to the supermarket, feeling grown-up. On the way they'd met Lucy, who never acted her age. When Lucy had asked "Where are you taking your dolls?" Sandra had replied loftily "We aren't taking our dolls anywhere." She'd done the shopping each Saturday morning since she was nine, so that her mother could work. Often she shopped in the evenings, because her mother was tired after work, and then Debbie would accompany her so that she felt less uneasy in the crowds beneath the white glare. This Saturday morning Debbie was shopping too.

The main road was full of crowds trying to beat the crowds. Boys sat like a row of shouting ornaments on the railing above the underpass; women queued a block for cauliflowers, babies struggled screaming in prams. The crowds flapped as a wind fumbled along the road. Debbie and Sandra manoeuvred their prams to the supermarket. A little girl was racing a trolley through the aisles, jumping on the back for a ride. How childish, Debbie thought.

When they emerged Sandra said "Let's walk to the tunnel and back."

She couldn't be anxious to hurry home to vacuum the flat. They wheeled their laden prams towards the tunnel, which fascinated them. A railway cutting divided the streets a few hundred yards beyond the supermarket, in the derelict area. Houses crowded both its banks, their windows and doorways blinded and gagged with boards. From the cutting, disused railway lines probed into a tunnel beneath the main road, and never reappeared, so far as Debbie could see.

The girls pushed their prams down an alley to the near edge of the cutting. Beside them the remains of back yards were cluttered with fragments of brick. The cutting was rather frightening, in a delicious way. Rusty metal skeletons sat tangled unidentifiably among the lines, soggy cartons flapped sluggishly, a door lay as though it led to something in the soil. Green sprouted minutely between scatterings of rubble.

Debbie stared down at the tunnel, at the way it burrowed into the dark beneath the earth. Within the mouth was only a shallow rim, surrounding thick darkness. No: now she strained her eyes she made out a further arch of dimmer brick, cut short by the dark. As she peered another formed, composed as much of darkness as of brick. Beyond it she thought something pale moved. The surrounding daylight flickered with Debbie's peering; she felt as though she were being drawn slowly into the tunnel. What was it, the pale feeble stirring? She held on to a broken wall, so as to lean out to peer; but a voice startled her away.

"Go on. Keep away from there." It was the old witch shouting from the main road, just as if they were little kids. To Debbie she looked silly: her head poked over the wall above the tunnel as if someone had put a turnip there to grimace at them.

"We're all right," Sandra called impatiently. "We know what we're doing." They wouldn't have gone too near the cutting; years ago a little boy had run into the tunnel and had never been seen again.

"Just do as you're told. Get away." The head hung above the wall, staring hatefully at them, looking even more like a turnip.

"Oh, let's go home," Debbie said. "I don't want to stay here now, anyway."

They wheeled their prams around the chunks that littered the street. At the main road the witch was waiting for them. Her face frowned, glaring from its perch above the small black tent of her coat. Little more of her was visible; scuffed black snouts poked from beneath the coat, hands lurked in her drooping sleeves; one finger was hooked around the cane of a tattered umbrella. "And keep away from there in future," she said harshly.

"Why, is that your house?" Debbie muttered.

"That's where she keeps her bats' eyes."

"What's that?" The woman's grey eyebrows writhed up, threatening. Her head looked like an old apple, Debbie thought, with mould for eyebrows and tufts of dead grass stuck on top. "What did you just say?" the woman shouted.

She was repeating herself into a fury when she was interrupted. Debbie tried not to laugh. Sandra's dog Mop was the interruption; he must have jumped out of Sandra's back yard. He was something like a stumpy-legged terrier, black and white and spiky. Debbie liked him, even though he'd once run away with her old teddy bear, her favourite, and had returned empty-mouthed. Now he ran around Sandra, bouncing up at her; he ran towards the cutting and back again, barking.

The witch didn't like him, nor did he care for her. Once he had run into her grass only to emerge with his tail between his legs, while she watched through the grime, smiling like a skull. "Keep that insect away from here as well," she shouted.

She shook her umbrella at him; it fluttered dangling like a sad broomstick. At once Mop pounced at it, barking. The girls tried to gag themselves with their knuckles, but vainly. Their laughter boiled up; they stood snorting helplessly, weeping with mirth.

The woman drew herself up rigidly; bony hands crept from her sleeves. The wizened apple turned slowly to Sandra, then to Debbie. The mouth was a thin bloodless slit full of teeth; the eyes seemed to have congealed around hatred. "Well, you shouldn't have called him an insect," Debbie said defensively.

Cars rushed by, two abreast. Shoppers hurried past, glancing at the woman and the two girls. Debbie could seize none of these distractions; she could only see the face. It wasn't a fruit or a vegetable now, it was a mask that had once been a face, drained of humanity. Its hatred was cold as a shark's gaze. Even the smallness of the face wasn't reassuring; it concentrated its power.

Mop bounced up and poked at the girls. At last they could turn; they ran. Their prams yawed. At the supermarket they looked back. The witch hadn't moved; the wizened mask stared above the immobile black coat. They stuck out their tongues, then they stalked home, nudging each other into nonchalance. "She's only an old fart," Debbie dared to say. In the street they stood and made faces at her house for minutes.

It wasn't long before Sandra came to ask Debbie to play. She couldn't have vacuumed so quickly, but perhaps she felt uneasy alone in the house. They played rounders in the street, with Lucy and her younger brother. Passing cars took sides.

When Debbie saw the witch approaching, a seed of fear grew in her stomach. But she was almost outside her own house; she needn't be afraid, even if the witch made faces at her again. Sandra must have thought similarly, for she ran across the pavement almost in front of the witch.

The woman didn't react; she seemed hardly to move. Only the black coat stirred a little as she passed, carrying her mask of hatred as though bearing it carefully somewhere, for a purpose. Debbie shouted for the ball; her voice clattered back from the houses, sounding false as her bravado.

As the witch reached her gate Miss Bake from the flats hurried over, blue hair glinting, hands fluttering. "Oh, have they put the fire out?"

The witch peered suspiciously at her. "I really couldn't tell you."

"Haven't you heard?" This indifference made her more nervous; her voice leapt and shook. "Some boys got into the houses by the supermarket and started a fire. That's what they told me at the corner. They must have put it out. Isn't it wicked, Miss Trodden. They never used to do these things. You can't feel safe these days, can you?"

"Oh yes, I think I can."

"You can't mean that, Miss Trodden. Nobody's safe, not with all these children. If they're bored, why doesn't someone give them something to do? The churches should. They could find them something worth doing. Someone's got to make the country safe for the old folk."

"Which churches are those?" She was smirking faintly.

Miss Bake drew back a little. "All the churches," she said, trying to placate her. "All the Christians. They should work together, form a coalition."

"Oh, them. They've had their chance." She smirked broadly. "Don't you worry. Someone will take control. I must be going."

Miss Bake hurried away, frowning and tutting; her door slammed. Shortly the witch's face appeared behind the grimy panes, glimmering as though twilight came earlier to her house. Her expression lurked in the dimness, unreadable.

When Debbie's father called her in, she could tell that her parents had had an argument; the flat was heavy with dissatisfaction. "When are you going trick-or-treating?" her mother demanded.

"Tonight. After tea."

"Well, you're not. You've to go before it's dark."

The argument was poised to pounce on Debbie. "Oh, all right," she said grumpily.

After lunch she washed up. Her father dabbed at the plates, then sat watching football. He fiddled irritably with the controls, but the flesh of the players grew orange. Her mother kept swearing at food as she prepared it. Debbie read her love comics and tried to make herself invisible with silence. Through the wall she could the song of the vacuum droning about the flat in the next house.

Eventually it faded, and Sandra came knocking. "You'd better go now," Debbie's mother said.

"We're not going until tonight."

"I'm sorry, Sandra, Debbie has to go before it's dark. And you aren't to go to anyone we don't know."

"Oh, why not?" Sandra protested. Challenging strangers was part of the excitement. "We won't go in," Debbie said.

"Because you're not to, that's why."

"Because some people have been putting things in sweets," Debbie's father said wearily, hunching forward towards the television. "Drugs and things. It was on the news."

"You go with them," her mother told him, worried again. "Make sure they're all right."

"What's stopping you?"

"You'll cook the tea, will you?"

"My mother might go," Sandra said. "But I think she's too tired."

"Oh God, all right, I'll go. When the match is finished." He slumped back in his armchair; the leather sighed. "Never any bloody rest," he muttered.

By the time they began it was dark after all. But the streets weren't deserted and dimly exciting; they were full of people hurrying home from the match, shouting to each other, singing. Her father's impatience tugged at Debbie like a leash.

Some of the people they visited were preparing meals, and barely tolerant. Too many seemed anxious to trick them; perhaps they couldn't afford treats. At a teacher's house they had to attempt impossible plastic mazes which even Debbie's father decided irritably that he couldn't solve – though the teacher's wife sneaked them an apple each anyway. Elsewhere, several boys with glowing skulls for faces flung open a front door then slammed it, laughing. Mop appeared from an alley and joined the girls, to bounce at anyone who opened a door. He cheered Debbie, and she had pocketfuls of fruit and sweets. But it was an unsatisfying Halloween.

They were nearly home when Mop began to growl. He balked as they came abreast of the witch's garden. Unwillingly Debbie stared towards the house. The white mercury-vapour glare sharpened the tangled grass; a ragged spiky frieze of shadow lay low on the walls. The house seemed smoky and dim, drained of colour. But she could see the gaping doorway, the coat like a tent of darker shadow, the dim perched face, a hand beckoning. "Come here," the voice said. "I've got something for you."

"Go on, be quick," hissed Debbie's father.

The girls hesitated. "Go on, she won't bite you," he said, pushing Debbie. "Take it while she's offering."

He wanted peace, he wanted her to make friends with the old witch. If she said she was frightened he would only tell her not to be stupid. Now he had made her more frightened to refuse. She dragged her feet up the cracked path, towards the door to shadow. Dangling grasses plucked at her socks, scraping dryly. The house stretched her shadow into its mouth.

Fists like knotted clubs crept from sleeves and deposited something in Debbie's palm, then in Sandra's: wrapped boiled sweets. "There you are," said the shrunken mouth, smiling dimly.

"Thank you very much." Debbie almost screamed: she hadn't heard her father follow her to thank the woman. His finger was trying to prod her to gratitude. "Let's see if you like them," the witch said.

Debbie's fingers picked stiffly at the wrapping. The paper rustled like the dead grass, loud and somehow vicious. She raised the bared sweet towards her mouth, wondering whether she could drop it. She held her mouth still around the sweet. But when she could no longer fend off the taste, it was pleasant: raspberry, clear and sharp. "It's nice," she said. "Thank you."

"Yes, it is," Sandra said.

Hearing her voice Mop, who had halted snarling at the far end of the path, came racing between the clattering grasses. "We mustn't forget the dog, must we," the voice said. Mop overshot his sweet and bounced back to catch it. Sandra made to run to him, but he'd crunched and swallowed the sweet. They turned back to the house. The closed front door faced them in the dimness.

"I'm going home now," Sandra said and ran into her house, followed by Mop. Debbie found an odd taste in her mouth: a thick bitter trail, as if something had crawled down her throat. Just the liquid centre of the sweet: it wasn't worth telling her father, he would only be impatient. "Did you enjoy yourself?" he said, tousling her hair, and she nodded.

During the meal her tongue searched for the taste. It was never there, nor could she find it in her memory; perhaps it hadn't been there at all. She watched comedies on television; she was understanding more of the jokes that made her parents laugh. She tricked some little girls who came to the door, but they looked so forlorn that she gave them sweets. The street was bare, deserted, frosted by the light: the ghost of its daytime self. She was glad to close it out. She watched the screen. Colours bobbed up, laughter exploded; gaps interrupted, for she was falling asleep. "Do you want to go to bed?" She strained to prove she didn't but at last admitted to herself that she did. In bed she fell asleep at once.

She slept uneasily. Something kept waking her: a sound, a taste? Straining drowsily to remember, she drifted into sleep. Once she glimpsed a figure staring at her from the doorway – her father. Only seconds later – or so it seemed at first – she woke again. A face had peered in the window. She turned violently, tethered by the blankets. There was nothing but the lit gap she always left between the curtains, to keep her company in the dark. The house was silent, asleep.

Her mind streamed with thoughts. The mask on the wizened apple, the skull-faced boys, the street flattened by the glare, her father's finger prodding her ribs. The face that had peered in her window had been hanging wide, too wide. It was the melting monkey from when she was little. Placing it didn't reassure her. The house surrounded her, huge and unfamiliar, darkly threatening.

She tried to think of Mop. He ran barking into the tunnel – no, he chased cheekily around the witch. Debbie remembered the day he had run into the witch's garden. Scared to pursue him, they had watched him vanish amid the grass. They'd heard digging, then a silence: what sounded like a pattering explosion of earth, a threshing of grass, and Mop had run out with his tail between his legs. The dim face had watched, grinning.

That wasn't reassuring either. She tried to think of something she loved, but could think of nothing but her old bear that Mop had stolen. Her mind became a maze, leading always back to the face at her window. She'd seen it only once, but she had often felt it peering in. Its jaw had sagged like wax, pulling open a yawning pink throat. She had been ill, she must have been frightened by a monkey making a face on television. But as the mouth had drooped and then drawn up again, she'd heard a voice speaking to her through the glass: a slow deep dragging voice that sagged like the face, stretching out each separate word. She'd lain paralysed as the voice blurred in the glass, but hadn't been able to make out a word. She opened her eyes to dislodge the memory. A shadow sprang away from the window.

Only a car's light, plucking at the curtains. She lay trying to be calm around her heart. But she felt uneasy, and kept almost tasting the centre of the burst sweet. The room seemed oppressive; she felt imprisoned. The window imprisoned her, for something could peer in.

She crawled out of bed. The floor felt unpleasantly soft underfoot, as if mouldering in the dark. The street stretched below, deserted and glittering; the witch's windows were black, as though the grime had filled the house. The taste was almost in Debbie's mouth.

Had the witch put something in the sweets? Suddenly Debbie had to know whether Sandra had tasted it too. She had to shake off the oppressively padded darkness. She dressed, fumbling quietly in the dark. Squirming into her anorak, she crept into the hall.

She couldn't leave the front door open, the wind would slam it. She tiptoed into the living-room and groped in her mother's handbag. Her face burned; it skulked dimly in the mirror. She clutched the key in her fist and inched open the door to the stairs.

On the stairs she realised she was behaving stupidly. How could she waken Sandra without disturbing her mother? .Sandra's bedroom window faced the back yard, too far from the alley to pelt. Yet her thoughts seemed only a commentary, for she was still descending. She opened the front door, and started. Sandra was waiting beneath the streetlamp.

She was wearing her anorak too. She looked anxious. "Mop's run off," she said.

"Oh no. Shall we look for him?"

"Come on, I know where he is."

They muffled their footsteps, which sounded like a dream. The bleached street stood frozen around them, fossilised by the glare; trees cast nets over the houses, cars squatted, closed and dim. The ghost of the street made Debbie dislike to ask, but she had to know. "Do you think she put something funny in those sweets? Did you taste something?"

"Yes, I can now." At once Debbie could too: a brief hint of the indefinable taste. She hadn't wanted so definite an answer: she bit her lip.

At the main road Sandra turned towards the supermarket. Shops displayed bare slabs of glazed light, plastic cups scuttled in the underpass. How could Sandra be so sure where Mop had gone? Why did Debbie feel she knew as well? Sandra ran past the supermarket. Surely they weren't going to – But Sandra was already running into an alley, towards the cutting.

She gazed down, waiting for Debbie. White lamps glared into the artificial valley; shadows of the broken walls crumbled over scattered bricks. "He won't have gone down there," Debbie said, wanting to believe it.

"He has," Sandra cried. "Listen."

The wind wandered groping among the clutter on the tracks, it hooted feebly in the stone throat. Another sound was floated up to Debbie by the wind, then snatched away: a whining? "He's in the tunnel," Sandra said.

"Come on."

She slipped down a few feet; her face stared over the edge at Debbie. "If you don't come you aren't my friend," she said.

Debbie watched her reach the floor of the cutting and stare up challengingly; then reluctantly she followed. A bitter taste rose momentarily in her throat. She slithered down all too swiftly. The dark deep tunnel grew tall.

Why didn't Sandra call? "Mop! Mop!" Debbie shouted. But her shouts dropped into the cutting like pats of mud. There might have been an answering whine; the wind threw the sound away. "Come on," Sandra said impatiently.

She strode into the tunnel. The shadow hanging from the arch chopped her in half, then wiped her out entirely. Debbie remembered the little boy who had vanished. Suppose he were in there now – what would he be like? Around her the glistening cartons shifted restlessly; their gaping tops nodded. Twisted skeletons rattled, jangling.

Some of the squealing of metal might be an animal's faint cry; perhaps the metal was what they'd heard. "All right," Sandra said from the dark, "you're not my friend."

Debbie glanced about hopelessly. A taste touched her mouth. Above her, ruins gleamed jaggedly against the sky; cartons dipped their mouths towards her, torn lips working. Among piled bricks at the edge of the cutting, a punctured football or a crumpled rag peered down at her. Unwillingly she walked forward.

Darkness fell on her, filling her eyes. "Wait until your eyes get used to it," Sandra said, but Debbie disliked to keep them closed for long. At last bricks began to solidify from the dark. Darkness arched over her, outlines of bricks glinted faintly. The rails were thin dull lines, shortly erased by the dark. Sandra groped forward. "Go slowly, then we won't fall over anything," she said.

They walked slowly as a dream, halting every few feet to wait for the light to catch up. Debbie's eyes were full of shifting fog that fastened very gradually on her surroundings, sketching them: the dwindling arch of the tunnel, the fading rails. Her progress was like a ritual in a nightmare.

The first stretch of the tunnel was cluttered with missiles: broken bottles crunched underfoot, tin cans toppled loudly. After that the way was clear except for odd lurking bricks. But the dark was oppressively full of the sounds the girls made – hasty breathing, shuffling, the chafing of rust against their feet – and Debbie could never be sure whether, amid the close sounds and the invisibility, there was a whining.

They shuffled onwards. Cold encircled them, dripping. The tunnel smelled dank and dusty; it seemed to insinuate a bitter taste into Debbie's mouth. She felt the weight of earth huge around the stone tube. The dimness flickered forward again, beckoning them on. It was almost as though someone were coaxing them into the tunnel with a feeble lamp. Beneath her feet bricks scraped and clattered.

The twilight flickered, then leapt ahead. The roundness of the tunnel glistened faintly; Debbie could make out random edges of brick, a dull hint of rails. The taste grew in her mouth. Again she felt that they were being led. She didn't dare ask Sandra whether the light was really moving. It must be her eyes. A shadow loomed on the arch overhead: the bearer of the light – behind her.

She turned gasping. At once the dimness went out. The distant mouth of the tunnel was small as a fingernail.

Its light couldn't have reached so far. Something else had illuminated their way. The taste filled her mouth like suffocation; dark dripped all around her; the distant entrance flickered, dancing. If she made for the entrance Sandra would have to follow. She could move now, she'd only to move one foot, just one, just a little. Sandra screamed.

When Debbie turned – furious with Sandra: there was nothing to be scared of, they could go now, escape – shadows reached for her. The light had leapt ahead again, still dim but brighter. The shadows were attached to vague objects, of which the nearest seemed familiar. Light gathered on it, crawling, glimmering. It had large ragged ears. It was her old lost teddy bear.

It was moving. In the subterranean twilight its fur stirred as if drowned. No, it wasn't the fur. Debbie's bear was covered with a swarm that crawled. The swarm was emerging sluggishly from within the bear, piling more thickly on its body, crawling.

It was a lost toy, not hers at all. Nothing covered it but moisture and unstable light. "It's all right," she muttered weakly. "It's only someone's old bear." But Sandra was staring beyond it, sobbing with horror.

Farther in, where dimness and dark flickered together, there was a hole in the floor of the tunnel, surrounded by bricks and earth and something that squatted. It squatted at the edge; its hands dangled into the hole, its dim face gaped pinkly. Its eyes gleamed like bubbles of mud. "Oh, oh," Sandra sobbed. "It's the monkey."

Perhaps that was the worst – that Sandra knew the gaping face too. But Debbie's horror was blurred and numbing, because she could see so much. She could see what lay beside the hole, struggling feebly as if drugged, and whining: Mop.

Sandra staggered towards him as if she had lost her balance. Debbie stumbled after her, unable to think, feeling only her feet dragging her over the jagged floor. Then part of the darkness shifted and advanced on them, growing paler. A toy – a large clockwork toy, jerking rustily: the figure of a little boy, its body and ragged sodden clothes covered with dust and cobwebs. It plodded jerkily between them and the hole, and halted. Parts of it shone white, as if patched with flaking paint: particularly the face.

Debbie tried to look away, to turn, to run. But the taste burned in her mouth; it seemed to thread her with a rigid frame, holding her helpless. The dim stone tube was hemmed in by darkness; the twilight fluttered. Dust crawled in her throat. The toy bear glistened restlessly. The figure of the little boy swayed; its face glimmered, pale, featureless, blotchy. The monkey moved.

Its long hands closed around Mop and pulled him into the hole, and then they scooped bricks and earth on top of him. The earth struggled in the hole, the whining became a muffled coughing and choking. Eventually the earth was still. The squat floppy body capered on the grave. Thick deep laughter, very slow, dropped from the gaping face. Each time the jaw drooped lower, almost touching the floor.

Another part of the dark moved. "That'll teach you. You won't forget that," a voice said.

It was the witch. She was lurking in the darkness, out of sight. Her voice was as lifeless now as her face had been. Debbie was able to see that the woman needed to hide in the dark to be herself. But she was trapped too efficiently for the thought to be at all reassuring.

"You'd better behave yourselves in future. I'll be watching," the voice said. "Go on now. Go away."

As Debbie found she was able to turn, though very lethargically, the little boy moved. She heard a crack; then he seemed to shrink jerkily and topple towards her. But she was turning, and saw no more. The taste was heavy in her. She couldn't run; she could only plod through the close treacherous darkness towards the tiny light.

The light refused to grow. She plodded, she plodded, but the light held itself back. Then at last it seemed nearer, and much later it reached into the dark. She plodded out, exhausted and hollow. She clambered numbly up the bank, dragged her feet through the deserted streets; she was just aware of Sandra near her. She climbed the stairs, slipped the key into the handbag, went into her room, still trudging. Her numb trudge became the plodding of her heart, her slow suffocated gasps. She woke.

So it had been a dream, after all. Her mouth tasted bitter. What had wakened her? She lay uneasily, eyelids tight, trying to retreat into sleep; if she woke completely she'd be alone with the dark. But light flapped on her eyelids. Something was wrong. The room was too bright, and flickering.

Things cracked loudly, popping; a voice cried her name. Reluctantly she groped to the window, towards the blazing light.

The witch's house was on fire. Flames gushed from the windows, painting smoke red. Sandra stood outside, crying "Debbie!" As Debbie watched, bewildered, a screaming blaze appeared at an upstairs window, jerking like a puppet; then it writhed and fell back into the flames. Sandra seemed to be dancing, outlined by reflected fire, and weeping.

People were unlocking doors. Sandra's mother hurried out, and Debbie's father. Sandra's mother fluttered about, trying to drag the girl home, but Sandra was crying "Debbie!" Debbie gripped the sill, afraid to let go.

More houses were switched on. Debbie's mother ran out. There was a hasty discussion among the parents, then Debbie's father came hurrying back with Sandra. Debbie dodged into bed as they came upstairs; the witch's house roared, splintering.

"Here's Sandra, Debbie. She's frightened. She's going to sleep with you tonight." Shadows rushed into the room with him. When Sandra took off her dressing-gown and stood holding it, confused, he threw it impatiently on the chair. "Into bed now, quickly. And just you stay there."

They heard him hurrying downstairs, Sandra's mother saying "Oh God, oh my God," Debbie's mother trying to calm her down. The girls lay silent in the shaking twilit room. Sandra was trembling.

"What happened?" Debbie whispered. "Did you see?"

After a while Sandra sobbed. "My little dog," she said indistinctly.

Was that an answer? Debbie's thoughts were blurred; the room quaked, Sandra's dressing-gown was slipping off the chair, distracting her. "What about Mop?" she whispered. "Where is he?"

Sandra seemed to be choking. The dressing-gown fell in a heap on the floor. Debbie felt nervous. What had happened to Mop? She'd dreamed – Surely Sandra couldn't have dreamed that too. The rest of the contents of the chair were following the dressing-gown.

"I dreamed," Debbie began uneasily, and bitterness filled her mouth like a gag. When she'd finished choking, she had forgotten what she'd meant to say. The room and furniture were unsteady with dimming light. Far away and fading, she heard her parents' voices.

Sandra was trying to speak. "Debbie," she said, "Debbie." Her body shook violently with effort or with fear. "I burned the witch," she said. "Because of what she did."

Debbie stared in front of her, aghast. She couldn't take in Sandra's words. Too much had happened too quickly: the dream, the fire, her own bitter-tasting dumbness, Sandra's revelation, the distracting object that drooped from the chair – But until Sandra's dressing-gown was thrown there, that chair had been empty.

She heard Sandra's almost breathless cry. Something dim squatted forward on the chair. Its pink yawning drooped towards the floor. Very slowly, relishing each separate word, it began to speak.

El Dia De Los Muertos

by Kevin Ross

Now what in the merry hell is all this?" grunted Steve Bell. He and Shep Garvey and Don Brent ambled their horses up the broad hillside past the cemetery outside the village of Colina Verde, just a few miles across the border into Mexico.

The three *americanos* had been part of a larger party that had recently completed a transaction involving a few dozen head of cattle and a couple hundred pesos per man. The fact the cattle didn't belong to any of the men wouldn't stop them from spending the pesos, nor would it prevent them from attempting similar transactions in the future. It was far too easy and profitable a venture for Garvey and his men, stealing cattle and horses in New Mexico and selling them across the border to *rancheros* in Old Mexico. They didn't get much money for their efforts, but they also didn't catch much of the blame since the stolen livestock would be found in the hands of Mexicans, if they were found at all.

It was a chilly evening in early November, and Bell and his companions were surrounded by villagers, men, women, and children of all ages. They moved through the streets bearing candles and torches, dressed in their best, most colorful clothes. What drew Bell's attention, however, were the masks worn by some of the revelers, for indeed, there was some sort of festival going on. Despite their crudeness, the skull-faced papier-mache masks nevertheless made an eerie spectacle in the flickering light and shadow.

"Day of the dead," offered Brent. "'s a Mexican thing." Brent was the quiet, smart one of the group. Dark-haired and dark-eyed, with a handle-bar moustache, and usually settled beneath a battered brown sombrero, he looked Mexican himself, but he hailed from Texas, and his ancestors were Irish.

Bell watched the villagers gathered in the cemetery. They placed flowers and plates of food and bottles atop the graves, and sat down next to them, chatting among themselves. Bell was about twenty-five, the newest member of Garvey's band of rustlers. He had drifted into New Mexico—eventually—from back east. Tall, blonde, and wiry, he carried a heavy Colt on his belt, and word had it that he had used it to fatal effect more than once. His tanned, unshaven face seemed set in a perpetual scowl.

"Bit late for Halloween, ain't it?" he asked.

"It ain't Halloween, Steve, it's a Mexican thing. All Souls' Day, Day of the Dead. Mexicans think this is the day the dead come back and wander around the village, so they put on their best duds and make food and drinks for the departed so they'll leave 'em alone." A handful of beaming children swarmed beside Brent's mount as he replied. Brent waved his hands, telling them in Spanish that he had no coins, no candy. Giggling and making faces, the kids drifted away back toward the village.

"Never heard of such a thing."

"That's 'cause you're from Missouri, Stevie, and there probably ain't many Mexicans up thataway," said Garvey. "Look at the bright side, there's lots of free food and drink laying around, if you wanna risk pissing off the spirits." Garvey, pushing forty, was the oldest of the gang. His grey eyes were cold and cunning. His grey-flecked hair and lined face told of a hard-lived life, though his pot-belly hinted that if he hadn't already gone a bit to seed, he was on his way. Still, the Remington revolvers holstered at his hip and across his belly bespoke that he wouldn't be put out to pasture without a fight.

"I'm more interested in catching a piece of tail, ta be honest. Wish I coulda gone with Drake. I hear that little wildcat of his has got a sister." Bell was keeping his eyes peeled for a cantina or a posada where he could wet his whistle. Both of 'em, in fact. Villagers mingled here and there, some in shawls and scarves, some with leering skull-faces that made Bell nervous.

"Shit, Stevie, why d'you think Gordo went with Drake? Reckon he's got dibs on the wildcat's sister."

"Goddammit, Gordo's already got 'im a wife in Laredo."

"Yeah, but he's got a thirsty pecker too," said Garvey, and all three men laughed. They drew up and dismounted in front of a bone-white adobe building with a sign outside reading "Posada". "Youngest pup gets to take the critters to the livery, Stevie, and that's you" said Garvey, handing the reins of his horse to Bell. He and Brent took their saddlebags off the horses. "Buy you a drink when you get back. Don't get lost." Garvey clapped Brent on the back and the two of them headed for the door, leaving Bell holding the reins of all three mounts.

"Come on, you club-footed bastards," grunted Bell, pulling the horses along behind him. He had seen a little stable just down the street from the posada; Garvey wouldn't want to be too far from the horses, just in case. Likely the posada had a room or two they could stay in. Bell hoped to find himself a woman with her own room, or at least drink enough that he wouldn't have to listen to Garvey's snoring.

A swarm of children, perhaps the same that had accosted Brent earlier, swirled around Bell and the horses, giggling and babbling in Spanish. They had weird little white balls in their hands, pressing them toward him, apparently wanting him to buy them. He looked closer and saw that they were miniature skulls, and he frowned, wondering what the hell this was all about. A little girl, laughing, bit into one of the skulls, and Bell realized it was some kind of cake or candy. He shooed them off with his free hand, exhausting his Spanish with "No gracias", "No 'ablo Espanol", and finally, in exasperation, "Vaya!" The children, still laughing, swept away.

Bell continued toward the stable. A shawled old woman within a low adobe structure pulled the shutters closed as he passed. A group of men passed a bottle between them, each man saluting or raising a toast when the bottle came to him.

Then Bell was startled when a black-clad figure stepped around the corner of a building within spitting distance of Bell and the horses. The young man's right hand flew to the Colt at his side, his left hand straining to hold the reins of the spooked horses as they shied away from the newcomer. Bell hissed in disgust as he relaxed. It was just another of these goddamn Day of the Dead folks. He wore a leering skull mask with black highlights where the eyes, nose, and mouth should be. Bell's appearance and demeanor had startled the skull-masked man as much as he had spooked the *americano*, and he spread his hands, bowing his head, as he backed away. Bell snorted, realizing he had frightened away Death.

"Goddamn Mex'cans," he muttered, dragging the horses into the stable. Inside he found two young Mexican boys duelling with wooden swords. They understood enough English that he could arrange to have the horses fed, watered, and put up for the night. He paid them a few coins, giving them his coldest glare to let them know that if anything happened to those horses he'd nail their hides to the barn door for it. They seemed to get the message.

The night was growing colder as Bell stopped outside the livery. He took out his makings and rolled himself a cigarette. Music and voices still echoed through the little village, but the streets were slowly emptying in the darkness. In the corner of his eye Bell saw three figures coming down the street toward him. Two wore serapes and sombreros, while the third, between them, was dressed in a cloak or robe of some kind that completely obscured its face and head. The other two men supported the third by the elbows, and the gait suggested that whoever he or more likely she was, she was old and infirm. As they passed, the two men turned toward Bell, and once again he found himself looking into papier mache skull masks. He smirked and started to nod at the men...

And then the third figure turned to face him.

It was just a brief glimpse, as the hood or whatever it was briefly fell open to reveal the head within. Pale, pitted flesh gleamed within the dark folds, and if there were eyes in those deep black sockets he didn't see them. The face seemed oddly short, and Bell wondered if part of its jaw was missing or something. He stood, gaping, as the trio shuffled past him and disappeared into the night beyond.

Only when his cigarette burned his fingers did he rouse from his astonishment.

"What the merry hell..." Shivering, Bell ground out his cigarette and started back for the posada. Did these crazy goddamn Mexicans actually dig up dead bodies and carry 'em around town like that? He needed a drink, perhaps several. He couldn't help shuddering as he passed a few other knots of villagers dressed in serapes, hats, and skull-masks. They drank and laughed merrily, but Bell couldn't shake the image of the far more realistic death-mask he had seen, so he hurried to find Garvey and Brent.

They were laughing too, when he found them in the back of the posada's tavern room. It was hot and smoky and stank of sweat, stale beer, and tobacco. Bell's friends had their feet up on a table, clay mugs in their paws, smiles on their faces.

"Hey gringo!" shouted Garvey, already buzzed.

Bell sat down. "Where's my drink?" Garvey waved toward a serving girl and pointed toward the newcomer at his table. "Cheer up, sonny. You got money in yer pocket, tequila on its way, and lots of soft, warm Mex'can girls jus' dyin' ta meet a pretty blonde gringo like you, long as you got the money for it."

Bell took his drink from the fleshy brown girl's tray and gulped it, wincing as it burned down his throat. It was *not* good tequila. "'nother," he croaked as the girl left.

"What's the matter, Steve? You run inta trouble out there?" asked Brent.

"Not a chance. I just don't like all this Day of the Dead shit goin' around. People dressed up as skeletons and dancing and drinking is one thing, but carrying around dead bodies is another. 'At's just sick, I tellya."

"The hell are you talkin' 'bout, boy? You smoke some loco-weed while you was out?"

"I wish I did. I saw these two hombres carrying somebody down the street. First I thought it was some drunk old lady, but I saw under her shawl and I'm pretty sure it was a goddamn dead body." At the table beside them, a slatternly middle-aged Mexican woman drew her hand from within the shirt of the young bravo she was draped over and said something Bell didn't hear.

"Bullshit!" drawled Garvey. He drew out a short stub of a cigar and scratched a match to light it. "You're seeing things. Just another mask is all."

"I'm telling you, it didn't look like no mask. Nothin' like these cheap shabby ones, anyways. It was a real skull, I'd bet. Skin looked all rotted and sick, and I think the lower jaw was gone." At the neighboring table, the whore crossed herself and took a long drink straight from the bottle.

"What's yer problem, woman?" snapped Bell. Garvey tensed as the young Mexican with the drunken whore turned toward them. His expression dropped menacingly, but Garvey, Brent, and Bell glared back at him. The Mex's gaze took in the gunbelts and dusty saddlebags, and his eyes slowly swiveled elsewhere. The woman looked from the gringos to her customer.

"Senor Vargas," she said to her man. He scoffed and pushed her away. Standing, he downed his drink in a single gulp, shot a glance at Bell and the others, and made his way toward the bar.

"Who's Senor Vargas?" asked Brent. "Quien?"

The whore looked around the room, drew her blouse up around her shoulders and clumsily slid her chair over to the *americanos'* table. She held up her cup and wiggled it, offering the men a smile that featured two chipped front teeth. Brent caught the serving girl's eye and motioned toward the woman at their table. "Christ on crutches..." Garvey muttered.

"Vargas?" coaxed Brent. The whore leaned forward conspiratorially and began speaking Spanish in a hushed voice. Bell didn't understand a word of it, but Brent listened, occasionally nodding and asking a question. The woman's glazed eyes widened, her tone lowered to a whisper. Through it all, the only thing Bell understood was "Senor Vargas"—the rest of it was gibberish to him. Garvey smoked his cigar, shook his head, chuckled softly, and drank, but he too half-listened to the whore's tale. Finally, Bell could take it no longer.

"So who the hell is Senor Vargas and what's he got to do with the corpse they was draggin' around?"

Brent held up his hand, urging Bell to be patient, then nodded at the woman to continue. Garvey chuckled at Bell's vexation. The whore's tale finished a a few moments later. Brent slid her a coin and thanked her. She scooped up the money quickly as she rose unsteadily to her feet. She shook her finger at the men and said something else with an expression that was so deadly serious that her drunken state made Garvey burst into laughter. He waved her off and she left, scowling. Garvey slapped her plump backside as she left.

"Well that was a steaming pile of bullshit if I ever heard one," said the older man.

"Goddammit, what did she say?" Bell waved the serving girl over and motioned her to bring them a couple of bottles.

"Senor Vargas is the town spook, far as I can tell," offered Brent. "He supposedly founded this little shithole town way back when. S'posedly he was with the Spaniards when they came over and explored Mexico and killed all the Indians an' took their gold. The Spaniards didn't like ol' Vargas much, as he was interested in all kinds of legends and books and such that weren't Christian. Said he was a *brujo*, a witch. So the Spaniards left him here and he settled this village and brought in other folks, not all of 'em witches, but just normal folks.

"Supposedly when he died nobody knew what happened to his body: he ain't got no grave that anybody knows of..."

"And here comes the bullshit part" said Garvey, grinning. Brent ignored him and kept on.

"So anyway, for years and years now—hundreds of years, supposedly—people o' this village still see old Vargas around." Brent paused thoughtfully. "Though come to think of it how they know it's the same guy I don't know..."

"Cuz it's bullshit?" offered Garvey.

"Anyway, Vargas, or whoever this guy is, is supposed to be this hundreds of years old ghost or spirit or whatever. He never seems to hurt anybody, but that gal there says every once in awhile somebody in the village disappears, and they reckon it's this Vargas, snatching people and sacrificing 'em to the Devil, or eating them, or whatever."

"Bullshit."

"I'm just sayin' what she said, Shep. Don't mean I believe it."

Bell drank, deep in tought. "I still don't get it, Don. There was three of 'em. If one of 'em was this Vargas, then who were the other two?"

"I dunno. I ain't even sayin' that was Vargas you saw. I'm just tellin' ya what she told me. I kinda think this Vargas fella is a story these Mexes tell to scare each other, get their kids ta behave and so forth."

"Or to get stupid gringos to buy drinks for their ugly drunk whores." Garvey laughed, claiming one of the bottles of tequila for his own, and not even bothering with his mug anymore.

"Very funny, Shep. I'm tellin' ya, them Mexes was carryin' a dead body with 'em."

"Maybe so," said Brent, pouring himself a mugful. "But maybe not. Maybe those hombres you saw were having a bit of fun with one of their dead kin. Did the dead guy move at all?"

Bell thought a second. "I think so, but I ain't sure. It was dark, and I really couldn't see that good."

"Maybe he was sick. If he looked as bad as you thought, he might have even been a leper."

"A *what?*" spat Garvey.

"A leper. You know what I'm talkin' about. That disease makes your flesh rot and pieces fall off of ya. But those other guys were taking a big risk touching the sick one if he was a leper. That shit's contagious as hell."

"Bullshit," spat Garvey, rising to his feet. He swayed drunkenly, grinning. "Gotta take a leak, boys. Save my seat." His companions watched him weave through the crowd of tables toward the back door.

Garvey eventually reappeared, and the three resumed drinking and talking. The discussion of the spectre Bell had seen, and Senor Vargas, faded quickly from their minds. The drink flowed freely, and the *americanos'* attitudes brightened as they grew drunker. Brent drifted away to dance with a young barmaid, while Garvey and Bell started singing Stephen Foster songs to drown out the mariachi tunes sung by the Mexicans. It didn't take long for the Americans to start wordlessly warbling along with the mariachis, and vice versa. Brent soon disappeared with the little serving girl, and the other two continued to drink themselves near blind.

At last Garvey and Bell staggered off to bed, arm in arm to support each other, though Bell did most of the carrying. Garvey was all but passed out, and Bell was dragging him and the saddlebags to their room in the back of the posada. Bell kicked open the door, threw the bags into a corner, and lugged Garvey over and dropped him onto a pallet on the floor.

"Whoops!" he snickered. "Sorry Shep."

He arranged the older man so that he was more centered on the pallet, then staggered back to survey his handiwork.

"There ya go, old man. Try not t' snore so goddamn loud t'night."

Bell sat down on the bench to take off his boots, then decided he would go outside for a piss and a cigarette before turning in. He put the saddlebags under Garvey's limp arms so that if anyone did come in they'd at least have to pull him off of them. Bell hoped he wouldn't be gone long enough for anything to happen in any case.

The young American swayed down the narrow hallway at the back of the posada. The handful of rooms off the hall were mostly silent: a couple of them were plagued by snorers, and from a third came the sounds of a grunting, huffing man and a low-moaning woman.

Bell cursed himself: he'd wanted to get some pussy tonight and instead he'd gotten stupid drunk. Oh well, there'd be time for that back in New Mexico soon enough.

He threw open the back door and was harshly greeted by the chilly night air. He shivered and fumbled in his shirt pocket for the cigarette he'd rolled earlier. Bell figured he'd be too drunk to make a good one when he needed it, and damn if he hadn't been right. He scratched a match alight off of a barrel stay and lit his cigarette, then weaved over to the wall and unbuttoned his trousers. With his smoke clutched between his lips, he leaned forward against the back wall of the posada as he pissed, sighing contentedly as his bladder emptied. Finished, he turned as he fumbled with the last button.

The corpse-man stood within arm's length of him.

Bell stumbled backward, the cigarette falling from his open mouth. Even as he started to yell he was reaching for his gun, drew it and aimed—except he *didn't* do any of those things. Bell wanted to—God, how he wanted to—and he thought he had moved and screamed, but instead he stood completely paralyzed before the skull-faced horror.

It was wrapped in the cloak-like garb it had been wearing when Bell had seen it earlier. It was wearing some kind of black coat and trousers, with the cloak or robe drawn up to hide its face and head, but this close there was no concealing the thing's dead face. A shock of dirty white hair was visible under the hood. The flesh was pasty white, the eyesockets dark sunken caverns with filmy eyes like translucent grub-worms at their depths. The nose was long, downturned, pointed, almost knife-like. But worst of all was the fact the lower jaw was gone, the lipless upper jaw studded with but a few teeth that jutted into open space. The flesh of the dead thing's arms and hands were the same sickly white as its face, but there were patches of skin missing, some exposing bone beneath. The corpse's fingers were almost entirely fleshless, mere bones strung together by sinew.

And Bell was paralyzed before it.

Now he noticed two other figures in the shadows behind the standing corpse. They were the skull-masked, sombrero-wearing companions he had seen earlier with the dead man. Their sombreros and masks were gone, but even in the shadows Bell could see that their flesh was pale and their bodies were too thin...

"Los otros?" one of them said. The dead man nodded, and the other two slipped into the shadows out of Bell's sight.

Bell was still frozen in place, helpless, unable to move or scream.

Senor, said the corpse-thing, though how it could speak without a full set of jaws...

El Dia De Los Muertos

Senor I welcome you to our humble village. You have come at a very special time, the day when the spirits of the dead are free to walk the Earth. Of course you know this is a childish superstition, but there is some truth to it, nonetheless. This time of year there are powers in the earth, the sky, and the stars that are stronger now than at other times. These powers are old, much older than even I am. And I am very old, my friend. I saw the last of the Aztecs exterminated, and I saw the foolish Spaniards burn their beautiful codexes with their quaint primitive depictions of truths the Catholics could not bear to see, let alone acknowledge. Aztec, Spaniard, Indian, white, I have seen them all come and go, live and die. Only my companions and I remain. And Those whose truths we acknowledge, of course. They will be here long after this world has crumbled to dust among the stars. Whether or not I will see that... Quien sabe? El Fuego Verde shall decide, not I.

Bell realized the dead man was somehow speaking directly to his mind, or something. How else could he be hearing the thing's thoughts? Or had he gone crazy, and these thoughts were somehow his own...?

You should listen, gringo. You do not have much time.

Bell felt his body moving, and found himself sitting down on the ground in the alley behind the posada. Then he was laying flat on his back, looking up at the narrow band of starlit sky visible between the surrounding adobe buildings. And then the dead man came back into view, impossibly tall, as if his bony scarecrow form reached into the stars above.

I must apologize, my friend, for what is about to happen to you. This body is old and worn out, and yours is young and strong.

Bell started to scream again—dear God, how he needed to scream!—but he couldn't. In the dim light of the alley he saw the dead man's form writhing beneath the clothes. Something poked through the flesh of its cheek, wriggling against the pale skin. More worm-like shapes pushed out of its eyes and forehead, their bodies twisting and turning and writhing. And then the worm-shapes began dropping onto Bell's body. Worse, he could feel them crawling onto him from where they had wriggled away from the dead man's legs. He could feel the worms—meal-worms, maggots, earthworms—crawling onto him, down his pants-leg into his boots, up his trouser-leg, inside his shirt, under his collar...

I'm afraid this will take some time, senor, but you will feel no pain. Still, it will not be pleasant for you...

He could feel the worms wriggling all over him. Hundreds, thousands, more. Inching, squirming, slithering, toward his nose, mouth, his eyes, his every orifice. Steve Bell screamed. And screamed and screamed—but only in his mind.

The dead man was true to his word. What happened took a very long time.

Brent and Garvey slouched outside the posada the next morning. They shaded their eyes with their hands, blocking out the bright sun. They spoke little.

They had been waiting about an hour when Steve Bell appeared up the street, dragging three horses behind him. He stopped before his companions, holding the reins of the shying horses.

"Steve?" asked Brent, his voice curiously gutteral, his smile crooked, as if he were uncertain how to do such a thing.

"No longer," answered the other.

"What now?" asked Garvey.

"We go north," said Bell, in perfect Spanish. "I think I would like to travel."

Treason and Plot
by William Meikle

I was late in reaching Cheyenne Gardens that night in early November. The whole length of the Embankment was closed all the way from Chelsea to Waterloo Bridge and the Underground system had been brought to a halt. "An Irish Plot," the *Thunderer* said, and the evidence of many policemen along the by-ways seemed to indicate that something was indeed afoot. But it was not enough to keep me from my appointment. Carnacki's card had intimated that he had a new tale to tell, and I was most eager to hear my friend's latest adventure.

On arrival I discovered that the others were there before me; they too showing a similar eagerness for a tale. As ever Carnacki kept us waiting until after dinner, but none of us complained as the meal was as usual magnificent, consisting of fine pheasant and mashed potatoes washed down with some particularly fine London Porter from the Chiswick Brewery that Carnacki favoured.

We retired to the parlour at eight-thirty and got our drinks charged and fresh smokes lit. Carnacki gave us several seconds to settle then launched straight in to his tale.

***

"My tale begins in the early hours of Sunday morning," he began. "I had spent Saturday in further examination of the deeper caves in Chislehurst and, being somewhat fatigued, had fallen into a deep sleep that I was loath to leave. But the insistent knocking on my front door would brook no argument and I was forced rudely from my bed to answer it.

"Three policemen stood on the step, which I am sure you'll agree is never a good sign, never mind at two-thirty on a Sunday morning.

"As it turned out, the policemen were nearly as clueless as I was regarding the situation at hand; they had merely been sent as emissaries from the Home Secretary. I soon discovered there was a bit of a flap on at Parliament; one that required my particular field of expertise. I was given scarcely ten minutes to do my ablutions and get dressed before I was hurried out into a carriage and off along the riverside. The driver was obviously under orders for we fair rattled across the cobbles and I felt quite shaken by the time we came to a stop outside Parliament.

"There were more policemen there. A cordon of them around a portly figure I quickly recognised as the Home Secretary. After a cursory hand-shake no time was wasted in leading me down to the bowels of the old building, deep into the sewers and tunnels to a spot that showed signs of having been there since the Medieval, and maybe even Roman era. At any other time I would have stopped to investigate the masonry, for it looked to be particularly finely tooled, but the Secretary was insistent that we keep moving, and his urgency even seeped into me so much that we proceeded at a fast walk through the warren of tunnels. I started to smell water and if my mental map was accurate I guessed we were nearing the Thames. My feeling was proved right when we came to a series of steps that descended down into the river. But that was not what I had been brought to see.

"A body lay on the ground inside a pentacle drawn in chalk, itself inside three concentric rings circled with a great many scrawled symbols. Burned-down candles sat at each point, cold now to the touch. The body had been burned beyond recognition; an amorphous mass of charred bone and ash.

"'I don't know what I can do here,' I said, kneeling beside the body.

The Secretary was staring at where the river lapped against the old stone steps, and he looked pale, almost sickly.

"'It is not the body we need you to examine,' he said. He motioned at the chalk pentacle, and the inscription drawn around its outer ring. 'I understand this is your area of expertise?'

"I did indeed recognise *some* of the symbols, but by no means all, and I could already see that it was the basis of a ritual I was unfamiliar with.

"'You wish for me to find out what he was doing?' I asked.

There was a *splash* out in the river and the Secretary started to edge away into the tunnels, dragging me with him.

"'No Mr. Carnacki,' he said, starting to walk faster. 'I need you to find out what he was doing wrong.'"

***

"Ten minutes later the Secretary had some colour back in his cheeks. It might have had something to do with the warmth of the fire, in his office two floors above the terrace in the main House. It also might have had something to do with the anger with which he berated the poor cleaning lady for cleaning his room when he needed it. I tried to placate the woman with a smile, but her scowl told me that she was not in the mood, and a curt Irish accent informing me to *Move aside sir*, showed me who was boss here. However I have a feeling that the redness in the Secretary's cheeks had more to do with the large snifter of Scotch he had downed as soon as we got up from the tunnels. And by Jove, I took to a drink of my own readily enough when he started to tell me the reason I had been summoned. As is usual with politicians, he took rather a long way round the subject.

"'What do you know about the history of the city?' he asked, chewing on the largest cigar I had ever seen. I might have replied with a display of my knowledge, but he did not give me an opportunity, merely continued straight on. 'You do of course know what date it is?' he asked, confusing me further.

"'But what you may not know,' he said. 'Is that every year at this time, for five days during and after Samhain, it has been necessary for us to appease the old god of the river lest it consumes us utterly.'

"He said it in such a matter-of-fact manner that at first I did not believe I had heard him properly, but when I pressed him, he repeated the assertion.

"'It has been going on for as long as we have been keeping records,' the Secretary said, and motioned towards a small stack of leather-bound tomes on his desk. 'The last time there was any *disruption* was back in 1605 when Guy Fawkes decided to try to stop the ceremony and let matters take their course. Since then all has been quiet… until tonight.'

"He had another chew on the cigar.

"'David Crowther had the duty for nearly twenty years with no problems, and, despite David's retirement and this being the first outing for a new man, we foresaw none last night. Young Peter Rogers went down into the tunnels at eleven-thirty. And the result is what you have so recently seen. We need you Mr. Carnacki; for if you cannot fathom what has happened then I fear that tomorrow the *Ancient One* will rise up completely from the river. And who knows what might happen then?'"

* * *

Carnacki paused to knock out his pipe and, never one to let an opportunity pass, Arkwright piped up.

"I say Carnacki, this politician chappie sounds just like you do. If I'd known they believed in spooks and ghoulies I might be a tad more keen to vote for them. I remember at the last Hustings I…"

Carnacki stopped him with a single upraised hand, and the rest of us breathed a silent sigh of relief, for we knew of old how quickly Arkwright could derail an evening if given his head. We were saved that ordeal as Carnacki went straight on with his tale.

***

"As Arkwright has pointed out, the Secretary did indeed sound like someone who was intimately familiar with my own area of *enthusiasm*. But I quickly found out that he only knew as much as he had already imparted, and that *details* were not his strong point. I requested leave to return to the tunnel, all the better to examine the pentacle drawn there, but I was refused, somewhat curtly.

"'The site has already been cleaned,' the Secretary said, almost as if he was proud of the fact. 'We cannot have anyone else discovering this particular secret. Can you imagine if it got out?'

"I believe that what I could imagine, and what he could imagine, would vary rather wildly, but I kept my mouth shut and merely asked just what I was supposed to do without the evidence from the tunnels.

"He waved towards the books on his desk.

"'The answer to all your questions is in there. And photographs were taken of the scene before you arrived. They are being developed as we speak and you shall have them anon. Now, if you'll excuse me, I must brief the P.M.'

"And with that I was left alone, with only the old books for company. I opened the office door to find two policemen standing guard and I was told in no uncertain terms that I would not be allowed to leave Parliament until the matter at hand had been resolved. Indeed, I am probably breaking several laws in merely relating this story to you chaps here tonight, such was the secrecy surrounding the facts of the case. I gave in to the inevitable and, pausing only to ask for a pot of tea to be brought, returned to the office and began my perusal of the books on the desk.

"It was not long before I had forgot about the policemen as I became transported back to a history of London I had never before been privy to; one that had purposefully been kept from the people to protect them from one simple fact. London only exists because a way was found to mollify its original inhabitant; a creature so old and so foul that the very sight of it could drive a man mad. It seemed to be a creature of paradoxes, a controller of flame that lived in the water, a vast monster that could encompass the city, yet disappear through the smallest of holes.

"The story was a long one, and its beginnings have been lost in antiquity. I will not bore you chaps with the Roman tales, nor the even older Druidic songs that came before. Suffice to say that over the centuries a means was discovered to keep the old thing in the river in check; but not before the city had burned, time and time again. It was only the stubborn refusal of the Romans to be beaten by a god that was not their own that led to the initial subduing of the river deity. It was they who started the tradition of lighting bonfires at strategic points along the river on Samhain and the days immediately following, a tradition that continues to this very day and indeed one that has grown far beyond its original intent—but I am getting ahead of myself.

"Over the centuries since its inception in Roman times the ritual has been improved and modified, yet essentially it has remained true to its primitive origins; a simple pentacle and a series of chants. In almost every case they have proved enough, if performed in the proper order on the proper dates, to keep the old thing in the river quiet.

"But not tonight. I had seen for myself the result of Mr. Rogers' attempt on the ritual. It was now my duty to ensure that such immolation did not happen again and, more than that, to ensure that the river stayed quiet for another year.

"Now before I go any further, I can see that Arkwright is full to bursting with questions, and I believe I know what these will concern. You are all no doubt anxious to know what part, if any, the Guy Fawkes story plays in my tale. It will not surprise you to learn that the passageway in which Fawkes was captured was the very one in which I had stood not an hour earlier. But the books before me on the Home Secretary's desk told a far different tale to the one all children know. And here I must plead secrecy, for the conspiracy that covered up the true story encompasses all the high ranks of society of its day, from Ministers to Archbishops, from Mayors to Monarchy. Suffice to say that Fawkes had no plan to blow up Parliament with gunpowder. No—his plan was to disrupt the ritual and to allow the ancient evil to do the job for him.

"As it turned out, Fawkes' capture allowed the government to re-instate the old system of protective bonfires on the prescribed date every year. Fawkes' act, instead of destroying Parliament as he desired, had the exact opposite effect, and has ensured the integrity of the House down to this very day.

"Until now. For if I could not discover what had gone wrong with the ritual then the *Old One* would rise up from the river. The older books were quite clear on what could be expected. One particular woodcarving stays in my memory. It was done sometime in the Norman era and shows a bridge over the river near Westminster. *Something* is crawling up out of the water, something amorphous and almost slug-like. Flames belch from several mouth-like orifices, and everything the beast has touched is charred and black.

"By the time I had finished with the books thin sunlight washed in through the window behind me. A young policeman arrived bearing a breakfast tray and a sealed envelope addressed to myself. I allowed myself a helping of tea and toast, and a most welcome pipe of tobacco, before broaching the envelope. As I had been promised, it was the photographs of the scene of the botched ritual. The photographer had done a dashed fine job of it, and all the symbols on the pentacle had been fully documented.

"Unfortunately for me, they also looked to be exactly as I would have expected. There was no sign of what might have caused the ritual to go so badly wrong."

***

Carnacki stopped and rose from his chair. We all knew from long acquaintance that this was a signal for a natural breaking point in the tale and a chance for us to refill our glasses and arrange fresh smokes.

Carnacki had also been right about Arkwright. Our old friend was close to bursting with questions.

"I'm jolly confused old man," he said, corralling Carnacki at the drinks' cabinet. "Are you saying that Fawkes wasn't a cad after all? Or is he still a cad, just a different sort?"

Carnacki laughed.

"Let us just say that he tried to dabble in the Outer Realms and, like other dabblers before him, got his just desserts. But we should not even be discussing such matters," he said. "I was informed most forcibly by the Home Secretary that should I disclose any part of Fawkes' tale then I, and any one that I told, could be tried for treason. I believe they still hang you for that, and I am rather fond of my neck thank you very much."

All the blood fled from Arkwright's face and he looked so stricken that only a friendly pat on the shoulder from Carnacki placated him.

"Come old friend," Carnacki said. "The rest of the tale is not a matter of national security as far as I know. You can listen to it without fear of the noose."

If any of us noticed that Arkwright poured himself a larger snifter than was usual, none of us spoke of it. Several minutes later we were once again settled in our chairs waiting for Carnacki to continue.

***

"As you chaps can see, I was now on somewhat of a sticky wicket for I had nothing to report when the Home Secretary looked in on me later that morning. I had spent hours poring over the photographs but still could see no sign of anything that might have caused the ritual to go wrong. I could only think that the poor chap who died had made an error in part of the accompanying chant. Judging by the transcript of the ritual I had found in the books, it was a fairly straightforward, if a tad dull, affair and difficult to get wrong if you had your wits about you.

"Indeed, my study of the ins and outs of the ritual had decided me on a course of action, and when the Secretary started to berate me for my perceived uselessness, I put my plan to him.

"I intended to carry out the ritual myself, to stand and face the thing in the river and determine what manner of thing it might be. The Secretary accepted my offer without hesitation, but would not allow me to leave the House to fetch my defences. Instead he sent two policeman on the errand and, while we were waiting on their return, treated me to a rather splendid lunch in the Member's restaurant. In the course of the meal he regaled me with tales of his adventures as a newspaper correspondent during the Boer War. I in turn told him of some of my own escapades. I was rather taken aback to find that he knew already about almost every case I have undertaken these past three years.

"He tapped at the side of his nose as he puffed on another huge cigar.

"'It's not who you know, it's what you know,' he said, and laughed so infectiously that I could do nothing else but join him. And so it was that I was in rather a splendid mood by the time my kit arrived and I was led once more down into the tunnels.

"The pleasant feeling lasted only as long as it took to reach the river. Once we were back on that cold shelf above the steps I felt a chill seep into me, one that threatened to sink deep into my bones. I warmed myself by setting up the pentacle for the coming night.

"I will not bore you with the details of the ritual; you have heard enough of my tales to know the basics of the protections involved in such matters. The main difference from my own system was that the pentacle I was about to employ had not come from the Sigsand MSS. That in itself gave me pause, for I did not have the luxury of familiarity that I normally have on these occasions. The policemen had brought my electric pentacle with them from my lodgings but I decided against its use at this time, preferring to stick with the ritual exactly as described in the book. I took extra time and care over the preparations, all the time aware that the damp chill was getting ever more intense. By the time I felt ready and stepped into the pentacle it was late evening. Any daylight that seeped through from beyond the steps into the river dimmed and faded and only a small oil lamp kept the growing darkness at bay.

"The last remaining policeman decided not to wait with me and I was left alone in that damp chamber. As I waited I ran the chant through in my mind, over and over until I was sure that I would be able to reproduce it exactly as it was written in the old book. What with that, and the smoking of a pipe, I achieved a certain degree of relaxation as the evening turned to night.

"As you chaps know, I have stood in some dashed tight spots in my time, but something about this one had me in a blue funk. My knees almost gave up on me and I felt that fine luncheon roil and bubble in my belly. Something *splashed* out of sight at the foot of the steps, just where they met the river, and that was almost it for me, but I'm glad to say I stood my ground, although my teeth clenched on the old briar pipe so much that I found grooves there later.

"I started the chant as transposed in the old book.

"*Servo mihi per totus vestri vires. Thrice inter orbis, reus subsido totus, malum nessum.*

"Now your Latin, like mine is probably a mite rusty, but it all sounded right and proper to me as I shouted it out. However it was having little effect on the *thing* that pulled itself up out of river. I saw the shadows it cast before I saw the thing itself. The walls of the tunnel took on a flickering orange glow as if afire.

"*Servo mihi per totus vestri vires. Thrice inter orbis, reus subsido totus, malum nessum.*

I called out again, with more urgency this time as a pale foetid thing slumped up over the step to lie directly in front of me. It looked remarkably like a bloated earthworm, but one cast entirely of flame. I had seen its image before; back in the woodcut in the quiet office I was now regretting ever having left. It reared up above me until what I took to be its head scraped against the ceiling of the tunnel, leaving a black charred scar to mark its passing. I could do naught but trust the ritual and repeat the chant.

"*Servo mihi per totus vestri vires. Thrice inter orbis, reus subsido totus, malum nessum.*

Something felt *off* with the chant; it did not carry any *resonance*, any sense of *command* that I might have expected.

The thing obviously felt the same way. It kept coming. The skin at my cheeks started to tighten as the heat grew almost unbearable. Round about then I regretted not having employed the electric pentacle, for the worm was already encroaching on the chalk defences on the floor, crawling over the outermost circle and making for me with some speed. I stepped back just in time to avoid being burned to a crisp and did the first thing that came to mind. I called out a banishing spell, one that had proved efficacious in other tight spots.

"*Ri linn dioladh na beatha, Ri linn bruchdadh na falluis, Ri linn iobar na creadha, Ri linn dortadh na fala.*

"*Damnú ort!*

The thing backed away, slithering down to the water and departing with a *hiss* of steam. I slumped, exhausted, against the too-hot wall of the tunnel and surveyed the smudged marks that were all that remained of my protective circle. Like Mr. Rogers before me, I had not succeeded in my intent. The old one was not placated and I had a feeling that it would return even stronger; I had failed completely."

* * *

Carnacki paused again, but only long enough to knock out his pipe on the grate before continuing.

"The Home Secretary of course was not amused. He did allow me a couple of hours rest that I spent sleeping fitfully in an armchair in the Member's bar before once more putting me to work on the books. I took to it with some degree of urgency for I now knew that the beast was certain to return that very night, and stronger than before.

"Remembering just how *hollow* the chant had felt I focussed my attentions on that. At first the transcribed ritual all looked as expected, but on closer inspection with a magnifying glass it soon became apparent that the chant itself had been tampered with. The last word, *nessum*, had originally been written *ressum*. Someone with a steady hand had added a tail to the first letter thereby rendering the chant completely ineffective. It could not be a coincidence that this had happened just as a new chap had taken on the job.

"The Home Secretary was apoplectic when I told him, his face redder than ever.

"'Bloody sabotage,' he shouted. 'But by whom? Those books are kept under lock and key in this very room. Only Rogers and I had access.'

"Of course I immediately saw something that would have been beneath his notice.

"'And your cleaner? Would she have been in the room alone? Did you ever, as you did with me, take Rogers to lunch leaving the books on your desk?'

"He went pale and abruptly left the room, barking orders at the policemen outside. Meanwhile I turned my attention back to the ritual itself. I now had to ensure that I expunged the older version from my mind and that, when I chanted, the modified word did not pop unbidden into the sequence. If you wish to know how this felt, you should try reciting your multiplication tables over and over again, then change one of the results, and keep it changed in all subsequent recitations. It is not as easy as it seems. And nor did it prove so for me.

"By the time evening came round again I was no means certain that I would be able to perform the task adequately. As a precaution I had the Home Secretary ensure that bonfires were lit along the length of the embankment for I knew from my reading of the books that this method had proved efficacious in the past in keeping the beast at bay. The Secretary was somewhat preoccupied with his hunt for the *saboteur*, but promised me that my request would be carried out forthwith.

"When I reached the steps in the tunnel under the House at dusk that night I was hoping that he had been as good as his word. A deeper chill had set into the chamber and the air was full with a sense of foreboding as I quickly redrew the protective circles. And this time I also added my electric pentacle, the rainbow glow from the valves lending me a degree of calm that I had been having difficulty in reaching otherwise.

"And it seemed I finished my preparations just in time. Once again I saw red shadows flicker on the walls, and once again the bloated worm slumped its way up the steps towards me. I chanted.

"*Servo mihi per totus vestri vires. Thrice inter orbis, reus subsido totus, malum ressum.*

"The blue valve of the electric pentacle started to pulse and flare in time with my voice and the chant took on weight and resonance.

"*Servo mihi per totus vestri vires. Thrice inter orbis, reus subsido totus, malum ressum.*

"The worm quailed and faltered as I raised my voice to a shout. The green valve of the pentacle began to pulse in time. Red flame ran across the body of the worm—but it came no closer and I felt none of the heat that I had the night before.

"*Servo mihi per totus vestri vires. Thrice inter orbis, reus subsido totus, malum ressum.*

"The worm retreated back down the steps.

"Almost as soon as it had began, it seemed to be over.

"There was a certain sense of anti-climax as I related the events to the Home Secretary back in the comfort of his office. He passed me a large shot of Scotch and a cigar.

"'Good show all round,' he said, smiling. 'Crisis averted, and we caught the bally cleaner too, trying to flee the country.'

"I did not quite know how to broach the matter I had now been considering, so I came straight out with it.

"'I believe that tonight I shall be able to banish the beast completely,' I said as I lit the cigar.

"The Secretary went pale again.

"'Banish it? Whatever for? Sorry old chap, but that can't be allowed. We have the tradition to consider.'

"'Surely the *risk* outweighs the needs of tradition?' I said.

"He smiled, and I saw the predator in him for the first time.

"'But consider this Carnacki... what if an enemy ever reaches our door-step? Do you not see what a weapon we will have as a final solution?'

"And at that I was dismissed."

* * *

Carnacki sat back in his chair and we realised with some confusion that his tale was over. Arkwright, forthright as ever, was not slow in voicing his displeasure.

"I say old man, you can't stop there. That's no kind of story at all. There's no end to it."

Carnacki gave a wistful smile.

"But there is indeed an ending... of sorts." He said. "You all saw it on your way here tonight. The Home Secretary has used his cleaner's treachery to create an anti-Irish flap. That in turn has allowed him to light bonfires all along the Thames, supposedly in *celebration* of the foiling of a new plot on the anniversary of Fawkes' original. The fact that none of this is true does not seem to bother the Secretary one little bit.

"The only gratifying thing to my mind is that his actions should ensure that the fires are continued to be lit on these nights for many years to come, and that the old thing that lurks in the water will be kept quiet as long as the ritual is maintained.

"Now, out you go," he said, and herded us through to the hallway and then out onto the Embankment. As I strolled home I watched the fires burning with a renewed interest in their history and tradition.

And I kept well away from the river.

The Dreaming Dead
by Joshua Reynolds

That which is not dead is eternally annoying," Charles St. Cyprian said, rubbing red-rimmed eyes as he glared out the window. It was November of 1919 and London was awash in red. Poppies clung to every lapel, collar and hat brim walking along the Embankment outside the window of his Cheyne Walk residence, marking a newly ordained solemn occasion. St. Cyprian wore no poppy, feeling that his scars earned him freedom from convention.

The scars, earned at Ypres the year previous, traced his evolution from a callow youth to a slightly-less callow man. It had been a quick one as such things went; two bullets deep and one long. His thigh ached abominably in the damp, but he was learning to live with the physical pain, if not the spiritual. He had had much occasion to ponder on the subject of the latter recently.

He had not slept in four days, and it showed. His dark Mediterranean features were haggard and two days' worth of stubble coated his jaw. He was dressed as fashionably as always, but lack of sleep had reduced his normal sense of tidy precision to sloppy half-heartedness.

"Which means what, exactly?" someone said from behind him.

"The past has a way of shoving itself into the present with regrettable consequences," St. Cyprian said, turning from the window to face his assistant. In contrast to her employer, Ebe Gallowglass was dressed unfashionably, but neatly. Braces held up men's trousers, and a man's shirt covered her slim cinnamon coloured limbs. She bared startlingly white teeth in a smile that didn't reach her dark eyes.

"You look like hell on toast," she said.

"I was afraid to check the mirror."

"Obviously; I take it that you're still having the dreams?" she said, offering him a cup of steaming coffee.

St. Cyprian ran his fingers through his hair and grunted, "Dream, singular." He took the cup, eyed it suspiciously and then drained it with a grimace. He sniffed the empty cup. "Turkish?"

"How should I know? I made what was in the can. Want a poppy? I'm wearing two, you know," Gallowglass said, snapping her braces and causing the poppies there to wobble alarmingly. "If you were wondering, it's one for me and one for thee."

"How civic-minded of you."

"One of us has to be," she sniffed. "You really don't look good."

"Thank you. Your opinion has been noted," St. Cyprian said sourly, falling into a chair in front of the fireplace. He dug the heels of his hands into his eyes. "It's getting worse. The dream, I mean."

"I didn't figure you meant the coffee," Gallowglass said, watching him carefully. She had only been with St. Cyprian for little under a year, and while it was better by far than the Cairo slum she had grown up in, she was still getting used to her new employer's peculiarities.

He ran his fingers up across his face and through his hair. "Something's in the air."

Gallowglass grunted. "Something is always in the air. Specifics would be nice."

"We don't deal in specifics," St. Cyprian said. "We barely deal in reality."

"Loaded word, that." Gallowglass made a face. "Who says what's reality, eh?"

"Why, us, of course," St. Cyprian said, essaying a smile. And that was true, as far as it went. Formed during the reign of Elizabeth the First, the office of Royal Occultist (or the Queen's Conjurer, as it had been known) had started with the diligent amateur Dr. John Dee, and passed through a succession of hands since. The list was a depressingly long one, weaving in and out of the margins of British history, and culminating most recently in one Charles St. Cyprian—the final arbiter of the margins and vagaries, the real and the unreal. At least until one or the other swallowed him up; which, unfortunately, something looked to be doing, only a year into his tenure.

"You've never told me...you know?" Gallowglass said, making a helpless gesture. "About any of that, about what happened over there...?"

"What's to tell?" St. Cyprian said. He pulled a silver cigarette case out of his coat pocket, flipped it open and selected one. He proffered the case to Gallowglass but she shook her head. He shrugged and held up a finger. A moment later a tiny flame sprang to life on the calloused tip and he held it to the end of the cigarette. Gallowglass raised an eyebrow but said nothing. She'd seen the trick before. "Men went to war. Men died. Men I knew. Men I liked. Men I didn't. It was all the same, in the end." Puffing meditatively on his cigarette, he continued, "The dream isn't like the run-of-the-mill nightmare one expects. Not like any nightmare I've had, at any rate. Usually it's just the vague sensation of being back there, of feeling the mud beneath your hands and tasting the blood in your lungs as gas rolls down the trench line and bullets hiss overhead like angry wasps..." He trailed off, staring at nothing. He shook his head, breaking the spell. Blinking, he looked at her. "It's more vivid than it should be."

"Vivid?"

"Like mud being stirred up off a river-bottom. I have a head for details. Faces, images, sounds, smells...and my dreams are never that specific normally. But these...I can see my surroundings as clear as day, and I recognize most of the men around me. Not in the sense of knowing who they are, but recognizing them all the same..." Puffing on his cigarette, he looked around the room. The house occupied a small plot on the Embankment, and was, along with certain other items, part and parcel of the position. It was only proper; after all, the Prime Minister had Number 10, Downing Street, and thus the Royal Occultist had 472, Cheyne Walk. St. Cyprian still didn't know what half of the stuff occupying the shelves did.

"So what's causing it?"

"A better question might be...who else is it affecting?" He snuck a glance down at his hand and the three strange steel rings that adorned his fingers. Each ring was inscribed with a series of characters that might have been Cyrillic or Hebrew or something else entirely. Like the house, they came with the office, their purpose lost to time. A brief memory rose and the old familiar burn of bile with it, of Carnacki, cut to shreds by artillery, shoving the rings to him through the mud of the street, his pale face going slack. He shook his head.

"How the hell do we figure that out?" Gallowglass said.

"I think we need to pay a visit to Bethnal Green." He rose to his feet abruptly. He looked at Gallowglass. "Feel up for a drive?"

"Let me just get my gun," she said, hopping to her feet.

They made the journey in a black Crossley 20hp with a well-stocked boot. Unlike the house and the rings and the statue behind the umbrella stand that cursed quietly in Aramaic, the Crossley was St. Cyprian's. The engine hummed as St. Cyprian put it into gear and took them out of Chelsea and towards St. Pauls.

"So why Bethnal Green particularly?"

"Why not Bethnal Green?" St. Cyprian said. He squeezed the horn and zipped around an oncoming bus. "*Blitha Healh*...'Happy Angle' or 'Blitha's Angle' or, more commonly, Bethnal. Edwin Drood—my predecessor's predecessor—wrote that it was one of London's 'sour tendons' and that it was better that no one knew the truth behind the Tudor ballad 'The Blind Beggar of Bethnal Green' or the whole neighbourhood would be abandoned to the rats within a fortnight."

"What's so bad about 'The Blind Beggar'? Other than it being truly awful, I mean?" Gallowglass said, grabbing the dashboard.

"He didn't go into detail, I'm not sorry to say." St. Cyprian looked up at the cloudy sky and frowned. His head itched, and had since he'd woken up. "To answer your earlier question however...Sergeant Robert Ogden is why we're going to Bethnal Green."

"Who?"

"A...friend, I suppose." He glanced at her and twisted the wheel to avoid a cab moving too slowly.

"You suppose?"

"Are you going to keep saying everything I've just said back to me? Yes, I suppose he was a friend, of sorts."

"I don't like that 'was'. Was implies he's not now. If he's not your friend now—"

"Well he's not my enemy, if that's what you're worried about."

"Are you sure about that?" She jerked her chin towards obvious shape of the Webley Bulldog revolver nestled in his coat pocket. He didn't carry a gun habitually, only carting the heavy little pistol around when he expected trouble. St. Cyprian didn't bother answering. Before long they were in the East End, and Bethnal Green Infirmary rose like a grim patch, with Whitechapel gloom stuck to the bricks like permanent shadows. It was a gothic toad of brick and bar, and that its purpose was healing took away little of the menace inherent in its facade.

"Never thought much of this place for a hospital," Gallowglass muttered, fingers tapping nervously against the butt of the Webley-Fosberry holstered beneath her arm. "How do you know this Ogden character is here?"

"He will be," St. Cyprian said, pulling the Crossley against the curb. "After all, he's the one who asked me to come."

The infirmary wasn't so much busy as crowded. Even two years after the war's end there were still more men than beds. St. Cyprian walked as if he knew where he was going and led them through the halls at a brisk pace until they came to a quiet ward. Men lay on beds or sat on chairs, speaking quietly amongst themselves. As the duo entered, however, all conversation ceased. Each of the men looked as battered as St. Cyprian, with pale faces and dark circles to attest to their lack of sleep. As one, those that could, stood and saluted, albeit half-heartedly.

St. Cyprian looked at them blankly, each face easily recognizable for all that he did not know them. Phantom faces that floated to the surface of the miasma of his nightmares. "Kemmelberg," he said suddenly.

"See lads? I told you old Charley would find his way here before too long." The speaker looked as haggard as St. Cyprian felt; his expression of weary satisfaction was offset by the pinned-up sleeve of his coat and the limp way his legs were thrown up onto a bed. In his good hand, he held a pocket-watch. As they turned to him, he snapped it shut with a sniff. "Four days Charley? Captain Carnacki—God bless and keep him—would have been here in two at the latest." He let the chair he was sitting in thump down and stood, saluting.

"At ease Sergeant,' St. Cyprian said. 'I'm not an officer these days."

"Once an officer, always an officer, sir, if you don't mind me saying," Ogden said, dropping his salute. He smiled crookedly. "More is the pity." His eyes slid sideways, towards Gallowglass. "Who's this then?"

"Ebe Gallowglass, say hello to Bobby Ogden, who left his arm at Kemmelberg and his heart in—where was it, Bobby?" St. Cyprian said.

"Charleroi, if you must know," Ogden said, his parade ground stance drifting into something altogether more relaxed. "You look like hell, if you don't mind me saying Charlie."

"I do mind, actually."

"You still look like hell." Dextrously, Ogden retrieved a loose cigarette out of his coat pocket and stuffed it into his mouth. "Gimme a light, Cap'n, if you please."

St. Cyprian snapped his fingers and a tiny plume of flame blossomed. Ogden accepted the light with a grin. "Love that trick, me," he said, winking at Gallowglass, who rolled her eyes. Ogden's own snapped back to St. Cyprian. "Glad you deigned to show up Charley."

"I'm a busy man, Bobby," St. Cyprian said, pre-emptively stifling Gallowglass' snort with a quick glare.

Ogden nodded. "I heard you had taken over the job. It's why I'm here, actually," he said. "Sorry to hear about Tommy, no two ways there." Both men fell silent. Gallowglass cleared her throat.

"How do you two know each other then, if I might ask?" she said, glaring at her employer. He grinned sheepishly.

"Bobby was—ah—invaluable in certain matters of a sensitive nature."

"Vampire," Ogden said matter-of-factly. "Vampires, really. Whole nest of the buggers under Saint Martin's Church. Tommy—Captain Carnacki—had my whole squad on pest control." He frowned and blew smoke from his nostrils. "Pretty sort of church though, for all that."

"You've never told me that story," Gallowglass said, looking at St. Cyprian, her eyes glinting with interest.

"I haven't told you a lot of stories," he said.

Ogden grinned. "Have you told her about that lass in Luxembourg with the teeth in her—" he began, but St. Cyprian cut him off.

"No. And neither should you. Been having any odd dreams, Bobby?" He looked around the room, at the other men. "How about the rest of you?"

Ogden frowned and he answered for everyone as he fiddled with his cigarette. "You been having them as well then, I expect."

"Yes. Bad memories, and far too vivid. I assume that they're why you called me?"

"If it was just me...no." Ogden blew a plume of smoke into the air. "But it ain't just me, now is it?" He gestured with his good arm. A murmur swept the room and St. Cyprian frowned. Ogden cocked his head. "Almost every man jack in the place has been having nightmares, waking dreams, hallucinations—whatever you want to call 'em. I did some digging on my own, out of curiosity, like."

"And?" St. Cyprian said.

"You tell me, Charley. You're the high muckety-muck now...let's see if Tommy taught you anything," Ogden said. Gallowglass looked back and forth between them.

"I sense yet another story I was never told," she said.

"Nothing to it really," Ogden said. "Just testing the waters. Captain Carnacki was a good man; what he didn't know, you couldn't learn. But Charley here barely knew his pentacles from his pentagrams last I saw him."

"He still doesn't," Gallowglass said.

"That's a bit harsh, I should think," St. Cyprian said. "I know one of them has five points. That's something." He cleared his throat. "Your dreams, if they are dreams, have two common elements...the fourth battle of Ypres, specifically that little village on the Kemmelberg, and the men involved in that battle." He looked around the room. "These men, specifically. The men of the 19th Western Division."

Silence fell. After a moment, Ogden nodded slowly, a halo of smoke surrounding his head. "And you Charley...don't forget yourself then."

"No." He cleared his throat. "I've done some digging of my own. In the past year and a half, since Ypres, men of the Western Division have continued to die. Of wounds mostly, but also exhaustion and in two cases, of no discernable causes."

"So?" Ogden said.

"So what if our dreams aren't simply dreams?" St. Cyprian said. "And what if, as men die, the dreams of the rest of us got stronger? Until now it's our turn..."

"For what?"

"I don't know," St. Cyprian said.

Gallowglass looked at him. "You've got that look."

"What look?"

"The look that says there's more to it," she said. "What are you thinking?"

"I—" St. Cyprian hesitated. He shook his head. The itch was back, but worse now than it had been. It was like something was caught in his scalp and it burned. Hands clenched, he fought to release the sudden tension that had filled him. He looked at Ogden, whose face was equally pinched.

St. Cyprian looked around. The other men in the room had similar expressions. One or two were rubbing their heads as well. He spun and motioned to Gallowglass. "Get the equipment...that electric dream-catcher of Carnacki's and the Pentacle as well. And some incense and the collapsible brazier."

"And what'll you be doing while I'm playing porter?"

"Clearing my thoughts." He smiled at her. "Besides, you are my assistant, after all. It's your job to play porter."

"Clearing your thoughts hunh? Shouldn't take long," she groused, stalking out of the ward.

"I like her," Ogden said.

"Of course you do." St. Cyprian turned in place, taking in the ward. Gray light dripped through the windows and crawled across the floor. It was a grim sort of place, which he supposed was only appropriate. He turned back to Ogden. "How much do you remember? About that last day, I mean?"

"It was a bad one, I recall that. Artillery, gas, the lot. Jerry wanted that spot and badly. When Froggy took over, I thought we were well out of it. Then, I had lost my balance," Ogden said, indicating his empty sleeve. "Nothing special about it really; it was just one more stupid stand in a series, yeah?"

"Yeah," St. Cyprian said, his eyes narrowing. "Or maybe no. There was something more to it..."

"But you don't know what?"

"That's why I'm here," St. Cyprian said. Gallowglass returned then, bearing a generator and a number of vacuum tubes, each of which was dyed a different colour. As St. Cyprian began to set the device up, Ogden watched him.

"Haven't seen that thing in a while," he said.

"It still works, if that's what you're implying," St. Cyprian said. He sat back on his haunches and looked around the room. "How many men are here, would you say?"

"There's Styles, Marsh, Bettingford..." Ogden rattled off a dozen names, pointing at the men in question.

"Fourteen of us in all," St. Cyprian said, raising a hand. "It'll have to do. We'll need to pull the cots into a circle around the pentacle far enough in that they're all within the protective circle." As the men did that, albeit awkwardly in some cases, St. Cyprian began setting up a series of collapsible braziers. In each brazier, he doled out a tiny pile of incense from a leather bag.

"What are you planning Charley?" Ogden said.

"Simple. I'm going to see exactly what it is that our dreams have been trying to tell us. The incense will aid your lot in falling asleep. The circle will protect us from anything waiting for that, and I'll get to the bottom of things."

"And how do you plan on doing that, exactly?"

St. Cyprian didn't reply. Once the cots had been moved, he directed the men to lay on them, including Ogden. He turned to Gallowglass. "Watch the door. Keep everyone out until we're done."

She patted the pistol hanging beneath her arm and gave him a worried smile. "No worries. Be safe, hey?"

"Always. Besides, I have insurance," he said, tapping his pocket and the pistol there. "I cut the Signs of the Saaamaaa Ritual into the bullets, which is enough to put the wind up anything." He hesitated. "But if I should look to be in trouble—if any of us look to be in trouble—turn on the pentacle. That should be enough to cut whatever it is off at the proverbial knees."

He situated himself within the center of the pentacle, surrounded by a halo of steel cots, the generator of the pentacle at his feet. He sat comfortably, legs crossed and hands spread. He cleared his mind with a precision born of practice and let the hazy, half-dreaming state settle on him like a blanket. The smell emanating from the braziers helped, and the world went sluggish at the edges.

Slowly, he pulled his jack-knife from his trouser's pocket and flipped it open. Then, he let the blade drift across his palm. In the *Sigsand Manuscript*, it said that blood was a certain attractor. Just what he was hoping to attract, he couldn't say however. Half-retrieved memories danced at the edges of his consciousness.

It was a simple enough plan. If there were answers to be found in the dream, then in the dream he would have to go. The shape of the pentacle would help him focus and to experience the dream outside of the dream, just as the blood would encourage the cause to show itself, at least theoretically. It would also open him up to attack. Carnacki had taught him the art of unconscious delving early on in their acquaintance, though it wasn't something to be undertaken lightly. The natural defences of the human mind grew thin and weak in the places between sleeping and waking, and spilling blood was sometimes akin to tossing a rope and a lantern down to the beast in the dark. Carnacki had almost been killed by the things that used focused dreams as entrances into the waking world, and while St. Cyprian had yet to face one of the Outer Monstrosities, he was in no rush to do so.

He sat in a state of half-sleep for what felt like hours until the pain in his palm had faded and he heard the distant hum of the past drawing closer. When his eyes opened, he could hear the rattle of a water-cooled machine gun as it filled the air with death. They were still in the room, but not, as the walls faded and returned like persistent hallucinations. The floor became mud, then stone, then wood. The men rose as one from their beds, but remained lying all the same. Ghostly echoes of the men they had been, whole and undamaged, carrying weapons of equal weightlessness. St. Cyprian looked around, recognizing the village of Kemmel on the hill's northern slope. It appeared as it had then, but also as it had been in ages past, as a Frankish pile under siege by implacable Roman expansion. Modern houses burned to wattle huts and dissolved into ectoplasmic smoke, becoming the walls of Bethnal Green Infirmary once more.

The ground seemed to rumble beneath his feet and he looked around slowly. The ground went vague, and he saw what might have been tunnels stretching away into an infinite blackness. He heard men screaming and smelled the acrid tang of blood and gunpowder. Artillery ripped furrows in the ground and he remembered that the Germans had seemed more intent on obliterating the village than taking it. Looking around, he saw gaps in the line. Missing men, left dead on the field the first time and thus were not here for the second go-round. He heard a voice, vaguely familiar, behind him.

"Up and at them lads," someone barked. St. Cyprian pushed through the marching forms of the men of the Bethnal Green Infirmary, moving back towards that voice, despite the tugging sensation that threatened to pull him in the opposite direction. He broke through, pushing past someone he thought might have been Ogden to grab for an extended arm, clad in the sleeve of an officer's great coat. Bullets chopped into the lines and he saw a man stumble and fall, clutching his chest. He jerked the arm's owner around.

Eyes without a face bored into his own and he recoiled instinctively from what he saw within them. "Fight is to the fore, laddie," the voice said, wavering from youthful timbre to a rusty rasp, as if the speaker weren't sure how a man should sound. "The enemy is that way." Inhumanly strong hands—were they hands?—seized him and tried to force him around, but he resisted, trying to see the face past those burning eyes that weren't eyes. Desperately, St. Cyprian reached for the blurred features with his wounded hand and his bloody fingers plunged into a cold wetness. When he ripped it away, the memory went with it and he saw the world as it was. Looking around wildly, he saw cancerous tendrils of globular blackness rising from the skull of each sleeping man in the circle. A burst of pain told him that he was not spared that deformity and, frenzied, he grabbed at the tendril extruding from the top of his head. It burned with slick acidity and he screamed as the flesh on his palms sizzled.

His memories crashed and rattled in his head like shards of broken glass. He felt the bullets entering his flesh again, the shock of their passage causing his body to whipsaw. He saw Carnacki fall again and saw the explosion that tore Ogden's arm off, even though he hadn't been a witness to the latter. Every memory of that war spun like a cyclone in his head.

His wrists were seized and wrenched away from his head. The eyes seemed to boil in their sockets as they glared at him. Frantic now, St. Cyprian struggled with his captor. The face was first that of a young man, and then an older one. It had Carnacki's face, and Ogden's and his as well. Something seized his throat and he found himself yanked upwards, as if his attacker were trying to choke him into submission. His eyes rolled back in his head and his dimming sight was drawn upwards, towards the true face of his captor.

Something horrible peered through a crack in the ward ceiling. The tendrils sprang from it in no appreciable order or arrangement, and its form seemed to be hidden behind blind-spots that crawled across the surface of his eyes. It shifted and scuttled, moving first like a slug and then like a spider and it seemed to swell behind its concealment as he watched. He caught a sickly-sweet whiff of battlefield stink. Clawing at the tendrils that held him, heedless of the pain, he caught the tattered edges of other memories, older than the Kemmelberg he had visited. He felt an iron spear pierce his side and tasted blood as a stone axe chopped into his shoulder.

Kemmelberg had been the scene of war for far longer than just the current century. It had been fought over for centuries without end, and this thing had supped on every moment, battening on every death-memory. Who could say why it had chosen to follow them here, rather than the Germans or the French. Maybe it had. Maybe like some abominable insect, it laid its eggs in the festering, wounded psyches of those who had fought there, and they, all unawares, carried the newborn nightmare home. Had something similar fed on the agonies of the Coliseum in Rome? Or followed Napoleon's armies on the march, eating the death-dreams of his soldiers?

It had grown hungrier lately, he knew and he wondered whether it was because of the holiday, when men's thoughts would turn more towards the war and the suffering that came with it, thus arousing the beast's appetite. Or maybe it was simply a cruel cosmic joke that this latest feeding frenzy had fallen afoul of the newly-named Remembrance Day.

Teeth without a mouth clashed together close to him. It rifled through his thoughts with brutal efficiency. Blindly, he reached for his pistol. Ripping it out of his pocket, he fired upwards. The tendrils tightened and the hungry cancer-shape sped towards him across the ceiling, moving on innumerable legs that clicked and splashed. A thrill of weak triumph filled him...he had hurt it, if only temporarily. He fired at it again and again, and its shrill, child-like cries filled his ears. It shuddered and squirmed and a foul liquid spilled across him, burning him worse than the tendrils. It's grip slackened and the bright black sheen of it grew dull.

In what he hoped was a dying frenzy, a face out of nightmare pierced the veil of blind-spots and shoved towards him, teeth clicking in ways no mortal creature's mouth could. Eyes like dollops of molten metal glared at him, full of animal pain. He took aim with a trembling hand and fired three more times, until the cylinder spun empty and the eyes had gone out like snuffed candles.

Then, like the sigh of God, there was a white flash and then he was falling to the hard floor with painful alacrity, the creature's fading screams still echoing in his head. The pentacle's generator sparked and popped, smoke rising from it as it growled to full power. Gallowglass stood over it, gaping at him. "Are you okay?"

"No," he rasped, rubbing his throat and rolling over onto his stomach. He pushed himself to his feet. "I was right. I hate it when I'm right," he said. He looked around the humming circle and then upwards, where bullet-holes pockmarked the ceiling. A strange stain was growing there, like rising damp. His eyes narrowed. Was it—

Something stung him across the back and he fell, an impossibly heavy weight clinging to him. Striations of fire bit into his limbs and he heard a satanic chitter in his ear. Then he heard Gallowglass curse virulently and her Webley cracked like thunder.

The weight was punched off of him and he toppled forward as whatever it was crashed into the edge of the pentacle's crackling current. It shrieked like a cat caught under the wheels of a car and then went silent as the three closest vacuum tubes burst, leaving the room smelling of burnt wire and an open grave.

"Is it—what was it?" Gallowglass said hoarsely, her eyes wide.

"Hungry. I think we gave it a belly-full though." She helped him to a chair and he continued, "It wasn't mature, whatever it was. Barely more than an infant, for which we can thank our lucky stars." He stared at the shattered tubes. There was nothing left of the thing but black stains on the floor.

Ogden was awake now and he as well as several others were leaning over the cot of one of the men—Styles, St. Cyprian thought. Ogden looked at him, his face drawn and frightened. "He's dead," he said. "Like his heart just—just stopped. What happened Charley?"

St. Cyprian stared at the stain and didn't answer.

Later, as he sat with Ogden and Gallowglass in a corner of the ward, inhaling a mug of steaming tea, he clarified. "It was a church," he said finally. "No. Not a church, a temple." He glanced at Ogden. Nurses swept in and out of the ward, seeing to their patients. They had removed Styles earlier. Luckily the ward was on the top floor and his shots hadn't perforated any innocent bystanders. "That was why the town was of strategic import, I think. There was a temple there. Carnacki didn't explain—he didn't have time, before—well. There were dozens—hundreds, even—of such places scattered all over Belgium and France. That was one of the reasons Carnacki was encouraged to take the shilling. Couldn't let Jerry get his hands on anything of occult import, could we? And once I was seconded to him, they became my focus as well. Areas of 'unpleasant attention' as he termed them. I never found out what that meant...I can guess, of course, but I never thought about it too much. It was destroyed in the artillery barrage on the third day. I thought that whatever we had been sent to deal with was destroyed along with it."

"But it wasn't," Ogden said, gingerly rubbing his scalp. St. Cyprian watched him, a faint sensation of revulsion sweeping through him. He resisted the urge to touch his own head and hoped that the entity hadn't left any eggs of its own behind.

"No. No, it seems to have come home with us," he said. He could hear the King's voice echoing out of the wireless somewhere, but distance muted the words into an unintelligible murmur. He looked around the ward at the wounded men, their bodies and their minds victimized by war even as his own had been. "Like so many things," he said, softly.

Entrée
by Donald R. Burleson

A flotilla of low black clouds drifted from in front of the moon in time to spread a wan wash of light over the grave just as Ned Crawford scraped the rest of the dirt off the coffin with his shovel and began to pry open the lid.

The exhalation from within would have made most people swoon, but Ned was not new to the miasma of rotting flesh. This activity was a regular nocturnal partaking, for him. He had long since perfected the art of covering up his indulgences to avoid being found out, and he had been doing this for years. There were laws against grave robbing and necrophagy, but these were wearisomely mundane laws, the naive scribblings of mere mortals. Ned obeyed higher laws.

With eagerness now, he partly lifted the corpse out of the coffin and propped it against the adjacent wall of dirt, the lower rim of the hole he had dug. The remains were perfect, precisely the right putrefaction, and he licked his lips in anticipation and thought of the Book.

It had belonged to his great-grandfather. Ned had been only nine when Grandpa had first read to him from the Book in the library of the old homestead back in Providence, Rhode Island, but he remembered, to this day, some of what he had heard.

"The power of the Old Ones," Grandpa's gruff voice had intoned, "shall dwell in those of faith. Great were They before the dawn of time, and great shall They be forever."

Ned had never wholly understood who the Old Ones were, but the Book had an aura of dizzying antiquity and authority, whatever its origins. Its massive cover was too worn to bear a title, and Grandpa only called it the Book, handling it with a dark reverence as pronounced as that with which some would have handled a rare edition of the Bible, but having in Grandpa's case nothing to do with any conventional religious sentiments.

Ned peeled remnants of clothing from the corpse and scooped up a handful of purulent flesh. It had a clabbered, chunky quality that he knew well, and he swallowed it with a thrill of delight.

"The Old Ones favor those who take the essence of mortals into themselves," Grandpa had recited, turning the hoary pages with the studied care of a librarian. "Let him who tastes the flesh know that power flows body to body, and a man, though one, may be many." After Grandpa had died, the Book was purchased from the estate by a wealthy collector of rare volumes, and Ned never saw it again. Nevertheless, recalling what he had learned, he had opened his first grave when he was seventeen, had first understood how rewarding life could be—had first eaten the dead.

Now he pulled aside more flimsy cloth and uprooted whole gobbets of wormy meat, eating slowing, leisurely, savoring the sensations, the texture, the flavor. How quaint, he reflected, that this was one of the world's great taboos, yet he felt no compunction about nourishing himself in this special way. The Book had been right—the Old Ones had spoken a timeless and immutable truth. "Power flows body to body," they had said, and he could feel it. Slipping a moldy shoe and a tattered sock off the corpse's foot, he sought out the delicacy he knew was waiting for him there, a cheesy sort of jelly; when he had been a child they had called this stuff "toe jam" (a term piquantly suggestive of edibility), but he had never dreamed, back then, how delectable a nectar it could be, at the proper stage of decay. He could hardly wait to go for the other foot.

At length the clouds wandered back across the bony face of the moon, and darkness enveloped the scene like the dropping of a velvet curtain on a drama played out. Ned, thoroughly satiated, eased the body back into the casket, closed the lid with a hollow thunk, climbed out of the hole, and began shoveling it back in, thinking all the while about what sort of evening it had been.

Thoroughly satisfactory, actually. How rich in opportunities for aesthetics these occasions were, at least when they went as well as they had gone tonight. Sometimes little things went wrong, somewhat spoiling the effect—a bit of bad timing, the light not quite perfect, a sudden access of some jarring sound like a barking dog—but tonight all had gone splendidly. It was like a flawlessly satisfying evening's visit to an art museum or a concert hall, a taste of the good life.

Finally finishing his task, he glanced about him at the rows of venerable gravestones, the somber trees, the mid-November sky that so resembled a shroud admitting a pale intimation of concealed moonlight just showing through, the stirrings of the wind breathing an eerie flute-song through the bushes. He shouldered his shovel and made for home, profoundly content.

The cemetery lay at the end of a long and lonely road winding through several miles of untenanted land, with no houses or buildings within sight of it and no one to see him coming or going. His walk home always gave him ample time to ponder how fortunate, indeed how privileged, he really was.

Back cozily ensconced in his den, stretched out in a comfortable armchair under a cone of warm lamplight, he put on a recording of Mozart's "Linz" Symphony in C Major, poured himself a glass of Lambrusco, and relaxed.

While he was sipping his wine he looked at the glass in his hand and wondered if perhaps he might have taken the wine with him on his visit to the graveyard. This sort of thing had occurred to him on a few occasions before, and again he thought it might have been good to have the wine along with the meaty morsels he had tasted. Then again, the wine was a pleasant way to follow up the whole experience, an after-taste of comfort, so maybe he was taking his sensual pleasures in their proper time and place after all. Still, the idea did stir some vague notion in the back of his mind, something to which he thought he might return later. For now, the elegant strains of Mozart kept the idea, whatever it was, subdued.

The next day in the office at the insurance company, he worked with his usual unobtrusive efficiency. Sometimes he wondered whether his coworkers thought his quiet smiles a bit enigmatic, though if they did they gave no evidence of it. They probably concluded that it was just his manner, being pleasant to everyone around him, and only he knew, of course, the irony behind his smiles, the inner truth that, were his colleagues to learn how he spent many of his nights, they would be horrified beyond words to be working alongside someone whom they would conventionally call a "ghoul."

What an unflattering, unfair term, when the more appropriate word would be "connoisseur" or "gourmet." Did not the Old Ones from Grandpa's well-remembered but long-vanished Book approve of his way of life? And they were said to be older than the cosmos itself. What could it ever matter, what a gaggle of tradition-bound narrow minds might think of him if they knew his little secret?

That afternoon in his cubicle at the office he realized what it was, that thought that had eluded him before, when he had been drinking his glass of wine at home and idly wondering whether he might have enjoyed it even more at the opened grave. The notion had suggested, subliminally, a more elaborate idea to him, one that he fully countenanced now and tended to approve of, the more he thought about it.

Thanksgiving Day was coming up in only a few days.

In truth, Thanksgiving had always been an important holiday to him. He had never had any religious beliefs, in the commonly accepted sense of the term anyway, but he did feel a deep sense of gratitude (though not directed toward any particular recipient) for the fact that in his childhood the Book, whatever its metaphysical underpinnings, had pointed him toward the best way for an artistically sensitive person to live. What could be more sincerely human than devouring the dead? What could be more of a tribute to one's departed fellow creatures than taking their essence to oneself? The depth of feeling inherent in this concept nearly brought tears to his eyes at times.

Usually he had Thanksgiving dinner at a restaurant, cheerlessly alone, and though this was always a melancholy departure from his preferred dining habits, it was always a time, as well, for him to reflect upon how proper it was for him to stop and feel grateful for all his good fortune. But now it dawned on him that there might be a better way.

The thought of taking the bottle of wine to the graveyard had suggested it to him, unconsciously at first. Now he saw it plainly, the idea that could make this year's Thanksgiving the best ever.

On the Wednesday evening preceding Thanksgiving Day, Ned bustled about the supermarket filling his shopping cart with the requisite items: carrots, green beans, yams, potatoes, pearl onions, cranberry sauce, cornbread stuffing, all the fixings for a memorable meal, or all but one anyway. He was a good cook, and this dinner would be done up to perfection.

At the checkout counter the girl eyed the items one by one as she rang them up. "Somebody's getting ready to make a nice Thanksgiving dinner. Did you already pick up your turkey?"

Ned smiled and moved his head in what might have been a nod in the affirmative, or might not. "The meat dish is all taken care of," he said.

On Thanksgiving Day he had only a modest breakfast and lunch at home, saving his appetite. He spent the afternoon cooking, humming to himself with more contentment than he had felt for a long time. The aromas of food filled the air. It was working out to be a wonderfully promising holiday.

While some of his dishes were preparing in his slow cookers, he visited the remote old graveyard, driving his car to save time, and did what he needed to do, to avoid having to let his side dishes get cold later that night. Virtually no one else ever visited this place, so he was safe from prying eyes, and finished his work in fairly good time, even as elaborate and laborious as it was. He had had plenty of practice, after all, and he knew how to get the work done in minimal time.

When he drove back to the graveyard after dark, he had a whole back seat full of cooked food, all in special containers to keep it warm.

Choosing a nice flat spot on the ground, he carefully arranged six of the seven bodies he had dug up—three men and three women, his friends (or his family) for the evening—arranged them in a tight circle around the seventh and fattest corpse, which he laid out flat on a tablecloth spread on the ground. As for the six bodies arrayed in a circle, he propped them upright as best he could. If they slumped over a bit, that was all right— one's friends and family should always feel at ease for Thanksgiving dinner. Satisfied with the way they looked, he went back to his car for the prepared food.

Tonight the waning moon was a little past full, but it was adequate, casting a chalky glow over the scene like romantic candlelight in a restaurant. Ned set out platters of fluffy mashed potatoes, stuffing, pungent yams, peas, pearl onions, and steamed carrots, with a large bowl of cranberry sauce, meticulously arranging everything around the meat dish, which added an aroma all its own to the medley of more customary aromas emanating from the side dishes; these smoked pleasantly in the chilly night air. He had not forgotten the wine glasses and a suitably chilled bottle of Merlot, which he distributed among himself and his six dining companions.

"Happy Thanksgiving, everyone," he said to them, beaming. For once he didn't have to eat his holiday dinner alone.

And it was a gourmand's dream, this meal. Sitting in the middle of the circle beside the main dish, he scooped up quivering forkfuls of the meat— a slice of leg, a bit of belly, a bite of maggoty arm, all interspersed with crisp peas and potatoes and yams and carrots. The pearl onions turned out to be a nice touch; they reminded him of the eyes that the center dish might still have had if Ned had gotten to him a bit sooner.

"How is everything, my dear friends?" he asked his company of corpses. They were silent.

"But of course," he said. What could he have been thinking? There was no excuse for being a negligent host. "I'm sorry. How inconsiderate of me. You can't very well serve yourselves, can you? Allow me."

He took bite-size portions of clabbered flesh, potatoes, and other comestibles and lifted them to the mouths of his guests, getting as much food between the unresponsive lips as he could. Poor chaps and ladies could scarcely do the chewing themselves, so he moved their jaws with his fingers to help. Two or three of them took on the appearance of made-up mimes, with bright splashy oozings of cranberry sauce outlining what was left of their lips. He felt privileged to be able to make it a nice holiday for them. In between these somewhat labored mastications he took an occasional extra bite of carrion or of vegetables himself, though he was getting full.

By the time he finished off the bottle of wine, drinking not only his own but also what he had poured for the others, since they seemed little inclined to do so themselves, he felt positively glutted, more so than he could ever remember being. The body on the tablecloth was picked clean to the bone, and though he had given liberal amounts to his guests, he had ingested a sizable share of it himself. His stomach ached, and without rising from where he sat, he bent over what was left of the corpse on the cloth, his head almost touching the denuded ribcage, and moaned.

He remained in that position until the discomfort in his stomach abated a little, and was about to straighten back up to an ordinary sitting position, when he noticed something peculiar.

One of the rotting guests had fallen with its head upon his arm. One of the ladies, he thought. Charming.

But now it was more than that. Now the fallen corpse, strangely animated, had buried her brittle teeth in Ned's arm just above the wrist. For a moment he almost didn't notice the pain, so great was the surprise. And that wasn't all, either.

In dwelling upon this development he had failed to notice that another of the guests, one of the men this time, had crouched over the other arm, skinning back the coat sleeve and sinking his yellow teeth into Ned's flesh. Someone was howling with pain now, and it took Ned a minute to realize that it was himself.

At some point his scattered senses registered the fact that all six of the circled corpses had collapsed upon him, holding him down, pulling his clothes open to find warm flesh.

In a moment of near-delirium that struggled with an impending unconsciousness, and even under a rising tide of hideous pain, a corner of his mind recalled the old passage from the Book: "Power flows body to body." That had certainly turned out to be true for all of the diners, one of whom now raised his lich-face to stare at Ned with sliding, liquescent eyes. It opened its ghastly jaw to gurgle a few thickly articulated words.

"For this food we are about to receive, may we be truly thankful."

The nightmare mouth barely got these words out before the remnant of a tongue came out too. The dinner guests were all six of them in various stages of dissolution, but, amidst all the screaming, they went right on with their Thanksgiving dinner just the same.

Keeping Festival
by Mollie L. Burleson

now crunched underfoot as Paul alighted from his car at the tiny mall. Marblehead on the twenty-first of December. The real Yuletide. He smiled. Wrapping his scarf tighter around his neck and pulling on his gloves, he headed towards the business area.

From the crest of the hill, the town spread out before him, and his artist's eye saw the beauty of the gabled houses that lay in various attitudes of disarray like a giant's toys scattered about. Lights were coming on in them one by one, giving an appearance of welcome to him. Somewhere off in the distance a dog barked and the wind blew flakes of snow about. The whole scene was reminiscent of the snow globe he had as a child. Beautiful.

As a mere lad Paul had read the stories of the writer H. P. Lovecraft and enjoyed them tremendously. But then he had grown up and had forgotten them in the world of trying to stay alive, trying to exist on the money his paintings brought. Not a rich life monetarily, but rich instead in the things that were real. He had forgotten those charming stories until the other day when in cleaning out his bookshelves he had come upon a few of those volumes and immersed him for a while in their otherworldliness.

That was when he decided to come to Lovecraft's Kingsport by the sea—Marblehead—and find out for himself just what it was about the town that had captivated and influenced the writer so much. Where had he read that phrase—Only the poor and the lonely remembered? Well, he was poor enough, and lonely enough, and he had remembered.

The shops were still open and he entered a bookshop filled with ancient tomes and which served hot cider and gingerbread. The cakes were hot and fragrant, and the cider warmed his insides.

He walked the crooked streets, trying to see the town as Lovecraft had once seen it. It was little changed from the writer's description, especially now at night when the small-paned windows were unshuttered and open for all to view their lovely insides. Great Christmas trees stood in silent parlors, their lights blinking in the darkness; braided rugs lay at their feet, and presents abounded. A lone skier swished by. The setting was a more

Dickensian one than one of horror. Still, Paul could imagine the spectral aspect of these seemingly untenanted homes, and the dark, narrow streets that led to even darker corners where anything could be waiting.

He climbed the hill to the cemetery then, looking over the town and the bay below. Ships in the harbor were strung with Christmas lights and rocked to and fro as the tide crept in. Now and then a ship's bell would ring, a lonely and forlorn sound, and even here high above the harbor, he imagined he could hear the waves splashing upon unseen pilings. He looked about him. The great old slate markers indeed looked more like the fingernails of some gigantic creature, clawing their way through the snow and out of their graves. He shivered involuntarily; that writer was quite a spellcaster.

He paused in his walk then, and listened. What was that sound? A great concrete slab grating against another? Surely it was a sound from the harbor, or a tree's limb rubbing against something. He shivered again.

As he cautioned his way down the steep path, he saw a dark shape before him. A man, similarly occupied, viewing the harbor on this night of nights. A tall man, almost completely covered from head to toe with overcoat, mufflers, and cap. Paul could barely see his face.

"Good evening," Paul announced.

"Yes, it is indeed a good evening," the man answered in a high voice and in beautifully enunciated English.

"There doesn't seem to be anyone else abroad tonight," Paul said. "You're the first soul I've seen."

The man said nothing, but fell into step beside Paul, who found it difficult to keep pace with him and his long-legged strides. He was so bundled that Paul could just barely see his eyes, which were dark and, in the street-light's glow, sparkled as if with some secret amusement.

The man said, "I know this town well. I have trod these lanes many times, and each time I like them better; especially at night."

Paul nodded agreement but said nothing, thinking that the man preferred a quiet companion.

"Would you care to go down to the harbor and watch the tide come in?" the man asked.

"I was about to do that very same thing myself, and I'm glad to have someone along for companionship. Somehow the water seems strange and forbidding to me now, and at this moment so does the town. The wind must have shifted."

The man made no comment, but continued down the shore. The water was indeed black and forbidding, and the tide hungrily lapped at the wooden pilings with a frightening sucking sound.

"According to some, this is the great Yuletide, the twenty-first of December. I've never really thought about it before, but I suppose it is. A celebration older than time."

The man nodded agreement and said, "Would you care to have me show you a special monument, a church on a hill?"

Paul heartily agreed, for he had grown accustomed to the stranger and his ways, so different from people one met today. A gentleman he was; a real gentleman.

The man led the way down darkened and silent streets and up a slight incline to a church perched forthrightly atop it. Alongside was the usual New England churchyard with ancient slate stones marking the resting places of the forefathers of Marblehead's residents. A cold wind blew snow into their faces, and the man shuddered.

"I think it's getting colder," Paul said. "Colder and damper."

The man told Paul that he could not tolerate the cold for very long, that he preferred the summer's heat.

"But," Paul said, "there's something to be said about the cold, something primeval and humbling, and I feel that the Yuletide coming on a sultry August day would not be the same."

"Of course you're right; but nevertheless, I cannot tolerate the cold." As the man spoke he wrapped his arms about himself as if for warmth.

"I wonder if others are observing Yuletide tonight, or are we the only ones?"

Some of the lights were beginning to wink out, and Paul saw that the hour was late. Then he heard, or thought he heard, voices far off. They seemed to be singing or chanting, and in the frosty air the sounds vibrated as surely as a bell would have when struck with its frozen clapper.

He turned to his companion to comment on the strange happenings, but found him gone. Where did he go? And how? Paul had not sensed his leaving. How very strange.

The voices were nearer now, and Paul left the church's steps and carefully went down the icy slope to the shelter of the houses across the street.

What he saw then amazed him, for hundreds of people, it seemed, came up the frozen walkway to the church. They were clad in long black robes and walked in a strange fashion. The first ones entered the church, followed by the next group and the next, and it appeared to Paul that the line of communicants would never cease. But finally the last one entered the dark church and disappeared from view.

Paul's curiosity was aroused then, and he made his way back to the church and up the steps, trying to peer in at the locked door. All was silent and dark. And as he looked down at his feet, no footprints but his own appeared in the sparkling snow.

Was it all a mirage, a fancy brought on by his recent reading of the Lovecraft tales? And his strange companion, what of him?

Paul retraced his steps down the darkened streets, toward where he had parked his car, musing all the while. He could not justify the whole evening, the strange man, the masses of people near the church, the eeriness of the tide, and he did not wish to. It was the Yuletide after all, and he, too, had kept Festival.

Wassail

by Tom Lynch

I sat in the Elders' longhouse, blinking back the irritation in my eyes from all the smoke. It felt like no breeze had been through in eons. The musty smell of old people, the tangy smell of sweat, and the thick smell of smoke filled the room. I decided I was going to do my best to breathe through my mouth.

"Young one," the Eldest said. "Do you know why you are here?" He sat on the far side of the fire from me, in the middle of the other four elders. His face was stern and soft at the same time.

"I confess, I do not," I answered, looking at the five firelit faces.

"Can you not guess?" barked the Second, leaning his pinched face forward.

"I assume you have a task for me."

"You are special," said the Eldest, placing a calming hand on the Second. "Have you not been aware of this these years? You spent most of your time with us, learning of our beliefs and our history while the other young men were learning to hone their battle skills. You were pulled aside and taught about nature, planting and the harvest, while the others your age were at the Beltane dances."

"You honored me with your teaching," I said quietly.

The Eldest smiled. "You are free to feel angry. Anger is a form of passion, and passion is a sign of youth. Were you not a youth, we would not be having this conversation. But yes, we have a task for you. It is the task for which we have been preparing you. Everything you've learned up to now, everything we've told you, it all culminates during this task. And this task is sacred to the goddess. We need her intercession to continue to grow and live as we have been, and you must be the one to make the request."

"I leave at dawn?"

"Such impudence," muttered the Second, while the Third and Fourth hid their smiles. The Fifth just shifted uncomfortably.

"I'm afraid not, my boy," said the First. "You leave tonight. Tonight is the end of our teaching and the beginning of your new journey."

"But—" I began. "The rest of the clan—"

"I know," the First's eyebrows knit in concern. "But what you do is for all of us, and will help shape the future of the clan for generations. I know the Yule celebrations are important to you, but this, young man, comes first. The honor falls to you."

I bit back everything I wanted to say, and simply nodded.

"You remember all you need?" the First asked. "Your supplies are in the ceremonial chest."

***

I struggled with the old wooden box, waddling my way to the sacred grove just outside our village. As I huffed along, revelers of all sizes and shapes passed by me, going toward the dances and merriment. Most didn't even acknowledge me, but some gave me sad looks, as if to say, "We're so sad you're missing the party of the season." That made me feel much better.

Once inside the grove, I dropped the chest in the snow and lifted open the lid. There was the virgin wool tunic, the cape, the ceremonial athame, and the sacred spore. Supposedly this was all I would need on this sacred quest.

I couldn't help but wonder if they considered the weather when the put this outfit together. Had it been early fall, two thin layers with no sandals or boots would have been fine, but this was midwinter. I was supposed to walk several miles in only this? And I was supposed to be capable of doing anything other than freezing once I got there?

Ah well.

I wrapped the spore in the lambskin pouch, and bound the athame to my arm. The metal was already chilling my skin, and I hadn't even left the village yet.

***

I pulled my cape closer, again wishing for more layers than the coming ceremony allowed, cursing the Elders for naming the winter solstice one of the best times for this summoning. The rest of the clan would be feasting in the great hall, spilling mead and shouting their hopes that the sun would rise at dawn.

Only one member was not so lucky. Only one member of the strongest clan in the forest was out this night. Only one member's feet were freezing in the snow and frost. Only one member was the recipient of this *great honor*.

Honor? Psh!

At this moment, warmth would be far more spiritually appealing than this oh-so-sacred task.

I crested the tallest hill bordering our valley and looked back. There, from my vantage point, I could see the firelight. I could even see the silhouettes of members of my extended family prancing around, frolicking in the festivities.

I chose this moment to urinate. I had to go anyway, and had to be clean to perform the ritual, so here was as good a place as any. I cursed the sudden breeze. Naturally it would kick up now.

I finished and strode away, stamping feeling back into my legs, thrashing my arms to keep myself warm. I headed down the far side of the hill to the Goddess' Clearing. As I picked my way among frozen roots, doing my best to avoid slicing open my bare feet, I guessed it was unfair to curse the elders.

Sacred texts handed down for generations named three ideal times for contacting the other side of the veil: Samhain, Yule, and Litha. Ah Litha. Why could tradition not place this particular celebration on Midsummer? I'd happily volunteer to go to the Clearing skyclad and perform the ritual. Twice! Doing this in the middle of winter is insane.

So yes, cursing the Elders is unfair. I curse the sacred tex—

I made a gesture to the gods in apology. I could not do it. Even in jest, I shuddered to think of the wrath I'd bring down on my own head, and the head of any progeny I might have. Of course, if certain parts of me got any colder progeny would remain a pleasant dream. Ah, to dream of the mother of that progeny, too. All I had to do was get Regan away from Breanainn, the chief's second son. I could show her the kind of love she *should* be getting!

And with that, I came to the clearing. The idle rambling of my mind had kept me warm enough to make the trip, now to leave my cape behind and experience excruciating cold for as long as this summoning took. I didn't even know how long that would be. I knew the ritual, sure, but I had no idea how long it would actually take, or if it would even work. All I knew was that I was supposed to follow my instructions. I shook myself, took a deep breath of icy air, make sure I had both the athame and the spore, and stepped into the clearing, as naked as when I entered the world.

***

I'd never been here before. As with so many other things, I knew all about them, but hadn't experienced them first hand. This. This was very different. I had stepped into a different world.

No, that's not accurate. I stepped next to the world. The silence was absolute. Gone was the whistling wind and the creaking branches of trees. I could not even hear my feet scuffing the frozen grass, nor could I hear the beating of my own heart. Silence ROARED over me.

As sweat-inducing as the silence was, the physical feeling was at least as startling. Yes, it was still cold, but the cold wasn't touching me. I could feel that I was cold, yet I wasn't. It didn't bother me, or interfere with what had to be done. My feet no longer throbbed with aching cold, they merely were. My hands, which held the sacred tools, no longer felt like my own. Yes, I could see that they were still attached to my arms, and my arms to my shoulders, but somehow, they were elsewhere as I walked/floated to the middle of the clearing.

I knelt, pressed my head to the frozen soil, again aware of the cold that was/wasn't. I muttered the incantation nine times, calling the goddess' name, desperately asking her approval and praying for her intercession. I reached up with the purified dagger, and drew it from above my left eyebrow, to the edge of my jaw by my right ear.

As the wound opened, so did my eyes and ears. I crashed my head to the frozen ground again, and again, bloodying the snow, daring my new sensations to feel pain. I could see colors that had no name and hear songs, music that words simply could not capture. Dawn broke, sun set, lightning flashed, thunder crashed, rain poured, all in the light of the moon. Sensations lifted and pulled me to the height of the heavens and dropped me back to earth so quickly and fully that I gasped.

I remembered to continue with the ritual. I raised the blade and again, pressed it into my flesh, drawing a crimson line of blood from my left shoulder to my lowest right rib. I stared down as the blood first oozed, then flowed down my body. I reveled in it.

Standing, I moved to the far end of the clearing, dancing, flowing to the music that the goddess had let me hear, weeping with the eyes that saw impossible rainbows. Again, I knelt, this time, before the Chosen Tree. This was the tree I'd known about. This tree was on our shields. This tree held the key to the strength of our clan. When we invoked the goddess, it was this tree that we pictured. It was this tree that we drew in the dirt as children. When ever we planted grain or vegetables, it was the everlife of this tree that we invoked for a fruitful harvest.

This tree.

And I knelt under it.

Just me.

Unblooded, never allowed to see battle.

Unwed, never allowed to know woman.

I would trade none of it now.

How petty my thoughts had been earlier of cold and bitterness. I sang with joy to be where I was, doing what I was doing. I sang to the tree, to the goddess. To all Creation and all Death.

I raised the athame, the purified silver dagger, and plunged it into the tree, raking downward. All the strength I could muster barely scratched the bark. Again, I cut. And again. My left eye stung with the blood that flowed from the wound on my face and most of my lower body was red with my chest wound.

I kept cutting.

Cut until you can insert the spore, said the Elders. They knew. The sacred texts had been passed down to them. None of them had done it, of course, but they knew.

I cut more, hearing colors and seeing sounds. My mouth went slack in an ecstasy of the senses: weeping eyes filled with unutterable sites, singing ears with songs of the stars, fingers tingling as I cut into the flesh of the earth. I felt, saw and heard everything; even those that I couldn't have known. I knew that Breanainn was pulling Regan behind a tree with amorous intent. I knew Regan wanted to go. I saw the Elders sitting in a circle around a low-burning fire, chanting. I felt their chant, not heard it. I felt it give me strength.

I thrust the athame into the tree, and it opened. I placed the spore into the wound in the tree, and caressed the embedded spore with my bloody hands. I rested my face against it, drooling into it, as I felt the creature start to stir. I could feel first a vibration, then a song. Its song. I sang, and it sang back.

Together our chorus raised its throngs to the darkened heavens above and again I saw. I saw Breannainn and Regan's son beginning his life. I saw the Elders reel back from the flame as it burst upwards with purple, scarlet, and ebony.

As we sang, I saw the Elders rise, link hands, and dance around the unearthly flame, their eyes on fire as well. I felt everyone's ecstasy as I felt my own, and they all powered mine.

I danced around the waking creature as we sang. As I danced, I felt the earth soften beneath my feet. The creatures birth and the blood from my wounds had created a thaw. It let the creature move. I felt stirrings under my feet. Oozing motion, pulling, pushing. Something was trying to stand. More I danced, spinning round and round. I slapped and beat at the creature-tree to wake it, to begin the process of the journey toward the longer, warmer days of summer. To fight the power of cold and darkness with fertility and growth. My hands and fingers tingled as they bled droplets onto the creature, feeding it.

I spun further out, stomping the ground, kicking away the frost to create my own private thaw.

A thrumming sound rose out of the earth, and the creature trumpeted.

"Awaken!" I cried. "Rise! Join the land of the living!"

Wailing, fluting sounds burst from the creature as it raised its hoofed foot to take its first step this Yule. Its branch-like arms flailed, less and less branch-like as it continued to wake, wave, and move.

My dance became a frenzy of movement as I lost track of conscious movement, giving myself totally to the feeling, sights, sounds, and smells now. Rich, loamy earth-smells filled my nostrils. These winter-black woods were coming alive. One of its children was rising.

The ground shook, and I ceased my dance. Weak and bleeding but elated, I gazed upon the new/reborn, and it gazed at me with its eyeless face, steam rising from its open maws. It trumpeted again, and I covered my ears as the sound struck either side of my head. I dropped to my knees. I raised my streaming eyes to behold the creature again.

"Iä!" I cried. "Iä! Black goddess of the woods! Praise to her dark young!"

And I gave myself as the first sacrifice of the season to bring spring fertility and strength to our valley that we would live and prosper.

Krampusnacht
by Joshua Reynolds

It was 1920, Christmas was in the air, and Oswald Rawdon was terrified. He huddled in the large wingback chair, a cup of tea clutched in his trembling fingers. The last of the Rawdons nervously slopped brandy-laced tea onto the knees of his trousers as he started suddenly at the sound of wood crackling in the fire.

"Nervous are we, Ozzy?" Rawdon's host said. "Try not to ruin the carpets, please."

"I'm sorry Charles," Rawdon said, swallowing a mouthful of tea. "It's just, I hear it everywhere."

Charles St. Cyprian nodded in sympathy, and took a sip from his own cup. "Perfectly understandable, old boy, considering the kind of life you've led."

Rawdon froze, and his eyes narrowed as he looked at the dark-haired man opposite him. The two men were a study in contrasts for all that they were of an age. Where Rawdon was a thin stretch of Teutonic paleness, St. Cyprian was dark and sharp-featured, with a Mediterranean exoticism to his features. Both men were dressed well, though Rawdon's suit showed distinct signs of hard living.

"What's that supposed to mean?" Rawdon said. "The kind of life I've led?"

"Don't be dense, Ozzy." St. Cyprian put his cup aside and pressed his fingers together. "You're a bit of a bastard, is all."

"How dare you!" Rawdon shot to his feet, the cup falling to the floor. Tea immediately soaked into the Turkish carpet, and St. Cyprian groaned.

"Now look what you've done," he said, leaning back in his chair. "Do sit down Ozzie. Your reputation as a complete and utter pillock is well deserved and you know it."

"Fine," Rawdon said, flopping back down in his seat. "Fine! But you don't have to say it with such relish."

"Hardly relish, chum." St. Cyprian sighed. "Granted, you're no Crowley, but you do tend towards the troublesome."

"If I'm so much trouble, then why did you even agree to see me?" Rawdon spat. Outside, the sound of church bells gave voice to the late hour.

"He's got a heart made of nutmeg and cinnamon," a new voice interjected. Both men turned as the speaker, a young woman, walked into the sitting room, dropping an armful of wooden boards and a hammer onto the floor as she did so. "Me? I'd have left you to the tender mercies of the—"

"Don't say it!" Rawdon barked, clapping his hands to his ears.

"Tea, Ms. Gallowglass?" St. Cyprian said, gesturing to the teapot and the extra cup and saucer sitting on a low table nearby.

"Don't mind if I do, Mr. St. Cyprian." Ebe Gallowglass said. Dressed in a frayed Guernsey and a man's trousers, she looked less than ladylike, with her short, dark hair, cut into a curl-edged bob, and slim, straight limbs the colour of cinnamon. A swath of freckles spattered across her sharp Egyptian features, and her grin was almost feral. Filling a cup, she knocked it back a moment later. "I've got the windows braced with birch boards and the upstairs chimneys blocked with sprigs of mistletoe, holly wreaths and holyrood. Oh, and the carollers have finally wassailed off."

"Excellent," St. Cyprian said. "See? You can uncoil now, Ozzy. We're safe as houses."

Rawdon lowered his hands. "Do you really think you can keep it out?" He looked nervously at the fireplace that dominated one wall of the sitting room, blazing merrily away. It was the only light in the sitting room save for the odd candle or three resting in the branches of the Christmas tree that occupied one corner of the room.

"Keep it out? No." St. Cyprian stood. "Direct its method of ingress, however?" He went to the fireplace and used the poker to shift the cherry-red logs, the three steel rings on the fingers of his left hand clinking against the metal of the poker. "Certainly," he continued, with all the assurance one expected of the Royal Occultist.

Formed during the reign of Elizabeth the First, the office of Royal Occultist (or the Queen's Conjurer, as it had been known) had passed through a succession of hands, starting with those of diligent amateur Dr. John Dee. The list was a long one, weaving in and out of the margins of British history, and culminating, for the moment, in one Charles St. Cyprian.

His position was an open secret, and the rather cluttered house on the Embankment that served as the hereditary abode of the office was equally open to any who might need a consultation. It had been that way since the tenure of Sir Edwin Drood in the earliest days of the late Victoria's reign, and St. Cyprian saw no reason to disrupt tradition, no matter how much he might occasionally wish otherwise.

Thus, Rawdon's breathless appearance on his stoop this Christmas Eve was not surprising so much in and of itself, though the fact that it was Rawdon who was doing the calling had thrown St. Cyprian for a turn. He hadn't seen Ozzy Rawdon since the end of the War, though he'd kept abreast of his activities via the usual outlets of Society gossip.

Rawdon was a rum one, no two ways about it. He was a gambler, a professional lout and a war hero.

St. Cyprian stabbed the fire again. A cascade of sparks swirled upwards. Still holding the poker, he turned. "Ebe, be a dear and get me the container on the third shelf of the second bookcase there."

"The one with a cat's head or the one shaped like a jolly fat man?" she said, sipping on her second cup of tea.

"The one shaped like a fish."

"That's supposed to be a fish?" Gallowglass said, peering at the shelf in question.

"Get it, please." St. Cyprian turned back to Rawdon. "Now, Ozzy, I'd like you to spill those guts of yours in the figurative sense, while we scheme to prevent the literal."

"There's not much to say," Rawdon said, licking his lips.

"That's a lie," Gallowglass said, handing St. Cyprian the container. "And I still say that this looks like a cat."

"Possibly a cat-fish, then?" St. Cyprian murmured. "And Ozzy isn't lying, are you Ozzy? Ozzy never lies. Ozzy just bends the truth into new and more advantageous shapes." St. Cyprian opened the container and took out a pinch of powder. Flinging it onto the fire, he looked at Rawdon. "I want the unbent truth, Ozzy."

"Fine way to treat a man who saved your life!" Rawdon said.

"Ozzy, it's because you saved my life that I didn't turn you away the minute a certain word tripped from those bud-like lips of yours." St. Cyprian frowned. "In itself, that tells me everything I need to know, really."

"You don't know anything," Rawdon protested.

"I know you, Ozzy. And I know what's after you. What I don't know is why it's chosen now to bring you to bay." St. Cyprian stabbed the poker into the fireplace again. Then he pulled it loose and examined the smouldering tip. "Now, I say again, why exactly is the Krampus after you, Oswald?"

The fire gave a pop, and Rawdon jumped in his chair. He visibly fought to control himself. "It's obvious, isn't it? I've been bad." Rawdon stared down at his hands. "That's why. I've always been bad, and it's always been after me and now, now, it's finally caught me.

"It was my gran who first put it on my trail, I'm sure of it, Bavarian biddy that she was. Did you know she was a Kraut, Charles?" Rawdon shook his head. "Hardly matters now. Besides, go back far enough, and most of the great families of fair Albion are either Frogs or Krauts."

"Or Punic, in my case," St. Cyprian murmured.

"What?"

"Nothing. Go on."

Rawdon grimaced. "Jokes on the block, Charles?"

"Not our necks getting the chop, now are they?" Gallowglass said. As Rawdon shot a glare at her, she held up the teapot. "More tea, Mr. Rawdon?"

Rawdon looked at his cup on the floor, and then shook his head. "Gran always told me that the Kra—*the gentleman in question*—would get me if I didn't mend my ways."

"Krampus. You can say it, Ozzy. He already knows where you are, after all." St. Cyprian stirred the fire again. "The word originates from the Old High German word for 'claw', which is appropriate given the demeanour and personality of the fellow." He looked at Gallowglass. "Anything to add, apprentice-mine?"

"Oberstdorf," Gallowglass said, tapping her chin. An ability to store and recall seemingly trivial facts was just one of the many talents which she had discovered as she assisted St. Cyprian in his investigations into obscure matters. "They're supposed to have a similar sort of chap. Except that he doesn't work for Father Christmas, I don't think."

"Neither does this thing," Rawdon said harshly.

"Is that experience speaking?" St. Cyprian said.

"It's been after me since I was eight, Charles. I've read up on the subject quite a bit."

"You mean, when you weren't trying to forget about it with opium, heroin or alcohol." St. Cyprian raised a hand. "No judgements intended, Ozzy."

Rawdon made a face. "I'm sorry that I'm not as brave as you, Charles. Not every man can face his demons head on," he spat.

"Got you there," Gallowglass said.

"Shouldn't you be making us some more tea?" St. Cyprian said. "Like a good apprentice?"

"Whoever said I was a good apprentice?"

"You'll be an unemployed apprentice if you don't pipe down," St. Cyprian said, glaring at her. Gallowglass stuck out her tongue and hefted the teapot.

"There's still a dreg or so in here, milord," she said. "If you're thirsty."

"Stop talking about tea!" Rawdon snapped. "I don't want to die, Charles!"

"Few of us do, Ozzy." St. Cyprian handed the fish-headed container to Gallowglass. "Make yourself useful and put this back." He looked at

Rawdon. "You said your grandmother put it on your trail?"

"She's the one who first mentioned it to me, at any rate." Rawdon shrugged. "Put the thought in my head. I stole a cookie from the kitchen, and she said the K-Krampus would punish me." He had to force the word out. His hands clenched and unclenched repeatedly. "That I would know he was coming by the clattering of his bells and the scratching of his—ah—his claws."

"And?" St. Cyprian said.

"And? And what? And I heard it!" Rawdon said squeezing his eyes shut. He ground the heels of his palms into his sockets, as if trying to wipe the images from his mind. "I heard it. Just a whisper of sound. It might have been anything. Bells on a carriage. Leaves on the roof."

As if to emphasize Rawdon's statement, from somewhere upstairs there came the sound of shutters being rattled violently. He started, looking around wildly.

"What was that?"

St. Cyprian glanced at Gallowglass. "We're edging towards midnight. Get the Pentacle."

"That old electric thing of Carnacki's?" Gallowglass said. "Think it'll be any use?"

"I wouldn't ask otherwise," St. Cyprian said. "Go on, Ozzy."

"The scullery maid." Rawdon ran his hands through his hair. "I was fourteen. And she was quite pretty." He looked at them. "It wasn't my fault she got pregnant!"

"Immaculate conceptions occur where you least expect them, I'm given to understand," St. Cyprian said. "You heard it again?"

"Gran was dead by then and good riddance. But I heard it all the same. Louder." He shook his head. "Father put her out, of course. Scandal, you know."

"Yes. I know." St. Cyprian's face was like stone as he turned to the fireplace and jammed the poker into the wood again. Soot tumbled down from within the chimney, and St. Cyprian's eyes narrowed.

If Rawdon had noticed St. Cyprian's tone, he gave no sign. "Do you remember that Felstead fellow? The Christmas Truce?"

"Vaguely. I was elsewhere at the time." St. Cyprian said, recalling the whirlwind months following the death of his predecessor Carnacki at Ypres. He could still see Carnacki's bloody fingers shoving the trio of rings that now decorated his hand through the mud of the trench towards him. He looked down at them, twisting his wrist so that the nearly invisible characters engraved on the rings caught the firelight. "You heard it then? During the truce?" he said.

"First Christmas I didn't," Rawdon said. "The first Christmas I was free of those damn bells." His smile was crooked. "I didn't hear it much, during the War."

"But when you came back?"

"Old habits," Rawdon said, making a loose gesture. "A man can't be blamed. Especially one who went through what we went through."

"The bells again, I trust?" St. Cyprian said.

"And the claws. Scratching over the windows and in the chimneys." Rawdon paused, head cocked. "I say, do you hear that?"

"Yes. Go on."

"But—"

"It's been seen to, Ozzy. Go on." St. Cyprian tossed another log onto the fire.

"Drinking, gambling. The usual." Rawdon wrapped his hands together and squeezed the air from between them. "Harmless fun."

"Vice and sin," St. Cyprian said. "Gossip as well, if I recall. How much did Lord Pettigrew pay you to keep silent on his son's doings?"

"Enough," Rawdon muttered. "A man has to earn a wage."

"Most men do it honestly."

"You're one to talk Charles!" Rawdon said, pushing himself up out of his chair. "You've never met a lie you didn't embellish!"

"All in the name of necessity," St. Cyprian said, after a moment, clinking his rings together gently. It sounded hollow, even to him.

Rawdon grinned mirthlessly. "Necessity depends on perspective."

"So it was your perspective that the younger Mr. Pettigrew was a threat?" St. Cyprian said. Rawdon jerked, and St. Cyprian nodded. "I have contacts at the Yard, you know Ozzy."

"He intended to kill me! He said his father had disowned him!" Rawdon protested.

"So you killed him first?"

"No!" Rawdon shook his head. "I mean, I—it was self-defense!"

"Perhaps the Krampus doesn't see it that way," St, Cyprian said. "You know, you could have solved all of your problems by simply changing your ways, Ozzy." St. Cyprian felt a momentary surge of pleasure at Rawdon's visible flinch. "Given up the dirty deeds and damnable deals and done something with your life."

"Easy for you to say."

"Easy enough to do," Gallowglass said, returning, a heavy electrical apparatus in tow. St. Cyprian winced as she drug it across the floor, leaving scratches in the wood. "If you've got the minerals."

"Minerals?"

"Stones. Rocks. Testicular fortitude," Gallowglass said. "One electric pentacle, as requested Cap'n." She tossed off a lazy salute to St. Cyprian.

"At ease," St. Cyprian said. "My predecessor created this device for situations such as this, when contact with an untoward manifestation could result in death. Or worse."

"Manifestation?" Rawdon said.

"Monster. Spectre. Long-legged beastie," Gallowglass said. St. Cyprian frowned and shot a glare her way. She shrugged in response.

"A manifestation of hostile intent," St. Cyprian said as he sank to his haunches and began to arrange the diverse apparatus of the device, which was composed of a central generator and five vacuum tubes. He swiftly stripped a section of the rug away from the floorboards, revealing a dark pentacle scored into the wood.

St. Cyprian set the generator in the center of the pentacle, and arranged the vacuum tubes at the corresponding points of intersecting triangles. "If you—come here Ozzy—if you stay within the pentacle, you should be safe."

"Should be?" Rawdon said.

"It's not an exact science, I'm afraid."

"It's not a science at all," Gallowglass said, snapping open the cylinder on a Webley-Fosberry revolver and spinning it experimentally. She loaded the pistol with brisk efficiency, and then flicked her wrist, popping the cylinder back into place.

"A good apprentice keeps her comments to herself," St. Cyprian said, situating Rawdon beside the generator. "Don't move, no matter what happens."

"I was just pointing out the flaws in your reasoning, Mr. St. Cyprian." Gallowglass rubbed her cheek with the pistol barrel.

"Duly noted, Ms. Gallowglass."

Something banged loudly across the roof. Rawdon started, his eyes widening. "It's here!"

"It's been here for some time, Ozzy, scampering across my roof and testing the runes on the windows." St. Cyprian flipped a switch on the generator and the vacuum tubes began to hum and spark. "Stay within the pentacle."

"Soot," Gallowglass said, simply.

St. Cyprian turned, loosening his tie and shrugging out of his coat. Soot tumbled down the chimney, and he could hear metal scraping against the brick. He strode swiftly to the fireplace and reached up, taking down the short-bladed sword mounted there.

Roughly two feet in length, and wide, the sword was a xiphos—a weapon that had been in St. Cyprian's family for centuries, and had purportedly been carried by an ancestor in the Peloponnesian Wars. Unsheathing it, St. Cyprian swung it experimentally. It cut the air with a near-silent hiss and he nodded.

"Rag," he said.

Gallowglass plucked a rag out of her back pocket and tossed it to him. The fabric was smeared with the juice of the holly bush. St. Cyprian rubbed the blade with it until the former was glistening. He sighted down its length.

The fire coughed and sputtered as chunks of brick and more soot fell into it. He stepped back, rolling up his sleeves. "I trust you took the proper precautions?" he said, glancing at Gallowglass.

"The bullets were prepared according to Alpine tradition." Gallowglass cocked the pistol. "They should do the trick right enough."

"Should being the operative word." St. Cyprian frowned. "We only have to hold it until midnight. Then, it should depart."

"There's that word again," Gallowglass said. St. Cyprian glanced at her. "Should," she elaborated.

Smoke suddenly billowed out into the room, carrying with it a foul odor, like wet dog and rotten meat. The trio gagged as the smell swept over them.

And then, with a clatter of rusty bells and a shower of sparks, the Krampus erupted from the fireplace, howling like a lonely wind coiling through the Bavarian peaks. It was a black shape, outlined by the flickering dregs of the fire at its back. It was so large that there was no conceivable way that it could have squeezed down the chimney. Chains draped it, and cowbells dangled between its oddly-jointed legs and off of its bony shoulders. Curving horns swept up nearly three feet off of its vulpine skull, and its hair was matted and filthy.

The carpet sizzled beneath its cloven hooves as it stepped forward, jaws working soundlessly. Eyes like red sparks rolled madly in its sockets as it swung its head back and forth.

Rawdon made something that might have been a hastily strangled whimper. The Krampus' jaw opened, revealing a forest of curved teeth that sprang like iron nails from the black gums. A long, impossibly red tongue slithered out of from the depths of the beast's gullet and tasted the air.

The Krampus snorted, and it stamped a hoof. Wood splintered beneath the carpet as it trotted forward.

"Stop right there," St. Cyprian said, stepping in front of the beast, arms spread. The Krampus reared back, head cocked. It gave an interrogative snarl. The sound might have contained words, but sounded for all the world like a distant avalanche.

"No. No, I think not." St. Cyprian gestured with the sword. "In fact, I think you'll return back the way you came, friend." He said it with a bravado he didn't entirely feel. St. Cyprian had seen worse things than the spectre before him, but none so close, and none so foul.

The Krampus was simply wrong. If Father Christmas, Saint Nicholas or Santa Claus, however you referred to him, was everything joyous about the season, then the Krampus was everything that was terrible and tragic and ill-fitting. The bells in his chains were funerary voices, and his breath was a fog on the air, showing ghostly images of fallen friends and starving children. Of the unfortunate and the lost, those for whom the season was anything but happy. A dozen ghosts were caught in the thick links of the Krampus' chain, bound to the beast for all eternity. Sinners all.

That was the Krampus' remit, after all. Where Father Christmas rewarded the good, the Krampus was responsible for punishing the wicked. And at that moment, it's eyes were solely for Oswald Rawdon.

Ignoring St. Cyprian, the beast raised a hairy paw and pointed one filth-encrusted talon at Rawdon, who shrank back. Then, it howled like a locomotive and leapt!

Straight over St. Cyprian's head it bounded, its hooves digging divots in the carpet as it landed and flung itself at Rawdon. There was a fat pop and crackle and then the hiss of sizzling meat and the Krampus hit the ground in a rattle of chains, rolling to its feet like a kicked dog. Carnacki's electrical pentacle had held.

"I told you that it would work," St. Cyprian said, raising his sword. "Now be a dear and shoot the bugger!"

"Gloating doesn't become you," Gallowglass said. The Webley bucked in her hands and the Krampus shrieked as a bullet rubbed in bear fat and mistletoe creased its hip. It staggered, tongue flailing like a serpent's head. Gallowglass fired again, stepping back to stay out of the beast's reach.

The Krampus lunged for her, but St. Cyprian moved forward, stabbing his sword down through a link in its chains and on into the floor. The beast yowled as it tried to pull itself free, and swung a thunderous backhand at the occultist. St. Cyprian hopped awkwardly back, losing his grip on the sword.

Gallowglass fired a third time, and the Krampus shrieked again as a blossom of blood burst into existence on its breast. It reached out with an impossibly long arm, swatting the pistol from her hands, and sending her skidding sideways. Then it spun, eyes blazing like twin torches. It grabbed the sword and began to jerk it from the floor.

St. Cyprian darted towards it, sweeping up one of the birch boards that Gallowglass had deposited on the floor. He brought it down on the

Krampus' arm, eliciting a yelp. Claws tore at his waistcoat, severing buttons. He swung the birch board again, shattering it against the Krampus' skull. The beast shoved him back and he slid across the floor, only stopping when he struck the wall.

Shaking its head, the brute yanked the sword free and hurled it aside with a victorious growl. Then it turned back to the crackling pentacle and Rawdon, who cowered within.

"No! No! Not me! I didn't do anything!" Rawdon said, twitching like a rabbit in a trap. "I don't deserve this!"

The Krampus hissed and slowly trotted around the pentacle, eyes narrowed. Brass claws trailed across the invisible barrier, leaving a trail of sparks in the air. Rawdon turned with it, his eyes pits of terror.

"Charles! Help me!" he shouted, pounding his useless fists against his thighs.

St. Cyprian pushed himself to his feet, head ringing. "Ebe?" he called out.

"I'm fine," Gallowglass said, scooping up her pistol. "Just knocked the wind out of me. Bugger's not so tough."

"He's not after us. And our precautions don't seem to have been that effective," St. Cyprian said, stooping to pick up the sword from where the Krampus had hurled it.

The Krampus stopped its pacing and eyed them warily, its red gaze flickering like dying embers. St. Cyprian stopped moving, and motioned for Gallowglass to do the same.

The Krampus could have killed them both, had it wished. But its prey had to have been judged and found wanting by whatever celestial court empowered the creature. The chains it wore were not symbolic, but real shackles, binding what had once been an old, wild nightmare of Pre-Christian times to the new ethos of this age.

The chains rattled across the floor as the beast crouched, digging its claws into the floor. Its hulking shoulders hunched and the wood began to give with a series of rending cracks.

And, as the floor gave way, the nearest of the vacuum tubes tilted, and, finally, toppled, shattering. The Krampus surged to its feet and lunged for the opening in the mystical barrier, its form twisting and billowing like a thread of smoke.

"Get Rawdon out of there!" St. Cyprian said, throwing himself towards the closest bookshelf. A number of containers sat amongst the books. Some held dust, or a variety of foul-smelling pastes. All had proven useful, once or twice.

As St. Cyprian shoved books out of the way and scrabbled for a solution to their problem, Gallowglass fired the Webley at the curling twist of Krampus-smoke, perforating it even as she tackled Rawdon out of the pentacle.

The Krampus began to reform, a look of brute hatred on its face as it moved to pursue them.

"Ha!" St. Cyprian barked, hanging off of the bookshelf. He hefted something that resembled a canopic jar and tossed it towards the pentacle. "Shoot it!"

Gallowglass shoved Rawdon off of her and fired her last shot. The bullet shattered the urn and a dark substance spattered across the floor, mostly in the spot where the Krampus had broken the power of the pentacle.

The Krampus turned back towards the opening, and then retreated abruptly with a howl. It turned in place, spinning so fast that its chains struck the barrier and cast off foul-smelling sparks.

"What was in that?" Gallowglass said, getting to her feet.

"A little concoction from the Tyrol region—rosemary, juniper and fat from a priest's grave. It'll only hold until it dries, but that should be long enough—ah." St. Cyprian dropped down from the bookcase and held up a hand.

Somewhere, church bells sounded the midnight hour. Christmas Eve had given way to Christmas Day.

The Krampus gave a long, low mournful howl as it writhed in its makeshift cell. Smoke and ash drifted from its hairy shape and soon it was completely obscured, save for the hot glow of its eyes. And then, even that was gone, as if it had never been.

Waving a hand to disperse the smoke, St. Cyprian moved to turn off the electric pentacle. Gallowglass stepped over Rawdon's still-prone form, and grabbed a bottle of sherry off of the book case. Pouring herself a snifter, she said, "Well. A merry Christmas to one and all, I suppose."

"What-what-what—" Rawdon said, staring at the space where the Krampus had been.

"It's Christmas Day, Ozzy. The Krampus has returned to wherever it goes for another year. Which means that you're safe, relatively speaking." St. Cyprian stood, and helped Rawdon to his feet. He pulled the other man close. "You have a year, Ozzy. Don't waste it."

Rawdon yanked his arm free. "What do you mean?"

"I mean, I might not be around next year to save your wretched hide." St. Cyprian's eyes narrowed. "And even if I am, I may decide not to."

"What?" Rawdon blinked.

"You never really answered my question, you know," St. Cyprian said. "About young Pettigrew."

"It's none of your business," Rawdon said. "And I'll thank you to stay out of it." He straightened his coat.

"Would that I could, Ozzy," St. Cyprian said.

Rawdon turned, his face a picture of confusion. There was an electric buzz as someone rang the front bell. Rawdon whipped back around. "What was that?"

"The police, I imagine." St. Cyprian motioned to Gallowglass. "Ms. Gallowglass, please show them in."

"The police? What is the meaning of this Charles?" Rawdon said. "What are you playing at?"

"I had Ms. Gallowglass ring the police while she was upstairs seeing to our defences," St. Cyprian said, pouring himself a glass of sherry. He held it up, and then took a sip. He didn't look at Rawdon. "Was it really self-defense, Ozzy? Or did you murder him because he called you on your black ways? Either way, the truth will out."

Rawdon didn't reply. A moment later, the police bustled in after Gallowglass, and Rawdon seemed to slump in their custody. He didn't resist as he was led out and away. St. Cyprian didn't turn around the entire time.

When Gallowglass had seen them out and returned, he sighed and set his glass down. She cleared her throat, and he turned.

"Are they off?"

She nodded. "Think he'll hang?"

"No. He has friends yet, and likely it was self-defense. Or it'll be seen that way." He looked up at the ceiling, noting the ash mark right over the pentacle. A reminder of the Krampus' visit.

"Think our visitor will be back for him next year, then?"

St. Cyprian was silent for a moment. Then, softly, he said, "Well, Christmas is a time for miracles, they say."

And somewhere distant, just at the edges of his hearing, it seemed that he could hear the clatter of funerary bells, and the tromp of black hooves.

The Christmas Eves of Aunt Elise:
A Tale of Possession in Old Grosse Pointe

by Thomas Ligotti

We pronounced her name with a distinct "Z" sound—*Remember, Jack, remember*—the way some people slur Missus into Mizzuz. It was at her home in Grosse Pointe that she insisted our family, both its wealthy and its unwealthy side, celebrate each Christmas Eve in a style that exuded the traditional, the old-fashioned, the antique. Actually, Aunt Elise constituted the wealthy side of the family all on her own. Her husband had died many years before, leaving his wife a prosperous real estate business and no children. Not surprisingly, Aunt Elise undertook the management of the firm with admirable success, perpetuating our heirless uncle's family name on "for-sale" signs planted on front lawns in three states. But what was *Uncle's first* name, a young nephew or niece sometimes wondered. Or, as it was more than once put by one of us children: "Where's *Uncle* Elise?" To which the rest of us answered in unison: "He's at his ease," a response we learned from none other than our widowed aunt herself.

Aunt Elise was without husband or offspring of her own, true enough. But she loved all the ferment of big families, and every holiday season she possessed as much in blood relations as she did in her tangible and intangible assets and investments. Nevertheless, she was not the conspicuously consuming type of rich bitch. Her house was something of an Elizabethan country manor in style while remaining modest, even relatively miniature, in its mass. It fit very nicely—when it existed—into a claustrophobic cluster of trees on some corner acreage a few steps from Lake Shore Drive, profiling rather than facing the lake itself. A rather dull exterior of soot-gray stones somewhat camouflaged the old place in its woodland hideaway; until one caught sight of its diamond-paned windows and realized that a house in fact existed where before there seemed to be only shadowed vacancy.

Around Christmastime the many-faceted windows of my aunt's residence took on a candied glaze in the pink, blue, green, and other-colored lights strung about their perimeters. More often in the old days—*Remember them, Jack*—a thick December fog rolled off the not-yet-frozen lake and those kaleidoscopic windows would throw their spectrums into the softening haze. This, to my child's senses, was the image and atmosphere defining the winter holiday: a serene congregation of colors that for a time turned our everyday world into one where mysteries abounded. This was the celebration, this was the festival. Why did we leave it all behind us, leave it outside? Every Christmas Eve of my childhood, as I was guided up the winding front walk toward my aunt's house, a parent's hand in each of mine, I always stopped short, pulling Mom and Dad back like a couple of runaway horses, and for a brief, futile moment refused to go inside.

After the first Christmas Eve I can recall—chronologically my fifth—I knew what happened inside the house, and year after year there was little change either in the substance or surface details of the program. For those from large families, this scene is a little too familiar to bother describing. Perhaps even lifelong orphans are jaded to it. Still, there are others for whom depictions of unusual uncles, loveable grandparents, and a common run of cousins will always be fresh and dear; those who delight in multiple generations of characters crowding the page, who are warmed by the feel of their paper flesh. I tell you they share this temper with my Aunt Elise, and her spirit is in them.

For the duration of these Christmas assemblies, my aunt always occupied the main room of her house. This room I never saw except as a fantasy of ornamentation, a hallucinatorium in holiday dress. Right now I can only hope to portray a few of its highlights. First of all holly, both fresh and artificial, hung down from wherever it was possible to hang—the frames of paintings, the stained-wood shelves of a thousand gewgaws, even the velvety embossed pattern of the wallpaper itself, intertwining with its swirls and flourishes, if memory serves. And from the fixtures above, including a chandelier delicately sugared with tiny Italian lights, down came gardens of mistletoe. The huge fireplace blazed with a festive inferno, and before its cinder-spitting hearth was a protective screen, at either end of which stood a pair of thick brass posts. And slipped over the crown of each post was a sock-puppet Santa, its mittens outstretched in readiness to give someone a tiny, angular hug.

In the corner of the main room, the one beside the front window, a plump evergreen was somewhere hidden beneath every imaginable type of dangling, roping, or blinking decoration, as well as being dolled up with silly bows in pastel shades, satiny bows lovingly tied by human hands. The same hands also did their work on the presents beneath the tree, and year after year these seemed, like everything else in the room, to be in exactly the same place, as if the gifts of last Christmas had never been opened, quickening in me the nightmarish sense of a ritual forever reenacted without hope of escape. (Somehow I am still possessed by this same feeling of entrapment.) My own present was always at the back of that horde of packages, almost against the wall behind the tree. It was tied up with a pale purple ribbon and covered with pale blue wrapping paper upon which little bears in infants' sleeping gowns dreamed of more pale blue presents which, instead of more bears, had little boys dreaming upon them. I spent much of a given Christmas Eve sitting near this gift of mine, mostly to find refuge from the others rather than to wonder at what was inside. It was always something in the way of underwear, nightwear, or socks, never the nameless marvel which I fervently hoped to receive from my obscenely well-heeled aunt. Nobody seemed to mind that I sat on the other side of the room from where most of them congregated to talk or sing carols to the music of an ancient organ, which Aunt Elise played with her back to her audience, and to me.

Slee—eep in heav—enly peace.

"That was very good," she said without turning around. As usual, the sound of her voice led you to expect that any moment she would clear her throat of some sticky stuff which was clinging to its insides. Instead she switched off the electric organ, after which gesture some of the gathering, dismissed, left for other parts of the house.

"We didn't hear Old Jack singing with us," she said, turning to look across the room where I was seated in a large chair beside a fogged window. On that occasion I was about twenty or twenty-one, home from school for Christmas. I had drunk quite a bit of Aunt Elise's holiday punch, and felt like answering: "Who cares if you didn't hear Old Jack singing, you old bat?" But instead I simply stared her way, drunkenly taking in her visage for the family scrapbook of my memory: tight-haired head (like combed wires), calm eyes of someone in an old portrait (someone long gone), high cheekbones highly colored (less rosily than like a rash), and the prominent choppers of a horse charging out of nowhere in a dream. I had no worry about my future ability to remember these features, even though I had vowed this would be the last Christmas Eve I would view them. So I could afford to be tranquil in the face of Aunt Elise's taunts that evening. In any case, further confrontation between the two of us was aborted when some of the children began clamoring for one of their aunt's stories. "And this time a true story, Auntie. One that really happened."

"All right," she answered, adding that "maybe Old Jack would like to come over and sit with us."

"Too old for that, thank you. Besides, I can hear you just fine from—"

"Well," she began before I'd finished, "let me think a moment. There are so many, so many. Anywho, here's one of them. This happened before any of you were born, a few winters after I moved into this neighborhood with your uncle. I don't know if you ever noticed, but a little ways down the street there's an empty lot where there should be, used to be, a house. You can see it from the front window over there," she said, pointing to the window beside my chair. I let my eyes follow her finger out that window and through the fog witnessed the empty lot of her story.

"There it once stood, a beautiful old house much bigger than this one. In that house lived a very old man who never went out and who never invited anyone to visit him, at least no one I ever noticed. And after the old man died, what do you think happened to the house?"

"It disappeared," answered some of the children, jumping the gun.

"In a way, I suppose it did disappear. Actually what happened was that some men came and tore the house down brick by brick. I think the old man who lived there must have been very mean to want that to happen to his house after he died."

"How do you know he wanted it?" I interjected, trying to spoil her assumption.

"What other sensible explanation is there?" Aunt Elise answered. "Anywho," she went on, "I think that the old man just couldn't stand the thought of anyone else living in the house and being happy there, because surely he wasn't. But maybe, just maybe, he had his house torn down for another reason," said Aunt Elise, drawing out these last words to suspenseful effect. The children sitting cross-legged before her now listened with a new intentness, while the crackling logs seemed to start up a little more noisily in the fireplace.

"Maybe by destroying his house, making it disappear, the old man thought he was taking it with him into the other world. People who have lived alone for a very long time often think and do very strange things," she emphasized, though I'm sure no one except me thought to apply this final statement to the storyteller herself. (*Tell everything, Jack.*) She went on:

"Now what would lead a person to such conclusions about the old man, you may wonder? Did something strange happen with him and his house after both of them were gone? Well, the answer is yes, something did happen. And I'm going to tell you just what it was.

"One night—a foggy winter's night like this one, oh my little children—someone came walking down this exact street and paused at the property line of the house of the old man who was now dead. This someone was a young man whom many people had seen wandering around here off and on for some years. I myself, I tell you, once confronted him and asked him what business he had with us and with our homes, because that's what he seemed most interested in. Anywho, this young man called himself an an-tee-quarian, and he said he was very interested in old things, particularly old houses. And he had a very particular interest in the house of that strange old man. A number of times he had asked him if he could look around inside, but the old man always refused. Most of the time the house was dark as though no one was home, even if someone always was.

"So you can imagine the young man's bewilderment when on that winter's night what he saw was not a dark house where it seemed no one was inside, but a place all lit up with bright Christmas lights shining through the fog. Could this be the old man's house, decorated so nice and cheerful with these lights? Yes, it could, because there was the old man himself standing at the window with a rather friendly look on his face. So, one more time, the young man thought he would try his luck and maybe get to see the inside of the old house. He rang the bell and the front door slowly opened wide. The old man didn't say anything, but merely stepped back so that his caller could come in. Finally the young antiquarian would be able to study the inside of the house to his heart's content. Along the way, in narrow halls and long-abandoned rooms, the old man stood silently beside his guest, smiling all the time."

"I can't imagine how you know this part of your *true* story," I interrupted.

"Aunt Elise *knows*," asserted one of my little cousins just to shut me up. And when my aunt cast a glance at me, it seemed for a moment that she really did know. Then she continued her true story.

"After the young man had looked all around the house, both men sat down in the deep comfortable chairs of the front parlor and talked a while. But it wasn't too long before that smile on the old man's face, that quiet little smile, began to bother his visitor in a peculiar way. At last the young man claimed he had to go, glancing down at the watch he had drawn from his pocket. And when he looked up again…the old man was gone. Naturally, this startled the young man, who jumped up from his chair and nervously checked the nearby rooms and hallways for his host, calling "Sir,

sir," because he never found out the old man's name. And though he could have been in any number of different places, the owner of the house didn't seem to be anywhere that the young man investigated. So the antiquarian finally decided just to leave without saying good-bye or thank you or anything like that.

"But he didn't get as far as the door when he stopped dead in his tracks because of what he saw through the front window. There seemed to be no street anymore, no street lamps or sidewalks, not even any houses, besides the one he was in, of course. There was only the fog and some horrible, tattered shapes wandering aimlessly within it. The young man could hear them crying. What was this place, and where had the old house taken him? He didn't know what to do except stare out the window. And when he saw the face reflected in the window, he thought for a second that the old man had returned and was standing behind him again, smiling his quiet smile.

"But then the young man realized that this was now his own face, and, like those terrible, ragged creatures lost in the fog, he too began to cry.

"After that night, no one around here ever saw the young man again. Well, did you like that story, children?"

I felt tired, more tired than I'd ever been in my life. I barely had the will or the strength to push myself out of the chair into which I'd sunk down so deep. How slowly I trudged past faces that seemed far off in the distance. Where was I going? Was I in want of another drink? Did I desire another dainty from the table spread with Christmas treats? What was it that was calling me away from that room?

No time seemed to have passed, but when I came to myself I was walking down a foggy street. The fog formed impenetrable white walls around me, narrow corridors leading nowhere and rooms without windows. I didn't walk very far before realizing I could go no farther. As it happened, though, I did finally see something. What I saw was a cluster of Christmas lights, their colors beaming against the fog. But what could they have signified that they should seem so horrible to me? Why did this peaceful vision of hazy wonder, which had transported the imagination of my childhood self, now strike me with such terror? These were not the colors I had loved; this could not be the house. Yet it was, for there at the window stood its owner, and the sight of her thin smiling face for some reason was not right.

Then I remembered: Aunt Elise was long dead and her house, at the instruction of her will, had been dismantled brick by brick.

"Uncle Jack, wake up," urged young voices at close range, though technically, being an only child, I was not their uncle. More accurately, I was just an elder member of the family who had nodded off in his chair. It was

Christmas Eve, and I had had a little too much to drink.

"We're gonna sing carols, Uncle Jack," said the voices. Then they went away.

I went away, too, retrieving my overcoat from the bedroom where it lay buried in a communal grave under innumerable other overcoats. Everyone else was singing songs to the strumming of guitars. (I liked their metallic timbre because it was in no way reminiscent of the rich, rotting vibrations of the church organ Aunt Elise played on Christmas Eves long passed.) Foregoing all rituals of departure, I slipped quietly out the back door in the kitchen.

I left that Christmas Eve get-together as if I had an appointment to keep, one of longstanding whose import I never knew or had forgotten. So many things I can remember from years gone by—and easily enough because I have led such an uneventful and solitary existence—but I cannot remember what happened next that evening. My mind was not at its best, and the dream I had earlier must have carried over into one I had when I went to sleep at home, though I do not recall doing that either. The one thing I do remember, as if it happened while I was still awake and not dreaming, was standing before the door of a house that no longer existed, a door that opened in a slow, weighty sweep. Then a hand reached out and laid itself upon me. What horror I felt as I saw that great, gaping smile and heard the words: "Merry Christmas, Old Jack!"

Oh, how good it was to see the old boy when he came to me at last. He had grown old but never grew up. And finally I had him, him and his every thought, all the pretty pictures of his mind. Those weeping demons, souls forever lost, came out of the fog and took away his body. He was one of them now. But I have kept the best part, all his beautiful memories, all those lovely times we had—the children, the presents, the colors of those nights! Anywho, they are mine now. Tell us of those years, Old Jack, the years I have now taken from you—the years I can play with as I wish, like a child with his toys . Oh, how nice, how nice and lovely to be settled in a world where it's always dead with darkness and always alive with lights! And where it will always, forever after, be Christmas Eve.

Letters to Santa
by Scott David Aniolowski

now fell with a hush on the bejeweled suburban sprawl. Lights of red and green and white twinkled from rooftops, and large plastic Santas and snowmen stood vigil in front yards, warmly glowing from within. Decorators of unwavering faith but questionable taste proffered tableaus of light-up Nativity characters. Wreaths hung on doors, and tiny sparkling fairy lights dripped from trees and buildings. Tasteful or tacky, the neighborhood was clothed for Christmas.

Inside the tall Colonial house at 615 Spruce Street, a man in his mid-thirties peered through a drape and watched the snow fall. All of the houses along the street shone with lights to ring in the yuletide holiday. All but one. The house at 614 Spruce—the one directly across the street—was dark save for eight little white lights that glowed in the front window. Jim envied the Blooms: they didn't have to suffer through the hell of Christmas every December. They lit their candles each night and played dreidel with their children and enjoyed a family holiday steeped in tradition and ritual instead of consumerism and greed. No tacky decorations. No bank-breaking shopping. No Christmas insanity. But best of all, no Santa Claus.

A puffed black and white cat, house-lazy and overfed, lay curled in a fat ball on one corner of the sofa. It stretched, yawned, and peered at the man through one squinty eye before rolling onto its back. Immediately it was asleep again, indifferent to its human companion and dreaming the dreams of cats. Jim rubbed the animal's belly but solicited only a feline sigh.

"He's fast asleep," purred a silky voice from an arched doorway. A lovely but homey young woman stood there. She glowed with the weary happiness of a parent of young children on Christmas Eve.

"Yeah. What a life, huh?" Jim smiled at his wife. He finished the last gulp of a now-tepid eggnog, wrinkling his nose.

"Another?" Maura asked, reaching for her husband's glass.

"No. I'll just wash it down with this," he said, filling his glass to near overflowing with brandy.

Maura squeezed in next to Jim on the couch. They snuggled and kissed and she played with his messy hair. The cat lifted its head to look at them and then rolled back into a ball and covered its face with its bushy tail. The room, cozy and glowing from the crackling fireplace and twinkling Christmas tree lights, looked for all the world like a carefully crafted department store window.

The pretty young mother plucked a chocolate covered cherry from a candy dish on the coffee table. She bit into the confection and clear red syrup drizzled down her chin. She popped the other half of the candy into Jim's mouth and then rubber her gooey chin on his playfully. "Come on," she stood and took her husband's hand, trying to pull him up.

He pulled his hand free and took a deep swallow of brandy. "You go on," he said, wiping the sticky ooze from his chin. He knew he needed a shave when he felt the prickly two-day stubble.

She made a kissing noise, brandished a spring of mistletoe and nodded toward the stairs.

He turned away, rebuffing her enchantment.

"Jim..." she started.

He took a deep breath and turned back to the window and the falling snow.

"Fine," she spat and headed toward the stairs. It was a fight she was used to. It had become as much a holiday tradition as putting up the tree or baking cookies with the kids. Every Christmas Eve it was the same. She'd almost gotten used to it. Early in their relationship it nearly drove them apart, but she'd finally accepted it. For their sake. And the sake of the boys.

"Hon, you know I have to wait up," he mumbled.

"For Santa?"

"Yes."

"Jim, we go through this every year."

"I have to be here. Ready. In case he comes."

"Jim, for the love of god, he's not real!"

"He is!"

Maura sighed deeply, resigning herself to the fact that this was not an argument she could win, nor one she wanted to escalate in case the children heard.

"Fine. I'll see you in the morning, then," she feigned a smile as she ascended the dark staircase. She knew that Jim would stay up until dawn waiting for Santa to come down the chimney. In the morning the boys would open their gifts in a whirlwind of colored paper and shiny ribbon while mom beamed at the magic of childhood and dad did his best to stay awake. Once the gifts were opened, Jim would trudge to bed and sleep the rest of Christmas Day away while the boys played with their new toys and his wife and in-laws visited. He'd appear again in time for Christmas dinner where he'd act as though everything was as it should be. Maura—and eventually her parents—became used to Jim's bizarre holiday behavior and just accepted it as one of his annoying yet endearing quirks.

Maura tried to be understanding. She'd heard the tragic stories from Jim's childhood. She knew he'd hated Christmas since he was a young child: since the Christmas when he lost his brother. When he went off to college he wouldn't even come home for the Christmas break. He spent Christmas Eve in Chinese restaurants with foreign students and Jewish families, staying behind long after everyone else had gone, playing mahjongg with the restaurant staff until early into the morning. Even back then, he slept through most of Christmas Day.

Jim's parents—now both dead—seemed to fair little better on Christmas. There were severe depressions and alcohol abuse. The years since Jim's dad died his mom didn't even put up her beloved Christmas tree. None of the family had ever gotten over the loss of Jim's younger brother Kyle. Kyle went missing one Christmas Eve when he was four and Jim had been five. There had been intensive police searches and investigations, but no trace of Kyle was ever found. Unofficially, it was assumed that Kyle had been snatched by some child predator, but officially the case was never solved; eventually the case went cold and the files ended up in the back of a drawer somewhere. Jim's own story of what happened that fateful night—described by psychiatrists as the imagination of a child's fragile mind trying to cope with a horrible tragedy—only complicated matters and led to years of psychotherapy and self-loathing. Eventually he learned to just not talk about it. Even Maura didn't know what Jim had seen that Christmas Eve so many years ago. When Jim's mom died he and Maura cleaned out her house and they found Kyle's Christmas presents still stashed in an upstairs closet, the paper faded and dusty and the ribbon frayed; his mom had held on to those gifts for over thirty years. Even that wasn't enough to get Jim to talk to her about it, and the packages were unceremoniously dumped into trash cans without another word.

Early in their marriage, Jim had fought with Maura about Christmas decorations. It was usually a compromise of a tree and a few other things. Once the boys came, however, it was a different story and Jim knew it best he acquiesce lest he risk the loss of his happy home and family. His one firm objection, however, was all things Santa. He refused to allow his wife to have any images of Santa Claus anywhere in the house, and in order to keep the peace she reluctantly agreed. So every December their house filled to bursting with ornaments and baubles and lights and shiny things. Holly and poinsettias and snowmen and reindeer and every other possible bit of Christmas decoration. Except for Santa. Maura and the kids baked cookies and built a gingerbread house; she sent cards with shiny embossed pictures and set out bowls of ribbon candy that looked as much like delicate bits of stained glass as sweet comestibles. Jim was able to tolerate it all for a few years, and was even beginning to reluctantly enjoy it. Until Jim Jr. and little Kyle were old enough to know who Santa was. They wanted to sit on Santa's lap at department stores and send him letters. That was too much for him. Inevitably, Jim and Maura would end up in a fight and she would take the kids and leave him behind, red-faced and fuming. He suspected that she secretly took the boys to see Santa, but tried not to think about it, and never asked outright. He didn't want to know. If he didn't know, it didn't happen.

Christmas Eve passed into Christmas Day as the clock moved into the small hours. The fireplace held only embers now, the crackling and popping long silenced. Jim turned off the television just as Scrooge woke from his visitation from the jolly Ghost of Christmas Past. Outside, the snow was falling harder, veiling the neighboring houses. Three light-up plastic wise men in the yard next door were buried up to their waists by blowing snow. Gauzy snowy halos gleamed around every twinkling light and glowing figure up and down the street. In a few more hours the sun would rise and Jim could relax knowing his own Ghost of Christmas Past hadn't come—his family was safe and he could start a new year (Jim considered December 25 as the first day of his New Year, and not January 1, like the rest of the world). He wouldn't have to worry again for twelve months.

The cat heard it first. Its head shot up, its eyes like saucers and its ears swiveling in on some sound Jim hadn't heard. It nervously leapt to its feet, it's back arched and tail puffed. A low growl grumbled from the cat's throat as it locked its attention on the fireplace. Jim sat up, scooting to the edge of the couch. He tried stroking the agitated animal but it hissed and ran off, skulking close to the floor with its ears back and tail dragging behind it.

Something made a sound on the roof. That time he'd heard it. Jim stood, listening. He moved to the fireplace, putting his ear near the hearth. A faint crumbling sound came from above, and bits of black soot fell into the fireplace. He poked his head in and looked up the chimney but could see only darkness. He could hear something moving... maybe even breathing. A shower of soot and ashes rained down, then the sound of something coming down the chimney. Something deliberate. Something large. Jim's heart raced. This was it. Just like thirty-some years ago. He was coming. Santa Claus was coming.

Jim retreated to the couch to retrieve something he had hidden beneath it. He was just picking himself up, cloth-wrapped parcel in his hand, when the black boots stepped with a hard crunch into the dying embers in the bottom of the fireplace. Before he could fully comprehend what he was seeing, an enormous figure in red pushed and squeezed its way out of the brick fireplace with a grunt.

The young father gasped involuntarily. The memories of his child-hood—the horror—came flooding back to him. The figure before him stood over seven feet tall and weighed five or six hundred pounds or more. It was clad head to toe in velvety red cloth trimmed with white fur. A long floppy fur-trimmed red cap adorned its head, the white fuzzy ball dangling over one shoulder, and a thick white beard and frosted wire spectacles obscured most of the purplish-red face. This was the Santa Claus of Jim's childhood and of his nightmares of thirty-some years.

Santa stood for a moment, studying the stunned figure before him. He cocked his head and a smile seemed to break across what little of his face Jim could see. "Ho, ho, ho!" the giant in red said as much as laughed. The whole of his elephantine bulk quaked fluidly as he made to laugh.

"I know you," Jim muttered breathlessly. "I remember you."

The red shape took a thunderous step forward, dragging a large cloth sack behind it and kicking smoldering ashes across the floor. It produced a strap studded with silvery jingle bells, shook it and filled the house with the crisp jubilant euphony. The sound burned through Jim's memory, sending him back thirty years. He grasped his head with his hands, trying to drive out the bitter recollections.

"No!" Jim shouted. He pulled the cloth from the pistol he'd sequestered beneath the sofa and shakily brandished it toward the towering form in red.

Santa laughed again, but this time it was a real laugh, deep and gurgling. "Jimmy. Still missing your brother?" it mocked.

Jim cocked the gun and pointed it at the mountainous form. Tears filled his eyes and his entire body shook.

"A gun won't kill Santa, Jimmy. Besides, do you want to wake up the rest of the family? Your wife? Your boys?" The last he said in a breathy whisper.

Somehow Jim knew that it was telling the truth. He knew the gun was impotent against the intruder.

"Why? What do you want? Who are you?" Jim sobbed.

"I'm Santa Claus," it gurgled.

"No. Santa's not real. He's just a story."

"Well, a useful one, then. How better to be invited in by children?"

"What? Invited?"

"I only go where I'm invited," it breathed heavily. "The letters. From the children."

"But..." Jim stammered.

"'*Deer Santa*,'" it began to read from a yellowed scrap of paper it pulled from somewhere in its coat. "'*I had been a vary good boy this yeer. Plees bring me a baskitball like the proes use and a bike and a trane set. I will leave cookys for you and carots for Rudof. Love Jimmy Hunter 22 Apple Orchard Drive.*'"

Jim's blood ran cold as he heard the words. The letter—the last letter he had ever written to Santa Claus when he was five years old.

"My letter..." he stared, the full reality of the horror dawning on him like a hazy autumn sunrise.

"I keep them all."

"You came because of me? My letter? I woke Kyle when I heard you. But then I was scared and I stayed at the top of the stairs. Kyle went downstairs. I peeked over the railing. It was my letter. It was supposed to be me? It was supposed to be me!" Jim crumbled to the floor, crushed beneath the weight of full comprehension.

"It's a burden being responsible for your brother. I abandoned my own brothers long ago. We were powerful once. We built great cities. But then we tired of our masters and turned against them. When we finally won our freedom my brothers squandered it. They were stupid and lazy. Worse— they were content. But not me. A few of us left. Thank Ubbo-Sathla, I left. Early on I was not much better than my brothers. Consume. Sleep. That was all. There was nothing to distract. Nothing to fill the long eternity. But then I began to watch you. To watch man. And eventually man grew. I found distraction. Release. You are wonderfully entertaining creatures. Your art. Your literature."

"What did you do to my brother? Kyle? Where's Kyle?"

The mountainous Santa stood for a moment, looming over Jim's comparatively small and frail figure. Then it bent low, its face inches from Jim's. "Why, I ate him, of course," it whispered, the stench of unguessable ages on its hot breath.

Without thought, Jim lashed out at the red giant, landing a solid blow to the face. The long white beard, frosty spectacles and red cap dropped off, and Jim's hand made contact with something that felt hot and gummy and soft. It wasn't flesh but some gelatinous stuff. And it burned. He pulled back a hand blistered and raw with burns and bleeding welts. Santa's face—or what should have been a face—was a formless fleshy lump with a toothless wet slit where a mouth should be and a couple blank bubbles for eyes.

"This doesn't have to be difficult, Jimmy," Santa gurgled, pulling off his gloves. Immediately the gooey purple hands began to slowly ooze like honey or melted wax. "Just let me get what I came for and I'll go," it headed toward the stairs. "I enjoy your holiday tradition. I gorge myself, too. Then I read a good book and sleep for a few months. It all helps pass the time. It entertains me. This King fellow writes nice long books," he paused, leaning in close to Jim, "but I think he knows."

"No! Please. Why here? What—what about someone else? What about the Blooms? Yeah. Across the street. They have three boys and a girl," Jim felt his soul blacken as he made the suggestion, but at this point his family was at stake, and he'd do anything to protect them.

Santa stopped. "The Blooms?"

"Yeah. Right there," Jim pointed out the window. "Right across the street."

"They don't believe in me. Besides," the disfigured giant continued, its voice deepening, "haven't the Jews suffered enough?"

Jim was dumbfounded by the response. His mind raced, looking for something else. Anything else. Some way to protect his boys. "Wait!" he yelled. "Wait. You said you only go where you're invited. I didn't invite you in. You weren't invited," he almost laughed. "Get out! Go away!"

Santa stopped, considering his companion. A crude smile yawned across its head, and the eye-bubbles burst open wide, making it look queerly like a jack o'lantern. A formless, gelatinous arm reached inside the enormous velvety red coat, pulling out a sheet of paper.

"'*Deer Santa*,'" the thing began to read. "'*My name is Jimmy Hunter Jr. My dad don't beleev in you but I do and my brother to. This yeer I want a new video game box. Bring my bruther some good kids stuf. We liv at 615 Spruce Street. You cant miss it it's the big white house with blak shutrs.*'"

"My god! No! Take me, then," the young father threw himself at the elephantine creature's feet. "You came for me thirty years ago, so take me now. Just leave my boys."

"No," it said simply.

"Why?" Jim stammered, feeling his life and mind slipping away.

"You're filled with poisons. Alcohol. Medicine. Other drugs. Years of school sports and the on-again off-again working out most of you do leave you tough. Tasteless. Children are tender and sweet. Fattened by the mystical enchantment of childhood. They haven't gotten unimaginative and bitter yet."

Then Jim Hunter was confronted by the most searing horror he'd ever experienced. From the darkness at the top of the stairs came a voice. A child's voice. His son's voice.

"Daddy? Santa?" it was Jim Jr.

"It's Santa! It's Santa!" came little Kyle's sweet voice, filled with the music of childhood excitement and wonder.

The two brothers stepped down onto the top step and into the dreamy light off the Christmas tree. Their sleep-creased faces glowed with amazement. Jim Jr. grasped the banister to steady himself while Kyle had a death-grip on a purple plushy animal.

"Ho! Ho! Ho!" laughed the gelatinous Santa and it shook its strap of jingle bells.

The boys made to move down the stairs.

Santa grasped his velvety coat in gooey hands and tore it open, a thick mass of sticky, ropey purple-red jelly spilling out onto the floor. Instantly the jacket and pants deflated. The black boots tipped over, emptied of their contents. Twisting tendrils groped up the walls and onto the ceiling while others wrapped snake-like around the fancy staircase spindles and flowed up the railing toward the boys. The bulk of the thing heaved and quivered near the bottom of the stairs, numerous weird eyes blinking open randomly and toothless mouths yawning and puckering. The whole thing had a horrible translucence about it, although it was nothing but churning ooze.

And from each of the mouths came the gurgling, slurping sound of "Ho! Ho! Ho!" in various tones and voices, like a chorus of drowned men.

Jim sobbed and screamed. He felt his mind clawing toward darkness, trying to shut out what it was unable to comprehend. He danced on the edge of consciousness, fire and pain throbbing through his head. In his mind's eye his baby brother begged for help, then his own children.

The broken man struggled for self-control, and in a final desperate moment snatched it from madness. Jim screamed again, begging for forgiveness. Tears burned his eyes, bile bubbled in his throat. He focused as hard as he could to steady himself, Kyle's face pleading with him across the years. And he raised the gun he still clutched in his hand. Above the gruesome mass of gelatinous flesh. To the top of the stairs. Taking careful aim.

Then he fired the gun.

Twice.

Keeping Christmas
by Michael G. Szymanski

omething was wrong at the Marshall house. The signs were evident to anyone who knew what to look for, and Martensen was a past master at the craft of observation. Ironic, then, that this observation should be made in the town where he lived, and right over there at the end of his block. He could see the modest New England cracker box from his upstairs study, even through the veil of swirling snow that had taken the night, darkness filling windows that once had glowed with light and life, driveway and sidewalk smothered beneath a deep blanket of snow that had fallen the night before last and had yet to be cleared away.

Marshall was of the breed that embraced winter, never wasting an opportunity to be out in it, whether to plow the first flake of the season from the drive or building armies of snowmen with his son and daughter, exuberant eight-year-olds who clearly favored their father in their climatological preferences. Martensen favored the opposing sentiment, having neither use nor affection for things wintry, especially with Christmas Day fast approaching and shopping still to be done and lights still to be hung.

He would have been content flinging tinsel at a Yuletide palm tree in Florida or Hawaii or any other tropical sanctuary but Molly was a traditionalist, and a pine tree in the house and snow on the ground for Christmas were key elements of that tradition. No room for negotiation there; Molly was a soft-spoken wall against which he could throw himself only to his own detriment. He bore no fondness for snow in his heart, but so long as it stayed clear of the roads when he needed them an uneasy truce was grudgingly maintained by both parties. There were compromises between the extremes though, so why was it they had settled in an obscure fishing village on the frigid wind-swept coast of Maine? Easy enough; New England was Martensen's hunting ground, his prey unique to this area where land met sea and where sometimes were spawned strange overlaps.

Flat, moisture-laden flakes of snow pattered against the window, clinging briefly to the glass before slipping down to collect at the bottoms of the panes. So, quiet, the night. Silent night. Holy night. That impending evening hung heavy in his thoughts as they did every year, when bittersweet memories played out in the sparsely tenanted theater of his mind.

Shrugging those memories into reluctant intermission, he continued his study of the Marshall house, hoping, praying that some sign of life would reveal itself to abate his dark misgivings. He didn't think that it would; no Christmas miracle here. Once again his antagonism for the holidays showed its scowling face; no, make that The Holidays, to separate them from all others, a carefully-honed mental weapon brandished against the madness of the season.

Molly suspected but didn't know for sure, so she kept silent about it. She would never confront him outright, he was sure, but he was equally certain that she was attempting to subtly win him over through the pleasure she took in the celebration of Christmas. How such pleasure could be possible after what they'd seen, what they knew, what they'd sacrificed...

He knew the history of the region well, knew of certain towns that appeared on no map but had played a pivotal role in the lives of far too many over the years. Cursed places, squalid clusters of decaying structures infested by those who harbored a peculiar, heinous decay unique to themselves and thankfully confined to those regions for the most part. These were dangerous locales where the curious could be swallowed whole with vicious speed or consumed by insidious increments, and where the sea is known to keep its secrets well.

Martensen had read much and surmised more, especially after consulting that musty report detailing a covert raid on the town of Innsmouth in 1927. Even the redacted version revealed a great deal, but Martensen had been allowed access to the original file, this achieved through numerous university affiliations and government contacts. It had opened his eyes onto a world of perverse alliances and unforgivable exchanges that, revolting as they were, did not come as much of a surprise to him, considering what he already knew, even then.

The history of this corruption of the human genome ran far and deep, deeper than the vast, abyssal seas that had given it birth. It rose from the tropic reefs of Ponape to spread its unclean taint around the world and into the lunatic fringes of human society, but nowhere was this morbid heritage more vital than in certain seldom-named fishing villages strung out along the bleakest sections of the New England coastline. It was a vile, repellant legacy, the heart of it ripe with the rot of avarice, weighed down by the effluence of power-lust and malign intent.

Martensen had come away from that reading convinced the government should have eradicated Innsmouth to the smallest shack and shed, the last plank and nail, leaving no two bricks conjoined to provide shelter for the obscenities that had tenanted there. But they had not done so and now he hunted.

He had stalked them, learning their spoor as he and Molly prowled up and down the coast through towns that reared squalid façades just beyond the casual eye of the summer tourist. He tracked them to their lairs, facing them down and taking decisive action with conviction of his righteous purpose. Now, his instincts were drawing him to the Marshall house and the horrid drama that might very well be playing out within its bright and freshly painted walls that had so recently basked in the multicolored glow of festive Christmas lighting.

Molly had brought the situation to light the previous weekend, as they were getting ready for bed. He'd just come up from stoking the wood and oil burner in the basement to find his wife peering between the curtains of the bedroom window, which faced onto the street. She squinted to bring the scene into focus, vanity refusing the necessity of eyeglasses.

"James," she called him over with a familiar quiet urgency. "Come look at this."

Late as it was, cold as it was, Jenna Marshall was about to take a trip. As Martensen watched, the attractive twenty-something brunette hustled to the trunk of the family car and tossed in a large, use-worn suitcase. Her movements were abrupt and spastic, those of a frightened bird, as she threw wary glances over her shoulder back at the house. Her posture was rigid, and even at this distance he could tell she was wound up tight as a spring in an emotional bomb that was primed to detonate at the slightest provocation.

"Marital problems?" He offered as he stroked his rust-hued beard, which had yet to suffer any taint of gray.

Molly shrugged. "*That* would be the best kept secret in town."

"Could be nothing." Martinson frowned; he'd been anticipating an uneventful holiday tucked deep in the warm comfort of his home, and he was reluctant to place that in jeopardy. "Still, it's one of the first signs, isn't it? Non-blood relatives pushed away, alienated, or done away with. Her leaving now is a good sign. And aren't those the kids in the back seat?"

"She bundled them into the car earlier, and they seemed awfully upset. Scared. We should watch this closely. Very closely."

"Don't worry," he assured. "I intend to."

What followed was an exasperating interval, filled with the unwelcome tasks of the season coupled with maintaining a casual surveillance of his neighbor. He'd stalled as long as possible before Molly's quiet scowls drove him into the cold to decorate the house. It seemed such nonsense to him, celebrating a pagan holiday to observe the birth of a prophet who was most likely born several months later. What did these garish lights, gaudy ornaments and exchanges of wildly overpriced and inappropriate gifts have to do with such a celebration?

Martensen had seen much in his life, the things he'd experienced having jaded him in ways he'd never suspected until they surfaced in response to some trivial occurrence or idle observation. The curse of being a realist was a stark view of life's trivialities and a substantial amount of intolerance for those who placed such importance on them. This glum attitude was more finely distilled the longer he was forced to remain out in the biting cold untangling and stringing silly damned multicolored bulbs over every square inch of his property.

This he resented above all else, those stupid glowing cords, bright and cheery and meant for younger eyes than his, eyes that Molly and he had not been allowed to bring into their home. The doctors said there was nothing wrong with either of them, that it was just one of those flukes that plague our lives before eventually moving on, but it hurt; it *hurt*. And this time of year was a knife driven deep into his soul. This was a season for *children*.

A tear froze to his cheek, a tear that Molly could never, *ever* know about. He worked mechanically in that silent night, allowing his sorrow and anger this single outlet. If by chance a group of carolers had paused at his fence just then, Martensen was certain he would have strangled them all with those damn Christmas lights, God bless us, everyone.

It was the tree, that damn *tree* that hit him hardest, every time he passed it. It stood in the corner of the living room, a living thing sacrificed to the season tricked up like a desperate hooker in glitter and tensile standing sentinel over its meager collection of presents; two each to one another, plus one or two perfunctory offerings from friends or, occasionally, neighbors. No toys, though; no need of *those*.

Martensen pulled his attention back to the lights. One string wasn't working, and he'd have to test each bulb to ferret out the offender. It was cold and bleak out there in the front yard and Martensen saw no beauty in it, perhaps because it too closely resembled the secret wasteland of his soul.

To his mind, the only good to come of the whole process was the opportunity to keep a closer watch on the Marshall house, for all the good that did. The place remained dark, revealing no sign of activity within.

It took another week to convince him. Marshall left the house on three occasions during that interval, each time bundled in a heavy coat and wide-brimmed hat that left his face in shadow. This signified little, but he could not disguise the slumped, bent back posture or the shuffling gait that grew more pronounced between excursions. The conclusion was unavoidable; Marshall was *changing*.

Martensen knew the Innsmouth look, had seen it all too often on the bloated visages of his quarry; bulging eyes, over-wide mouth and flaking, scaly skin gone a color of nothing healthy or natural. It was a hated look, the countenance of the shunned and despised, the mark in human flesh of a bargain struck in hell.

There had been a terrible *interbreeding* at work in Innsmouth prior to that classified raid. The inhabitants there had polluted themselves with the alien genetics of a monstrous species from the abyssal depths of the sea, a species that worshiped deities even more repugnant than themselves and whose motives were diametrically contrary to the well-being of the human race.

Martensen had learned of the Innsmouth spawn at an early age, the revelation spurring him to the intensive study of biology and in time, genetics. He'd assaulted both subjects with obsessive dedication, earning high academic honors and a position at one of the leading research facilities in the nation following his graduation. Five years there saw the accomplishment of his goal, and not long after he and Molly, then his fellow researcher and fiancé, resigned their positions and relocated to New England. The moving cartons remained unopened when Martensen began to hunt.

Ten years traveling by motor home up and down the coast had imbued them both with a level of experience that could never have been achieved at any university or research facility, no matter how well equipped or generously endowed. All that experience told him now that the Innsmouth look had crept into his hometown and into his neighborhood.

The situation came to a head on Christmas Eve. Molly was downstairs in the living room, putting the *final* final touches on the tree and Martensen was in the study posting a few last-minute holiday e-mails. Amazing how many acquaintances they had accumulated over the years, and each simply had to be wished well at this time of year. And when it was over and done, everyone could go back to being themselves, which usually entailed—but was not limited to—cutting one another off in right there in the church parking lot after Christmas service. T'is the season...

Of course the e-mails were an excuse, something to get him out from under Molly's eye for a few minutes. He'd slipped; not much, but he had slipped and he needed time, just a little time to recover.

They'd gone into town for dinner at the Blue Oyster Café as part of a holiday tradition that culminated in a meandering drive home so Molly could take in all the decorations one last time before the Big Day. *Christmas lights*, Martensen growled to himself, thinking of that old Stooges routine. *Slowly I turned...* Molly "oohed" and "ahhed" at each new display and Martensen sank deeper into his sulk. The car grew quieter, with each passing block until:

"I'm sorry."

Martensen blinked, startled by the statement. "Beg pardon?"

Molly gestured vaguely at their surroundings. "For all this. For everything."

Martensen was mortified. He'd let his darker thoughts out for a walk, and they'd been spotted by the one person who meant more to him than life. Without missing a beat, he slipped into recovery mode.

"Dinner was pretty good," he forced a lightness into his voice. "As close to home cooking as you'll ever get. And the lights are nice..."

"James, stop."

They drove in a soundless hell for an unending span of time, aware of nothing beyond the dashboard, festive holiday displays a forgotten, smarmy joke. Desperate to set things right, he had ventured into the silence.

"You know, I always get a little depressed around the holidays. Miss my folks, I guess. I think of them more often at this time of the year."

Another extended silence, but then: "And that's all?"

"That's all, hon. I swear." And felt a lying hypocrite for saying it. But it pulled them back from the edge, and by the time they got home an hour later they were laughing and lighthearted.

Now, as he set clicking off one e-mail after another, he at last came to terms with the fact that he actively hated Christmas. It was the kids, he knew, or rather the gaping void, where they should have been. After all, Joseph and Mary hadn't even been trying and look what *they* got. Why then, were he and Molly denied what so many others took for granted, and all too many, damn them, saw as an inconvenience, an intrusion into their self-centered existences?

Could it have been the treatments? He wondered, but shied away from that possibility. If true, it would surely break him...

"James." Molly's voice was sharp and filled with sudden tension. "There's someone at the Marshall house."

He was out of his chair and at the window in a swift, fluid motion, parting the curtains just enough to bring the house on the corner into view. "Damn," he muttered when he recognized the car.

Leaving the window, he returned to his desk and retrieved the .357 magnum he kept there in a locked drawer. Next to the gun was a mahogany pen case which he also scooped up, tucking it into his shirt pocket as he raced for the stairs.

"It's Jenna's car," Molly greeted him as he stalked into the living room.

"Come to try for a Christmas reconciliation. I should've seen this coming. I did see this coming, but I just didn't want to deal with it." He grabbed his coat and headed for the door.

"Wait," Molly called after him. "I'll get the shotgun."

"Give me a head start and follow after. Too many people barging in all at once might drive Marshall over the edge."

He turned to the door, but she gripped his arm, hard enough for him to feel through the thick wool of the coat. "Be careful."

He leaned in and pressed his forhead to hers. "Always."

He stepped outside and the cold stung him like harsh words from a loved one, but he ignored it in his rush to reach Jenna before she opened the front door of her house. As it was he had to yell from the street to draw her attention.

"Mr. Martensen, hello." Her voice was uncertain and tight with the stress of her circumstances. "This isn't a good time..."

"I agree, which is why you shouldn't go in there."

Her brows beetled in puzzlement, but irritation lurked there as well "I don't understand..."

"Your husband was changing, wasn't he?" She didn't reply, but he could see affirmation in her eyes. "He has a genetic anomaly, an inherited family trait that evidences in patients of his age." Now came confusion. "I know it's a lot to process, but you must understand that Colin's condition has deteriorated since you left, and confronting him now could be dangerous for both of you."

"That's insane. Colin is sick and I should be with him. It was a mistake to leave in the first place." She turned toward the door, but Martensen grabbed her arm, spinning her back.

"*Think*, Jenna! Remember how he looked when you saw him last; his face, the color of his skin. Remember that and tell me it was some benign ailment."

The dam cracked but did not burst. "God, it was horrible," she sobbed, slumping back against the door. "He was so *deformed* and gasping for breath but he wouldn't go to the hospital, refused to go. He seemed to know what was happening, and had already given in to it. He forced us to leave, for the children's sake, he said, and I went. I was a coward, terrified of what he was telling me and I left him here alone to face it. What kind of wife, am I?"

Martensen leaned in, took her face in his hands and looked into her wide, glistening eyes. "The kind who came back," he told her, admiration weighing heavy in his voice. That offered her something to cling to and she took it; her spine straightened as she wiped away her tears on the sleeve of her coat.

Molly arrived then, shotgun in hand, which rocketed Jenna to a whole new level of anxiety. "What's that for?" She demanded, voice raising an octave.

Martensen brought his own weapon from concealment. "For doing whatever might become necessary. I'm going to insist you stay out here with Molly for now; I wasn't joking about the danger."

"But it's just *Colin*..."

"Maybe. But maybe not. Stay here, Jenna. One way or another, we'll know for certain in a few minutes."

He didn't wait for her protests, trusting Molly to distract the woman from what was about to happen inside. They made a good team, a rapport honed through long years of undesired practice. Easing open the front door, he slid inside and closed it behind him.

The house felt colder than the open air outside, the sensation subsumed by the redolence of the sea, an icthyc stench that had infiltrated every open space of the domicile. Martensen was compelled to breathe through his mouth just to penetrate even a short distance down the entry hall, from where he could see a faint, flickering glow creeping through the living room doorway. The cloying odor was a sure sign that his suspicions were correct, and he now berated himself for delaying this inevitable confrontation for so long. Always best to get the unpleasantness behind you, especially in situations of this nature.

The stench approached physical proportions as Martensen stepped into the living room; it crawled down his throat, coating it with an oily gluten that threatened to wrench up the full contents of the stomach. No matter how many times he encountered it, Martensen could never accustom himself to that horrid olfactory assault.

A feeble fire huddled in the hearth, weakened glow casting a dingy, depressing pallor over the room, a grimy gray cloak that accreted around the slumped, shrouded figure hunched into an armchair pulled up before the guttering flames. This figure was the undisputed source of that malodorous taint, and thus the object of Martensen's search. This was the pivotal moment and, as usual, he moved into it with calm and quiet.

He allowed the figure time to become aware of him, all the while keeping a firm grip on the handgun, which he kept concealed behind his back. The figure of Colin Marshall started and half turned towards him, offering a glance of sickly, scabrous skin, a single overlarge and bulging eye and a portion of a mouth far too wide for the visage that harbored it. It froze then, stopped breathing altogether as it considered its next stratagem.

"I suspect your name was originally Marsh," Martensen sent gentle words into the tension. "You may not be aware of that, or even that your family has its roots in a town called Innsmouth." A reaction there; so this was not a revelation. "You know, then, just as you must know about that town's history and the curse it's carried for over a century. Why else send your family away when the change was upon you?

"You must understand on some level what's happening to you, what you are becoming. But will you embrace this change or deny it? That's what I'm here to find out."

Marshall made no reply; by now his vocal cords were no doubt beyond the ability of human speech and tending toward the thick, guttural utterances of his new genus. But he understood, of that there was no doubt. He turned back to the fire, his gaze occupied by something he held in his hands, though Martensen could not see what that was.

"I'm here to end this Colin, and trust me, one way or another it *will* end. The how of it is up to you." He paused, regarding the batracian hulk before him. "Are you a man, still, or are you given over to Dagon and that worse atrocity sleeping in R'leyh? Show me what you are, Colin."

At first, the figure of Colin Marshall did not stir, and for a moment Martensen suspected that his words had been lost on alien ears. But then the transformed man rose from the armchair to face his guest. He was all but gone into the change, very near the moment he would seek out the sea and leave the world of men behind for all time. His was now a slick and bloated form bearing unpleasant resemblance to certain amphibious frogs Martensen had encountered in his researches, made doubly repellant by the spark of intelligence at work behind the swollen, bulging orbs of his eyes.

There was something in his webbed and malformed hand, a single scrap of paper that had suffered from the ravages of constant, clumsy handling. Marshall shuffled forward, prompting Martensen to swing up the gun and draw back on the hammer in a swift, fluid motion. The appearance of a weapon in no way deterred Marshall from his course; Martensen increased pressure on the trigger, already planning what he would say to the man's widow.

A scant two feet separated them when Marshall came to a halt, the closest Martensen had ever been to such a being, a position that he did not find in the least comfortable. Then Colin Marshall leaned forward until his misshapen forehead touched the yawning barrel of the handgun, whereupon those horrid, bulging eyes rose to meet Martensen's and trapped them in a gaze of abject misery.

One misshapen hand rose in a slow arc, the hand that held the use-worn scrap of paper. It was a photograph. In it, Marshall stood with his wife and children before the brightly decorated tree of some past, far happier

Christmas observed in this very room, illuminated by the warm, cheerful light of the hearth which now threatened to extinguish at the faintest breath of air. It was an image of contentment, of hope and pride and love expressed at a time our species came closest to being truly *human* beings; a portrait of all that was now lost to Colin Marshall.

Martensen's gaze returned to the other's eyes, and was shocked by what he saw there. From a bulbous, nictating orb flowed a single tear, the liquid measure of human grief upon the visage of that which was utterly inhuman.

But no. This man, this *man*, held to his humanity, and far beyond any limit Martensen ever believed possible, clinging to memories of family and holding close the true spirit of a season most, including Martensen himself, took so lightly. Faced with a monstrous fate he'd neither sought nor embraced, he had fought back with the weapons dearest to his heart, his *human* heart, and in the hour of his soul's peril, Colin Marshall had kept Christmas, in truth and in earnest. Martensen's decision was clear.

Lowering the gun, he tucked it into his waistband as he spoke. "You've done well to hold out this long, but the crucial moment is near. I'm sorry I waited so long, but there's still time if we act quickly." Reaching into his coat, he retrieved the mahogany pen case and brought it out, opening it so that Marshall could view its contents.

"I told you once that I used to be a geneticist." He lifted the syringe from the case. "This is why. I couldn't have accomplished this without Molly, especially in those last days when the change began to assert itself. 'Physician, heal thyself' is an apt adage, and that's what I struggled so desperately to do from the night my blasphemous heritage was revealed to me. What afflicts you now was in my blood as well, and I wanted it no more than you, that damned Innsmouth gene that was inflicted on our DNA to set our fate from the day of our birth."

Martensen indicated the clear fluid within the syringe. "This is my life's work. It weakens the tainted gene that brings on the metamorphosis, allowing the human genome to reassert itself. I've offered it to many since I tested it on myself, and now I'm offering it to you. Will you accept?"

In reply, Marshall let the blanket fall from his pallid, glistening arm and held it out to Martensen.

"This is *not* a quick fix," he cautioned as he administered the injection. "It took a year and a seemingly endless series of injections to completely reverse the process in me, and you are somewhat further along than I was. That said, I see no reason why you shouldn't be celebrating next Christmas with your family here in this very room.

"It will be sometimes difficult, but your wife will be with you, as she is even now, and I will always be available if you need a… kindred spirit to talk with."

Marshall said nothing, could not, yet this did not deprive him of eloquence as he placed his hand, that taloned appendage of what most would see as a monster, hesitantly upon Martensen's shoulder and gently squeezed. The gratitude invested in that simple gesture nearly broke Martensen down, and that most unique and wondrous sensation was the true reason that he hunted, why he would continue to hunt until the day this subversion was expelled from every soul that did not welcome it.

As he returned to the front door to assure the women that all was well, Martensen could not help but feel shamed. He'd come to think of Christmas as an extravagant and glitzy sham and ridiculed its observance with sour contempt and bitterness because of what was lacking in his life. The long years of the hunt had affected him far more than he'd suspected; so many years passed in darkness, he'd very nearly forgotten the light.

And then Colin Marshall, a man in desperate need of a miracle, had found it on this frigid New England evening, this Christmas Eve that he would remember always as the night when saviors truly walked the Earth; and it had been given to Martensen to deliver that miracle. Here was a gift of profound extravagance, to pull a soul back from the abyss and return it to the circle of Humanity.

Time ran true, and when Martensen stepped out of the Marshall house it was Christmas day. The decorative lights, suddenly not so gaudy to his eye, illuminated the street and pushed back the darkness, denying this place to the wretched calamity of the Innsmouth look.

The source lay out there still, deep beneath the waves where neither light nor warmth nor compassion penetrated, plotting with malign intent and shuddersome purpose against all of humankind, against all that was natural. Such a thing demanded confrontation, but it would not come today. For now, he would enjoy the satisfaction of another successful hunt and, following Marshall's example, keep Christmas warm and joyous in his most human of hearts.

One month later to the day, Molly, informed him that she was pregnant, and the world changed forever.

The Nativity of the Avatar

by Robert M. Price

ew manuscript discoveries, like that of the famous Dead Sea Scrolls, always cause a stir, at least briefly till the jaded public's attention flits away to some new momentary stimulus. Perhaps the last place one would expect to find a new cache of ancient documents would be the British Museum, where every scrap of antiquity has long been catalogued and filed away. But, as the reader may remember, a few years ago it was announced that a wealth of "new" documents had in fact been discovered, lying concealed on the very same sheets of papyrus which well-known texts were occupying. They were palimpsests, sheets already bearing writing but, given the scarcity of writing materials, erased to afford room for new texts. Various such documents had been discovered and deciphered before, but new infrared techniques now made it possible to recover the original layer of writing without removing the more recent ink. This scientific boon opened the vault, so to speak, of a whole unknown library of ancient works, and it has taken some years to decipher any significant portion of them. There were new copies of familiar Greek dramas, Platonic dialogues and other philosophical works, and what not. Many of these have been published in English translation, though only specialists are likely to have paid much attention.

My name is Alasdair McKenzie, Professor of Ecclesiastical History at Brichester University. I expressed my interest in the project early on and was happy to be assigned what appeared to be an apocryphal gospel of sorts. In particular, it may be classed among the Infancy or Nativity Gospels, whose better known members include the Infancy Gospels of James, Matthew, Thomas the Israelite, and the Arabic Infancy Gospel. Each of these has fascinating features well worth studying, especially the surprising Zoroastrian connections in the Arabic Infancy Gospel. But the new one, assigned to my care, was in some ways radically different. Having translated it to the best of my ability, I herewith offer it to readers, who may decide for themselves what to make of it. One note: it may seem out of place to employ the Sanskrit word "avatar" in the translation of a Hellenistic Greek document, but it represents κατάβασις, "descent," which is also the meaning of "avatar" (*avatara, anvantara*), denoting a god coming down to earth.

Finally, I have inserted chapter and verse numbers. Most readers will know the Bible was written without these divisions and that they were added many centuries later to facilitate reference. So why not here?

***

1 [1] He who has ears, let him hear. He who has a mouth, let him bear witness to the truth of what we say. For this is the true account of the entry among men of the Avatar.

[2] In the last days of Herod the Blessed, three monks of Yian-Ho on the Plateau called Leng arrived in Jerusalem and gained audience with the king. [3] "O mighty Lord, we have learned from the midnight star that shines in the Cavern of the Elementals that the Avatar has been born in your kingdom, as a reward for your service to the cult of Set-Typhon.

[4] The light of the Elder Pharos has shone upon us as we made our way over many miles and mountains. [5] We have come to worship him, to take him in hand and to prepare him for his mission. Where, with your permission, may we find him?"

[6] Withal did King Herod summon the brethren of the monastery of the Naassenes in the Judean desert. [7] These are they who maintain the secret worship of him who is called Father Yigael and Leviathan and Nehushtan, and whom Egypt knows as Set the Old Serpent. [8] And he put it to them, "Where may the new-born Avatar be found? I, too, would go and bow down before him."

[9] And the monks of Yig confessed that the One they sought should be found in the village of Beth-Lehem, chosen on account of its ancient shrine to the god Dusares. [10] For it was from there that Balaam had prophesied the Avatar should arise. Now this is he who in the latter days should vindicate the Serpent and depose his ancient conqueror Jehovah. [11] Father Yigael had waited for many thousands of years, but soon he should regain his rightful mastery.

[12] And as he gave them provisions and horses and an escort of his troops, Herod told the brethren from Leng that he would offer all the infants of Beth-Lehem as a sacrifice to welcome the young Avatar into the world he should one day rule. [13] And Herod wept, knowing that he should never live to see the day of that final triumph.

[14] And as the company came near to Beth-Lehem, behold: the night was filled with the batlike forms of the gaunts of the night, and the number of them was so great that they blotted out the stars above. [15] And the gaunts chattered in no human tongue. But the men of Leng understood their meaning which, being interpreted, was, "Lo, the long night of Jehovah is ended, and the dawn of the Avatar is at hand! [16] And you, O men, see that you spread the tidings to all who cherish the secrets of the Olden Gods. But as for the rest, cast not your pearls before swine!"

[17] Thus they arrived at last where the child was. He lay in a manger between the dead bodies of his parents, for his birth was attended by many ill-omens, even the deaths of all the livestock in the place, [18] so that the owner of the stable and his servants had stoned the family. But the child they could not kill. [19] And now he lay wide-eyed, awaiting those who should take charge of him. [20] No childish cry did he make, but seemed to follow the movements of the men of Leng as a master observes his servants at work.

[21] As the company, carefully bearing the babe wrapped in swaddling, passed through the dark streets of Beth-Lehem, they were greeted by the sounds of violence and of the screaming of infants, [22] for Herod had sent his troops on the heels of the men of Leng and their guards. [23] The monks listened quietly, as if the screams contained some message that none but they could hear. [24] And thus was fulfilled the words of scripture, "Out of the mouths of babes and sucklings thou hast brought forth perfect praise."

2 [1] None hindered their journeying as they passed on into the land of Egypt after many days. Palm dates were their food, but also the lizards and scorpions of the desert. For these, too, may nourish the body when the soul is fitly prepared. [2] The men of Leng made their way at once to the great Sphinx, to the hidden adytum known but to the adepts, and it was to these that they entrusted the child.

[3] Within the deep chambers under the Sphinx and within the Pyramids did the child grow in stature and in learning. [4] For, though he was in truth the fleshly embodiment of One whose ways are from of old, yet his fleshly mind must be brought to remembrance of those secrets he had known before.

[5] There in the immemorial land of the asp and the viper, of the jackal and the crocodile, did the Avatar wipe away forgetfulness. [6] There did he learn again the arts he himself had created before the very foundation of the world. [7] The Pyramid adepts came to know him as Hermes Trismegistus, as their ancient forbears had. And they presumed to instruct him and to initiate him. [8] And this they did with fear and trembling lest they make some error that their disciple should recognize, and make them pay dreadfully.

[9] Some days he would embark up the Nile, which he said was the extended form of Set-Typhon himself. [10] And he said that, just as the boat of Osiris would reach the end and sink down into Amente to resurface like an underground spring back at the point of departure, [11] so had he gone down into the great Vault below, where the ghouls cavorted among the rock tombs of Neb. And these did teach him the mysteries of the worm.

[12] At length he was ready to return to the land of his birth. The men of Leng had grown old and died in the meantime, [13] but he did not depart Egypt alone, for it was said that great leopards followed him and licked his hands.

[14] When he had reached the age of twelve, a second embassy from Yian-Ho journeyed to the land of Israel to observe and to guide him. [15] They asked no one the way this time, but proceeded unerringly to the temple in Jerusalem, where they found him in heated debate with the elders. [16] These explained to him how the temple had been founded on the great navel stone of the world, and that the world itself could not survive the destruction of the holy place, [17] since it was only the sacrifices offered there that dissuaded Jehovah from visiting the world in judgment.

[18] But he said to them, "Do you see this temple made with hands? The day will come when I will destroy it and will establish another, in which you and your children shall be offered unto older gods. [19] The world you know will end when it returns to its rightful owners. In truth, you are like wicked tenants who took the vineyard for their own, saying, 'The master is long delayed; he will never return.'"

[20] The elders of the Jews were enraged at the saying, and they spoke no more with him. [21] As he made to depart from the temple, the men of Leng came to meet him, explaining that it was time for him to come with them back to the monastery, [22] where he should learn the secrets pertaining to his destiny. And he went with them obediently.

[23] They must needs cross the borders of Rome's empire and that of the neighboring Parthians, but none waylaid them. [24] Their provisions were renewed as needed as they were greeted by certain hermits and barbarian sorcerers who had been warned of their passing in dreams and premonitions. [25] The journey was long, and the company gained advantage in some places, losing it in others, as they followed ancient, hidden routes to the great plateau they sought.

[26] And he arrived at the monastery to the acclaim of all, seated upon a yak, as all the brethren spread their blood red robes upon the rocky ground before him. [27] There the Avatar learned things which may not be uttered. [28] There they prepared him for the exercise of the office to which he was born, that of the High Lama of Leng, for the day he should be invested with the

yellow robes and the silken mask. [29] But that day was not yet, for the one who then sat the throne would keep his post for a few more years before his successor should welcome the brethren to the sacred feast of his flesh.

3 [1] When he reached his thirtieth year he embarked upon the journey back to Israel, and this time he journeyed alone. [2] He suffered much along the way, but the time passed quickly as he meditated on all he had learned, upon that which he had been brought to recall, dispelling the stupor of the flesh.

[3] The Avatar commenced preaching in the meeting places of the Jews throughout Galilee, and each time he preached, he was cast out by the elders until word went around, and he was welcome nowhere. [4] For he brought a message strange and hateful to their ears. It was the tidings of a coming kingdom that would blot out all that came before it, even all that was. [5] "He that seeketh to save his life shall lose it, but he that loseth his life shall find it." And many other such things he told them.

[6] Once as he preached a man possessed of an unclean spirit cried out, saying, "What have you to do with us? We know who you are!" [7] But he answered, "Blessed are you! Come, follow me!" [8] And the man passed through the crowd, who one and all shrank away from him, and he followed him.

[9] Another time he found a youth who foamed at the mouth and threw himself into the fire, and none could stop him. [10] The Avatar saith unto him, "Come, follow me!" And immediately he did so.

[11] Again, he came to shore in the region called the Decapolis, as if he had arranged to meet someone there. [12] And there came out to greet him a man who went naked and lived among the tombs, gashing his own flesh and breaking every chain the people might put on him. [13] He was tormented by the earthbound souls of those buried in the cemetery, for, being in the Decapolis, it was unclean ground. [14] Seeing him, he said to him, "Name yourself!" And the fellow cried out, "Legion, for myriads of us live in him!" [15] And he bowed before him, and asked that he might follow him. And the Avatar gave him leave to do so. [16] And they got into the boat and returned to Galilee. And many of the harlots and sinners followed him.

[17] And the Romans sent spies to watch his movements, but he knew of it and cared nothing. [18] One day he sent one of his followers to the spies. "Be sure that you say to them, 'My Master says, "One day your proudest cities will fall to ruin and sink into the ground from which they were hewed. [19] In a single night they will fall, and all the tribes of the earth shall mourn when they behold their doom descending upon them. [20] Sea bottoms shall be exposed to the gaze of men when the valleys are raised up and rough places are made a plain. And you will quail at what you see there."'" [21] And the Romans did not understand him, but they began to look for an op-

portunity to arrest him.

[22] And it happened one day as they took their rest in the village of Chorazin, that he asked those who were with him, "Who do men say that I am?" [23] And they answered, "Some say you are a false prophet. Others say Belial, and others the Antichrist." [24] And he said, "But who do you say that I am?" And Legion said unto him, "You are Nyarlathotep, the Creeping Chaos."

With

The Strange Dark One,

W. H. Pugmire collects all of his best weird fiction concerning H. P. Lovecraft's dark god, Nyarlathotep. This avatar of the Great Old Ones is Lovecraft's most enigmatic creation, a being of many masks and multitudinous personae. Often called The Crawling Chaos, Nyarlathotep heralds the end of mortal time, and serves as avatar of Azathoth, the Idiot Chaos who will blow earth's dust away. Many writers have been enchanted by this dark being, in particular Robert Bloch, the man who, through correspondence, inspired Wilum Pugmire to try his hand at Lovecraftian fiction. This new book is a testimonial of Nyarlathotep's hold on Pugmire's withered brain, and these tales serve as aspects of a haunted mind. Along with stories that have not been reprinted since their initial magazine appearances, The Strange Dark One includes "To See Beyond," a sequel-of-sorts to Robert Bloch's tale, "The Cheaters", and the book's title story is a 14,000 word novelette set in Pugmire's Sesqua Valley. Each tale if beautifully illustrated by the remarkable Jeffrey Thomas, who is himself one of today's finest horror authors.

Coming soon from

Miskatonic
River
Press

They Lie not Dead, but Dreaming...

Dissecting Cthulhu
Essays on the Cthulhu Mythos

Edited by S. T. Joshi

Non-Fiction
Now Available
from
Miskatonic River Press:

The Cthulhu Mythos is H. P. Lovecraft's most dynamic invention. His bold vision of a cosmos filled with baleful "gods," forbidden books of occult lore, and a constellation of richly imagined New England cities was the perfect vehicle to express his "cosmic indifferentism." The Mythos has become one of the most imitated tropes in horror literature, and hundreds of writers have made their own extrapolations on it.

But many misconceptions remain about the Cthulhu Mythos. Its very name was not invented by Lovecraft, but by his disciple August Derleth. Derleth altered the Mythos in significant ways, and it is only recently that scholars and writers have returned to the purity of Lovecraft's own vision.

This collection of essays, gathered by pre-eminent Lovecraft scholar S. T. Joshi (*Black Wings, The Rise and Fall of the Cthulhu Mythos, I Am Providence: The Life and Times of H. P. Lovecraft*) prints many of the seminal essays on the Cthulhu Mythos, ranging from pioneering articles by Richard L. Tierney and Dirk W. Mosig that strip away Derleth's misconceptions about Lovecraft's pseudomythology, to penetrating studies by Robert M. Price, Will Murray, Steven J. Mariconda, and others probing key elements of the Mythos—its use of gods, books, and topography; the influences that Lovecraft absorbed in fashioning it; and its wide dissemination by generations of later writers. All told, this book provides an invaluable guide to Lovecraft's most intriguing but most misunderstood creation.

Miskatonic
River
Press

Thomas Ligotti is beyond doubt one of the Grandmasters of Weird Fiction. In *The Grimiscribe's Puppets,* Joseph S. Pulver, Sr., has commissioned both new and established talents in the world of weird fiction and horror to contribute all new tales that pay homage to Ligotti and celebrate his eerie and essential nightmares. Poppy Z. Brite once asked, "Are you out there, Thomas Ligotti?" This anthology proves not only is he alive and well, but his extraordinary illuminations have proven to be a visionary and fertile source of inspiration for some of today's most accomplished authors.

Coming from
Miskatonic
River
Press

CPSIA information can be obtained at www.ICGtesting.com
Printed in the USA
BVOW031513280212

284016BV00012B/36/P